DONATED TO:

If You Only Knew!

by
Helen Splane-Dowd

Helen Splane-Dowd

PublishAmerica
Baltimore

© 2005 by Helen Splane-Dowd.
All rights reserved. No part of this book may be reproduced, stored in a retrieval system or transmitted in any form or by any means without the prior written permission of the publishers, except by a reviewer who may quote brief passages in a review to be printed in a newspaper, magazine or journal.

First printing

ISBN: 1-4137-5413-9
PUBLISHED BY PUBLISHAMERICA, LLLP
www.publishamerica.com
Baltimore

Printed in the United States of America

Dedication

Special dedication in memory of those unforgettable people who have gone from this life: my parents, Jessie and Allyn, whose lives inspired this story; Aunt Florence, my mother's sister, who not only encouraged me to write, but also supplied me with many of her stories about their childhood; my sister and her husband, Clara and Stanley, killed in a car accident; our "love-son," my half-brother Wilfred, who spent much of his childhood with my husband and me, but who drowned at the age of twenty; and my beloved Uncle Bill, Dad's brother, for whom we cared during his last days, and who died in my arms; my high school principal, who read my manuscript and passed on helpful criticism; among others, who influenced my life and contributed inadvertently to this account.

Helen Dowd: Website: www.occupytillicome.com E-mail: hmdowd@telus.net
41-6900 Inkman Rd., Agassiz, BC., V0M 1A1. Ph. 604 796 3367

Acknowledgments

It's hard to know what to label this story. Although it is a biography, it has a hint of fiction: a few of the names have been changed, and some events are fictitious. However, for the most part, the facts are actual. How they came about, and in some cases, the exact dates of events may not be accurate. After all, I wasn't there, or wasn't old enough to understand what was going on, for a good part of the story.

I wish to thank all who contributed to the writing of this book: my dad, who supplied me with much of the information; my husband, who encouraged me from start to finish and would never let me give up; my cousins, who added valuable input by sharing their memories; my aunts and uncles for their accounts of shared experiences; my own brother and sisters for their invaluable contributions; Jessie's nursing contemporaries, in their late eighties at the time of my research, who willingly answered my questions and shared their memories; and my many friends and members of my family, for reading portions of the manuscripts and passing on constructive criticism.

TABLE of CONTENTS

Part I

	Prologue	11
1.	Jessie	13
2.	Growing Pains	18
3.	"Huddy"	24
4.	"Huddy," the R.N.	28
5.	Lower Ten	32
6.	The Saxophone Player	37
7.	Tibby Gives Up	43
8.	The Farm Up North	46
9.	Utopia?	53
10.	That's Not *My* Baby	59
11.	"Dat's *My* Baby"	63
12.	Lumpy Bread & Grasshoppers	66
13.	"The Devil's Payroll"	72
14.	Sunshine & Light	81
15.	The Theater	86
16.	Lettuce 'n Do'nuts	91
17.	"Angels and Demons"	98
18.	And Then?	101
19.	The Plan	107
20.	"Wither Thou Goest"	115
21.	The Spring	118
22.	New Beginnings	122
23.	School	128
24.	Make Her Cry	133
25.	Lily	142
26.	Three Quarters	148
27.	The Fleece	153
28.	Fire!	157
29.	The Shadow of Death	160
30.	Mad Dog	169
31.	Hayrack	172
32.	"And The Meal Wasted Not" I Kings 17:16	175

33.	And Four Makes Nine	181
34.	A Quiver Full	188
35.	"Pauly, My Baby"	195
36.	A No-Win Situation	199
37.	The Hitchhiker	203

Part II

	Prologue	211
1.	Surprises in Store	213
2.	Adjustments	219
3.	Medicine Hat	225
4.	"A Lot of 'Splane'n"	231
5.	The Singer Sewing Machine	234
6.	A Reason to Cry	236
7.	The Victory Garden	239
8.	"Train Up a Child"	243
9.	One Bleak November Morning	248
10.	The Invasion	251
11.	To Entertain Strangers	257
12.	Blind?	267
13.	Full Circle	271
14.	"That's Not Flu"	274
15.	Only a Miracle	280
16.	All is Well — Or is It?	284
17.	The Coat	287
18.	The Coronation	293
	Epilogue	298

PART I

Prologue

October 1939

She picked up her bag and purse and stepped out into the clammy darkness of the late-October morning. A tear slithered under her horn-rimmed glasses, trickled down her cheek and into her mouth as she turned to take a final look at what she was leaving behind: the smoke from the rusty stovepipe, spiraling downward, wrapped itself around the lamplight radiating through the frosty panes, and danced with it. Ghost-like shadows, floating from one window to the other, joined in the gyration.

Brushing the tear from her face, she recalled what she had thought when she had first seen the log shack, the shack that her husband had built: its two, four-paned windows—one slightly lower than the other—placed on either side of the slab-wood door; its slightly peaked roof; its rough, shabby appearance, had reminded her then, of a vacant-minded man, staring out over the fields.

As she stood now, trembling in the cold, she imagined she could hear the children crying, *Mama, come back. Come back.* Her heart lurched. Another tear snuck down her cheek.... She took a deep breath, threw back her shoulders, and walked away, away from this life. Away into? —

The distant yipping of coyotes, and the closer replies of local dogs; the scream of a catfight nearby; the lonely *hoo-hoo* of owls; and the crunch of her footsteps on the gravel road, all mingled together with the turmoil of her thoughts. Like the floating fog around her, bits of conversation she had recently had with her visiting sister drifted through her mind: "Why?" her sister had asked, shuddering at the Spartan surroundings. "You had a career. And... and you threw it all away for... for this? Why?"

"'Why,' indeed!" she said aloud now, kicking at a pebble as she scuffed her way along the lonely road. She let out a long sigh. "Oh, my dear sister, if you only knew the half of it. If you only knew!" Her shoulders slumped. Her eyes misted. She stumbled on a rut in the road. How could she do this? How could she walk away? —

Chapter 1 — Jessie

1902 –1910

A cool breeze whispered through the poplars, the leaves trembled. Coyotes howled their protest of the dying night. Birds, one by one, joined in chorus to announce the dawn of Sunday, August 10, 1902. While Hugh Hudson paced the floor outside his bedroom on the main floor of their three-story house in Douglas, Manitoba, his five daughters and two sons, clad still in their nightclothes, sat huddled in the living room — waiting, waiting.

"God gives, and only God can take away," is what Hugh had told the doctor eight months previously when he had suggested an abortion for Maria, and it screamed in his ears now, as he paced. Oh, what was taking the doctor so long?

As the pink tongues of dawn began to silhouette the inky fringe of the quivering trees surrounding the house, a muffled cry was heard. Hugh expelled his pent-up breath, flinging himself through the bedroom door. The children scrambled to follow, but the door slammed in front of them, denying them access.

Collapsing by her bed, Hugh grabbed Maria's clammy hand. He stoked the saturated hair from her brow, peering into her face. Alive! She was alive! His head slumped onto her chest.

The bells of a little white church with Gothic windows, stone steps, and a stately steeple, designed and built by Hugh Hudson, rang out.

For the tiny town of Elton, November second was a special day. The three-month-old daughter of Hugh and Maria was christened "Rosalind Jessie Viola Hudson." And on that same day, in the same church, "Jessie's oldest sister, nineteen-year-old Caroline, was married to Fred Vague, a local farmer.

Five months later, in a grain wagon pulled by a team of oxen, Hugh moved his family and possessions to his newly claimed homestead near Stoughton, a small town in the southeast corner of Saskatchewan.

"Mama?" Jessie's eyes glistened with tears, as they did every time her mama recounted the story of Hannah and Samuel. (I Samuel 2) "Why did Hannah's little boy have to go away from home?"

"Because Hannah promised God that if He should give her a little boy, she would give the child back to Him." Maria touched Jessie's soft curls with her lips. "So when Samuel was about your age, Hannah took him to God's house to live. God had lots of special things for him to do; and Samuel learned all he could, so that he could *do* those special things when he got big."

"Oh, Mama!" Jessie threw her arms around her mother's neck. "I don't *ever* want to leave you."

Maria hugged her daughter close, the rocker keeping time with her heartbeat. Should she tell her daughter now? Was this the right time? Maria took a deep breath. "I love you, too, Little One," she said at last, a shudder-sigh escaping with her words. "And I, like Hannah, am giving *you* to God. But you won't be going away. You must stay here with your daddy, and brothers and sisters. It is I who will be going away... soon. God wants me to live in Heaven with Him. But He's got lots of special and important things for *you* to do." She gave her daughter another long hug.

Jessie pushed away. What could her mama mean? *Going away to live in Heaven.* A puzzled frown creased her brow as she unfastened, then fastened, the twenty-five buttons on the front of her mother's gray woolen dress. Then flopping against her mother's chest she fell asleep.

Her chin resting in her hands, Jessie sat swinging her feet back and forth. "Nobody remembered it's my birthday, 'cause Mama's in the hospital." She gave her feet a final kick, bounded from her chair and ran to the kitchen.

"Oh, Gertie! You did remember," she squealed when she saw the cake her sister was carrying, adorned with five flickering candles.

Hugh went to the mantle, returning with a brightly decorated box, which he thrust at Jessie. "For you," he said, a half-smile struggling across his face. "Mama told me not to forget your birthday." He had spent two hours that day looking for the gift his wife had described to him.

"Oh!" she gasped, reaching into the box and lifting out a doll with a delicate china face, china hands and legs, and a soft cloth body. "You're so pretty," she whispered, touching its face. "I'm gonna name you *Hannah*." Her fingers danced lightly over the frilly white bonnet, silky anklets, and the shiny, black shoes. Embracing the doll, she ran to her dad, throwing her arms around his neck. 1

To Hugh, a strict Methodist, Sunday was a day of rest, rest from everything. Just as Jessie was bolting for the door to join the family in the wagon for the twelve-mile ride to church the following day, her dad stopped her. "Hold on there, young lady," he said, wresting the birthday doll from her arms. "Today is the Lord's day."

Her eyes misting, she watched her daddy toss Hannah onto a shelf. How her arms ached to hold her doll in church, as she had seen other little girls do. Shuffling behind her dad, head down, she blinked to keep the tears from spilling. After church that day, as on every other Sunday, Jessie sat silently with her family in their expansive living room. Her eyes were glued to the mantel above the fireplace. Hannah looked so uncomfortable, stuffed on that shelf—and so lonely—with only a blue vase, a golden bell, and two tall silver candlesticks for company. She pretended she was up there, too, holding poor Hannah, instead of perched on an over-sized easy chair, waiting for the day to be over.

"I wish Mama was here." She sighed a long shuddering sigh, gathering her feet into the chair. Sleep soon rescued her and carried her through the long, Lord's-day afternoon.

One Saturday afternoon the following June, Jessie stood in her room in front of her mirror, frowning at her reflection. Everyone should be happy to have the whole family home. She was. She had her nephews to play with, Carrie's Harry, and Bell's Glen, both three. Two days ago her sisters and their families had arrived at the homestead—Carrie and Fred Vague, from Manitoba, and Bell and her husband, Will Todd, a blacksmith, from the nearby town of Stoughton.

As she stood now in her room, frowning at her frilly blue dress, she stamped her foot. Things were just not right. Why was she told to put on her Sunday dress, on a Saturday? And why were the grown-ups always talking in whispers, or shuffling her and the little boys off with twelve-year old Maude some place, whenever they all got together? Her eyes roved the room until they fell on Hannah. She ran to her, snatching her up and hugging her.

"What does *'funeral'* mean?" she asked the doll. Nobody, not even Maude, would tell her *anything*.

What is a funeral, anyway? she wondered, climbing into the wagon. *Maybe it's like a hospital.* She brightened. *Maybe that's where we're going, to see Mama in the hospital.* For the rest of the silent ride into town, she sat between her sisters, swinging her feet.

Gripping Maude and Florence's hands at the end of the journey, she jumped from the wagon and skipped between them. But at the door of the church she stopped. Why were they going into church on a Saturday? She shot a sideways glance at fourteen-year-old Florence, then at Maude. Her brows tightened. Why were her sisters crying? Then, as her brothers, Eugene and George, slid into the pew, she saw them wiping their eyes, too. In the row ahead of her, Gertie, her dad, and her two married sisters with their families, were settling in, and some of them were crying. What did it all mean?

Suddenly, into her mind flashed the talks she'd had with her mama, so long ago, it seemed to her now, about her going to live with God. She pulled Maude's head down to hers. "Has Mama gone to live at God's house?" she whispered.

While the minister droned on, it hit Jessie: *Mama's not coming back. Ever. Who would look after her, and Maude, and Florence, and George, and Dad...? Would Gertie?* She had always been there to look after them when Mama was sick, but Gertie was going away soon. Jessie puckered her brow and worried throughout the remainder of the service.

A year before, Gertrude had asked her dad's permission to marry the farmhand. His refusal had been sharp and final. So, deciding to postpone her marriage until she was twenty-one, when she would no longer need his consent, she had taken a course in dressmaking and tailoring. Her course now finished, she was eager to begin her career. 2

But now, what about the children? After a few heated discussions between Gertie and her dad—and many a tearful night for her—

twenty-year-old Gertie was designated to become mama to her younger brother and sisters.

Ten months later Hugh moved his family to Vancouver, British Columbia, leaving the homestead to his oldest son, Eugene. "I want you children to have a good city education," he said, hiding the real reason for his move: he hated homesteading, and wanted to get back to his building trade.

Jessie crouched beside the couch where Maude lay. With her elbows resting on the edge, her chin in her hands, she stared into her sister's pale face. "Why do people get sick?" she said to herself, thinking about her mother's long illness. Her eyes flooded with tears. "When I grow up I'm going to make sick people better," she whispered to her doll. She watched her sister's eyes flutter, then open. "D'you wanna play, Maude?"

Reaching for her little sister's hand, Maude whispered, "No, but you can talk to me."

"Wanna hear the story of Hannah and Samuel? The one Mama used to tell?" Jessie jumped up and stood by the couch, hugging Hannah to her.

Although she'd heard Jessie tell it many times before, she said, "Yes, I'd like that." Maude's eyelids drooped shut.

"Are you goin' to Heaven to live with Mama?" Jessie touched her sister's cheek at the end of the story.

Smiling, Maude fell asleep holding Jessie's hand. She died shortly after that, from what the doctors called pernicious anemia.

Footnotes:
1 The doll, faded, cracked, and torn, resurfaced in the family in 1942. Jessie gave it to her second daughter, who repaired it, and kept it until she left home.

2 Gertie never did marry that farmhand. She married Art Knight, another farm worker.

Chapter 2 — Growing Pains

1910 – 1921

Florence yanked her clothes from their hangers, flinging them onto the bed. "I'm getting out of here," she said to Jessie, dragging her suitcase from the closet. "She's impossible! And Dad goes right along with her. He's afraid of her. That's what he is. Afraid of her! Oh, Jessie—" Bursting into tears, Florence flung her arms around her sister. "Our family's simply disintegrating."

Four years after his wife's death, Hugh had married Maria's sister, Eliza. At first, Jessie had been excited about having a mama again. But motherhood was not for Eliza. *Auntie,* as the children called her, was cold, uncaring, and self-centered. And life had changed drastically for the family: Gertie had taken a job in downtown Vancouver and had moved into an apartment near her work; George had joined the army (since Auntie had succeeded in causing a rift between him and his dad); and with Florence, Eliza fought constantly. As for Jessie, she could have been invisible, as far as Auntie was concerned; she scarcely gave her a sidelong glance.

It was just after a fierce argument with Auntie that Florence had stormed into the bedroom and begun packing. "They say—Dad and her—that, 'what with the war and inflation and everything,' that we'll all have to tighten our belts if we want to keep this house." Florence clung to her sister, her tears wetting the back of Jessie's dress.

"Well, who wants it?" she continued. "Oh, Jessie, I'm sorry, but I just have to get out of here. Away... from *her*. I hate to leave you alone to battle old... old—"

Jessie pushed her sister from her, and with her handkerchief she wiped Florence's eyes. "Don't you worry about me. I wouldn't want you to stay... just for me." She picked up one of the dresses from the bed, and as she began to fold it, she buried her face in the soft material. The familiar fragrance of her sister's perfume brought a stabbing realization of how unbearable life would be without her. "You go," she said, placing the garment slowly into the suitcase. "I hate seeing you so unhappy. Besides—" She gave a feeble laugh. "Auntie doesn't bother me. Remember? I don't exist, as far as she is concerned."

The two sisters hugged each other again, both half-laughing, half-crying. *How can I bear to live without you?* they each thought, tears sparkling in their eyes.

World War I had been over for nearly a year. Jessie's dad had moved with Auntie and her to Empress, Alberta, where he had found employment building barns.

One day, while flipping through the newspaper, Jessie's eyes fell on a notice, written in bold print: *"All schools and public gatherings will be closed until further notice. The influenza epidemic is threatening..."* She flung the paper aside, bolting from the house.

"*Nothing* is going to stop me from graduating. *Nothing!*" Her whole life, Jessie had lived for the day when she would finish school and begin nurses' training. *It's just not fair!* She snatched her books from her school locker, frustration and anger threatening to explode inside her.

A few days later she called at a friend, Louise's, house. After only a few minutes, she returned, slamming the door and fleeing to her room. "Why, God? Why?" she cried. "How could You do this? You're supposed to be a God of love." Her hands flew to her head. "You—" She stood in front of the mirror in her bedroom, tears streaming down her cheeks. "Why do You always rob me of the people I love? First Mama, then Maude, and now Louise. Why God? Why can't You stop this terrible influenza? This death? Oh, God... Oh, God... Oh, God..." She flung herself onto her bed, pounding the pillow with her fists.

Hugh glanced at his daughter picking at her food. "Jessie, Jessie," he said. "What's the matter with you lately? You never laugh or sing;

you never play the piano anymore—" He got up from the table and walked to where his daughter sat. Squeezing her shoulders, he continued, in a less soothing, more scolding voice: "For the past month you've closed yourself in your room; you seldom speak; you hardly eat. You know, there's more to life than just studying. Come, girl." He gave her a slight shake. "Buck up. Finish eating; then go in and play the piano. Let's have a sing."

Jessie twisted, shrugging off her dad's hands. Her eyes blazed. If his remonstrations had meant to soothe her, they had done just the opposite. She turned, catching a glimpse of Auntie's icy eyes on her. She wanted to say, *What do the two of you care? You never feel other people's pain,*—but knew she dare not. Instead, she pushed from the table and fled to her room. Sobbing, she hugged her pillow, rocking back and forth on her bed, until from exhaustion she slept.

The influenza having abated, the schools reopened after a two-month's closure. Just before the end of the school year, Jessie, reluctantly, went with a friend to a Nazarene church service. During the congregational singing, she glared straight ahead, her eyes riveted on the leader. She wished she hadn't come. She could have been home studying.

This foolishness about God, about His love— All this turmoil was... was... *His* fault. Once, she remembered, she had loved Him. As a small child, by her mother's knees, she had asked God into her heart. But now, He'd forgotten her—and the whole world. He didn't care. Why just today at school there had been talk that the graduation exercises may be canceled, because only a handful of students had been able to catch up enough to complete the year. Even that, God could have prevented, if He'd wanted to. *It's just not fair!*

The minister stood to the pulpit, announcing the Scripture text: "Isaiah, chapter forty-five."

Jessie flipped absently to the chapter. She knew her Bible—of course she did! After all, her father was a Methodist, strict in his insistence on church attendance. Her eyes followed along: "I am the Lord, and there is none else, there is no God beside me: (v.5 a) I form light, and create darkness: I make peace, and create evil: I the Lord do all these things." (v.7) She jerked forward in her seat. Did the minister shout those last words? Was it really God who created evil? Why?

"Woe unto him that striveth with his Maker...! Shall the clay say to him that fashioneth it. What makest thou…?" (v. 9) Were those words actually there? She clutched her Bible, bringing it closer to her eyes. She re-read the words, nearly choking on the lump in her throat. That's exactly what she had been doing. Striving! Blaming God! She! Nothing more than a piece of clay, the Bible said, arguing against God, the Creator of *all* things.

"Our text tonight, friends," said the minister, "is verse two and three of this chapter. 'I will go before thee, and make the crooked places straight…'"

God was saying to *her* that He would make her crooked places straight? That He would direct *her*? That He would save *her*? He had called *her* by her name? She didn't hear the rest of the exhortation. A private sermon was being ministered inside her.

The service over, an invitation for prayer was given. She sprang to the altar, and through a bath of cleansing tears; she gave herself to God, dedicating her life to His service. *He knows me by my name. He hasn't forgotten me.* Peace flooded her heart.

Graduation. At last! Her life could begin. She'd waste no time in pursuing her goal. Tomorrow she'd tell him. Tomorrow, the day after graduation.

Her stomach in her throat, her hands clenched into tight fists behind her back, but her head held high, Jessie walked up to her father. He was on his knees, laying a hardwood floor in the living room. "Dad?" She gave her head a toss, her auburn curls flipping to one side of her head. She cleared her throat. "I… ah… I… want to enter nurses' training… In Calgary. I… could stay with Florence, and—"

"You want to do what?" Belying his sixty-plus years, Hugh bounded to his feet, chucking his hammer aside. Stretching to his full five-foot-eight-inch height, he stuffed his hands into his pocket and glared down at his daughter.

"I want to—"

"I *heard* what you said. Girl, use your head." He began pacing. "What do you think I'm made of? Money? I can't afford to put you through three or four more years of school. And a nurse, of all things! Carrie, Bell, Gertie, Florence, they all made it on their own—without some fancy career. Who do you think *you* are? Besides, you're still a child—not even eighteen." Hugh turned his steely gray eyes on his daughter. "But *you're* lucky. Just yesterday Florence sent some money for you, but not for any highfalutin nurse's course. *You* are going to business school."

"But—"

Her father strode toward her, laying his gigantic hands on her shoulders, his bushy eyebrows nearly touching her forehead. "There's a good secretarial school in Winnipeg," he barked. "I've already looked into it. That's where you're going. The course starts next week." He turned, and dropping to his knees, he picked up his hammer. "That's where you're going," he emphasized, giving the floor a whack with it.

"Winnipeg?" Jessie swallowed, turned, and fled to her room. *"Winnipeg!"* Flopping onto her bed, she buried her head in the pillow. "Will I ever get to be a nurse? Oh, Florence, Florence, I was so looking forward to being with you again."

"I will make the crooked places straight." (Isaiah 45:2) The verses from the sermon of a month ago penetrated through her despair. It didn't look like it now, but God had promised; she would trust Him. She fell asleep.

One week later she was in Winnipeg, and Florence was there to meet her. "You're too young and innocent to be in a big city by yourself," she said. The sisters fell together in an embrace. "Dad could have sent you to Calgary for the course." Florence picked up Jessie's travel bag. "There's a good school there. That's what I expected him to do when I—"

"I know. But who can argue with Dad?" Jessie flashed Florence a knowing smile. "Thanks for sending the money. At least it got me away from home. And thanks for leaving your Calgary job to be with me—you didn't have to, you know…. But I'm glad you did. Oh, how I've missed you!"

Just before Jessie had completed her course, she got a letter from Florence, who, loathing Winnipeg and her job there, had returned to her old job in Calgary: "Dear Jessie," she wrote. "There's an opening for you here at the office… Please come. I miss you!"

For a year Jessie trudged to work five-and-a-half days a week, plunked herself at her typewriter and pounded out perfect letters for her boss. Even his high praise didn't take the drudgery out of stenography. She knew what she wanted to do.

"I hate being stuck behind a desk all day," she wrote to her oldest sister, Carrie, one day. "It seems so pointless, when there are so many sick people in the world... I've inquired into nurses' training. I'm registered to begin this fall at the Calgary General. Dad won't like it — he has some aversion to nursing — but, as he pointed out to me, you all made it on your own. So that's what I intend to do..."

Chapter 3 — "Huddy"

1922 –1924

Miss Eddy, Superintendent: The letters stood in bold print on the window to the right. On the wall to the left was a calendar, the date, October 2, 1922, circled with heavy red crayon. Today. The day she'd worked for, longed for, since she was seven. Jessie stood with her hand on the doorknob, listening to her heart pound, partly from fright, but mostly from the realization that she was finally in control of her own life. To become a nurse was *her* decision, no one else's.

Opening the door, she flashed a self-conscious smile to the roomful of young women lining the walls, each holding a sheet of paper, waiting for her turn to be called. Afraid that even her sigh of relief that she wasn't late would be heard in the silence of the room, Jessie slowly exhaled. She should have been here fifteen minutes sooner, but she'd missed the streetcar by seconds. Wiping the sleet from her hair with her scarf, she tiptoed to the window to pick up her registration form, and then took her place among the women.

The next morning, dressed in an ocean-blue dress, a white ankle-length apron, and black knee-high boots, Jessie sat squashed between two like-clad strangers on a hard wooden bench, waiting for the initiation speech to begin. Behind a podium in the center of the Spartan classroom at the Calgary General Hospital, stood Miss Eddy. Her black hair, streaked with gray, was pulled tightly into a bun at the back of her head. Standing erect, in her dazzling-white, stiff-starched uniform, she stretched her slim body to her full five-foot-nine-inch height. With a grim and severe expression, unless you caught the slight twinkle that played at the corners of her eyes, she peered at the thirty unfamiliar faces before her.

"Your probation period," she began, "will be three months. That is, of course, unless you drop out—or are kicked out—first." A titter trickled through the room, melting the icy atmosphere of unfamiliarity. For the next hour the superintendent's raspy voice pelted out the duties, responsibilities, and requirements of this trial period.

Jessie's head spun: *thousands of rules, it seemed.* She thought her father had a corner on those.

That evening, Evelyn Kadey, Jessie's appointed roommate, introduced her to her friend, Sadie Nash. Jessie and her two new friends joined a young woman standing beside the piano in the nurses' lounge. The pianist, Mana Rummel, flashed a quick smile at the group, later introducing herself and her friend, Ida Huxley, the young woman by the piano. A five-some-friendship was born, a friendship that was to flourish over the years, a friendship born of common interests: a love for God, a love of music, an interest in people, and a fondness for skating.

It was through her love of skating that Jessie met Allyn. Among the new class of "Probies" the following fall, was Claribel Splane, a shy young woman, who attended the Crescent Heights Baptist Church. One Sunday Claribel introduced Ida Huxley—"Huxley"—to her eldest brother, Allyn, who from then on tried his best to date her.

A few days later, when Allyn telephoned the nurses' residence asking for Huxley, someone mistakenly called "Huddy," Jessie's nickname.

"Hey! That call was for 'Huxley,' not 'Huddy,'" said a red-faced Jessie, returning a few moments later to the lounge where her friends were gathered around the piano. "Do you know an Allyn... Allyn somebody?" She giggled. "He was jabbering on and on, until suddenly he realized he wasn't talking to 'Huxley'; then he spluttered and stammered and banged down the receiver. He sounded kinda'— Well, I'd... I'd like to meet him, this Al, your boyfriend."

"Boyfriend!" she snorted. "You can *have* him." She threw out her arms, as if tossing him her way. "He's a pest... and he's *not* my boyfriend, just Claribel's brother. Boyfriend!"

Jessie joined in the titters that tricked around the room.

Later that week, Allyn called at the residence with the pretext of taking his sister skating. (Actually, he was hoping to snare Huxley.)

"Why don't we all go?" suggested Claribel to her newfound friends. "Okay with you, Al?"

"0' course! 0' course!" Allyn bolted for the car before the girls could notice that his face had turned scarlet. His heart pounded in his ears: not only would he get to be with Huxley, but as a bonus, he was actually going to get the meet the mysterious "Huddy" he'd spoken to on the phone the other day.

Grabbing the crank from under the seat, he jammed it into the starter box at the front of the engine. "Start, baby," he said, giving the crank a pull. "Won't I be popular at the old Crystal Rink tonight! Six women! Even if one is my sister."

Chug-chug-splutter-splutter... Whir. "Purring like a kitten," he said, sliding behind the wheel.

A couple of hours later—it seemed like ten minutes—Jessie glanced casually at her watch. "Girls!" she gasped. "We'll be late. And if we are we'll lose our late-passes."

"Hey! Don't worry," shouted the now, not-too-shy Allyn. "Grab your shoes. Change in the car. Tin-can-Tilly'll get you there on time." Dashing out in his skates, Allyn cranked up the old Model T. Off they tore, Allyn still in his skates, driving like a madman. It was the first of many such excursions.

Letter writing was not a top priority with Jessie during training. One night after lights-out, near the end of her Intermediate year, she sat hunched on her bed; and by flashlight, she answered her sister, Carrie's, two-week-old letter. "About 'that farmer,' as you called my friend, Allyn," she wrote. "He's just that—a friend—someone to go skating with, and to church sometimes.

"Actually, he isn't even a farmer. He owns a farm up north, but he's never even seen it. He works for the Canadian Pacific Railway, and sells life insurance on the side. (He sold my friends and me policies.)

"I like him. True. He's dashing, vibrant, a daredevil—yet shy.... But romance? Hardly! He takes *six* of us girls skating, including his sister. So set your mind at ease. No wedding bells ringing for me!

"You probably never had a chance to be foolish, Carrie, being married so young. Well, Saturday, Rummel and Huxley, the two friends I often talk about—always the mischief-makers—talked me into doing something really hare-brained. Me! Dubbed 'Miss Serious' by my classmates.

"I had a couple of bags of laundry to go to the laundry room in the basement (via a spiral fire-escape chute). My friends suggested, 'Huddy, you go down *with* the laundry. It's fun. We've tried it.' After a lot of persuasion on their part, I climbed into the chute, the laundry bags ahead of me. The girls shut the flap, promising to be at the bottom to open the trap door. I shut my eyes to shut out the darkness, waiting long enough for them to get to the basement. Then I went spiraling, spiraling down into an abyss—into nothingness. Thump! I hit something, bringing me to a stop. I waited. Waited, in the pitch-blackness. The earth had swallowed me, surely. I pounded on the door. No one came. I pounded again. Was it time to panic yet? Suddenly, a burst of dazzling light, and kerplunk! The door burst open, and I, along with the laundry, landed in a pile on the floor. When my eyes became adjusted to the light, I gazed into the tomato-red faces of my buddies.

"About to splutter some curses on them for leaving me in such a plight, I spotted Miss McNeil, the assistant superintendent, in front of me. Her fat little hands on her podgy hips, her moon-shaped—usually jolly—face looking like a thundercloud, she bellowed, 'Hudson! I wouldn't have expected such behavior from you. Just what do you have to say for yourself?'

"While I clambered to my feet, trying to think how I would talk my way out of this, my most embarrassing situation, she turned and waddled toward the door. I started to splutter an apology, but she was already on the other side. It was then I heard her laughing, a real, cackling, 'Ha! Ha! Ha!' laugh.

"I'll tell you, Carrie, I'll never pull a stunt like *that* again; although I must admit, the trip down the chute was quite a thrill, worth the panic and humiliation...."

Chapter 4 — "Huddy," The R.N.

1925 -1926

Tuesday, May 5, 1925. Huddy groped her way through the boxes piled around the eight-by-twelve-foot room in the residence of the Isolation Hospital, her home for the next few months while she completed her training time. Putting her belongings into place would just have to wait. This was the day she'd longed for, dreamed of, and worked toward all her life. She must look her best. Standing in front of the dresser mirror, she fastened her stiff-starched, calf-length apron over her frocked white dress.

"Good-bye, cumbersome ankle-length apron," she said to her reflection. She tilted the mirror, checking to see that her seams were straight on her white silk stockings. "And good riddance, ugly knee-high boots." She buffed her white oxfords. Pinning on the perky white cap with the narrow black strip, she tucked a wayward curl beneath its crown. With her handkerchief, she shined her nurse's badge, picked up her bouquet of roses and carnations, a gift from the School of Nursing to each of the graduates, and headed for the auditorium.

"Jessie Viola Hudson..." After what seemed an interminably long time of listening to baccalaureate speeches and congratulatory messages, her moment of triumph had come at last.

"*Registered nurse. Registered nurse. Registered nurse,*" pounded inside her chest and gushed through her ears. With her certificate clutched in her hand, and her head held high, she floated back to her seat.

Huddy had a feeling of euphoria as she began work at the Isolation Hospital. At last, she felt like a real nurse, allowed to make decisions on her own.

When a diphtheria epidemic hit, however, swelling the numbers at the hospital, her euphoria turned to sadness. With an aching heart, she began her rounds in the twenty-four-bed children's ward on the third floor, where she had been assigned. After looking on the paper-white face of four-year-old Bessie, admitted just yesterday, and brushing the hair from her fevered forehead, she went to where Timmy lay gasping for breath. She sponged his forehead and took his pulse. He stared up at her, his eyes glassy. Her eyes darted to little Mickey's bed: it was empty — stripped and stark. She took a sharp breath. Only yesterday he had laid there, his eyes glazed like Timmy's were now, imploring her to help him breathe. She forced her eyes back to Timmy. Her heart constricted. He, like Mickey, was only three years old! Would he be next? She blinked back tears.

The jangling of an alarm clock exploded inside Jessie's head. Her arm shot out, grabbing at the offending noise and stuffing it under the covers. Why wasn't she up? She always beat the alarm. She tried to raise her head. It flopped back onto the pillow. She tried again. Her head felt like a lump of lead.

Come on, Huddy. Slowly she moved her foot to the edge of the bed and began the process of forcing herself to a sitting position. Her hand went to her throat. It felt like fire, yet she was shivering. She draped her housecoat around her, groping for her soap and towel, then stumbled down the hall to the bathroom. Maybe she'd feel better after a shower.

"Why now?" she scolded herself, turning on the taps. "I can't afford to be sick."

"Hudson… Hudson…" A faraway voice was calling her. She felt herself floating in slow motion towards it. "Hudson… Hudson…"

Urging her eyes open and squinting to adjust to the light, she could just barely make out the forms standing by her bed. *Supervisor, Miss Hood…? And Assistant Supervisor, Miss Robinson…? Why? Why were they there, by her bed?*

"Oh, I'm... I'm so... sorry," she managed to say, forcing a wan smile. I guess I fell... back to sleep." She struggled to sit up. "I guess I'm... late... for work."

"Hudson," said Miss Hood, adjusting Jessie's pillow and pushing her gently back onto it, "you've missed three *weeks* of work. We're just glad you're back in the land of the living." She flashed a patronizing smile at Jessie, patting her hand. "You gave us quite a scare. We thought we'd lost you."

"Three weeks...? Did you say...'three weeks'?" Jessie stared wildly around her. She strained to sit up. "I remember taking a shower —"

"Yes, and if your friend, Rummel, hadn't gone in right after you, you'd have drowned."

"That was three weeks ago," confirmed Miss Robinson, nodding her head up and down. "Diphtheria." She cleared her throat, placing her hand on Jessie's still-fevered brow. "Get some sleep now."

Huddy lay thinking of her illness, angry that such a block of time was completely obliterated from her life. *For what purpose? What a waste!*

Gradually, however, bits of sub-consciousness began to invade her memory. Was it a dream? A vision? Or just a strong impression? *It was like... there were angels, standing with outstretched arms. Waiting. Waiting for someone. Me? "Why?" I remember thinking then: "Am I dying, or dead? I can't be. I'm so close to being... to reaching my goal."*

I remember, too, hearing a voice — not one of the angels': 'My child.' The words were clear, but the voice sounded like the ringing of a bell — a golden bell, like one I remembered on our mantel when I was a child. I felt as if I were in a cloud. And I was alone with only the voice. 'My child,' the voice repeated, 'I have a special work for you. Are you willing to do it? It will not be an easy path you will walk, but I will walk with you.'

The bell-like voice faded; the cloud vanished. But the angels still lingered for a few seconds. Then, they too began to fade, and as they did they put down their arms.

That's when I awoke and saw the nurses by my bed. Jessie opened her eyes. She sat up. "I don't remember if I answered the voice," she said aloud. Flopping back on her pillow, she said, "But I must have, because I'm here... and I'm willing to do whatever God wants me to do."

With the snapping of the clasps of the suitcase, Huddy's heart did a flip-flop. In two hours she'd be boarding the train. Six years, it had been since she'd seen her dad. Incredible! She shuddered, recalling the unpleasant scene she'd had with him the night after her high school graduation... But she had done a lot of growing up since then.

Her hands clammy, she checked her purse: *Ticket Dad sent, money, bankbook.* She stroked her passbook, the balance in it making her snicker. *Three hundred dollars. Hmm! Not bad, I guess. At five dollars a month for the first year in training, ten a month, the second; and twenty-per, for the third; that adds up to four hundred and twenty dollars. What with having to buy my books and uniforms, and replacing the thermometers I broke over the years, I'm lucky to have that much. Of course, I had three hundred dollars in my account when I started training.* She sat down in front of the mirror, plopped her bankbook back into her purse, grinning at her reflection. She tilted her head to one side, straightening her hat and securing the pin.

"So!" she said aloud to her mirror: "Jessie Viola Hudson, alias 'Huddy,' begins her new life where she left off three-and-one-half years ago, with three hundred dollars." She stood up, squaring her shoulders as she picked up her purse and suitcase. Giving her reflection one last check, she said with a sassy toss of her head, "But one thing I have now that I didn't have before: I have 'R.N.' behind my name." She placed her free hand on her nurse's badge and walked out the door.

Chapter 5 — Lower Ten

April 1926

Clickety-click. Clickety-click. Jessie closed her eyes, letting out a long sigh as she settled into her seat on the Trans-continental Express train bound for Toronto. The rhythm oozed into her subconscious, draining the tension from her body. *Four days of doing nothing. Ah! She'd read when she felt like it, pace the aisles if she wanted exercise, and she'd sleep. Ah, yes, she'd sleep. Read, walk, eat, and sleep, for four whole days. What luxury!* She rolled her head on the seat back, peering out periodically at the flip-flip of the telegraph poles and at a few snow-patched, soggy farm fields. There was nothing else to see.

When she returned from the dining car after her evening meal, her berth had been made up for the night.

"*What! Why so early? Oh, well.*" She yawned. "*I'll get ready for bed and cozy in with a book.*"

She became so absorbed in her book she failed to notice the train's lack of movement, until she heard a commotion. She lifted the blind a crack, peering out into the darkness. "Winnipeg! Still?" She glanced at her watch. "We should have left here an hour ago. What's up?"

"There's a young lady in lower ten that fits that description," she heard a male voice say.

Lower ten! That's me! With a single motion Jessie turned out her light and slithered under the covers.

"Open up, Miss," the voice bellowed just outside her curtain.

She pulled the covers over her head. Maybe he would go away.

"Miss. This is the police. Open your curtain."

"The police? What... what? Who? What... do you... want?" She tried to make her voice sound as if she'd been sleeping.

"We want to ask you some questions."

"Questions?" She clambered into her dressing gown. "I may not have the answers." As she was fumbling with the buttons on the inside curtain of her berth, trying to open them, a hand yanked them aside. Trembling, she gazed at the three uniformed men standing before her, a police officer, the porter, and the trainman.

"Miss," growled the police officer. "Where did you board this train?"

"In Calgary. Early this morning. Why?"

"I'll ask the questions. You answer them," he snapped. "Where are you going?" The officer, notebook in hand, jotted something down.

"To Toronto." Her voice shook. She was annoyed with herself. She had nothing to hide.

"What is the purpose of your trip to Toronto?"

"To visit my father."

"What's your name?"

"Jessie Hudson." She tossed her head and sniffed. "What is this?"

Throwing her a scathing look, the policeman continued his jotting, a scowl on his mustached face.

"And just what *is* your father's name?"

"Hugh Hudson. Why?" The scowl on Jessie's face matched that of the officer's. "What *is* this all about? I demand an answer." Inwardly, she was trembling. What could it all mean?

The officer shot, "How old are you, Miss?"

"Twenty-three. Soon to be twenty-four."

Looking at her doubtingly, the officer scrutinized her from head to toe. "What's the name of your school?"

"*My school?*" She couldn't believe it. Why would they want the name of her school? "What school? I am a registered nurse." The words gave Jessie a thrill.

"Got credentials?"

"Credentials? For what? I mailed everything on to Toronto."

"Your *high school* credentials. That's what I'm talking about." The officer gripped his pencil, his knuckles showing white.

"Sir." Jessie plunged her clenched fists deep into her gown's pockets. "I graduated from high school six years ago. I am a regis—"

"How old did you say you were?" interrupted the officer.

Jessie let out a long sigh. "I told you. Twen—ty-thr—ee."

"Gonna' stick with that?"

"I have to. The calendar verifies it."

"Okay. Okay." The officer eyed Jessie again and began writing, glancing up now and then through his black, bushy eyebrows. "About five-foot-three; eyes, blue; complexion, rosy—peaches-and-cream." He rolled his eyes, licking his lips. "Hair bobbed—"

"My hair is *not* bobbed." She gave her head an indignant toss. "We were not allowed to have bobbed hair in training." She wore her hair in a modest knot at the nape of her neck, but for the night, she had braided it and pinned it to the back of her head.

"Let's have a look at your clothes." The policeman moved further into the compartment.

Jessie's hand shot out, protectively covering her neatly folded clothes.

"Something to hide, miss?" He lifted her hand.

She yanked it away, placing it again into her pocket. She watched, her face burning, as the men slung her undergarments across the bed head. They began their listing: "Dress, navy-serge; shoes, brown walking oxfords, matching purse; hat..." Turning to the closet, the men continued their report: "Coat—Hm! Expensive looking! What kind of fur would you say this is?"

"I dunno furs. My wife don't have none." The porter threw a broad smile at Jessie. He winked.

"Looks like Fitch to me." The trainman ran his hand officiously over the soft, white fur.

"Okay. Fitch." The policeman made a notation on his pad. "Hm! Fits. Expensive taste," he said under his breath. "Certainly fits the description."

Fitch... Fitch... Jessie's mind roved, *What is Fitch?* Suddenly, it snapped into place. She had seen a Fitch coat once, in the window of the Hudson's Bay store. "Fitch!" she said aloud, recalling the price tag attached to the coat on the mannequin. "And me just out of nursing school? How could I afford? —"

"Beats me," sneered the officer. "You name it then."

"It's prairie badger. And it was not expensive. It was my sister's. She gave it to me when she moved to Hawaii." Oh, why was she telling them all this? It all seemed so idiotic.

"Sister?" His eyebrows shot up. "S'pose your sister's name's the same as yours? Hudson, was it?"

"Sister," he said to himself. *"Doesn't fit. No sister."*

"Yes. Hudson. Florence Hudson. Same surname as mine — as long as we both remain unmarried." Jessie spat the words at the officer, fed up with his impudent questioning.

He gave an amused one-sided grin.

The men glanced at one another. The policeman shook his head. "How old —? He broke off his question. "That's 'bout it, Miss." The trio turned abruptly and left the compartment.

What was that all about? Jessie scrambled to button the curtain.

"One more thing, miss." The police officer shot his arm back in, yanking at Jessie's hair, pulling her ten-inch braid loose from its pins. The jolt made her bite her tongue.

"Was that necessary?" she hissed, putting her hand to her mouth.

The men had already disappeared down the corridor.

Tut-tut-clickety-click. The train moved on. The rhythm, no longer soothing, chanted in her ear, *What did they want? Why me? What did they want? Why me?*

The next morning, after a restless night, Jessie dragged herself to breakfast. From snatches of conversation overheard in the dining car, and from the porter later on, she began to piece together the reason for her ordeal of the night before.

"Well, ya' see, miss," explained the porter, "dere's dis here gal, sev'nteen, on'y chil', missin' out o' Winn'peg. Her daddy... big name, lots o' money... He thinks his little gal run away to dis good-fo'-nuthin', low-down..., an' she gonna' marry him. Her daddy, he be'n stoppin' trains in an' out o' Winn'peg. An' ya' know, Miss?" The porter moved close to Jessie, shoving his face near to hers. "Yo was da' on'y sev'nteen-year-old-lookin' gal on dis here whole train. Good thing ya' didn' have bobbed hair. 'Cause the missin' gal, she have bobbed hair." The porter moved away, singing as he continued his morning duties.

"Seventeen, indeed!" Jessie chuckled. Loosening her hairpins, she let her auburn tresses tumble around her shoulders. *I wonder if dey caught da' little bob-tailed rabbit befo' she runned down da' rabbit hole. But dis long-tailed fox, she got away!* She closed her eyes, a smile playing at her lips. She was going to enjoy the next three days.

Footnote: Chapter material taken from a story written by Florence, Jessie's sister. Used by permission.

Chapter 6 — The Saxophone Player

Spring 1926 - Fall 1927

"Not exactly the way I had visualized nursing." Jessie kicked off her shoes and slid into the corner of the breakfast nook. She had been working at the Toronto General Hospital for two weeks now, having been assigned ten long-term patients. "But then," she took a sip of the hot tea Auntie had pushed at her, "someone has to look after them.

"Today I asked Mrs. Emory how she was." Jessie looked up from her cup to where Auntie stood washing dishes, and then continued her one-sided conversation. "Poor soul stared at me with vacant eyes, her toothless mouth twisting into contortions. She wanted so badly to talk. I know she did. I took her cold, gnarled hand and held it, while I sang, 'Does Jesus Care?'" Sure that Auntie wasn't listening, she went on anyway. "I saw tears in those old eyes when I came to the words, 'I know He cares.' But just then the supervisor burst into the room. 'Hudson,' she bellowed, 'you have nine other patients to attend to. Get to them. This is a hospital, not a church.'

"Oh, Auntie, all my life I've pictured myself helping people get well. People like Mrs. Emory are never going to get better." She looked up, yearning for some response, some communication. Instead, all she received was a cold stare, while Eliza, with exaggerated deliberation, wiped her hands on her apron and left the room without having spoken one word.

Jessie swallowed the last of her tea. An explosion of loneliness such as she had never experienced—not even during her secretarial days, after Florence had moved to Hawaii—erupted inside her. Slowly, she rose from the table, carried her cup to the sink, rinsed it, and walked into the living room.

She sat down at the Mason and Risch piano, which had been in the family as long as Jessie could remember. As her fingers touched the keys she was transported back in time, sitting next to Mama—her mama, whom she'd barely known—and listening to her play and sing. A tiny bit of her loneliness trickled away.

"Does Jesus Care? I know He cares." As Jessie played and sang the strains of the song, melancholy wrapping its arms around her, her thoughts drifted to her friends in Calgary. Then, she thought of Florence, a world away. Oh, how she longed to see her just now. Her heart feeling like a sack of rocks, she sat with her hands resting on the keys, her chin quivering. She was so alone. So lonely.

When her dad asked her to accompany him to a Salvation Army meeting a few weeks later, Jessie's heart soared. Never in her entire life had she been any place with *just* her dad.

The atmosphere at the meeting was friendly, the singing lively; her mind drifted naturally to her friends back west. Again, loneliness grabbed at her heart, draining her spirit. She slumped in her seat, closing her eyes, trying to visualize herself back among her old friends.

Suddenly her heart gave a leap. Her eyes popped open. She grabbed her dad's hand and beamed into his face. A young man was playing a saxophone solo.

The following day Jessie sat down to make out a check for her insurance premium. Sitting for a moment, the end of her fountain pen making an indentation in her cheek, she mused, *I wonder… would it be bold of me to enclose a note…? Well, bold or no, here goes.* "Dear Allyn." Her heart beat a little faster than usual. "Last night at church, a man played a saxophone solo. I was reminded of you."

(That note, short and inelegant, was the beginning of regular correspondence between Jessie, and John Allyn Splane, the saxophone player, who toted six women to the skating rink in his Model T, and owned a farm up north, and worked for the Canadian Pacific Railway, and sold life insurance on the side.)

"It feels so good to share my thoughts with someone," wrote Jessie in one of her subsequent letters to Allyn. She told him about her patients: Mrs. James, who wouldn't leave her clothes on; Mrs. Franks, who thought she was seven, and chased imaginary chickens around the room; Mr. Alexander, who grabbed her, and wouldn't let go of her; and about the supervisor, always grousing at her for spending too much time with each patient.

Each time she wrote to Allyn, and each time she received an answer, a little of her desolation dissipated.

"There's an opening in the hospital here in Stettler..." Jessie clutched her sister's letter, her heart racing as she read on. "... if you're interested —"

Jessie's eyes darted to her watch. Letting Bell's letter tumble to the floor, she grabbed her coat and bolted from the house. She reached the telegraph office just seconds before closing time. "I... want to send... a telegram," she puffed.

That evening as Jessie sat at the piano, her father slid onto the bench beside her. Resting one calloused hand on the keys, with the fingers of his other hand, he traced the letters, "Mason and Risch," etched in the brass on the face of the piano. "No one plays it anymore, except for you," he said. "I want *you* to have it. Take it with you."

As he began to rise from the bench, Jessie grabbed his arm, pulling his face to hers. She kissed the tear that trickled down his leathered cheek.

Three weeks later, gliding past the bench at the far end of the Crystal Skating Rink in Calgary, Jessie collided with a young man. "Sorry," she apologized, feeling her face flush when she saw that it was Allyn.

"Whoops!" he said at the same time, grabbing her arm to steady her. "Oh! It's you!" His heart skipped a beat. He swallowed his Adam's apple. "S... seen Claribel...? I told her... I'd meet her here." Actually, Allyn had been *hoping* that Jessie would be at the rink. He'd seen her only once, briefly, since she had returned to Calgary a week ago.

Falling into the rhythm of the "Blue Danube Waltz," Jessie and Allyn glided together around the rink for nearly an hour, talking of nothing of importance, but feeling comfortable together. Then casually, as if discussing just the weather, Jessie announced, "I leave for Stettler tomorrow."

"What! So soon?" Allyn skidded to a stop. "You just got back." He skated ahead a few feet, hoping to hide his disappointment.

"My job at the hospital starts Monday. I came to Calgary a few days early to find an apartment for my— Oh, yes, I guess you wouldn't know." Jessie reached out and touched Allyn's arm. "I brought our family piano back with me—the Mason and Risch I told you about in one of my letters? Dad *gave* it to me. Mana and I are sharing a suite, whenever I'm in Calgary. And my piano's there."

The couple floated hand-in-hand for several more loops around the rink, saying little to each other, lost in their individual thoughts. Claribel and Mana—and everyone else—were forgotten.

"Jessie," Allyn said at last, clearing his throat while tightening his grip on Jessie's hand. "From… from the time I first talked to you on the phone… Remember? When I thought you were Huxley? I… ah… I knew—" He swallowed. His face burned. He felt himself turning sick. Why had he started this conversation? But he had, so he'd have to continue. "Then when I heard you sing… and… when we used to go skating with the girls… and go to homes with the church young people. And… when you'd send me your premium checks—" He swung her to the side of the rink and turned her to face him. He squeezed his eyes shut and lowered his head. "But… but… it was when you wrote me that note about the sax player—" He popped his eyes open, clutching Jessie's hands again. He knew he wasn't making sense, so he blurted, "I knew I loved you. That's when God told me… when I knew you were to be… my—"

Jessie pulled her hands free from Allyn's, dropping her eyes. With a shy smile playing at the corner of her lips, she said, "My sisters told me not to—"

Allyn's head jerked up. "What a fool I am!" he said to himself. "What a fool! Of course she wouldn't want to marry me." He pushed away from her, speeding across the ice, his hands clasped behind his back; his head drooped to his chest. "Who am I? I have no skills, and I'm certainly not handsome." He removed his CPR cap, rubbing his ungloved hand across his head. His hair—what was left of it—was a medium brown with a russet tinge to it. Jamming the striped cap back onto his head, he continued skating at top speed, zigzagging in and out among the other skaters.

"Allyn," called Jessie, cutting across the rink to intercept him.

"Wait!" She grabbed his arm, spinning him around. "You didn't let me finish. I... I... wrote my oldest sister, Carrie, after you first sold me life insurance. I told her about you. How you owned a farm up north. Everything. I had no idea what... what you thought of... of me. Or what I thought of you, for that matter. I just told her about you; that's all. And I told my sisters, Bell, and Gertie, and Florence. I didn't say anything about... about the future. There was nothing to say. But—" She skated to the bench at the side of the rink and began to untie her skates. "It was on the night I heard the sax player—I wrote you about him. I hadn't heard a thing at the meeting—I wasn't even there, except in body. Suddenly, 'Heavenly Sunlight,' came floating into my ears, flooding my heart. It was then—" She gave her skate lace a yank, sneaking a look at Allyn. Suddenly she was shy. She could feel her cheeks burning. She swallowed, then continued. "It... it was then that I heard a... whisper: *Jessie, remember Allyn, the saxophone player?*" There she stopped. She struggled with a knot in her second skate lace.

Allyn stood above her, gazing down at her. Never had he seen a picture so beautiful. Frost crystals on her toque and on her hair sparkled like diamonds. She looked up at him, her limpid blue eyes in the dim light looking like twinkling stars. She smiled, and his knees turned to water. He dropped in front of her, his fingers flying to untie her skate lace. Then he reached for her hands. "Jessie!" he said, his voice barely above a whisper, his eyes scanning the rink as if he were about to steal the crown jewels. The music had stopped; the rink had been vacated—when, he hadn't noticed. The haloed glow of the light bulb at the corner of the rink was their only company. The stillness of the night threatened to deafen him. "Jessie," he whispered again. "Will... will you be my... wife?"

Twisting a curl that had escaped from beneath her toque, Jessie lifted her shimmering eyes. The *Golden Voice* of her recent past flashed to her mind: *I have a special work for you...* Why she thought of it now, she didn't know. "Oh, Allyn!" she whispered. "Yes! Yes, I will. I will be your wife."

Jessie walked toward the nurses' lounge of the Stettler Hospital, rubbing her neck to relieve the stiffness. She had just finished a twelve-hour shift and was looking forward to climbing into a hot shower. Down the hall, hurrying towards her was a man.

"Oh," she gasped, when she saw who it was. "I wasn't expecting to see you. Today's Christmas."

"I... ah... I have something for you." Allyn fumbled in his pocket, pulling out a small, crumpled bag. "Here." He shoved the package at Jessie, then stood twisting his cap and shuffling his feet while she opened it. "It... it isn't much. I... I couldn't afford a big one."

Jessie placed her fingers on Allyn's lips. "Sh!" she whispered. "It's beautiful." She handed the ring to Allyn. With her finger extended, she said, "Here. You put it on."

Chapter 7 — Tibby Gives Up

April 1928

In that interim between winter and spring in the foothills of the Canadian Rockies, one can expect anything Mother Nature chooses to hand out. This year she had been kind: the snow had melted, and the ground was beginning to don a coat of green; the warm air had nudged the trees out of their winter's sleep, and the branches were responding by showing a swelling at their tips; pussy willows on the bushes that crowded the coulees and ditches, shimmered and squirmed in their delight of the soft spring breeze.

On the greening lawn surrounding an expansive house, on a quarter section farm on the outskirts of Calgary, two robins played hopscotch, tilting their heads as they listened for their lunch. The veranda of the house, on this fifth day of April, was decorated with pink and white streamers; and over the front door, hung a golden-colored, paper bell.

T. J. Bennett—a retired Baptist minister—and his wife, were long-time friends of Allyn's widowed mother, Clara J. Splane (known to her friends as "Tibby.") It was here, on Bennett's farm, that eight people gathered for a wedding.

For nearly a year this had been "home" to Allyn. So when a month ago Allyn had asked Reverend Bennett to perform the wedding ceremony, he had been delighted. "Of course," he had said. "You're part of the family."

The ceremony was about to begin. Allyn paced up and down the veranda steps, twisting his fedora in his hands. Until a minute ago it had been on his head; but Tibby, seeing her son with his hat plastered on his head, had knocked it off.

Tibby stood shaking her head. Why, oh why, hadn't he worn one of his tailored suits, or at least rented a black one, as she had suggested? But at the very least, he could have had this one sent out to be pressed. It wasn't exactly wrinkled, but it just didn't look fresh. She shuddered. Why, for his own wedding, did he look so disheveled?

Her eyes slid toward her youngest son. She smiled. He stood beaming up at his big brother, his hand extended, handing him a carnation boutonnière. Eleven-year-old Dick was dressed in a black three-piece suit, a black bow tie, and a dazzling white shirt. *Except for his miniature size*, thought Tibby, *he looked more like what a groom should look like.*

She forced her eyes back to her eldest son: she grimaced. She *knew* she should have picked his clothes for the wedding—even though he *was* twenty-seven years old. Under his green, pinstriped suit jacket, Allyn wore a blue shirt and black tie. At least his *brown* shoes were polished! In one hand he held his gray fedora, in the other, the carnation boutonniere, now crumpled. Why wasn't it on his suit?

Muriel Splane, the wife of Allyn's cousin, Sydney, was Jessie's only attendant. She wore a powder-blue suit, with hat, gloves, and pumps to match. She was with Jessie now in the Bennett's bedroom.

Jessie took a deep breath, glancing into the mirror for her final inspection. She had tailored her own suit, of soft rose-colored linen, with calf-length skirt. The jacket, fitted at the waist, flared slightly over her hips. Her white silk blouse, with a triple ruffle in front, she had trimmed with tatting, done in a variegated pink. Her pumps, a deep rose, matched her self-designed hat, which featured a row of miniature daisies, nestled in a bouffant of pink netting. Muriel had styled Jessie's hair in an upsweep fashion, a few curls cascading beneath her hat, tumbling around her neck, and encircling her face. A slight nervousness had blushed her cheeks.

"Well, Jessie!" Tibby sighed, her eyes combing her son in a final once-over. "I hope you know what you're in for." Although they had met several times while Jessie and Allyn were courting, Tibby had never really gotten to know Jessie, not well, anyway.

Her surface impression of her soon-to-be daughter-in-law was that she was serious—too serious, perhaps—quiet and sincere. Would she be up to handling this infuriating man? (Whom Tibby loved beyond words.)

She could feel her temples tightening. She drew in her breath, running her hand over her soft-green woolen suit. She'd be glad when this ordeal was over.

Jessie picked up her white Bible, covered with tiny pink roses. She took a deep breath, the words, *...not an easy path...not an easy path...* throbbing through her head. And, *What would my family think of Allyn?* She turned, smiling at Muriel. She was ready to begin her walk down the long spiraling stairway, into a whole new life.

Tibby's mind snapped to attention when she heard a scuffle inside the house. "Allyn," she hissed, turning suddenly back toward her son. "Your boutonniere." She pointed frantically to her left shoulder. "Put it on."

Allyn glanced down at the wilted carnation he was crumpling in his hand. "Oh!" He fumbled unsuccessfully for the proper place to put it, then stuffed the flower into the top buttonhole of his jacket. With a flip, he tossed his hat to the side of the veranda. He slid into place by his cousin, Syd, a grin on his face. He was ready for his bride.

His mother moaned, pressing at her temples. Grabbing Dickie by the hand, she walked to the chair on the lawn.

Jessie began her descent. Mrs. Bennet, sitting at the organ in the living room, struck up the chords of the "Wedding March." The marriage ceremony of Jessie Viola Hudson, youngest daughter of Hugh Hudson, and of John Allyn Splane, eldest son of Clara J. Splane, had begun.

"He's all yours!" sighed Tibby, watching Jessie take her place by Allyn. "He's all yours!"

Chapter 8 — The Farm Up North

April 1928 - Spring 1929

The walls of the small apartment at the Bennett farm, home to Jessie and Allyn since their marriage, began to close in on Jessie. Not that she wasn't happy — Bennetts treated her like a daughter; or that she wasn't busy — there is always plenty to do on a farm; but she wanted to be with Allyn, alone. She wanted them to start their new life together. And secretly, she wanted to get back to nursing.

"Honey," she said one night, snuggling close to Allyn. "The Bennetts have been wonderful. But—" She took a deep breath. How could she approach this subject tactfully? "But... we'd have more privacy if... if we moved into an apartment in town... Maybe my apartment? Mana's not there anymore, and—"

"Your apartment?" Allyn swung away from her, switching on the light by the bed.

"You'd be closer to your work," Jessie added... *Oh! Oh! That was the wrong thing to say.* One of the reasons they were here was so that Allyn would be handy to his work. Quickly, she came up with another argument. "And I could get a job nursing. Soon we'd be able to get a bigger place."

"Listen, honey. Let's get one thing straight." Allyn took Jessie into his arms. "I won't have you working. I'm the breadwinner in this family. I'm making enough to support us both." He kissed her, then said, "Move to your apartment? It's too small, smaller than this." He passed his eyes over the room and frowned. "We should stay here a while longer, just until... until—"

Jessie pulled away from his embrace. She felt trapped, captured—like an animal caught in a snare. They'd been married only a month, but already she felt stifled. She longed to get back to nursing, to be involved, to live her own life.

Allyn turned her face toward his: he read her look of despair. "Yea," he said. "Maybe you're right." He pulled her to him, kissing her again. "Your apartment *would* be a good idea." He switched off the light and slid down into bed, pulling her close. "But you're *not* working, and that's that."

Jessie had been fighting depression for a week. And today she felt especially agitated. The summer heat poured into their cramped third-floor apartment, and she felt as if she would suffocate.

Allyn thumped his bike against the wall of the house and bounded up the stairs three at a time. "It's sure swell to come home to my little wife after a hard day at work," he said, grabbing Jessie by her waist and twirling her around.

"Sure! Things are always *swell* for you." She struggled from his grip and shoved away from him. His remark—and his cheeriness—irked her, as did many other things about him and this apartment, of late. She began slamming dishes onto the table. "You, at least, get to go to work. I'm stuck up here in this stuffy attic all day." Her eyes filled with tears. "What do you think I spent three-and-a-half years training to be a nurse for...? Here." She flung a letter onto the table and fled into the bathroom, slamming the door behind her.

"Jessie. Honey?" Allyn tapped lightly on the bathroom door a few minutes later. "I've got something to tell you, something exciting." Lowering his voice, he added, "Honey, I'm sorry about this miserable place." It wasn't in Allyn's nature to remind Jessie that it had been *her* idea to move to the apartment. "Please, honey," he continued. "Come, listen to this letter from my brothers."

Jessie opened the door. She slipped her hand into Allyn's, and together they walked to the kitchen.

In 1924 Allyn had seen an ad in the Calgary Herald for the sale of an hundred-and-fifty-acre homestead, near the town of Colinton, about one hundred miles north of Edmonton. With life insurance money from the death of Ernest, Tibby's second oldest son, Allyn had bought the real estate, sight unseen, for seven hundred dollars. It was to be a family project, but as yet, Allyn had not been to see it.

Just before Jessie and Allyn's wedding, Tibby's middle sons, Bill and Erwin, by their mother's persuasion, had covered a wagon, loaded up their belongings, hitched up a team of horses, and headed north to Colinton, over three-hundred-miles from Calgary.

"Listen to this, Hon." Allyn spread Erwin's letter in front of him and began reading. "'Dear Allyn: Quite a trip we had... This is real pioneering...'" Erwin went on for two pages about the *homestead*, as he called it. "'But, why don't you and Jessie come see for yourselves on your next days off? Maybe Jessie could stay on for the summer. That is, ahem...! If you could spare her... ahem!'" Allyn snorted. He could just hear his eighteen-year-old brother titter at the thought of his leaving his bride of three months with two bachelor brothers. He stole a glance at Jessie: she was smiling.

"The rascal! Think I can't take care of myself?" she said. "Go on with the letter."

Allyn continued: "'What's on the farm?' you ask. 'There's a well and a house — I should say, shack — Anyway, come see for yourselves. Oh, yea, and there's a good outhouse... Hope ta' see ya' real soon.'"

He stuffed the letter back into the envelope. With a twinkle in his eyes, he took Jessie into his arms.

Together they said, "Let's go see it."

"*Anything* will be better than the nauseating heat of this apartment," Jessie had said to Allyn as she was packing for the trip. But now, with the buggy tipping from side-to-side as it bounced over ruts and rocks en route from the station in Colinton, to the farm, she wondered, *Would it?*

Along the way she had seen an occasional shack, hiding as if embarrassed, amidst a few straggly trees. As for livestock, not so much as a dog had crossed their path since leaving Colinton... And Colinton. What a one-horse town! *Only she hadn't seen even a horse, except for the one pulling the buggy she was riding in.* From the train station, all that could be seen was one elevator, a store, and a few shacks.

Jessie had never before been north of Edmonton. She glanced around her. *How could one survive in such wilderness? Nothing but scrub and brush.*

Bill steered the horse onto a narrow trail—more scrubby brush along the side of the road. They rounded the bend. Before her lay a vast field of... of... she didn't know what to call it: clumps of dirt; bits of collapsed buildings scattered here and there; long-since-abandoned, rusted-out machinery; and boulders—not little pebbles, nor even what one might call rocks. These were boulders—everywhere—boulders, with blades of grass, gasping and strangling, trying to poke their heads through to the sun.

At last, through a mirage of rippling heat waves, she viewed what looked like a settlement. Surely that couldn't be the house—shack—Erwin had mentioned, that pile of logs in the distance? Surely not! As they drew closer she saw the unpainted door, hanging at an angle; the low, four-paned windows; the flat, thatched roof; the gray horizontal log walls; and puffs of smoke belching from a rusty stovepipe. Her stomach hit her throat. This *couldn't* be the place. It just *couldn't* be!

All during the trip from town Allyn and Bill had been carrying on an animated conversation—or agitated, she wasn't sure which—oblivious, it seemed, to their surroundings. Didn't Allyn see what kind of wasteland they were in? Couldn't he see what *she* was seeing? Maybe this wasn't the place after all. Maybe they'd pass on through—to something better. She glanced at Bill. He had cut off his conversation and had turned to watch her, a bemused grin on his face.

Bill reined in the horse, pulling it to a stop by the door of the shack. Inwardly she grimaced; then subconsciously she noticed the *"good"* outhouse Erwin had mentioned. She couldn't help but smile.

Allyn had already jumped from the wagon and was running around the yard looking at... what? Jessie didn't know, nor did she care. Her vision blurred. Her stomach heaved... *This* is what she had chosen? She turned her eyes from Bill. She wasn't going to let him—or Allyn, for that matter—know how she felt.

Forcing a smile, she quipped, "So! *This* is my summer home. Hope Erwin has supper on. I'm starved." Actually food was the last thing she wanted. Her stomach was churning: maybe it was the buggy ride, or perhaps the July heat, or was it because of... her summer home? She climbed from the buggy.

Entering the shack she gazed at the kitchen-cum-living room, its whitewashed walls grimy with grease and soot, its windows opaque with smudge. The one bedroom, with its slab-wood door closed, did not reveal its condition... One bedroom? Where would everyone sleep?

Jessie's mind was swirling, so was her head. For some reason — she didn't know why — as she stood in the middle of the floor staring at her surroundings, she thought of her piano, all crated, ready to be shipped. But shipped to where? Certainly not *here!* She felt a sneer creep to her lips.

Erwin had the table set, man style, the dishes thrown helter-skelter over the table. But the food, Jessie had to admit, forcing herself to take control of her feelings, smelled appetizing. "Chicken," she said, smiling at her young brother-in-law. "Smells good." Maybe she *was* hungry, after all.

Two days later as Allyn was preparing to return to Calgary, Jessie kissed him, and in a more reassuring voice than she felt, she said, "It... it won't be so bad here. I'll be so busy, I'll— Oh, honey, about the piano."

Allyn looked puzzled.

"Well, we can't have it here." Her eyes made a circle of the place while she dug into her purse and pulled out an envelope. "Here. This is Fred and Carrie Vague's address. Remember? My sister in Kingman, just north of Camrose? The farmers? I'll ask her to keep it for me. I'll let them know you're shipping it." She gave Allyn a fading smile.

Oh, how she would miss her piano! Even though she'd had it such a short time, only while they'd been in the apartment, it felt like a part of her. But... oh, well! There was no turning back now. They had closed the apartment, despite Jessie's protest. As they were packing to leave for the north, Allyn had said that he'd rather go back to Bennett's for the summer than to live alone in the apartment. "We'll have the piano shipped," he had assured her at the time, "as soon as we see the place."

Near the end of July, Allyn, along with his mother and young Dick, arrived at the farm for a visit. As the group sat down to supper Erwin remarked, "Wow! Allyn, you sure did snare a winner when you trapped Jessie." His eyes twinkled. "Isn't this terrific?"

"Yea, and look at this place." Bill waved his hand around. "Hardly recognize it. Counter and floor covered with linoleum, not to mention—" He swung his arms around again. Not only had Jessie made curtains for the windows, but she had also sewn together Hudson Bay blankets and strung them up for a partition at one end of the kitchen, to curtain off an area which Bill and Erwin used as a bedroom. For the day she turned the two cots into settees, converting the area to a sitting room. The one bedroom, the men had given up to Jessie.

"And another amazing thing about Jessie," continued Bill, " apart from the meals — don't have to choke anymore on our own cooking — " He gave a quick, sideways glance at his younger brother, "is how she's always singing. Even in *this* dump." He swung his arms in an arch again.

"Okay, you guys. Watch it!" Allyn slammed his fist on the table in mock anger. "She's mine. I think I'd better take her back. I'll—"

"All right, boys." Tibby set her fork on her plate with a forceful clink. "That's enough. I can see that Jessie—" Tibby had been sizing up the situation. Her daughter-in-law had been here nearly a month. She figured — well, she didn't know what she figured, but she didn't go along with all this flattery. She had been married at nineteen; she'd had to put up with a lot worse than *this* in her day. It wasn't, in her opinion, good for a young bride to be given too much praise. Jessie had a lot to learn about hardship — Tibby figured, at least.

Jessie's hand flew to her face and she fled from the room.

Puzzled, the men looked at each other. Allyn jumped up to follow her, but his mother put her hand on his shoulder, pushing him back. "Go on with your meal," she commanded. "I'll go."

When Tibby entered the bedroom Jessie was wiping her eyes. "Oh... Mother," she sniffled. It had been difficult for Jessie to learn to call her mother-in-law, *Mother*, in that she had been robbed of her own mother when she was only five. "I've made such a fool of myself. I just don't know what's wrong with me lately. I just... seem to want to cry at... nothing. And —" She swallowed, choking back tears. "And I feel so... rotten— "

Tibby sucked in her breath, adding—it seemed to Jessie—two inches to her five-foot-seven-inch stature. To her, Mother Splane had always seemed so stern, so right, so confident—so intimidating. But right now, she needed someone to talk to—a woman. Her tears began to flow again. "Ever since, oh, I don't know how long, but I just don't know what's wrong with me. I love Allyn. I'm happy to help here at the farm, too. And I think the world of Bill and Erwin. But oh, Mother—" She sniffed, trying to stifle the sound of her crying.

"You silly girl," Tibby said, pushing Jessie onto the bed and sitting down beside her. She knew what was wrong. *She'd* been through it *six* times. "There's nothing *wrong* with you." With her index finger, she tilted Jessie's head so that she would have to look her in the eye. "Everything is *right*. You are in the family way." She gave Jessie a stiff smile. "*You* are going to make *me* a grandmother."

Chapter 9 — Utopia?

1929

"A baby. My own baby." Jessie's greatest joy in nursing had been handing a newborn infant to its mother. And soon *she* would be a mother. No longer were her days dreary. No longer did she lament that her career was going down the drain. In fact, she was so busy getting ready for the baby (back in Calgary, in an apartment on Ninth Street, East), that she barely noticed the winter passing. During the evenings while she sat knitting or embroidering some design on a baby garment, she and Allyn would talk, planning their future and dreaming. Never had Jessie been happier.

On Sunday March twenty-fourth, in a private hospital in Calgary, owned by a friend of Allyn's mother, that familiar first-cry of an infant entering the world filtered into Jessie's fuzzy mind. All the pain of the last few hours melted like the frost on a windowpane when the sun hits it. *"This one is mine,"* she said, sinking into unconsciousness.

"Mrs. Splane. Mrs. Splane." The nurse shaking her and the lusty shriek of an infant budged her mind back into semi-focus. "You have a beautiful seven-pound daughter. I think she's going to be a blue-eyed, blond-haired soprano. At least she certainly has a healthy set of lungs." The nurse smiled and handed Jessie her baby.

As she snuggled her daughter close she whispered, "I don't have to pass *you* to anyone. You're mine, all mine."

Whenever, throughout the winter, Jessie and Allyn had discussed names, Jessie had insisted, "We can't name a baby we haven't seen." So when Allyn peeked for the first time at his daughter, he whispered, "Well, Mama, now we've seen her, what'll we call her?"

Shutting her eyes for a moment, then popping them open, pretending she'd just thought of a name, Jessie replied, "Clara. Let's call her Clara, after your mother." The name had come to her instantly, upon peeping for the first time at her daughter. She had tried out "Clara Maria", after the two mothers, but the names didn't flow smoothly. "And I've always liked the name, Louise," she added, peering into her husband's sparkling eyes. "I had a friend once, by the name of Louise." Her mind flashed briefly to her high school chum, who had died of influenza.

"Clara Louise." Allyn tried the name, smiling at his mother, who was just then walking through the door, holding Dick by the hand. "Clara Louise. I like it. It's bright." He felt all-aflutter, like a dandelion puff soaring to the clouds.

It'll be heaven to be able to raise my family on the farm. Clean air. Good earth. Hard work. No city corruption." Plunking the crates containing the family's belongings onto the train platform, Allyn emphasized each phase of farm living, as he saw it.

Jessie didn't have as glorified a picture of farm living as her husband had. She'd lived there? He hadn't. They had talked many times about moving to the farm, weighing the pros and cons, and now it was actually happening. "How are we all going to squeeze into that little shack, Allyn?" she had asked as they packed, hoping to discourage her impetuous husband from so hasty a move.

And now as the train spit and hissed into the station, Jessie paced nervously up and down the platform, rocking Clara.

"Don't look so worried, Honey." Allyn, always the optimist, glanced at his frowning wife, hunched over the baby to protect her from the shower of cinders being spewed from the engine. He grabbed her by the arm and helped her board the train. "Everything'll be swell. We'll find a way. We'll find a way."

"Sure. Swell!" she said to herself as she walked down the aisle to find a seat. She remembered last summer how difficult privacy was, but now with the baby — She buried her face in Clara's blanket, as if to bury her worries. They had burned all their bridges: no more railway passes, too far from any hospital to work. And — But settling into her seat, she looked into Allyn's radiant face. She smiled at him. She'd make the best of it.

"We can work our own land, then hire ourselves and our machinery out to the neighbors." Allyn jumped behind the wheel of the 1928 Model T Ford, which he, Bill, and Erwin had just bought. They had been to the bank and had financed a four-cylinder, 1530 McCormick Deering tractor, and a breaking plow, as well as the car.

The future looked bright in 1929: an ideal spring, a warm summer with just the right amount of moisture — great prospects for bumper crops.

"Yea, and with a good crop ourselves, and when the neighbors sell their harvest and pay us what they'll owe us for our work —" Bill added.

"We should be able to pay a good half of our bank loan by the end of the harvest season," Erwin concluded.

The talk on the way home from town was light and spirited.

"Tell Jessie we'll be in for supper in a little while," Erwin shouted as he and Bill jumped from the car and headed for the bunkhouse.

Early in the spring Bill and Erwin had begun homesteading alongside the present farm. Unbeknown to Jessie and Allyn, until they arrived at the farm, the brothers had thrown together a bunkhouse for themselves for sleeping. But they still had their meals at the house.

"At a buck twenty-five a bushel for our wheat — that's last year's price; should be better this year — we should be able to..." While Jessie did the last-minute preparations for supper, Allyn shared with her the plans he and his brothers had discussed on the way home from town.

"Honey! We should be able to get our own place after this fall's harvest." Unable to contain his excitement any longer, he jumped up from his chair and gave Jessie a bear hug. "And then we'll send for your piano," he added, kissing her.

Jessie smiled while shoving her husband from her. He and his brothers labored long hours on their own land, and now they would be working their neighbors', as well. She shook her head and let out a long, slow sigh.

"I've just put Clara down for the night," she said. "She's not asleep. Pick her up if you want, while I put supper on the table."

The harvest was over: not only had Allyn and his brothers had a fair crop, but the crops they had harvested for their neighbors had been even better. Maybe as soon as they could sell their grain, they could pay the bank right off and still have money left over. Perhaps they'd even be able to begin building the promised house.

The enthusiasm of Allyn and his brothers gladdened Jessie's heart. She didn't mind putting up with a few hardships, as long as her husband was happy.

But then the Great Depression hit: the economy plummeted.

Allyn splashed water from the basin onto his face, spluttering into his hands. "We're washed up. We'll... we'll have to return the machinery... if things don't improve. Bank's already sent us several dunning notes." He flopped onto a chair at the table. "Last year wheat sold for a buck-and-a-quarter a bushel. This year it's down to four-bits: and even then, we can't get our money. No one has any — even to live, let alone pay us for our work." He dropped his head into his hands.

Forcing her voice to be light, Jessie said, "Hope your supper's still all right. It's been sitting in the warming oven for two hours." Despite her cheerful exterior, Jessie felt a momentary panic seize her. Poor Allyn! For six months he had been working so hard to be a farmer, to make it his life. For a while she had had hopes for him, but it just wasn't working. Even if they'd gotten their money for their work — even if — he just was *not* a farmer. It wasn't that she never saw him from sunup to sundown that bothered her. It was what farming was doing to his spirit. He tried so hard to put on a cheerful front, but she'd watched him when he didn't know she was watching. It ripped her heart apart to see him so dejected. Not just now, but every night. And she didn't know what to do to help?

She joined him at the table, pouring herself a cup of coffee. "What'll you do if you can't make a go of farming?" she ventured, after several moments of silence.

Allyn took a forkful of roast chicken before he answered. Don't know, Hon... Boy this supper's good! And thanks for the peppermints you stuck in my lunch. Where'd you find 'em? Kept me goin' all afternoon." He took a mouthful of scalding coffee. "It's too late *this* year to find other work—even if I could," he continued, in answer to Jessie's question. "We'll get through the winter somehow. See what comes of the spring. Bill's fed up. He's going back to Calgary for the winter. Not Erwin, though. He's the real pioneer. He'll struggle it through... somehow."

Jessie handed Allyn a piece of pumpkin pie. "Clara helped me make this."

"Mm! Good!... Should be enough vegetables from the garden for the winter," he continued, snatching Clara from her highchair and setting her on his lap. She grabbed his suspenders, giving them a snap—her favorite game with Daddy. "And we'll kill off the chickens and pigs." His spirit was lightening, as it usually did after being in from the field for a while. "We'll get by." He shoveled a chunk of pie into the baby's mouth, chuckling at the face she made at the spicy tang. "We'll get by."

"Well, Mama, guess it's back to farming—if that's what you call it." Allyn plunked the flour, salt, lard, and yeast he'd just brought from town, onto the table. "I scouted all day for a job. No work. No money. Radio was on in the store. Nothin' but depression talk everywhere—depression, depression, depression. They were saying how bad it was in the cities—'specially the U.S. People jumpin' out of windows; blowin' their heads off; thousands of dollars lost in the stock markets."

Going to the porch, he poured a dipperful of water into the basin, splashed cold water onto his face; then buried his face in the towel. It was like a moan Jessie heard: her heart wrenched.

"Honey." She walked over to him, placing her hand on his shoulder. "We're not destitute. We have each other, our family, and best of all, we have our faith in God." She went to the table, picked up the twenty-pound sack of flour and emptied it into the bin. "I saw a robin today. Oh, yes, and a gopher."

"Gopher," mimicked Clara.

Allyn turned to his daughter, picked her up and threw her over his head. Her infectious giggle, as always, made him forget about his trying day, his worries.

"My kid brother—twenty—knows exactly what to do. Me? Bungle, bungle, bungle. I'll never make a farmer." Allyn dropped an armload of wood into the wood box, splashed water onto his face, and sat down for his late evening meal. "Today the horses went in one direction, while I was left holding the plow, facing the other way. And yesterday, I broke the harrow. Tried to fix it with haywire, but no-go. Caput!"

Jessie stifled a smile as she set Allyn's plate in front of him. She placed her hand lightly on his shoulder as she passed. Hiding her own feeling of anxiety, she suggested, "Why don't you try again for something different? Anything. Something unrelated to farming." She pulled a chair back from the table and sat down to join him. It frightened her to see her sanguine husband so depressed.

"If only I were in the city," she said to herself, "I could go back to—" Just then her stomach gave another heave, as it had been doing a lot, of late: and she knew. But should she tell Allyn? Would it cheer him up? Or would it just add another worry, to know he'd have another mouth to feed by September?

Chapter 10 — That's Not *My* Baby

September 1930

"Bill and Erwin said they'd keep an eye out for you while I'm gone." Allyn dropped a load of wood onto the floor. "I should be back before that baby gets here," he said, chucking the wood into the wood box.

Bill worked for the CPR. His Job, filling grain cars, was sporadic, so right now he was back on the farm, as harvest was about to begin.

"Here." Jessie pushed her husband aside. "Let me do that. You make such a mess. Look at the floor. I just swept it. Your mother's coming this afternoon for Clara, and I don't want the place to look like a pigsty."

"They've promised to keep you stocked with wood," continued Allyn, ignoring his wife's rebuff. "Sorry I have to be away right now." He kissed her and hurried out the door.

Earlier in the summer Allyn had left farming, and was now doing odd jobs wherever he could find them. Right now he was heading north to dig wells, before the winter set in.

Jessie opened her eyes, squinting at the clock. It was Sunday, September seventh. "Claribel's birthday!" she said aloud, reaching for her housecoat. Just as she did, a searing pain ripped through her abdomen. *"It can't be time yet."* She gasped for breath. *"Not for another week."* The perspiration was pouring off her, but she began to shiver.

She staggered to the kitchen, built a fire, and while waiting for the kettle to boil, she lifted the curtain, her eyes scanning the yard. Uneasiness began to stir within her: she couldn't see the car. Erwin had met a young lady, Olive Brown, and was spending a lot of time in Colinton, where she lived.

Clutching at her stomach as another pain seized her, she subconsciously glanced at the clock: seven thirty. Quickly, she dressed; then added a stick of wood to the fire, setting the teakettle off to the side of the stove. "I'd better skip the tea," she said, heading for the men's cabin.

Just a couple of feet from their door, she staggered, as another pain--mingled with panic--grabbed her. "Where's the car?" she said aloud. "And where are the men?" No smoke was coming from the chimney. "Bill? Erwin?" she called as she entered. The clammy fall air hit her nostrils: no fire had been built. She headed for the barn.

At the entrance she crumpled to the ground, involuntarily screaming, "Oh, no! What'll I do? I'm alone. Alone!" Her mind began rehearsing childbirth procedures, and her panic grew.

"Jessie!" Bill, hearing her scream, dropped the milk bucket at the stall. His face ashen, his arms shaking, he lifted his sister-in-law from the ground. "What's wrong?" he shouted in her ear, while steering her toward the cabin. "Sorry it's so chilly in here. Thought I'd milk Bossy and slop the pigs before I lit the stove." He eased her onto a chair and scrambled to light a fire.

"Never mind the fire... Bill," gasped Jessie, "where's the car? Where's Erwin? I need... to get to the hosp... to Athabasca. Now. My pains... are... are close."

Dropping the stick of wood he had been holding. Bill spluttered, "Pains...? What pains? Jess— Is... is it? —"

A weak smile struggled on Jessie's face. "Yes, Bill. If I have my guess, before this day is up I'll have my son—your first nephew. And on your sister's birthday, at that!"

Bill turned red. "Er... Erwin didn't come home," he spluttered, twiddling his fingers against each other. "He... he took... Ollie to a meeting in Amber Valley last night. Some church thing. Her parents said he could sleep on their couch if... if he got home too late. Guess he did. Any chance he gets he—Well, he's like a love-sick cow lately." He laughed a dry, humorless laugh.

When he turned again to Jessie, she was grasping her middle and gasping for breath. He sprang into action. Grabbing his CPR cap, he lunged for the door. "I'll... I'll throw the harness on Lady... and... go for Erwin. Be back in a flash. You be okay? Want to go back... to your cabin where it's warm?"

"Never mind, Bill. Just go. I'll be fine. I'll go get my bag ready." Actually, she'd had her hospital gear ready for two weeks. "Hurry!" she added.

Jumping from Lady's back and leaving the reins dangling, Bill bounded up the stairs, three at a time, to Brown's apartment above the post office. "Erwin, Erwin, come quick. Jessie's got the urge." He burst into the kitchen without knocking. He hadn't even taken time to notice whether or not the car was out front.

Two bewildered faces stared at him from the breakfast table. Mrs. Brown set the coffee pot onto the stove. "Erwin's not here," she said. "He and Ollie have gone to a meeting." She looked from Bill to her husband, then back to Bill. "The urge to what, Bill? What... what's... wrong with Jessie?"

"Didn't Erwin tell you? That... that... Jessie was... was... due?" Bill turned away. He could feel his face turning red.

"Due? You mean... the baby? Already?" Mrs. Brown's face crumpled with concern. "Oh, if... if I'd known—"

"Never mind, Mother." Mr. Brown clunked his coffee mug onto the table, wiped his mouth on the back of his hand, stood up and brushed the crumbs from his overalls. "I'll go get her and fetch her to the hospital. Get my keys. I'll take the Olds." As well as running the post office in Colinton, George Brown was in the second-hand car business.

Prying her eyes open when the nurse nudged her, Jessie squinted at the squirming bundle being pushed at her: a scowling red face, a shock of straight, russet hair, and tiny fists flailing out from under a faded pink blanket. She threw back the blanket. Gasping, she said, "That's... that's not *my* baby." She shoved the wiggling, screeching bundle from her. "Take it away. Take it away."

"Well!" said the nurse, laughing. "It's the *only* baby in the nursery, and you are the *only* mother in the maternity ward. Where would you like me to take her?"

"Her?" squeaked Jessie, rubbing her eyes. "Did you say, 'Her?' I already have a girl. This... I wanted... this one was supposed to be a boy! You must be mistaken. This must be someone else's baby."

The nurse stood by her bed, looking down at her, shaking her head. "Mrs. Splane," she said, an amused smile tickling her lips. "There's been no mistake. *This* is *your* baby."

Elbowing her way to a sitting position, she reached for the wriggling package. "Well then, let's have a look at you." She lifted back the blanket again. Putting her finger into the curled-up palm of the baby's right hand and feeling the involuntary squeeze, she pulled the wee mite's arm to its full length. "And so puny, at that!"

"Five pounds, two ounces," informed the nurse.

"For one thing—" Jessie yanked the pink blanket off the baby, tossing it to the foot of the bed. "We'll get rid of that." She reached into her bag, pulling out a *cuddle sheet,* as eighteen-month-old, Clara, had called it when she had seen her mother folding it and putting it into her hospital bag. "It's for our new baby," Jessie had explained to her daughter at the time.

Wrapping the soft blue blanket around her infant, Jessie looked into the wizened face. "You have a face only a mother could love," she said, kissing the wrinkled forehead and pulling her to her breast. After several unsuccessful attempts at sucking, the baby screamed and pulled away.

"A real red-head," said Jessie, falling exhausted onto the pillow, passively allowing the nurse to take the screaming infant back to the nursery.

As she lay there thinking about names she and Allyn had discussed--all boys', her mind drifted to her family. Just recently she had met her brother's daughter, a pretty girl of sixteen, with bright-blue eyes, freckles, and curly rust-colored hair: *"Evelyn,"* she mused, her eyes popping open. *"Her name was Evelyn."* She remembered how pleased she had been to have had a visit from a member of her family. She hadn't seen Eugene since she herself was about sixteen, but having met his daughter seemed to bring the family together again. How she had enjoyed Evelyn's happy-go-lucky, bubbling personality!

"Evelyn," she said again, this time thinking of her nursing friend, and roommate, Evelyn Kadey. Her mind floated into the haziness that comes just before sleep, and the names of her sisters floated in her head: *Caroline...Isobel May... May... May* — She fell asleep.

When she awoke two hours later, it was to the screech of her baby. "Evelyn May," she said, taking the screaming, squirming bundle from the nurse. "That's what I'll call you. Evelyn May."

Chapter 11 — "Dat's *My* Baby"

Fall 1930 - Spring 1931

Jessie threw up her hands, saying aloud: "Mother and Dick for the winter! Well, if I thought we were crowded before—" She dropped the letter she was reading, hurrying to her screaming baby. "I wonder what your grandma will say about you, you little screech owl." She lifted Evelyn from the bassinet. "Just three more days and you'll get to meet your big sister," she whispered in her infant's ear. Her heart flip-flopped at the thought.

As she kissed the wrinkled brow, an indescribable fatigue enveloped her. She leaned her head on her hand while waiting for the bottle to warm. *Oh Allyn, Allyn, why aren't you here? I need you, oh, how I need you.* The sting of her mother-in-law's words burned in her mind: *I may be of some assistance to Jessie.* (Her letters were always addressed just to Allyn.) *I have been successful in potty-training Clara while she was here. I had all my youngsters trained long before they were eighteen months old. Clara is a bright child and learned quickly.*

"Of course she learned quickly," spat Jessie, shifting the baby to her shoulder and shaking a few drops of milk onto her wrist. "She was practically trained before she went there."

While she sat struggling with her fussing baby, urging unwanted nourishment into her tiny mouth, she could not keep her mind off the letter from Allyn's mother: *I must go north... during Father's illness... shall be leaving Dickie with you. This will crowd you... build a lean-to... giving you and Jessie some semblance of privacy... When I return I will be staying on with you...*

It was that last part, *"staying on,"* that bothered her. Her shoulders sagged; her back ached; her head felt as if it were about to explode. She wanted to close her eyes and sleep forever. Her head dropped to her chest... She jerked, suddenly alert: she had almost dropped the baby. It was then she noticed that the letter had slipped to the floor. As she reached to pick it up, her eyes passed the Bible, open at *Psalm 31*. With the letter still in her hand, her eyes drifted to *Verse 24*, underlined in red by Allyn: "Be of good courage, and he shall strengthen your heart, all ye that hope in the Lord." She tossed the letter onto the open Bible.

"Oh, Lord," she prayed, "How I *do* need your strength right now."

The door burst open. She jumped. In two leaps Allyn was at her side. "Came as soon as I could. Just heard yesterday about our new daughter." He crouched beside Jessie, lifting back the blanket and wrinkling up his face to match the scowl on the baby's face. "Just as ugly as your daddy," he said, grabbing her by two corners of her blanket. "Here, Mama, let me take her."

"Allyn!" Jessie gasped. "Be careful! "She's— Oh what's the use!" She sighed and smiled at the same time, seeing that no harm had come to the tiny infant. She went to the stove. "I'll make us tea. Glad you're home. Read your mother's letter." She pointed to the Bible.

"Want to see your new baby sister?" Jessie gave Clara a long hug; then carried her to the bassinet, which once had been hers. She folded back the "cuddle sheet" to let her little daughter look at the baby.

"Dat's *my* baby." Clara struggled from her mother's arms, reaching her hand in under the blanket and grabbing the baby's hand. "Cara look after *dis* baby." And she made it her job from then on.

After Dick was settled into school in Colinton, Mother Splane left for the north, where she stayed until after her father's death, several months later.

Winter hit with a vengeance, in early November. Even with the cabin being banked with bales of hay and the cracks chinked with plaster, the only place the family could keep warm was within a two-foot radius of either the stove in the kitchen, or the pot-bellied heater in the lean-to.

One morning Allyn burst in from the barn, blowing on his hands. "Baby! It's cold! Bet it's forty below." He turned to Dick. "Better skip school today. It's far too cold for you *or* the horse." He stretched out his hands over the stove.

Dick gave his brother a scathing look.

"Allyn, you don't understand." Jessie pushed him aside to drop a stick of wood into the stove. "You just don't understand." She shook her head. "Dick hasn't missed a day of school in his life. Have you, Dick?" She turned, smiling at her young brother-in-law. "I remember, I was like that, too. I'd rather walk to school in a blizzard, than miss. School was my life."

"Well... it's just *getting* there," sighed Dick, stuffing his foot into a woolen sock. "If only I could get Lady warm enough to take me. The school barn is pretty warm—better than here." He curled his lips, glancing in Allyn's direction, while continuing to dress for school.

Jessie stood pinching her lips between her thumb and forefinger, puckering her brow. Suddenly she snapped her fingers, "I know!" she said, turning to Dick. "Go get Lady. Take her in there." She nodded her head toward the lean-to. "You can warm her up while you're having breakfast... Then we can put blankets on her—"

"Great!" Dick bounded to his feet. "Thanks, Jess." He grabbed his coat and rushed for the barn.

"Now you really *are* a lady," he said, patting the horse's soft muzzle. He set down a small dish of chop for her and went into the kitchen to have his breakfast.

Chapter 12 — Lumpy Bread And Grasshoppers

1931

"What's the matter with that baby?" Mother Splane had just arrived back from her stay in the north and had been kept awake most of the night by the baby's screaming. "Look at her, four months old and the size of a newborn. Don't you have her on some kind of formula? She should be, if you're unable to nurse her. She's sickly. Straight cow's milk is no good. Girl, you're a nurse. You should know that."

Jessie busied herself at the stove while the scolding went on. What could she say? Could she tell her mother-in-law that *formula* had already been suggested to Allyn? Could she say that it had been *her* son that had insisted that cow's milk—and faith—was sufficient? Could she tell her that there was no *money* for formula? Of course she couldn't, so she said nothing.

"'*Horlicks*,' that's what she needs." Tibby cradled the baby in her arm. She had been to town and had brought back the powdered formula, used for invalids. "I raised all my babies on Horlicks," she said, urging Evelyn to open her mouth. "You watch. She'll stop fussing, and she'll gain weight." (She was right. Evelyn soon became a happy, healthy baby.)

"*Lumpy bread, my eye!*" Jessie slapped the dough onto the counter and began kneading it. "Tibby, Mother! Tibby, Mother!" she said with each punch. She never called her mother-in-law, "Tibby," to her face. "I'll show you good bread. I'll show you! Only you complain about my cooking. Of course I can't cook like you can. Wait 'til I've had as much practice. Just you wait!"

In the two weeks that Mother Splane had been back, her scolding and criticism had been continual. Jessie never answered back—out loud; but she said plenty under her breath, as she was doing now. Giving the dough a final slap, she heaved it into the greased pan and covered it with a clean towel.

"And a good housekeeper?" she said, picking up the broom to sweep the flour from the floor. "Look what I have to work with." She clutched the broom handle and took stock: a cracked cook stove with rusted chimney; a table made from three planks nailed to two sawhorses and covered with cracked oilcloth; six wooden chairs, rungs missing from the back (one with *no* back); wooden orange-crates nailed together for cupboards; cooking pots mended with screws and washers—no handles; and a broom so worn— She looked down at the straggly pieces of straw at the end of the handle, saw the absurdity of it all and laughed aloud.

Finished sweeping, she went to check on her sleeping children. She flopped onto her bed, glad for the privacy of the lean-to. She sighed. *I'll be glad when June comes and Mother goes back to Calgary.* She knew that her mother-in law was right. She knew she wasn't the best of housekeepers, or the best of cooks. Even though she resented it at times, she was thankful for what Tibby was teaching her. "Auntie could never be bothered," she muttered, shutting her eyes and falling immediately to sleep.

In the early part of that summer, in exchange for Allyn's having cleared a stand of trees for him, the owner of a lumber mill in Athabasca had built Allyn a three-roomed, shingled house. This simple building, situated about a hundred yards from the log shack, was built on skids, so that it could be moved at a later date. It was Allyn's intention to add on to it when he had decided where on the property would be the best place for a permanent dwelling.

It was to this place that the family had recently moved, leaving the log shack for Allyn's mother, and Dick, when they returned in a week or so.

Pulling her hands out of the slimy water, Jessie clutched her back, straightening from where she had been hunched over the washtub, in the yard, where she always did the washing on good days in the summer. With her waterlogged fingers, she pushed back a strand of hair from her perspiring brow. Lifting her apron, she wiped her forehead and looked around. "Just two more shirts to wash and we'll be all finished." Her lips struggled to form a weak smile at her daughter, while she dropped the shirts into the water to soak.

"A'most finished." Clara sighed, putting her hand to her back, the other hand pushing imaginary hair from her eyes. She had been "doin' wash" alongside her mama, scrubbing her doll clothes on her tiny washboard, in the little washtub Grandma had given her.

"Come along, Clara. Let's go to the well before your sister wakes up." Jessie picked up the water buckets and two tin cups. She handed Clara two lard pails.

A miniature adult, she thought, as she watched her daughter skip down the path ahead of her. *No wonder, with Grandma and young Dick both tutoring her. Why, she can practically read! Good thing my little lady isn't the spoilable type.* Jessie smiled, thinking of the many times during the previous winter, while they still lived in the lean-to of the shack, that Clara, after having been scolded, would stamp her rebellious little foot and say, "I go Gamma's." Then she would stomp off to "Gamma's" side of the house.

"Goin' to the well for buttamilk, Mama?" Clara said now, stopping to wait for Jessie. She loved going to the well. "Just me and Mama." She swung her pails, running ahead again.

Lifting the lid on the well, Jessie carefully pulled up the tub, where she kept her perishables: butter, eggs, milk, et cetera. She set the tub onto the ground, took the jar of buttermilk, filled the two tin cups and handed one to Clara. She sat down on the rough bench Allyn had slapped together, Clara beside her on an overturned water pail. It felt good to relax, even for five minutes.

"We'd better hurry, before Evie wakes up." Jessie released the rope on the water bucket, sending the pail whizzing down into the well. She stood back, watching the handle spin, unwinding the rope. *"That's what my head feels like,"* she said to herself.

"Spash!" Clara jumped up and down. She loved the sound of the bucket hitting the water.

Jessie jerked the rope: the bucket filled. Slowly, slowly, she turned the handle, struggling to bring up the heavy pail of water. "Three months without rain." Every time she came, it seemed the water level was lower. Some of the neighbors' wells had already dried up. She let out a long sigh as she poured the water into the carrying pails.

As mother and daughter neared the house a reoccurring oppression threatened to suffocate Jessie. *I could have had a career. A cynical smile trickled over her lips. A lot of good it did me to graduate third in my class. Here I am, six years later, stuck on a so-called farm, in debt, a husband gone most of the time, two babies, an unfinished house —* A dry laugh escaped her throat. *I wonder what Evelyn Kadey, or Mana Rummel, or Sadie Nash, or Ida Huxley are doing?* As she said the names of her nursing friends, she thumped her foot, and the water from the bucket splashed onto the hem of her dress, down her stockings, and into her shoes. *I bet they have bank accounts.*

She set the pails of water by the door and scanned her surroundings. A shudder rippled through her. How she hated this country! The grasshoppers creaked through the air, stinging her on the cheek, strangling in her hair. On the clothes drying on the line, they had left tobacco-like stains, and on the windowpanes, a gray, gluey substance. Hungrily, the creaky monsters had eaten her garden, the grass, the flowers; and what leaves the tent caterpillars hadn't stripped in June, the gray-gobblers had riddled in August. Dust and smoke hung in the air, and the cloudless sky looked scorched and desiccated.

She closed her eyes, trying to squeeze away the dizziness. She knew that tomorrow would be no different from today, just different chores: she would stoke up the fire, so unbearable in this August heat; she would set the four sadirons on the stove. *I wonder why flat irons are called, "sadirons?"* she thought, feeling one side of her face form a grin—although she was in no smiling mood. *Guess because ironing is such a sad job;* she would spread flannelette sheets on the table to serve as an ironing board—while Clara, by her side, would be using her toy iron to iron her dolly clothes on the little ironing board Grandma had given her. *At least she has an ironing board,* thought Jessie, with a little childish jealousy.

Jessie continued wallowing in self-pity while scrubbing the remaining two shirts she had left soaking. She dumped the slimy wash water onto the ground and used the rinse water to scrub out the porch and outhouse. Glancing at Clara, so happy doing her work, she sighed. *She does everything I do, yet she does it so cheerfully. Why can't I be like her?*

"Mama. Mammaa!" Evelyn wailed impatiently. At eleven months, she was still not walking, or saying words, as her sister had done at that age. Her only word was *Mama.*

"Cara will look after Evie, Mama." Clara dropped her wet doll clothes on the ground and ran to get Evelyn.

Picking up the tiny clothes, now covered with dirt, Jessie smiled. She felt her spirit lighten. "Do I really need a nursing career?" she said. "After all, I have a more important one, being a cheerful wife and mother. Thank you, little Clara, for being such a good teacher."

It was late that night, after the children were asleep, that Allyn came bouncing through the door. "Jessie, Mama. Good news! Good news!" He dropped his gunnysack full of dirty clothes on the floor by the door.

Jessie's face lit up. "Good news? I need some." She poured out two cups of steaming, amber tea, and placed a plate of fresh-baked oatmeal cookies on the table. "What's the good news?"

"I got a job where I won't have to be away so much." He stuffed a cookie into his mouth and began sloshing sugar into his tea; then he looked at Jessie, who sat expectantly waiting for him to continue.

"What kind of job?" she said, when he didn't go on.

"Well," he began. "I heard they needed someone to play a saxophone in a band." He took a swallow of scalding tea, waiting for his wife to ask him more about the job.

She sat cross-legged, swinging her leg back and forth. She rested one arm on her knee, holding her cup in mid-air in her other hand. She waited for Allyn to continue. He didn't; so she asked, "What band?"

"Well..." He choked on a mouthful of tea. "It's a band that... plays for concerts, and parties and... and—"

"You mean a dance band." It was a statement, not a question. "Have we really come to that?" Her voice was flat. She set her cup on the table, shook down the ashes in the stove and said, "I'm going to bed."

"It's... it's not like *I'm* dancing," protested Allyn, following her into the bedroom. "Couldn't if I wanted to. Never learned. It's... it's just a way of making money. It won't be for long. I promise." He pleaded, trying to coax her to say something. Anything. "What do you want me to do? I have a family to support." Now his voice had taken on an edge. "Everyone's out of work. Besides—" He got undressed and jumped into bed. "I've already signed the contract. I start this weekend."

Jessie turned over, feigning sleep. But she didn't sleep. She was angry; angry with God for allowing things to get so bad; angry with Allyn for stooping so low as to play for a dance band. But mostly, she was angry with herself for feeling the way she did. What *was* Allyn to do? He was doing his best and always had.

She lay fuming, even too angry to cry. Then, softly, like a breeze from heaven, came snatches of promises—voices from the past: *Isaiah 45* "... I the Lord do all these things...." (v. 7); "Look unto me..." (v. 22); "...I will make the crooked places straight: ..." (v.2); and, "It will not be an easy path you walk, but I will walk with you." Sleep came at last.

Chapter 13 — "The Devil's Payroll"

1931-1932

I wonder what Mother will think of her son's job. Jessie swiped at the stove with the paper, her eyes combing the rest of the room. *Sure glad we have our own place now. No kitchen is big enough for two women.* Backing out of the shack and pulling the door shut behind her, she shooed two cocky roosters away from the doorway. *And what would my father say? We were condemned to hell if we so much as listened to dance music while walking past a dance hall. And now my own husband plays in a dance band.* Then snorting, she said aloud, "Well, I'll not be the one to tell my family."

In the very depth of her soul Jessie knew that God had promised to make the crooked places straight — and this certainly was one of those places — but she couldn't condone this present means of making a living.

As she entered her own place, glad that the girls were still sleeping, she scanned the unfinished walls of the wood-framed cabin. She shook her head and sniffed.

Two months later Jessie was still fuming over Allyn's job. And to make matters worse, Mother Splane was blaming *her* for his having taken it on. "Well what can I do about it?" she said to herself just now, chucking dirty clothes into piles for washing. "I'm stuck here at home. I can't drive — even if there was something to drive. I can't go anywhere with *two babies, one of them barely able to stand on her feet. If I could, I'd get a job — anything — maybe washing clothes for neighbors...?"*

She dropped the clothes into the hand-powered, agitating washing machine Allyn had brought home for her two weeks ago. She pumped the handle back and forth. *You could be scrubbing your knuckles raw on a washboard still,* came a taunting thought. *And remember last night? Allyn offered to have your piano shipped out? Wasn't that nice?* She squeezed her eyes shut and pumped the handle faster. Well, she didn't *want* the piano here. She was in no mood for music.

Maybe sewing. Maybe I could take in sewing. She forced her mind to change directions, as she turned the handle of the wringer. *Oh, what's the use of dreaming? Who, out here in these sticks, has any money anyway?* She shook out the sheets she had just put through the wringer, noticing how much dryer, lighter, and even brighter they were than when she had had to wring them out by hand. She noticed, but refused to admit.

But I cannot, I will not reconcile myself to his playing in a dance band, even though... With each sheet she pinned on the line a niggling reminder of another convenience her husband's extra money had provided for her and the girls pricked her mind.

After all, at least he has a job. That's more than a lot of people have these days, came that nagging voice again. *What's the matter with you?* With each bucket of dirty water she carried outside and emptied onto the ground, she spilled some of her misery, trying to drown out the voice: *Where is your trust in God? What of His promise to walk with you? Is He not with you now?*

With December, came the snow. Each day it crept further and further up the walls of the cabin, until it was nearly level with the bottom of the windowsill. Even though Clara would plough her way to Grandma's every day — and she was always welcome — it was too cold and the snow was too deep for Evelyn to get out.

Every day was the same, and the walls began to close in on Jessie. "I've got to get out, away from this place, even for a day," she screamed at the ceiling one day. "I'm going mad, stark-raving mad!"

With those last words, like a bolt of lightning, came an idea. She could hardly wait until Dick dropped in that day for his daily chat and cookies.

"Hey! What a super idea!" Dick reached for his fifth cookie. "I'll suggest it. Are you volunteering?" He chuckled at his own joke.

"You bet I am. That is, of course, if your mother will mind the girls."

"What about Allyn? Won't he object?"

"So what if he does!" Jessie stuck her nose in the air, and set her jaw. "I'll do it anyway. He doesn't own me." She smiled, and placed her hand on Dick's shoulder. "Let me know what the school says."

Jessie kissed her daughters, thanked her mother-in-law for watching them, and despite Allyn's earlier protests over her decision, left the house. She felt like an Egyptian mummy, all decked out in a pair of Allyn's overalls over her dress, and two pairs of his woolen sox over her shoes, as overshoes, as well as her own coat, mitts, and toque.

Although the snow was deep and the air crisp, it was a beautiful, sunny mid-December day. She kicked the snow ahead of her. *Oh, it feels so good to get out, away from the house, away from the worries. Yes! Ah yes! And even away from my little darlin's for awhile.*

Spotting a mouse skittering across the snow, she stopped. A big jackrabbit lopped ahead of her, hopping along on his hind legs for awhile, then dropping on all fours, zigzagging back and forth, before diving out of sight. The snow sparkled on the ground like a diamond-studded carpet. Each step Jessie took, her head felt clearer, her heart lighter. She felt like shouting, like opening her mouth and singing at the top of her lungs. She felt like — like a youngster again. Clutching the books under her arms, she hastened her steps. She was going to enjoy this day.

Dick sat alert and expectant in the front row of the class.

"Students," the teacher began, bringing the class to order, "This is Jessie Splane, Dick's sister-in-law. She has kindly offered to give lessons in Red Cross first-aid, something entirely new for our school. Mrs. Splane is a registered nurse, and I understand from Dick —" She stopped to smiled at her star-pupil. "I understand from Dick, that she comes with wonderful credentials: she graduated third in her class of twenty-eight.

"Mrs. Splane, the class is all yours. Take all the time you need." The teacher sat down among the students.

Jessie was in her glory. She executed her teaching superbly. "Thank you, students," she said at the end of the class. "Your attention has been encouraging." She smiled. "Next month we shall begin practicing on each other, the things I've shown you today. So please study your notes. See you in the New Year."

Her head was in the clouds during her three-and-one-half-mile walk home. It was four o'clock: the sun was beginning to spill its color across the horizon. "This is exactly what I've needed," she said, tipping her head back and taking a deep breath. She was in no hurry to get home.

Christmas. Although Jessie didn't feel like celebrating, for the sake of the children she must muster up enough spirit to do something special. It was just Allyn, herself, and the girls now. Two days ago, as soon as school had broken for the holidays, Mother Splane and Dick had moved back to Calgary. "I think it will be better for Dick to finish his last year-and-a-half in the city," she had said, not wanting to admit the real reason for leaving the north: her only daughter was expecting a child in about six months. Claribel had lost her first child at birth, so she wanted to be close to her when this baby was born.

"There's nothing here on the farm anymore," Tibby had said. "Erwin and Oilie have their own place now. And even the cow is gone. I'm not needed here any longer."

Bill had long since gone back to Calgary, where he now worked full-time for the railway.

"One-thirty in the morning, and I'm just getting home. And Christmas, at that! Oh Mama, how I hate playing in that band." Allyn stumbled through the door, bringing in a blast of wind and snow with him. He blew on his hands, heading for the stove. "I hate the music. I hate the loud cackling laughter, the swearing, the smoking, the—" He stopped short of mentioning the drinking. There wasn't much, admittedly, but the very thought of it would just have upset Jessie further. Surely she knew that he would never partake in any of their activities. To him it was just a job—a hateful job, but a job, nonetheless. Surely Jessie *must* know that.

"Well why don't you quit then." Jessie spat the words at Allyn.

"I have to play one more time. New Year's Eve. Then I'm calling it quits... I promise."

He sounded so lonely. Jessie knew she had been shutting him out lately, and how she loathed herself for it, but the very thought of his job made her blood boil.

"Oh! I have a surprise for you." His voice was cheerful again. "I called at the post office." He dashed out to the porch and hauled in a large box. "From your sister." He grabbed a knife and cut the string.

"Allyn. Wait. I save all that. Here, let me do it. You go look after the stove." Jessie pushed her husband aside, carefully folding the paper and string as she unwrapped the parcel. It was from Gertie's address, and in her handwriting, but inside were packages from Carrie, Bell, and even from Florence, in Hawaii. *Gifts of love,* popped into her mind. Her eyes spilled over: she felt so undeserving.

The young couple set aside their differences and their problems on Christmas day. They laughed and played with the girls, helping them open the dolls and toys from their aunties, and enjoying the expressions of glee and squeals of delight at the new dresses their mama had made them, and the snow-candy their daddy had made.

Jessie felt warm and content, nestled beside Allyn in bed that night. She lay awake for some time, just listening to the breathing of her girls, and the snorts and snores of Allyn. She felt wrapped in Peace — The Peace of the Christ-child of Christmas.

"But you promised that New Year's Eve would be the last time you'd play for that dance band." Jessie flung Allyn's freshly ironed shirt at him, glad that the girls were sleeping and wouldn't hear her outburst. "It's Easter, and you're still promising to get off the devil's payroll."

Jessie's eyes burned with the tears of anger and frustration that hung in them. She ran to her bedroom and shut the door. Closing her eyes, she tried to block out how much easier life had become since Allyn had not had to be away from home, how many extras his steady income had provided: the girls each had her own bed now; all the walls had new coverings; the floor and counter in the kitchen had new linoleum; Allyn had fixed up a sink with a drain, so that she no longer had to carry out slop water; he had installed a reservoir, to eliminate having to go to the well so often; he had dug a cellar under the kitchen for the perishables. All these improvements loomed before Jessie; and had she been writing them down, she could have listed many more. She dropped to her knees by her bed and tried to pray, but the words, *"devil's payroll, devil's payroll, devil's payroll"* throbbed in her head.

Grasping her hair, she lifted her head and cried, "Oh God. Oh God." At first it seemed that her words went only as far as the ceiling; but soon the tears came, and she heard the familiar whisper of the bell-like voice: "I will walk with you."

And then she began to pray: "Oh God. I feel so desperate, so wretched. I don't know what to do. I need your help. Help me hold my peace about Allyn's job. I know he's doing his best. He, too, is unhappy about his present way of life, but I've been no help. "I pray for Your strength and wisdom. In Jesus' name. Amen." She felt peace returning to her troubled heart.

She rose from her knees and went out to apologize to Allyn for her outburst, but he had slipped quietly away. *"Poor Allyn. He never argues back. He just goes merrily along, letting my cutting remarks bounce off him like a rubber ball off a wall. I wonder what he really thinks."* She went back inside, determined that her attitude toward her husband would be different.

Jessie was at the oven checking on her bread when Allyn burst through the door. "Jessie, Mama," he called, dropping a load of wood onto the floor. "Remember me telling you about Aberhart, my high school principal? What a godly, upstanding man he was? Well, guess what?" He chucked the wood into the wood box, helter-skelter, as he talked.

Jessie brushed grease on top of the hot bread, dropped a stick of wood on the fire, pulled the teakettle over to bring it to a boil, placed some tea leaves into the teapot, then sat down to listen to the news about her husband's old principal.

"Aberhart's been goin' around the country trying to create an interest in folks, about a new, ah—kind of political idea." Allyn pulled out a chair and sat down at the table. "Some people call the idea *social credit*," he continued. "So far, it's been catching on like wildfire. Folks around are so fed up with this present system—"

It wasn't until about two years later that the Social Credit party became a reality, when they won the next provincial election. **1**

"What... what exactly does *social credit* mean? I know nothing about politics, if that's what you call this... new idea you're talking about." Jessie cut off a slice of steaming bread, and handed it to Allyn. She poured out two cups of tea.

"Well." He bit into the fluffy bread. "Aberhart read about an idea, that to get the economy of the country going again, money needs to circulate. He thinks if people were given money—"

She listened patiently to Allyn's explanation about the new political idea, but she didn't understand how it would affect *their* lives. "I hope *you* don't intend to get mixed up in this political stuff, Allyn, " she said, going back to the sewing she had started before Allyn had come home.

He jumped up. "Gotta get back to town. Be home around supper time." He kissed her, ran out the door, spent a minute or two to throw the girls over his head, kissed them, and was off down the road on the run. What he hadn't told Jessie was that he was *already* "mixed up in the political stuff."

"My wife doesn't know anything about this," he had told the group who had recruited him a couple of weeks ago. "So I may have to back out on short notice."

"Oh well," he said to himself now, as he ran down the road, *"I'll stay in 'til things get too hot at home."* He enjoyed being involved in public activities.

Jessie heard about Allyn's involvement in "politics" about a month later, when a neighbor stopped by. "Just thought I'd stop by ta see if ya needed anythin' in town, Missus." Mr. Goetes jumped off the wagon to meet Jessie. She had noticed him stop and had walked to the gate to see what he wanted. Neighbors rarely stopped, and Jessie hardly knew the Goetes.

"Heard ol' Al's been kickin' up a lot o' dust in town." Goetes guffawed, and spit a stream of tobacco juice into Jessie's flower garden.

Jessie took an instant dislike to the man. Straightening up to her full five-foot-three-inch height, she sucked in her breath. "What do you mean, *'kicking up dust?'*" Her voice was like ice.

"Well, I mean, like all that political garbage. Like the stink he's be'n makin' 'bout puttin' in a road past this place, to Meanook, to cut off a mile or two. And 'bout this Aberhart stuff." He spewed another stream of tobacco juice, this time hitting the pansy patch. He continued, "We don't need no religious fanatic runnin' our country. This Aberhart... your man, Al, he be'n on the bandwagon tryin' to promote his fanatical political rots. He—" This time when Goetes spit, he knocked a petal off a poppy.

"Thank you, Mr. Goetes. I don't need anything in town. Now, if you'll excuse me, I have to get back to my children." She felt sick. Her head was spinning, and the baby inside her began to churn. She would have to lie down. She turned and headed for the house.

"Mama?" Allyn stomped through the door. The kitchen was empty. There was no sign of supper being ready. "Mama? Where are you?" He made a mad dash through the kitchen into the bedroom, where in a matter of seconds, he had sized up the situation: the girls were playing on the floor amidst a mixture of water, crumbs, and honey—they obviously had made their own lunch; the cat was frantically licking his paw to rid it of a sticky knife; and Jessie was in bed, asleep.

"Mama?" Allyn lunged toward the bed. "What's wrong?" His head snapped toward the girls. "What's wrong with Mama?"

Hearing Allyn's voice, Jessie woke with a start. "Oh... oh, I guess... I guess I must have dozed off. What time is it?"

"Seven-thirty." Allyn dropped to his knees beside his wife.

"Seven-thirty?" Jessie looked around her, her eyes dazed. "In the morning? At night?" She began to swing her legs over the edge of the bed.

"No. You stay there." Allyn pushed her gently back onto the bed. "Come on, girls. Let's go make supper."

Through a semi-conscious stupor, Jessie heard pots and pans being banged around in the kitchen.

After the children had been fed and were in bed, Allyn carried a tray, all nicely set up, into his wife. While she ate, he cleaned up the mess on the floor.

"Mm! Good!" she said, after taking a few sips of chicken soup. "Who taught *you* how to cook?" A weak smile inched its way across her face.

"You did. Who else?" Allyn leaned over the bed and kissed her.

Jessie didn't mention her visitor of earlier in the day. She didn't have to.

"Mama, I want to talk." Allyn pulled a chair near to the bed. "You've heard about the politics. I'm sure you have. And about the trouble I've caused over the road to Meanook? But you've never said anything. And I've promised and promised to quit the dance band; then I broke all the promises; because, even though I've hated the job, I've liked the money. Well, let me tell you something." He took Jessie's tray and set it on the floor. He swooped up Tiger, who, having finished his cleaning, was sleeping on the foot of Jessie's bed. Setting the cat on his knee, he began stroking him under the chin with the fork from the tray. "I've been so miserable over my way of life," he continued, "and so unhappy about the disregard I've shown you. Today, kneeling in the barren, boulder fields, I spent hours just calling on God."

"Oh, Allyn!" Jessie's heart gave a leap of joy. "How I've been praying for us!" She sat up.

"Today, Mama," Allyn went on, pushing Tiger from his lap. "Today I made a decision." He reached into his pocket and pulled out a few crumpled bills, throwing them onto the bed. "That's the last of the dance band. And no more politics either.

"There's an evangelist coming to town. I'm going to the meetings. Maybe we'll all go, if you'd like. They begin tomorrow night. I'm not sure where to begin, but... I want to start... a new way of life."

"I'll make a fresh pot of tea," said Jessie, easing her way out of bed. "I feel much better — in fact, better than I have in a long time. See if the girls are still awake. Let's celebrate."

"A party! A party!" Clara bounded from her bed, onto her sister's. She hugged Evelyn, and the two of them scrambled to the kitchen.

"Po'corn! Po'corn!" Evelyn clapped her chubby hands. "Fro up, Daddy. Fro up." She lifted her arms for her daddy to throw her over his head. After popcorn and milk Allyn took the girls back to their beds, but before tucking them in, he knelt with them to hear their prayers. Jessie always did this, but Allyn hadn't for a very long time.

"Dear Jesus," Allyn began.

"Let's have a prayer meeting," interrupted Clara.

"Pway awnight," chimed in Evelyn.

Allyn had barely begun to pray, when he heard the girls snoring. He lifted each one tenderly, tucking her into her bed; then he went to the kitchen to join a happy Jessie.

Footnote: **1** Social Credit, the theory that the profits of industry should be distributed to all consumers by a system of dividends so as to insure a high level of consumption and allay the possibilities of economic depression. The theory was originated by C.H. Douglas."
(The New Lexicon Webster's Encyclopedic Dictionary — Canadian Edition, p. 941)

Chapter 14 — Sunshine And Light

June to November 1932

"Repent, brother. We're living in the last days. Give yourself to God." Allyn handed a gospel pamphlet to each man gathered outside the General Store in Colinton.

"Haw-haw! Listen to Preacher Splane," derided Goetes, while he and his companions contested to see who could spit tobacco juice the farthest. "Last month he was playin' at our dances, and kickin' up a fuss 'bout some road, and spoutin' politics. Now look at 'im, spewin' religion—not that there's much difference, seems now'days. What's it gonna be next month?"

The men guffawed. And the more the people scoffed, the more enthused Allyn became about his new way of life. Conversion for everyone he met—young or old. Catholic, Jewish, or Protestant—was his goal. He was on fire for God! It got to be that whenever he would approach, some of the men would hide.

It was at this time that he wrote a letter to Miss Thomas, of the Canadian Sunday School Mission (C.S.S.M.), in Three Hills, Alberta, asking her if she knew of anyone who could help him start Sunday schools in the area. He wasn't sure how to begin this new life, but he had decided, and nothing was going to stop him.

"A great day to have supper on our new outdoor table. First day of summer. Right girls?" The family bowed their heads while Allyn gave thanks, and the family began eating.

Rattle-bang-bang-chug-chug-splutter-splutte. Four heads turned.

"What? What's that?" Allyn jumped up from the table, running to the gate, Jessie and the girls on his heels.

The noise stopped. Out of the billow of dust that accompanied the racket, emerged a tall, young man. Brushing himself off, he sprinted toward the family.

The girls peeked from behind their mother's skirt, staring in the direction of the noise — a Model T Ford — from which the man had just crawled.

"Oh, don't be frightened of *him*," said the visitor, noticing the children staring in the direction of his car. "That's Lamentation. He does a lot of crying and spluttering, but he gets me around."

He looked again at Allyn. "My name's Cliff Neilson. I'm looking for a preacher, a guy named, '*Splane.*' You wouldn't know him, would you?" He chuckled. "The folks in town told me to head out this way."

Allyn took a step forward, extending his hand. "Name's Splane. Al Splane. This is my wife, Jessie, and daughters, Clara and Evelyn. What can I do for you?"

Jessie herded the girls back to the table, leaving Allyn to talk with the stranger.

"You sent a letter to Miss Thomas from the C.S.S.M. — about Sunday schools?" said Cliff, pulling a letter from his pocket. "I'm from Prairie Bible Institute, in Three Hills. Ever heard of it?"

"No. Can't say I have. But I did write the Sunday School Mission."

"Well, this Bible school was started ten years ago, by a Mr. Leslie Maxwell." Cliff chatted about the school and about how God was blessing hearts and changing lives. Allyn listened, kicking the dust with first one foot then the other, as the two men progressed slowly toward the picnic table.

Over cups of fresh tea, the men discussed Sunday school plans.

"Of course, it would be wonderful for you to go to this Prairie Bible school, but —" Jessie frowned. "But it's —" All summer Allyn had been telling her of the wonderful things he had heard from Cliff about the school. "But how can a man with a family go to school?" she continued, glancing at her over-extended abdomen. "Our baby's due any day now. It's just not possible." Jessie set the mashed potatoes onto the table. "You said yourself that the harvests are poor, and work is scarce. And all *we* have to our name is this miserable house and... a pig. In another month you won't have even any wells to dig."

Jessie felt miserable. Why did she always squelch his ideas? Why? She wished as much as he did that he could get into preaching — go to Bible school. She poured gravy onto Evelyn's potatoes, put a bib on her, and sat down herself for the evening meal. "It's just not possible," she said again, after the family had begun eating.

"Anything's possible with God," Allyn replied, in a small, peeved voice. "Anything's possible." He took a swallow of tea, his eyes glued to his plate.

"Wasn't Clara excited about going to Calgary with Grandma?" Jessie tried to change the subject, but Allyn made no reply.

"I think I'd better go into Athabasca tomorrow," she said, after several more minutes of strained silence between them. "Erwin and Ollie offered to take Evelyn until after the baby's born. I hope it won't be too much for Ollie, being four months along herself."

On Thursday, September twenty-ninth, after four false alarms, Jessie was admitted to the hospital. Through the cobwebs of her anaesthetized mind, filtered the husky cries of her infant. "My son at last!" A smile on her lips, Jessie slipped into pleasant unconsciousness.

Some indeterminable time later Jessie was budged from her stupor by the voice of the nurse. "Mrs. Splane, Mrs. Splane. Here's your little gypsy girl."

"Gypsy girl... gypsy girl..." Jessie fought her way back to reality. "Girl?... Did... you say, *'Girl'?*" Rubbing her eyes and struggling to a semi-sitting position, she reached for the bundle the nurse was shoving at her. Flipping back the blanket, she gazed with disbelief: this... this... *gypsy* with the olive complexion, a mess of black hair, a long nose nestled on chubby cheeks, between eyes (almost slanted); this bundle, so still she could have been a doll; this was the son she had so much wanted? The son she had counted on? This... this... gypsy girl?

"*A third girl!*" She slumped back onto her pillow, willing sleep to overtake her.

She awoke some time later to the fussing of her daughter and to the urging of a kind-faced nurse. "Mrs. Splane, you must try to nurse her? You must try."

Jessie stirred unwillingly. For the next hour she struggled to feed the infant. *Not another one I can't nurse?* She could feel hot tears forming behind her eyes. *Why?* Had God forgotten her? How could they afford to buy formula? Couldn't God at least have given her milk in her own body?

She shut her eyes, the baby lying death-still in the curve of her arm. She felt as if God were stepping on her heart. Maybe it would all go away. Maybe it was just a bad dream. Maybe when she awoke she'd be sitting up, nursing a lively son. *Take it away. Take it away*, throbbed through her head as she drifted once again into unconsciousness.

Allyn bounded into Jessie's room that evening, his face looking like the moon on a cloudless, full moon night. "We're sure good at makin' girls, ain't we, Mama?" he teased, bending to kiss his wife.

Jessie turned her face to the wall. She was in no mood for his cheeriness. He didn't know what it was like to hope and plan for nine months for a boy—a son for him. She had wanted so badly to award him for his patience and love. She had wanted to present him with a son. How dare he come bouncing in, all smiles and cheerfulness. She'd failed him—

"Jessie, Mama," Allyn said, tenderly taking her hand in his. "I don't care that we have another daughter. Our girls are wonderful. I wouldn't care if I had fifteen daughters and no son. I have you. You mean more to me than ten—"

"But, Allyn," moaned Jessie, turning at last to face him. "I can't even feed her. How can we afford—? Oh, Allyn, I wanted everything to work out for you. You want to go to Bible school. And I *want* you to go. I wanted to give you a son to show you how much I love you. I think God is punishing me for being so... so critical, so—" She burst into tears.

Then suddenly she sat up, and with tears still standing in her eyes, she smiled at Allyn. "What'll we name her? Have you seen her? We didn't think about names for a third girl!" Jessie pulled up the sheet, and while wiping her eyes with it, she giggled—a silly, school-girlish giggle.

"I think we should call her Helen—'Sunshine and Light.'" Allyn reached over the bed and gave his wife a bear hug. "Your face looks like the sun just popped out from behind a cloud."

Together they laughed.

"Helen." Jessie closed her eyes and tipped her head back. Taking a deep breath through her nostrils, as if savoring the name, she breathed, in a loud raspy whisper, "Yes." Her eyes popped open. "Yes! Helen. And how about 'Marjorie?' Helen ...Marjorie...Splane."

"Anders said he'd buy this house. Says he wants to drag it into Colinton to use as a shed at the store. Eight hundred, fifty bucks, he'll give me. That'll pay off our bills. And--" Allyn dashed sugar into his tea, leaving the usual sugary trail across the table. "He agreed to drive us to Three Hills... But best of all—" He picked up the letter and waved it at Jessie. "About the Bible school buying your piano. They will. Not only that..." His excitement had grown to such a pitch that he was no longer able to wait for Jessie to read the letter herself. "The school will even pick up the piano from your sister's. They're gonna give us—you—a hundred, forty bucks for it. That's enough for tuition. Oh... and... you know what else?"

"I *would,* if you'd give me a chance to read the letter myself." Jessie scowled. She liked to read her own mail, but with Allyn, she rarely got the opportunity.

Just then the baby began to stir. "You'd better read the letter to me while I fix the baby." She let out an exasperated sigh, lifting the infant from her improvised crib—a dresser drawer. She set the bottle on to warm, then changed Helen's diaper, while Allyn's voice droned on about the piano, pigs, potatoes, and PBI.

Footnote: Prairie Bible Institute (PBI) was born on October 9, 1922, when Leslie E. Maxwell, a graduate of Midland Bible Institute in Kansas City, was invited by a group of Central Alberta farmers, to teach the Bible to a group of their teenage children, in one of their homes. From this, the school grew to what is now known as Prairie Bible College.

Chapter 15 — The Theater

November 1932 - March 1933

    While Allyn fumbled with a padlock on the door, Jessie let her eyes wander to the post office across the street and to the dingy shoe-repair shop next to it. Down the street the other way was a grocery store, a barbershop, a clothing store, a pharmacy, a hotel, and although she could not see the church, she could hear its bells chiming out their noonday hymns. A feeling of comfort crept through Jessie at the sound. Not wanting to take a second look at the apartment before her — not yet, anyway — she turned to face north. Beyond the scattered shops and the few tar-papered shacks, up the dust-and-dry-snow-mixed road, just barely visible from where she stood, were the tops of a couple of buildings. "So that's the PBI I've heard so much about." A relaxed smile spread slowly across her face.
    Prairie Bible Institute had grown from eight local teenagers, desirous of studying God's Word, just ten years before this, to its present two hundred or so, staff and students. Many of the students, like Allyn, had brought their families to the area. And now, six weeks after school had started, all suitable living accommodations had apparently been taken — except for this one at the rear of the Lyric Theater, on Main Street.

Jessie turned back to where Allyn still struggled with the lock. Despite the cold November wind that was whipping dry, stinging snow around her ankles and into her face, she felt warm all over. She hadn't, until this moment, realized just how lonely for "civilization" she had been.

"Got it." Allyn dropped the padlock onto the ground and blew on his fingers. "Never was any good with locks." Turning the knob, he kicked the door; it didn't budge. Leaning his shoulder against it, he shoved. The door creaked open a foot, then stopped. He squeezed through the opening.

"Ice," he yelled, pulling Jessie through. They stood looking down at the stalagmite icicle blocking the door.

"Ten dollars a month for this!" Jessie gave her head a quick shake. "Well, let's get busy." She plopped her purse onto the table, looking around at the two rooms, littered with pop and beer bottles, crumpled cigarette boxes, empty food cans, newspapers, and dirty dishes.

Allyn clattered the rusty lids off the stove and scratched around at the ashes. "We'll have a roaring fire in here in no time," he said, crumpling some paper and throwing it, along with a few sticks of kindling, into the stove. The fire flared momentarily, then the room filled with smoke. "I opened the drafts," he choked, rubbing his eyes.

"Well, look!" Coughing, Jessie pointed to the stovepipe. "Look at the hole."

They turned and faced each other, bursting into laughter, tears, aided by the smoke, running down their cheeks. That evening, thanks to the help of the Walls at the grocery store, who had told them about the place, as well as several other shop keepers in town—who not only saw to the repair of the chimney, but also supplied pails, brooms, soap, rags, and even lunch—the lean-to apartment, next to the town theater, looked cozy and warm.

Clara, having been with Grandma since before the baby was born, rejoined the family. Life quickly settled into a new routine: Monday through Friday Allyn would arrive home from school, chuck his books on the kitchen table, toss the girls into the air, kiss Jessie, peek at the baby; then he would run out to chop wood, haul water, and shovel snow off the walk. Back in the house, he would join his family for a meal of potatoes, bread, and eggs—or meat, if by some chance they had some. After evening devotions he would clear the table while Jessie got the children ready for bed. Then, spreading his books on the table, he would open his Bible, and be lost in his studies.

Jessie had asked God to guide her to a way of bringing in money. One day while she was shopping, about a week after they had arrived in Three Hills, she asked the grocer if she might know of anyone in need of having sewing done.

"Mrs. Splane," said the grocer, her round, jolly face crinkling into a smile, "if it's sewing you want, you just write out an ad and pin it right here." She took Jessie by the arm and led her to the bulletin board. "Put one in the post office, too. You'll get all the sewing you can handle." And she was right. Jessie never lacked for sewing jobs.

"I just wish I didn't have to sleep," said Jessie just now, adjusting the one electric light, dangling by its cord from the ceiling, so that it would benefit both her and Allyn. "I can't seem to get at my sewing until I'm so tired I can hardly keep my eyes open."

"What 'ja say?" grunted Allyn, absorbed in his thesis on *The Fall of Man*. "Listen to this." For the next hour he read aloud about how God's plan of salvation was woven all through the Scriptures, from Genesis to Revelation. "Isn't it wonderful?"

Jessie would have loved to be able to study, too, but with the children, and her sewing, she had no time for even reading, except her Bible. So she was happy to have Allyn share his studies with her.

Tuesday evenings. How Jessie dreaded them! On Tuesday, as on any other weekday, Allyn would go through his routine. Except, instead of studying after supper, at seven-fifteen he would pick up his Bible, kiss his wife and girls, and head up to the campus for the mid-week prayer meeting.

But that wasn't the worst thing about Tuesday evenings. She recalled their first one, about a month before. As soon as Allyn had left for his meeting, she hauled out her sewing machine to work on some curtains for the kitchen windows, ignoring the ruckus and laughing outside. Suddenly there erupted through the air, an explosive, thunderous roar, raucous music, angry reverberating voices, and the rat-a-tat of gunfire, as the mystery movie, *Dr. X*, came blaring through the theater wall.

With a spine-chilling, ear-splitting scream, Clara sprang from her bed and scrambled onto her mother's lap, Evelyn right behind her. As Jessie comforted her little ones, she smiled, not sure from which side of the building more noise was coming, theirs, or the theater's. "It's a picture show next door," she explained, stroking her girls' hair.

"What's a picture show?" Clara pushed away from her mother, looking her in the eye.

She lifted the girls from her lap, setting them on the table; she sat on a chair facing them. Looking into two pairs of teary, blue eyes, she proceeded to explain: "Remember those books Grandma gave you? The ones with the pictures? They tell stories, don't they?"

Clara nodded and Evelyn copied her.

"Well, a picture show tells a story, too. Only the pictures are not in a book; they're on the wall. You wait; tomorrow I'll take you next door and show you where all the noise is coming from."

"But... but... there's bad people out there," protested Clara.

"No. Look!" Jessie hoisted the girls to a chair by the window. "There are no *real* people out there; it's just a story about bad people."

It took Jessie an hour of singing, praying, and playing with the girls after that episode to settle their fears.

From that day on she had made sure that the children were asleep before the show started. But to quell her own dread of Tuesdays, Jessie would, during the blaring shows, engross herself in her sewing, praying aloud, trying to drown out the cacophony next door.

One Tuesday about half way through the term, Allyn burst through the door. "Jessie, Jessie," he said. "Someone's coming to stay with the girls this evening, so that you can come with me to the prayer meeting."

"Who? Who'd want to sit with three babies?" Jessie gathered up her sewing scraps from the floor, brushing past her husband to drop them into the stove.

"A teenage daughter of one of the staff members is coming over at seven," he answered. "I just found out about it. It's a free service the school provides so mothers can get out. You do want to come, don't you?"

"Yes." She hesitated. "But I'd better hurry."

"Well? How did it go?" asked Jessie, when she and Allyn returned from the meeting.

"Fine. Fine." Olive reached for her coat. "I'll sit for you anytime you want," she said, her brown eyes sparkling. "When it was time for the girls to go to bed," she continued, "I said to them, 'Now get down on your knees, and say your prayers.' Clara looked up at me with insult in her starry blue eyes, and said, 'We don't say our prayers in this house, we *pray!*' She folded her hands, and with her face uplifted to the ceiling she began: 'Dear Lord Jesus...' then she carried on a conversation with the Lord, just like she would talk to me—or you. That little girl's really going to *be* somebody some day." With a toss of her brunette head, Olive headed for the door. "See you next week."

Jessie smiled at her dramatization of the incident. "And that young lady's going to be somebody some day, too!" (And she was. Olive became a missionary.)

Several times after that Jessie accompanied Allyn to the prayer sessions. Not only did it give her a break from the humdrum of her daily routine, but also she came away feeling refreshed and uplifted, reassured of God's presence and power.

Chapter 16 — Lettuce 'n Do'nuts

March - August 1933

"Lac La Biche?" Jessie whirled around from the washtub. "What do you mean, 'Lac La Biche'?" Her heart sank. How could she uproot her family and go away up there, out to the sticks again? "Allyn. We can't. We just can't. Is there nothing you can do here?" She felt as if all the blood were draining from her body; she flopped onto the closest chair, leaning her head on her hands.

Allyn had just told her his plan to join a fellow-classmate in mission work for the summer.

"Mama... I..." He jumped to his wife's side, falling on his knees beside her. "I wasn't... thinking about taking the family. God's looked after us all winter. He'll provide for you and the babies here, while... I go... up there. And I'll send... I'll find brush cutting, or something. I'll—"

"Brush cutting! Who has money up there for brush cutting? For anything, for that matter?" She stood up, took a deep breath and went back to her washing. It was Monday, March 24, Clara's fourth birthday. She hadn't reminded her that it was her birthday, and now she was glad. She didn't feel like celebrating anything. And she didn't feel like arguing with Allyn. During the winter, while Jessie held her audible, solo prayer meetings—during the blaring shows—she had asked God to help her control her tongue. "Set a watch, O Lord, before my mouth; keep the door of my lips." Psalm 141:3, she had prayed. So now, she just sucked in her breath and swallowed the words that her mouth so badly wanted to say.

Hardly daring to breathe, Allyn waited, waited for Jessie to reply, to rebuff him. When she said nothing, he spun around and went out to his chores.

Through the window Jessie watched him talking with the girls, who were splashing in the melting snow. She said aloud, "I have four children, three girls and a boy." She recalled her mother-in-law's words of a couple of years before: "Jessie," she had said, putting her hand softly on Jessie's shoulder, a rare gesture for her. "You have a special job in life." At the time, Jessie had recalled the voice of years before: *I have a special work for you to do.* "You are perhaps the only woman in the world who will be able to put up with Allyn's eccentricities and peculiarities," her mother-in-law had continued. "He's not an easy person to live with. Take care of him. He's not... like my other sons..."

Just now Jessie felt her insides warming. She was reminded of Esther in the Bible. Esther had been raised for the special job of delivering her people, the Jews, from destruction. It flashed into her mind again now, that *this* was the special job she had been spared for—when diphtheria had nearly snatched her away during her nurses' training days—to love and help her impetuous husband and to guide and lead her children. A reassurance that God would be with her and the girls while Allyn went north, flooded her soul. He had promised, *You will not have to walk the path alone.*

"Maybe a few month's separation will be good for us both," she said to herself. It certainly wasn't that she didn't love him: she loved him deeply. But often she grew tired trying to keep up with his jumping, restless nature.

Clara's birthday came again to her mind. *Well, he wouldn't remember it anyway. I'll wait a couple of weeks, 'til he's gone and the warm April sun comes out; then I'll give her a party.*

By the time Allyn and the girls came into the house, Jessie had finished scrubbing the floor with the rinse water. She had put leftover potatoes into the frying pan, had set the table, and was cracking eggs into a pan.

Allyn, having forgotten the earlier tension, helped Evelyn off with her coat. "You girls are getting to be a big help," he said.

"I'm glad spring is in the air," said Jessie, as the family began supper. "Maybe I'll be able to get outdoors more with the baby. She worries me. She's not gaining like she should, only three pounds since birth. And at six months, she should be more active, trying to roll on her tummy, or sit. She seems content just to sleep. She rarely cries, rarely laughs; in fact, it seems she's hardly aware of her surroundings."

"Hm!" Allyn stabbed a piece of bread with his fork. He didn't know much about babies; but he'd been glad that while he studied, she *had* been a quiet one and hadn't cried constantly as Evelyn had. "Maybe it's some real food that she needs." He jumped up, grabbed her by two corners of her blanket—stork-style—and set her roughly in his lap, propping her head against his arm. He sopped a lump of potato in his egg and held it to Helen's lips. Jessie gasped; the girls giggled; the baby sucked at the fork, cooing as the food oozed from her mouth. "See? She's just hungry."

"Pretty smart daddy you've got," Jessie said the following morning as she spooned oatmeal and milk into Helen's mouth. She had tried a few solid foods before, but the baby had refused them. She had expected to be up the whole night nursing a sick baby. "That greasy food your daddy gave you last night would have killed your big sister, Evelyn, when she was your age."

"That Old Goat!" Allyn slammed the door behind him. It was the day he was to leave for Lac La Biche. "He told us we could rent this place 'til next spring. Now, because I told him I was going to be gone 'til October, he wants us out. 'I ain't havin' no grass-widow livin' in my place, payin' no rent, starvin',' he said. 'You Bible punchers, spoutin' 'bout livin' on faith. Pshaw! Ain't no faith you be livin' on. It be so-si-yety. People like me. No way! You go? You take your wife and brats wit' you.'" Allyn threw his cap onto the table, went into the bedroom and hauled out the trunk.

"Hold on!" said Jessie, sucking her finger to stop the bleeding from the diaper pin stab she had received when Allyn came storming into the house, startling her. "I'll do the packing, if there's any to be done. Just wait. I'll go talk to the 'Old Goat.'" Jessie grabbed her sweater and went out.

Fifteen minutes later she was back. "That Old Goat!" she said, pulling clothes from the shelves and stuffing them into the trunk. She didn't say, and Allyn didn't ask, what conversation had gone on between her and "Old Goat."

Earlier in the day, after leaving the theater manager's, Allyn had inquired at the real estate office to find another place to rent, but could find no affordable place.

"We'll leave the dishes," Jessie fumed, as she gathered last-minute things and squeezed them into the trunk. "If he thinks we owe him anything, he can have *everything* we leave. Come on, girls, let's go."

Clutching a cardboard box containing his clothes under one arm, Allyn tugged at the trunk, bumping and scraping it along behind him for the four blocks to the train station. Jessie followed behind, carrying the baby in one arm, her dangling purse bumping her as she walked, her other hand grasping Evelyn, almost dragging her along. Clara stumbled behind, crying.

It was fifteen minutes to train time. Jessie figured, although she hadn't checked, that she would have enough money for her fare to Edmonton. The children could ride free. After Edmonton? Well, she'd decide that when the time came. Too angry and too tired even for tears, all she knew right now was that, no matter what, she wasn't going with Allyn all the way to Lac La Biche.

The train hissed and spit as it screeched to a stop at the station. The girls stood with their hands over their ears, watching. Allyn boosted Clara up the steps of the train and turned to reach for Evelyn.

"Splane. Splane. Wait!" Both Allyn and Jessie turned to see who was calling. "Wait. *Puff-puff.* I'm sorry. I changed m' mind." It was their landlord. "You kin stay. Come back. Missus. You kin stay 'til nex' spring, like I promised. I ain't no hard-hearted ol' goat, like your missus said." He paused for a breath, his head turning toward Allyn, then back to Jessie. "You stay for nuthin' all summer. Missus. You sew for my missus an' you don't pay nuthin' for my place.... I'll fetch your trunk and take it back." He turned and ran to where the luggage was being loaded.

The train belched. The conductor droned, "'board!"

With a gasp, Jessie thrust the baby at Allyn, bolting up the steps of the coach to retrieve Clara, who had already made friends with several of the passengers.

"A' board!" The conductor swung to the coach door. The train sighed and began to shunt into action.

With a quick peck on his wife's cheek, while passing Helen back to her mama, Allyn, still clutching his clothes box under one arm, grabbed the railing, running alongside the train. Then he was aboard.

The family stood watching, until the train became a speck on the horizon. Turning slowly, Jessie said, "Come along, girls. Let's go home." To herself she said, "We'll discuss my sewing for 'Old Goat's missus' later. I'm no one's fool. I'll sew for the 'missus' all right, if she'd like, but she'll pay, like everyone else. And I'll pay the rent, like always."

The following Saturday was bright and warm. "How would you like to have a party tonight at supper?" Jessie asked Clara. "For your birthday."

"Oh, Mama, could we?" Clara danced around her mother. "And could we have our party at our little table that Gramma gave us? With the little tea-party dishes? And our little chairs?"

"And what would you like to have at your party?"

"Ah, I would like do'nuts, n' lettuce, n' —" Clara put her index finger on her cheek, like she had seen her mama do when she was thinking. "An', ah. That's all. Just lettuce 'n do'nuts."

"All right. You and Evie go now to the farm for the milk. When you get back you can have your party." Jessie gently pushed the girls, pails in hand, out the door. "Remember now, go the way you always went with Daddy. And Clara, you look after Evie. She's never gone before."

The girls headed north, past the school, to McElheran's farm, one-and-one-half miles away. Jessie worried about sending them so far by themselves, but with Allyn gone, how else could she get the milk?

Although she was used to trusting God for daily needs, Jessie was worried. She checked her purse. "Two nickels and two pennies. Not enough to buy lettuce, let alone doughnuts." She peeked over at the baby. "And Lord," she said aloud, a touch of anger in her voice. "What about tomorrow, and next week? And what about the small request of my little girl for lettuce and doughnuts for her three-week-late birthday party? What about it, Lord?" She could feel Satan laughing at her. *What of your faith now, Jessie? Where's it gotten you? Where's the Lord that promised to walk with you?*

She could feel her anger rising, anger at Allyn for having left her alone with three small children — and he'd been gone for over a week now and she still hadn't heard from him — anger at God for... for what? Hadn't He looked after her up until now? Then ashamed, she was angry with herself for her lack of trust.

She went to the girls' bed and pulled out the little table from under it, taking it to the basin to wash it off. *Blessed be the Lord, because he hath heard the voice of my supplications...My heart trusteth in him, and I am helped.* These words from Psalm 28:6 and 7 echoed in her ear. She began to hum, then to whistle her old standby, "Only believe... all things are possible, only believe."

The girls burst through the door, Evelyn tripping on the doorstep, nearly spilling her pail of milk.

"Mama." Clara set her milk on the table. The lady let us pet the new calf."

"He thuck my hand," lisped Evelyn, holding up her right hand.

"Can we have our party now?" Clara dropped her coat and ran to her little table.

"Not yet. First we have a few things to do." Jessie was stalling. It was five-thirty, suppertime, and nothing in the house; except for a cup of flour—not even enough for pancakes—some salt, some tea, and now, milk. She had used the last three eggs and the potatoes last night for supper, and the last oatmeal and bread, for breakfast and lunch. She had hoped that the lady whose coat she had finished would have come for it today. That couple of dollars would have helped. But now, she wouldn't come until Monday.

She kept the girls busy until nearly six o'clock. When she knew she could no longer stall, she made a ceremony of setting their table. "Here Clara, put this little tablecloth on. Now, Evie, place the spoons carefully. Clara, be sure your cup and saucer is in its proper place, like I showed you."

"Mama, will you make tea for our little teapot? Real tea?" Clara asked.

The table was set, the tea steaming from the small pot in the middle of the table: Jessie knew she could stall no longer. "All right, girls," she said, "you can sit down now and say the blessing."

"Dear Jesus," prayed Clara, "thank you for this nice birthday party with lettuce 'n do'nuts."

"Don't forget to pray for Daddy," prodded Jessie, thinking of anything to prolong the agony of telling her little girls there would be no lettuce and doughnuts, only tea and milk. Her heart believed. Her head did not.

IF YOU ONLY KNEW

"Amen," came Clara's voice to Jessie's ears.

"'men," echoed Evelyn.

A soft *knock, knock,* at the door, came just as Evelyn was echoing her *Amen.*

"I had these perishables left over from the store," whispered the caller, Mrs. Wall, while glancing over Jessie's shoulder to where the girls sat with empty plates, at their birthday table.

"Think you could use them?" She set two bags on the table. "They'd only spoil by Monday; that would be a shame." The store proprietor patted Jessie's hand, smiled and left.

Jessie knew they'd be there—the lettuce and the doughnuts.

While the girls sipped tea, munched on crisp lettuce and nibbled at their doughnuts, Jessie, with her heart bursting with thankfulness, put away the *perishables:* bread, butter, eggs, coffee, flour, fruit, cheese, bacon, chicken, and peppermints.

"Perishables Indeed!" she cried. "Oh God, how could I have doubted?"

Footnote: "Only Believe"—By: Paul Rader: c. 1929/1949 The Rodeheaver Co.

Chapter 17 — "Angels And Demons"

August 1933 - January 1934

The winds, hot sucking winds that seemed to come from all directions at once, blew constantly. Again, as she had many times during the summer, Jessie folded her sewing away to protect it from the dust which filtered through the door and window frames, the cracks, even the walls themselves, and settled on everything.

It was the last day of August. The dust hung in the air, fogging the eyes and clogging the nostrils. Jessie felt as if she would suffocate. She had to get out, just for a while, although it was no better outside.

A train whistle blew. Jessie's thoughts turned to Allyn. It was that way every time the faraway whistle of the bi-weekly, mixed-train sounded.

"Let's go for a walk," she said to the girls, picking up Helen's bonnet and tying it on her.

The girls raced each other to get the wagon for the baby.

As if drawn by some giant magnet, she headed west toward the train station. Her eyes misted when she saw the steam puffing from the old engine and heard its *chu-chu*, as it sat, as if impatient to be on its way, at the terminal. "Oh, Allyn" she sighed, "How I wish you were here! I miss your cheerful laugh, your optimism." October was still so far, far away.

"Daddy! Daddy!"

A lone figure was hurrying up the path, two screeching little girls bounding toward it.

"Allyn! Oh, Daddy, it *is* you." Jessie dropped the wagon handle and ran into his waiting arms. "It's only August. I thought—but I'm glad you're back... so glad!"

"I'm glad, too. God's been so good. But we'll talk about that later." Allyn swung his wife around. "How I've missed my family!" Setting Jessie down, he snatched Helen from the wagon, throwing her into the air, as he had done with his other daughters. "Where'd my baby go? You're all growed up."

That winter, life was a little easier for Jessie. The girls, now aged four-and-one-half, three, and one, entertained each other with books and toys, while Allyn studied and Jessie sewed. Because of Allyn's heavier schedule, he had agreed, at Jessie's request, to stay home on Tuesday evenings, the movie nights.

One Tuesday evening near the end of January, Jessie put her sewing away early. She glanced at the Big Ben alarm clock on the warming oven: *nine o'clock.* Despite the blaring movie next door, Allyn had climbed, exhausted, into bed. His thesis, *Angels and Demons,* due in two days, lay on the table waiting for Jessie. Because the teachers had difficulty reading Allyn's hen-scratch-like writing, Jessie had offered to copy his assignments for him. By doing this she also benefited from the Bible studies.

The day had been cold and blustery. Yawning, Jessie pulled on her boots and coat and headed to the outhouse. The wind, now on its way east to the neighboring province, Saskatchewan, had harrowed the snow. The air crackled in rhythm with the dancing northern lights; the sinister-looking moon peeked from behind a remaining cloud; eerie music exuded from the theater; a halo-like reflection from the dangling electric light in the kitchen, seeped through the frosty window. As Jessie crept along the path back to the house, her skin crawled; her hands trembled; she looked around her, and then grabbed at the doorknob. Once inside, she slammed the door behind her, shoving a chair up against it. Slowly she let out her breath.

What's the matter with me? she scolded herself. *I've never reacted like this before.* She shuddered. Having made a fresh pot of tea, she sat down to begin copying Allyn's manuscript. Ephesians 2:2: (*Satan...the prince of the power of the air.... The prince of demons or fallen angel...*) Jessie wrote in rhythm, it seemed, to the ticking of the clock.

When next she looked up from her writing, it was twelve-thirty. She stoked the fire, located the flashlight, turned off the light, and crawled into bed, snuggling close to Allyn. He didn't stir.

She was just about asleep when she heard a *whir-buzz-rattle*. Bolting to a sitting position, she turned her ear toward the children. Hearing the peaceful breathing of each of them, and the snorting and thrashing of Allyn beside her, she settled down once again.

Brr-whir-rattle-whine. There it was again. She shivered. "Wake up, Allyn," she rasped, shaking him. I think someone's at the door."

"What? What?" Allyn turned over.

She shook him again. "Listen!"

He bolted up. Putting their breath on hold, they both listened.

Whirr-brr-rattle-bang-whine.

"It's... it's the wind." Allyn flopped back onto the pillow.

"No. There is no wind. I just got to bed. It's as calm as the eye of a hurricane out." Jessie eased herself down beside her husband. There it was again—the noise. Louder now.

Allyn took the flashlight. He crept out of bed, tiptoeing to the door. Moving the chair, he peeked outside. The moon cast a silvery sheen over the freshly swept snow: silence whispered. He crept back to bed, slithering under the covers. "No one's out there," he whispered, pulling Jessie to him.

Sleep had all but claimed them when they heard the noise again. This time it was on the theater side. They sat up, Allyn putting his ear to the wall. The noise moved: now it was above them, now on their left, now on their right, then in the kitchen, then at the window. "I don't know what this is all about," he rasped, "but I think it's some of Satan's demons, left behind in the theater." He grabbed Jessie's hand. "I think we'd better pray and plead the blood of Christ."

Had it not been that Allyn had been asleep when Jessie had first heard the sounds, she may have put it down to the fact that the topic of the thesis, *Angels and Demons*, was playing on her mind. But he was hearing the sounds, too. So they were real... or, were they?

But whatever, she knew prayer wouldn't hurt. Together, the couple crawled out of their warm bed, knelt on the icy floor and prayed for God's protection. Together, they quoted the scripture from Psalm 34:7. "The angel of the Lord encampeth round about them that fear him, and delivereth them."

The fear left their hearts. They climbed into bed and into each other's arms. They were safe. The noise never returned.

Chapter 18 — And Then?

April — October 1934

There had been times when Jessie had looked forward to the end of Allyn's Bible School days; but now, here she was packing. It was over. She was sorry to be leaving the friends, the involvement of Allyn's studies, the security of knowing that he would be home at the end of each day. Then as she looked at the bare-board floors, the sagging door, the cracked and rusty stove; and as she thought of the blaring movies — all the things the family had had to put up with for the past eighteen months — her heart gave a leap of hope. Maybe things would get better, life would be easier.

"Hmph! With Allyn? Fat chance!" She shrugged her shoulders and plunked the large cast iron pan into a box. "Life with Allyn will never be easy."

Abraham went and lived in a tent, Allyn would often sing. "If life gets easy we forget God. *Here have we no continuing city* — Hebrews 13:14. That was the principle *her* husband went by.

Jessie clapped one hand over her mouth and the other onto her stomach as a wave of nausea swept over her. In the background she could hear the girls squabbling over some toy; then a blood-curdling screech from Helen pierced her ears. She squeezed her eyes shut and clenched her fists. She wished right now that the whole world would go away.

"Mama!" Allyn burst through the door. "The Mission has just given me my appointment for the summer." He kicked off his rubbers.

Jessie shuddered as she watched. Ever since their marriage, she had tried to persuade her husband to wear proper shoes. His reply to her was always the same: "Why wear rubbers *and* shoes? Leave me alone." But right now, what aggravated her more was his stalling. She knew his stalling games. Whenever he had a bombshell to drop—something he knew she wouldn't like—he would stall.

She waited. Allyn stalled.

Turning at last to where her husband sat peeling off his wet, muddy socks, her heart melted. Shaking her head while stifling a smile, she said to herself, *"He's just like the girls, always stepping into, not around, puddles."*

And still she waited. And still Allyn stalled.

"Allyn," she crooned, as if to one of the children, when after several more seconds of silence he still had not informed her of his assignment. "*Where* is the Mission sending you—us?"

"Ah... ah, they're coming for our stuff in the morning." He made an exaggerated effort of removing his last sock.

"Who? Who's coming for our stuff? And where are *they* taking our stuff?"

Allyn stood up, moved to the stove and shoved the teakettle on to boil. "Well." He waved his hands over the stove, warming them, before continuing. "We'll be going north." He blew on his hands.

"North! Where north?" Jessie swung around, dread gripping her heart. "Unless you mean—? She could feel the blood draining from her face.

"Mama." He jumped to her side, throwing his arms around her. "God will provide. Has He ever let us down? Has He?"

She shrugged away and went back to her packing.

Was it from the joggling of the hayrack, where she and the girls were squashed amidst the family's possessions that caused Jessie's stomach to churn? Or was it because she knew now where Allyn was taking them? Or was it because—?

Jessie glanced at her husband, perched like a bird on the frame of the hayrack, chattering away to the driver as if he were being driven to a palace in a limousine. *Doesn't anything bother that man of mine?* A wave of anger, mixed with the nausea, engulfed her.

She looked around her, recalling the first time she had seen this country, seven years before. Despondency settled on her at the thought of having to spend another summer of dust, mosquitoes, black flies, caterpillars, grasshoppers, and drought, in this godforsaken place.

As she sat brooding, half conscious of the girls' giggling, she heard a voice: "Have not I commanded thee? Be strong and of a good courage; be not afraid, neither be thou dismayed; for the Lord thy God is with thee whithersoever thou goest." Joshua 1:19. She jerked her head around, expecting to see Allyn standing over her; but then she realized that the voice had come from within. She closed her eyes, breathing deeply. Slowly, like water trickling into a glass, peace replaced the dread. She opened her eyes, seeing, as if for the first time, the countryside around her.

"Look, girls!" she said. "Look at the lambs frolicking and jumping over their mamas... 'I am Jesus' little lamb; Happy all the day I am.'" She sang the little chorus she used to sing with her mama, clapping her hands in time with the music. "'I am His, and He is mine. For I'm His lamb.'"

The girls sang along, giggling when the bumps made their voices wobble. Soon, one by one, they dropped off to sleep, leaving Jessie alone with her thoughts.

And then, there it was in the distance: the shacks; the rusted machinery; the barn, with its sinking roof, and the cabin; the shabby cabin, with the four-paned windows, the peeling paint of the trim against the weathered gray of the adjacent logs, the thrown-together lean-to. The slab-wood house, of course, was no longer there; it had been hauled off the property as soon as it was sold.

"Well," she said, forcing a smile to her lips, "at least we won't have to share the place this time with Mother Splane and Dick." Her mind drifted to her young brother-in-law, now in college. She recalled how exasperated she used to get with him—and how delighted he was with her exasperation. Before he would even reach the house, he would detect the aroma of fresh-baked cookies and dive for the cookie jar, often devouring the whole batch. She smiled now, remembering how she would try everything she could think of to save her cookies: she'd clean every trace of her baking away, find hiding places for her treasures, then be busy at something unrelated to cooking by the time

Dick arrived home from school. But, alas! He could still smell them: "Aha!" he would say. "Coookeeez!" Then his search would begin. He'd look in the cupboards, the warming oven, under beds, under mattresses, in clothesbaskets, on shelves, up in the rafters—she'd run out of hiding places—until he'd find them.

Well, she mused now, nestling Helen's head in her lap, *at least he didn't find anything lacking in my culinary skills.* She smiled again, recalling how severely his mother used to criticize her cooking.

Settled once again in the familiar surroundings, Jessie's days were pretty much the same: dressing and feeding the children, soothing hurts, wiping tears, settling squabbles. And always, always the nausea and a deep-settled depression.

"Why?" she questioned herself as she scrubbed socks on the washboard. "Why do I feel this way? I want this baby. Oh, yes, I want you," she said aloud to the unborn child. "I don't even care whether you are a girl or a boy. Just be healthy." She had never been this nauseated, or for this long, for a pregnancy. And, of course, she hadn't seen a doctor, but then she'd never seen one for her last two babies either, except for their births. But a niggling worry dogged her: *What if something was wrong?*

She shook out the clothes and pinned them to the line, wishing that she could as easily shake off the cloud that seemed to be hanging over her.

It was late September. The poplar, aspen, and birch trees had exchanged their summer attire for a wardrobe of gold, orange, and brown; and the underbrush looked like a multicolored plush carpet. The air, fresh and clean after a rain, had a nip to it. During the days the skies were an amphitheatre of caterwauling Canada geese on their way south. Had it been spring instead of fall, Jessie would have thought their honking to be euphonious; but now it was a bitter reminder of the imminence of winter.

She stood outside the door of the shack, watching, as the Master Artist spilled His pallet of color across the sky, portraying the close of another day. While her artist-eyes were reveling in the beauty of God's creation, her heart was rebelling at her circumstances: *How can I bear it, Lord? How can I spend another winter here?*

She turned and went inside, her head trying to tell her heart that she wasn't alone, that God had promised to walk with her. But she couldn't rid herself of the heaviness that seemed to be dragging her down. She longed to be… back with friends in Three Hills? With her family…? Where…? She didn't know. Anywhere but here.

The girls had finally settled down for the night. She reached into her apron pocket, pulling out Carrie's letter. She'd longed for this minute ever since Erwin had dropped off the letter early in the day. Wanting to read it when things were peaceful, she had stuck her sister's letter into her apron pocket. Throughout the afternoon, whenever she had put her hand into her pocket and touched the envelope, a feeling, like a surge of warm water, ran from her fingers to her heart and through her whole body. Her family was still out there, and they cared enough to write her.

And now at last, taking a sip of refreshing amber tea, she read, *Dearest Jessie: We got your letter… we detected a feeling of dejection…* Carrie told of the many happenings on the farm in Kingman. "And by the way," she wrote in conclusion, "Gertie, Art, and the girls, Edith and Beatrice, arrived from Froud, Saskatchewan, the other day. They'll be spending the winter with us. It will be good to have them and to have the extra hands around to help with the harvest. Tell Allyn, if he wants work, it's here… Tell him to bring—"

A pang of longing for her family stabbed at Jessie's heart. As she folded the letter to place it back into its envelope, a smaller envelope, with the words, *For you, for emergencies,* printed in miniscule letters, dropped to the floor. She reached down to pick it up, opening it slowly.

Ten dollars! She slumped onto a chair, placing her head on her arms on the table. Oh, what she wouldn't do to see her family. But she knew Allyn wouldn't— She knew how he felt. She knew how her family resented him for taking her away from a promising career, into— She knew he would never— Would he?

Suddenly she lifted her head, washed her face, stoked the fire, and poured herself a fresh cup of tea. Her mind mulling over the words of the letter, she plotted ways to approach the subject with her husband, discarding each one.

Late that night Allyn came home. Setting his supper in front of him, she sat down at the table with him. "Got this from Carrie today," she said, pulling the letter from her apron pocket and rubbing the pages between her fingers. When he didn't reply, she continued, "She said... she asked... she said that there's work—harvest... and that all of us should—" She freshened her husband's tea, setting the letter on the table beside him.

He slopped three spoonfuls of sugar into his cup, noisily stirring the tea with the sugar spoon, and then plunging it back into the sugar bowl. "How could I take the family?" he snapped. He slurped a mouthful of tea. "If I go, I go alone." He shut his eyes in his "I-don't-want-to-talk-about-it" manner.

Jessie sighed. She picked up the unread letter and tucked it into her purse beside the ten dollars. She would not bring up the subject again.

As she lay beside Allyn that night listening to his agitated tossing, she was surprised that she felt no anger.

But in her mind, a plan began to formulate.

Chapter 19 — The Plan

October 1934 - December 1934

September bumped into October. Jessie, so busy working out her plan, gave little thought to her nausea. It was there — as bad as ever — but she pushed it back into the background; she had to make sure every detail of her plan was in place. Even her oppression had lifted. She awoke each morning, humming.

On this particular morning she was humming the tune: "Are you weak and heavy laden. Burdened with the load of care...? Take it to the Lord in prayer." She lifted the curtain and peeked out. Patches of fog floated like ghosts through the air; clumps of dank leaves lay sprawled on the sodden ground or over frost-smitten bushes. An odd snowflake fluttered through the air, lingering awhile like a lost stranger, before landing on the unfriendly ground. "I know just how you feel," she muttered consolingly to the flakes. "And I don't blame you one bit for not wanting to stop here. I feel the same way." A smug, foolish grin spread over her lips, and she said aloud, "But I have a plan."

As she was turning to the stove to build up the fire, it hit her — the dread, the depression, the claustrophobia. It was back. Allyn would be home from Kingman any day now, and as the thought struck her, so did the gloom. Why should she feel this way? After all, she had a plan. But what if it didn't work? What then?

She dragged herself through breakfast and morning chores, the aggravating chatter of the children buzzing in her head.

"A car! A car! It's Daddy! It's Daddy!" Clara's shriek cut like a knife through Jessie's ears.

She shuffled to the window; and with the little finger of her flour-dredged hand, she pulled back the red gingham window curtain. "Oh no!" she groaned. Her nephew and his fiancée had brought Allyn home. "He'd better not be bringing them in, me looking like this." She slapped the work-soiled apron covering her elephant-sized abdomen, her floury hand flying to her bedraggled hair. "I'm a mess."

Carrie had written many glowing reports about George's lady friend, and she had looked forward to meeting her. But now, with her looking as she did at the present, was certainly not the time.

Erupting through the door, Allyn grabbed the girls one by one, tossing them into the air and kissing them. Then he turned to Jessie. "They're coming in for coffee," he said.

"You entertain them then." She spun around, disappearing into the bedroom. A full-blown surge of nausea hit her. She flopped onto the bed.

Having already insisted that she and George couldn't stop, Bernice alone followed Allyn into the house. He pointed to the bedroom, and then ducked back outside.

Bernice tiptoed into the bedroom. "I'll just stop a minute," she said. "Must get back to Edmonton for tomorrow." Then, while looking over her shoulder, she said in a stage whisper, "I've a letter for you from Gertie. She asked me to deliver it to you in person."

Jessie had been lying on the bed, facing away from the door, when Bernice entered. She swung to a sitting position, hot tears stinging her eyes. "Thanks," she whispered, too embarrassed to look up.

Bernice patted her hand, smiled at her, and then left.

Jessie tore open the letter. Her hand trembled as she read: *Dad will be visiting at the farm for the winter...arriving mid-November... So sorry you were unable to have come with Allyn. He said you were unwell. You should have come. We would have looked after you ...*

Tucked into the folds of the letter was a ten-dollar bill.

With tears splashing onto the paper, she finished reading the letter; then tucked it and the bill into her purse next to Carrie's letter, and the other ten dollar bill. She stood up, brushing her hand quickly across her eyes. She smoothed her apron, rubbed her hand over her hair, straightened her shoulders, sucked in her breath, and went out to the kitchen to greet Allyn, a forced smile on her face.

It was six a.m., Wednesday, October 31. Jessie awoke, grasping her stomach. She sat up. She felt as if she were crawling on her hands and knees through a train tunnel, a mile-long train on top of her. A low backache and a cramp through her middle made her feel cut in half.
"Allyn! Quick!" She grabbed him by his shoulder, shaking him. "It's time! Get Mrs. Strang. Quick!"
"Wha—? Who—? What did you...? Time?" He rolled out of bed and jumped into his pants. Gripping the collar of his shirt between his teeth, he hopped on alternate feet, shuffling into his socks. At the door he stepped into his rubbers, rammed his arms into his shirt, and tore out to hitch the team of horses for the four-mile trip to Mrs. Strang, the midwife. A hand plow Allyn had given to the Strangs in the spring was advance payment for Mrs. Strang's midwifery.

She knew she must make every push count. She had determined not to lose consciousness during the birth, but she was now no longer in control of her senses. She was sinking into a black hole. A far-away voice was calling her... calling her... calling her: it was the whine of the wind in the trees beckoning to her, pulling her. She was a leaf, fluttering... fluttering.
"Jessie... Mama," the wind was whining. "We have a—"
"Mrs. Splane. Mrs. Splane."
Now rising from the hole, now falling from the tree, she landed on the ground. A searing pain ripped through her: she was herself again. She groaned and tried to force her eyes to open.
"Mrs. Splane. Here's your eight-pound Halloween pumpkin." The midwife smiled and nestled the red-haired, red-faced baby into Jessie's arms.
The baby yawned and stretched, reaching for his mama's face.
"A boy?" croaked Jessie. "We got our little Alfred Hugh?" She peered down at the wizened little face, and grinned the grin of a Cheshire cat. His face *did* look like a pumpkin, so round, so shriveled,

so... perfect. Dropping her head onto the pillow, she closed her eyes, the little namesake of hers and of Allyn's father, nestled in the curve of her arm.

For over a week now, ever since the birth of her son, Jessie had eaten, slept, and breathed, with her *plan* uppermost in her thoughts. But Allyn was always at her side, always trying to help—always underfoot. When he was not attending her, he was pacing the floor, always restless, always pacing.

"Why don't you go, Allyn?" she said one morning. "Go find a job, get back to your mission work." She wanted him to go—almost prayed that he would—but she must not seem too eager. Her plan *must* work.

"Are... are you sure, Mama?" He jumped to her side. "Sure you'll be all right?" While asking, he was already picking up his cap and bag. He turned to kiss her. "Are you—?"

"I've never felt better." She patted his shoulder, forcing a smile.

No sooner was her husband gone from the yard—should she wait just a bit? But, no. Allyn never returned once he left. Always on the run, he would do without, rather than turn back. So, no sooner was he gone, than Jessie began to carry out her plan, cautiously at first, just in case.

She pulled out the battered suitcase from under her bed and dusted it off. With the children's clothes packed on top of her own few, she snapped the clasps shut. After filling six bottles of milk—she couldn't nurse this baby either—she wrapped the bottles in diapers, tucking a few sandwiches in beside them in the knapsack. The coats, mittens, and overshoes were laid out. She checked her purse.

With each heartbeat, the inside of her head swished with a deafening gush. She felt as if it would burst, if Mrs. Strang didn't soon arrive. The mid-wife had promised to check in on Jessie on this day—ten days after the birth—and Jessie was ready.

The log she had placed in the stove had died to a glowing ember. Already the room was beginning to cool off. She hoped she would not have to add another stick to the fire.

She heard a car stop in front of the shack; she sprang to the window. *Good!* She felt as if she had just exploded. *She's here.*

"How are you—?" Her neighbor's smile turned to a quizzical look when she saw Jessie helping the children on with their coats.

"My friend," replied Jessie to the unfinished question. "I'm fine. In fact, I've never felt better. Could I impose on you to take us to town?"

"Of course! It's no imposition." Mrs. Strang helped the children on with their boots, then led the way to the car.

Her eyes sweeping the room for a final check, Jessie lifted the sleeping baby into her arms and pulled the door shut behind her.

Allyn slapped the reins against the horses' backs. "It'll be so good to see my family again. Betcha Alfred's grown." It seemed like two months, not two weeks that he'd been away.

Oh, I have so much to tell Mama. Good meetings, Sunday schools started... and guess what? He was bursting to tell her *this* news. *Guess what?* he would say. *Someone wants to buy the farm. Oh, will she ever be glad to hear that!* Allyn's mind was whirling.

"Sure been a lot of snow." He rounded the last bend. As he neared the house he slowed the horses. Something was wrong—terribly wrong. Where was the cozy look that always made his heart glow? The smoke spiraling from the chimney? The trodden snow around the door? The —?

Panic seized him. Snow had drifted around the house, against the door. The windows, rimmed with snow, stared back at him like an unsighted man. He dropped the reins and jumped from the sleigh, scuffing through knee-deep snowdrifts, to the house. He pushed at the door. A swish of dry snow engulfed him, following him in.

"Mama? Clara? Evelyn?" He ran through the house and back into the kitchen. "Jessie...? Where is everyone?" He stood gawking at the polished stove, the scrubbed floor, the tidy wood box. He ran back into the children's bedroom. Empty shelves. In his and Jessie's room, he stared at the neatly made bed. His eyes roved wildly about, spotting the nails in the walls, where the clothes usually hung on hangers. Most of Jessie's scanty wardrobe was gone. He dropped to his knees, his eyes scanning under the bed. No suitcase. Racing back to the kitchen, he checked the table for a note. No note, nothing to give him a clue as to the whereabouts of his family. His hands flew to his head; if he'd had hair, he would have yanked it out.

"Oh, God," he shouted. "Where are they? Oh, what have I done to my family? My whole world has vanished—gone. I'm finished." How long he stood in the middle of the floor, his hands stretched to the ceiling, his head thrown back, tears spilling from his eyes, he wasn't aware.

Suddenly he snapped into action. Grabbing his cap and running from the house, he jumped into the sleigh, lashing the horses all the way to Colinton.

"Any mail?" he cried, grabbing the storekeeper by the arm. "Oh, there's got to be some mail."

Startled by Allyn's sudden outburst and by the look of panic on his face, the storekeeper shook his head from side-to-side. "No. I'm sorry, Al... But I did see your missus and the little ones boarding the southbound train 'bout a week ago. I... ah... Mrs. Strang, I think... brought 'em in. Didn't stop in here, though. Went right to the station."

Allyn leaped from the store. Yanking on the horses' reins, he steered the team towards Strang's. "Oh, God, what am I going to do?" he shouted to the sky. Tears froze on his face. He couldn't ask, "Why?" He knew why. Hadn't Jessie been hinting—no, outright, telling him—that she couldn't spend another winter in that cabin...? But he thought she had reconciled herself to it; she hadn't mentioned it lately—

Oh, what was he to do? Hadn't God called him to mission work? Hadn't He? Oh, he'd give it all up, to have his family back, his Jessie. Hadn't she always encouraged him to do what God prompted him to do? Hadn't she been behind him?

He jumped from the sleigh, shoved open the gate, and pounded on the door of the big white farmhouse. The door opened a crack. In the opening, appeared the face of a little girl.

"Is your mama in?" Allyn pushed at the door.

"No," said the little girl, slamming her foot against it.

"Where is she? When will she be back?" Allyn pushed again at the door.

"She went to Colinton to born a baby," said the girl, throwing her whole body against the door. "She'll be back tonight maybe, if the baby gets borned. Go away!" She slammed the door in Allyn's face.

His shoulders drooping, his heart feeling like a lump of lead, he shuffled back to his team. "Oh, Prince," he sobbed, throwing his arms around the neck of his big chestnut plough horse. "What am I going to do? Take me home. Take me home." He climbed into the sleigh, leaving the reins slack. He was oblivious to the bitter wind that blew snow around his face, and to the frost that nipped his cheek.

After tending to the horses he went into the icy cabin, sweeping the snow back outside. He built a fire and made himself a cup of strong tea. He flipped open his Bible — always his source of comfort — to one of his favorite passages, Psalm 27.

By the dregs of the fading daylight he read the familiar passage, down to the last verse, verse 14: "Wait on the Lord; be of good courage, and he shall strengthen thine heart: Wait, I say on the Lord."

"Wait! Wait for what?" he shouted. "The family's not going to come out of the cracks, or up from the cellar. They're gone. Gone. Wait for what, Lord?" He slammed his fist on the table, angry with himself, angry with Jessie for doing this to him, angry at God. "Where are You, God?" He dropped his head onto his folded arms on the table. He sobbed.

Clammy darkness had wrapped its arms around him by the time he next looked up; he shivered. Slowly, as if in a trance, he rose from the table. The words: *Wait! Wait! Wait!* throbbed in his head as he shuffled to the stove to drop in a few scraps of kindling to catch the embers. He lit the lamp; and since he hadn't eaten since breakfast, twelve hours before, he climbed down the six rungs of the ladder to the cellar, hoping — but not expecting — to find something he could fix for a meal.

"What!" A flash of anger hit him. On the shelves, all lined neatly, were bottles of vegetables, chicken, berries, jams and jellies. *She's been planning this 'escape' for quite some time.* He grabbed a jar from the shelf.

As he climbed back up the ladder, he remembered something, something about Carrie's letter, back two months ago. Jessie had let something slip. He remembered, because she had gasped, clasping her hand to her mouth. What was it? What had she said?

While he warmed up the chicken and sliced off a hunk of stale bread he'd found in the breadbox, his mind mulled: *What was it she'd said? Where would she go? Now what? How can I live without my family?*

He was stoking the fire for the night when he heard a car. He lunged for the door, opening it just as Mrs. Strang was about to knock. He snatched at the letter she was handing him. Without a word the neighbor retreated to her running car.

He stood with his mouth agape. He wanted to call after her, *Where did you take my Jessie?* But instead, he stared at the envelope he was holding. It was addressed to Mrs. Strong, but it was in Jessie's handwriting. He turned it over. It had been opened. As if in a slow motion dream, he reached into the envelope, pulling out another envelope, unopened, addressed to him.

His hand trembled. He read the letter. He read it again. After reading it for the third time, he dropped his head into his hands, his elbows resting on the table.

The next time he lifted his head, the house was cold, the lamp out of oil. He stoked the fire in the dark and flopped, fully clothed, onto the bed. *Well, I won't go after her. I won't! I won't!* He fell asleep.

Footnote: "What a Friend" — By: Joseph Scriven/Charles C. Converse

Chapter 20 — "Wither Thou Goest"

December 1934 - Spring 1935

Jessie couldn't remember when last she'd felt so relaxed. How wonderful it was to see her father again. He was alone now. Auntie had died some years back. And for the first time in her life, she was getting to really *know* Carrie. She'd been married the day Jessie was christened... And what luxury it was to be able to sit at the piano and play by the hour, if she liked. But maybe best of all, she enjoyed being spoiled, and mothered again by Gertie, the sister who had practically raised her. Since Edith and Beatrice, Gertie's young girls, were always eager to herd Jessie's three little ones off to play, it gave her a holiday from their constant care.

It was the opportunity she needed to rest, and to think, and to pray.

Sitting at the desk, in a comfortable chair in her evenly heated bedroom at her sister's house in Kingman (just north of Camrose, Alberta), her writing material in front of her, Jessie pulled out the letter she had just that day received from Allyn.

The electric light shone directly onto her writing paper — not the back of an old envelope, like what Allyn had used to write her. She glanced over at Clara, to the bed that she and Jessie shared. Her wavy blonde hair was splayed across the pillow, a cherubic look on her sleeping face. She thought of her other two daughters, asleep in their warm, soft bed in the next room. She peeked at her son, so sweet-looking in his crib—not a dresser drawer like what Helen had spent her infancy in. Her mind relived the many pleasant hours she had spent with her family during the winter.

Pulling her eyes back to the letter before her, her mind flipped to Allyn. What would he be doing tonight? Would he be sitting on a broken chair, leaning his elbows on a rough table, reading the Psalms by the dim glow of the kerosene lamp? *"I wonder if he's ever cleaned the chimney, or trimmed the wick,"* she thought. A smile snuck to her lips as she visualized him filling the lamp earlier in the evening, spilling coal oil all over the table, then sopping it up with a towel, and chucking the towel onto the top of the wood box.

Comfortable in a cozy bathrobe and slippers of Carrie's, she thought of her husband in his bare feet, jumping up now and then to throw another stick of wood onto the fire, a shower of ashes covering him and everything in sight.

Saturday night, she thought. *Bath night.* Oh, how she had enjoyed the baths she'd had in the tub here at her sister's. In contrast, she recalled the bath nights back where Allyn was: the steaming boiler on the back of the stove; the washtub in the middle of the kitchen floor; the baths, each child in order of age; then, after the children were tucked into bed, how she would heat the water up, climb into the tub herself—folded up like a jackknife—bath quickly, then dress while Allyn used the water; and how, before throwing the water away, she would scrub the kitchen floor, and the porch.

Her mind swung back again to the desk at her sister's house. She twiddled her pen; then chewed the end as she reread Allyn's few scribbled lines. There wasn't a single hint of accusation in his letter, nor had there been in any of his other correspondence with her. But she felt guilty—yet justified—at having deserted him. But was she justified? Hadn't she promised to love, honor and cherish him until the day they were parted by death? Her heart twisted with hurt for him. Tears welled in her eyes.

She dipped her pen into the bottle of ink, but she couldn't see through her tears, to write. She closed the ink, wiped off the pen, and crawled into bed beside her sleeping daughter.

In her dream she was with Allyn, up north in the shack that she hated so much. They were standing before Rev. Bennett, holding hands, looking into each other's eyes. She was saying, as she had on her wedding day: "... for whither thou goest, I will go; and where thou lodgest, I will lodge: thy people shall be my people, and thy God, my God:" Ruth 1:16... Then Allyn faded. She reached for him; he wasn't there. She called; he didn't answer.

She sat up. With dazed eyes, she looked around her; she jumped out of bed. Switching on the light, she grabbed her pen and wrote the letter she couldn't write the night before. She knew she loved her husband; she knew she wanted to be with him.

As Jessie lay snuggled in Allyn's arm that first night home, she felt so at peace. She lay listening to her husband's snorts and grunts as he slept. How much she had missed him! She knew she would never desert him again — until death. Mentally, she renewed her wedding vows: *...for better, for worse, for richer, for poorer. ... in sickness and in health...*

For her, she knew there would be no *richer* — but she was already rich. She had Allyn, and Clara, and Evelyn, and Helen — all precious treasures — and she even had the *over and above*, promised by God: her little Alfred Hugh. She sighed a contented sigh, and fell asleep.

Chapter 21 — The Spring

May - June 1935

Meanook, a town with two general stores and one elevator, is nestled amongst the hills of the beautiful Tawatinaw valley, ninety miles north of Edmonton.

On a knoll about two miles in circumference, in the eastern portion of Jack Rolland's land, about a mile-and-a-half north of the quiet little town, Jessie stood with Allyn, viewing the spot he had chosen to build their house. She tilted her head, looking up at the stand of trees to the north. To their south was the plowed field through which they had just driven.

"That's old 'Teapot' Rolland's closest field. All his other fields are about a mile in that direction." Allyn pointed west.

Between where she and Allyn stood, and the field to which her husband was pointing, was a coulee, with a coulee on the east side as well, both thick with bush and shrubs. Jessie took a deep breath, filling her lungs with the intoxicating fragrance of chokecherry and Saskatoon blossoms, mixed with the pungency of worm-like pussy willows, soon to burst into leaf. The setting was tranquil.

"What about water?" Her eyes involuntarily scanned the area again... "Careful, girls. Come away from the edge of that cliff. Helen, you stay with Mama." To Allyn she said, "I really like it. There's such a panoramic view, and there should be plenty of berries. But it's water

I'm worried about. Let's scout the valley. There. In that direction." She pointed west.

Back on top, after two hours of searching unsuccessfully for water, Jessie spread a tablecloth on the ground, took out a bottle of chicken, some baking powder biscuits, and a bottle of blueberries. "Good thing we brought this with us," she said, pouring water into five tumblers.

After lunch Jessie nestled Alfred and Helen into the wagon for a sleep. Clara and Evelyn scurried away, looking for early spring flowers, or bugs, or just looking, while Allyn trotted off to continue his search for water.

He had explained to Jessie during lunch, that on the knoll was the only place he could build. Rolland had lent him the spot in exchange for his taking off a quota of trees, which had been sold for fencepost. "If I cut the trees and haul them to the mill in town," Allyn had told her, "the guy who bought the trees will give me lumber for my roof and floor. Also, old 'Teapot' Rolland said I could have all the logs I wanted for building, and for firewood.

While the little ones slept Jessie sat on the ground, leaning against a wheel of the wagon. Her mind drifted to Isaiah forty-one, a chapter she knew well, one she had looked to for comfort many times, especially verses nine and ten, and thirteen: "I have chosen thee, and not cast thee away. Fear thou not... I am thy God: I will strengthen thee. ..." And: "Fear not, I will help thee."

Pulling her Bible from where she had tucked it amidst the diapers and baby bottles, she flipped to the familiar passage. Her eyes drifted over the verses until they rested on verse eighteen: "I will open rivers in high places, and fountains in the midst of valleys: I will make the wilderness a pool of water, and the dry land springs of water."

It was like the Lord was shouting, "There's water here." She jumped up, saying aloud: "That's it! There's water in this valley."

"Girls," she called. "Go find Daddy. I need him."

Scarcely had the girls left on the run to find their daddy, when Jessie saw all three of them running back in her direction.

"Mama, Mama. I've found it," puffed Allyn. "I found water."

"I know," she said, sprinting to meet him.

"I was running through the valley, praying, when a verse from Psalm 104 popped into my head. Verse ten, I think. Yea, verse ten: "He sendeth the springs into the valleys, which run among the hills." I stopped and retraced the area we walked this morning. I remembered seeing a valley *in* a valley—kind-of a lower place. I went back and forth just a while ago, looking for it. Then I stopped. I heard something. A rippling. I went toward it and stepped right into the spring." He glanced at his wet, sock-and-rubber-clad feet. "It's a spring, a running spring—underground—surfacing just in that one low spot. Come. Let's go look."

Each carrying a sleeping child, the couple headed for the spring, followed by two excited little girls. Along the way Jessie told Allyn about her verse from Isaiah. They stopped by the spring of water to thank God for His answer to their prayers.

Three weeks later the wagon, piled high with the family's possessions, pulled out of the yard. Jessie refused even to turn to take a final look at the shack they were leaving—the shack she had hated so much. They were headed down the road to a new beginning.

As they rounded the last bend in the trail, Jessie got her first glimpse of their new home. The log cabin, with its two front windows—one slightly lower than the other—placed on either side of the slab-wood door; its slightly peaked roof; it's shabby appearance, looked so much like one of Allyn's creations. It reminded her of a vacant-minded man, staring out over the field. She smiled, a warm, fuzzy feeling flowing through her. *Well, at least he looks friendly; and he has no history—a fresh, clean start,* she thought. To Allyn, she said, "I like the six-paned windows in the front."

"It's... it's not quite finished." Allyn turned to help Jessie and the children from the wagon.

As Jessie approached the twelve-by-twenty-four-foot cabin, she frowned. "Allyn?" She hesitated, peering through the cracks between the logs. "Shouldn't... shouldn't the logs be peeled before putting them together?"

"I know. I know." His voice was impatient. "But I had no time." He shifted Alfred to his other hip. "I'm gonna put mud plaster inside and out, then whitewash it," he said in a softer tone.

Jessie entered the two-roomed cabin. Allyn had built shelves on the wall to hold the dishes, and a wide, lower shelf for the water buckets and washbasin. He had made a rough cupboard to store food, the top to serve as a counter for bread making and dishwashing.

Studying the structure, she smiled: he had built the room as close as his capability allowed to the blueprint she had drawn him.

"Rolland gave me that table, the chairs, and cupboard." Allyn dropped the armload of things he had brought in from the wagon.

She glanced at the battered kitchen table and straight-backed chairs. But when she saw the factory-made cupboard with three deep drawers on one side and a double bin on the other side, her eyes lit up.

"At last, a place for flour and sugar," she said to herself.

The bedroom was the full width of the cabin and about one third the length. Under a four-paned window on the west side, Allyn had built a bed, fastened head and side to the walls, the only post standing at the outer corner. Lining the wall, nailed at eye-level, were wooden orange crates, to serve as clothes cupboards. On the other side of the room, he had nailed the crates lower, for the children's clothes. A similar hewn bed had been built into the east wall, under a lower four-paned window.

She smiled at her husband, who had followed her into the bedroom and was standing beside her. "Adequate," she said, taking his hand. "Quite adequate. All three girls can easily sleep on this bed. We'll put Alfred's crib here by the wall in the middle; and I'll hang Hudson's Bay blankets to divide the children's room from ours, for the time being.

"Let's have lunch." She turned abruptly and went back to the kitchen.

When she noticed the stove, a large McClarey with a reservoir and a warming oven, her smile spread wider. "Where did you find that stove?" she asked.

"Some guy staying in an old cabin of Rolland's left the country, and the stove was there. Rolland gave it to me. Like it?"

"Oh, yes. It's fine. Fine. Nice and big." The look on his wife's face assured Allyn that she was pleased.

Footnote: It was later in the day that Jessie learned the reason for Rolland's being known as "Teapot Rolland." When Allyn had introduced Jessie to him, she had responded in her usual, soft voice. He shot back, "Whadja say, lady? Speak up." With that, he had reached under his shirt, whipping out a horn-shaped hearing aid, with a teapot-like handle.

Chapter 22 — New Beginnings

August – September 1935

Having finished clearing the stand of trees for Rolland, Allyn had gone north to do brush cutting, resuming his mission work at the same time.

The stench of grasshoppers, which had landed in droves, eating everything in sight, filled the stifling August air. One morning about a week after her husband had left, Jessie awoke at 6:00, gasping for breath. She eased her way out of bed, shuffling to the kitchen to light the stove.

"Maybe when I have a cup of tea I'll feel better," she said to her reflection in the cracked six-by-nine-inch mirror hanging over the washstand. All her married life she had wanted a full-length mirror, but today as she looked at her sunken eyes and her gray face, she was glad she didn't have one. She grasped her shoulder-length braid, undid it, and began brushing her hair, noticing a few gray strands at the temples. Before she could twist it into a bun and pin it to the nape of her neck, she had crumpled to the floor.

"Mama! Mama! Wake up. Wake up."

"Mama! Mama!"

"Ma-ma!"

She forced her eyes open. Clara was kneeling beside her, shaking her, wailing at her, "Mama, what's wrong. Mama? Why did you fall?"

Her eyes began to focus slowly, as if she were in a foggy cave. Standing above her, holding hands and crying, were her other two daughters. A husky wail penetrated her fuzzy mind. "Oh... the baby." She began to struggle to her feet. "Is... is he all right?"

"Mama," said Clara, helping her mother to her feet. "I'll look after Alfred. You'd better make some tea." She glanced over at the large enamel teakettle, pouring out volumes of steam.

Jessie wobbled toward the stove, concluding that her suspicions were correct. She didn't know whether to laugh or cry. *Oh Allyn, why are you always away when I need you the most?*

While she sat sipping her tea, still in her nightgown, her hair hanging down her back, she studied her girls, also in their nightclothes. Clara, always angelic looking, with her wavy blonde hair and fair complexion, was acting right now more like sixteen, than six. She sat on the floor, feeding her ten-month-old brother, the bread and milk she had fixed for him. His red head bounced up and down as he kicked his feet, impatient for his next mouthful.

Helen, soon to be three, stood in her wet nightie, sucking her thumb as she watched her big sister feeding the baby. Jessie noted again the close resemblance of the two sisters. But with Helen's dark hair and olive complexion—a contrast to her light blue eyes—and her more pronounced dimple, her looks could be described as "cute," rather than angelic. Jessie turned to where Evelyn, her little shadow, stood at her elbow. She smiled into the limpid blue eyes—so like her dad's—wide with concern. Reaching out she rumpled the mass of tangled russet curls that circled the freckled face of her second daughter.

Oh, how she loved her children. But another one? She sighed a deep, trembling sigh.

Hearing the rumble of wagon wheels, Jessie pushed back the freshly hung curtains she had made from the outer parts of worn-out sheets, and trimmed with red gingham scraps she had saved from the curtains of the other house. "Daddy's home," she said, dropping the curtain and hustling to gather her sewing to put it away.

The girls, in the midst of preparing for bed, scrambled to the window, pushing at each other to get the first peek. It had been nearly a month since they'd seen their daddy.

"Mama," squealed Evelyn, turning toward her mother. "He's got junk in the wagon. Lotsa' junk."

Seconds later Allyn burst into the house, giving his family his usual greeting of throwing the girls into the air and twirling his wife around. After the mind-boggling excitement of greeting was over, Allyn spun around. "Now," he said, "I guess I'd better explain all that stuff." He nodded in the direction of the wagon, then headed for the door.

"Mama. Come with me. I got lots o' stuff t' show you," he said, leading her toward the wagon. "I did some clearing for a farmer. No one has any money, but those people are so generous. Look!" He began chucking things from the wagon. "A couch, mattress and cover aren't much, but maybe you can repair them? A rocking chair, a few rungs missing, but we can fix that; a chair, quite nice, high-backed. All painted nice and white." He tossed the crude chair with the chipped white paint onto the ground. "It'll help fill the room, anyway, won't it? Oh, yea, and here's a big cooking pot. You said you wished you had one."

Jessie furrowed her brow at some of the stuff: old boxes, dented pots and pans, harnesses, chicken wire. *Chicken wire?* It *was* junk, just like Evelyn had said. Oh, well. She'd sort through it later. "Where'd the farmer get all this stuff?"

"Had it stored in his barn. And—"

"Do you have chickens some place? I hear something."

"Oh, yea. I forgot." He dropped what he had in his hand and clambered to the front of the wagon. He began chucking off boards and scraps of lumber until he came to a wooden crate. "Five hens and a rooster," he said, shoving the box at Jessie.

"Hm! That's a good start. If they survive the winter." She placed the crate on the ground, carefully opening it. "We'll build them a pen," she said, remembering the wire she'd wondered about earlier." Cautiously she put her hand into the box, feeling a mass of warm feathers crowded into one corner.

"Mama, see all this lumber?" He tossed more wood scraps onto the ground. "I'm gonna crib the well and build a better shelter for Prince and Gilly for the winter. I think… I hope… Gilly's gonna have a colt in the spring."

"Speaking of having a colt—Oh, never mind… I'm going to take the chickens in to show them to the kiddies," she said, picking up the box and heading for the house.

"Whatcha got?" asked Evelyn, holding the door open for her mother.

Jessie set the box on its side, smiling at the reaction of the children as they watched the chickens stumble out like drunkards and stagger around the rough-board floor.

"I'll get some rolled oats." Clara scurried to the cupboard, returning with a cupful of cereal.

"An' I'll get water." Evelyn ran to the water pail.

"Me, too. Me, too." Helen dragged a chair, inch by inch, to the cupboard to reach some bread.

When Allyn entered the house a few minutes later, the three girls, on their tummies, were watching the chickens gobbling the goodies they had supplied. Jessie, on the floor, too, was laughing, holding the flailing hands of her son, who had already tried strangling one of the flock; while Buddy, the kitten, stood with his back humped and his tail puffed, hissing at the mass of moving feathers which had invaded his domain.

Allyn dropped to the floor to join his family. "Boy, it's good to be home," he said. "Oh, I almost forgot." Rolling to one side, he reached into his pocket to retrieve some change, which he tossed onto the floor.

"I got one," squealed Evelyn, grabbing at a coin rolling near her tummy.

"I got three." Clara pounced on the falling coins. "And now I got three more."

"Wha' 'bout me?" Helen didn't know what was going on, but she did not want to be left out.

"Here. Here's one for you." Jessie picked up a penny and pressed it into her little daughter's hand.

This coin-scramble was a game Allyn had instigated when Clara was eighteen months old. After tossing out the change from his pocket, he would help her count it. By the time she was two she was able to add the pennies and the nickels.

"Here, Daddy," said Clara, when she was sure she'd found every last coin. "I got the most."

"Let's count," said Allyn. "Three nickels, one dime, and eleven pennies. Good. That's—"

"Thirty-six cents," Clara finished. "How much you got, Evie?" She grabbed at her sister's money.

"I count. I count." Evelyn stamped her foot at her sister, then began, "I got a brown penny, and a silver penny, and a big silver penny."

"No, silly. That's a penny, and a dime, and a nickel. That's sixteen cents. I got the most."

Jessie retrieved the penny from Helen's mouth and added it to the pile the girls had placed on the table, a total of fifty-seven cents. "That'll buy a few groceries," she said to herself later, shaking forty-two cents from her purse to add to it.

After settling the children into bed, she pushed the teakettle to the hottest part of the stove, then went to the cupboard to cut some bread. "Let's see. What'll I get for a meal for Allyn?" She pursed her lips and wrinkled her brow. "Rose hip jelly, a tin of sardines, and bread. Well, I guess that'll do."

"Oh!" Allyn had just sat down at the table. He jumped up, and in his stocking feet, rushed out the door. "Here," he said, returning seconds later. He pushed a package wrapped in a not-too-clean strip of cloth at Jessie. "The farmer gave it to me. It's bacon. I'll have some of that."

Jessie took the bacon, cutting off a strip.

"Drop this in, too," he said, handing her the bread.

As soon as she had dropped the bread into the pan of sizzling grease, she grasped her head and her stomach at the same time. "You'd better do it," she gasped.

"What's wrong?" He jumped up, grabbing her arm and easing her onto a chair.

"Pour me a cup of tea... and I'll tell you." She leaned her head on her arms while her husband poured out the tea.

"Remember when you told me about Gilly's having a colt in the spring? I started to tell you something? Well..." She took a gulp of tea. "We, too, are going to have an addition to the family."

"What!" Allyn held his cup in mid air, his mouth agape and his eyes lighting up. "When?"

"About the middle of March, I'd guess. Hand me that calendar."

Her husband lifted the three-foot-long calendar from Hunter's store off the wall, and handed it to her. He shuffled closer to her while she flipped to the back page, where the following year's months were laid out in small squares.

"Yes. I think it should be sometime around the middle of March. At least most of the winter will be over by then. I don't think I could stand having a baby in the middle of winter." She gave a weak laugh.

"And another thing I want to discuss with you. Something I've been thinking about a lot lately." She shoved the calendar aside and turned so that she could look Allyn in the face. "Next month is September. School starts." She let the words sink in before going on. "Clara is six-and-a-half. Are we going to send her? What I've been thinking is—" She stopped, swallowed, and even though *she* didn't want one, she poured out two refills of tea. While Allyn was dribbling sugar between his cup and the sugar bowl, she continued. "Clara has been to Grandma's so much over the years, and she's been tutored and schooled by Grandma and Dick, she's ahead, I'm sure, of most beginners. You saw how quick she was with the money tonight. And you know that she can read all the books Grandma has given her. She knows her sounds, her alphabet, and her numbers..." She got up and began clearing the table.

"Mama! What are you getting at? Sit down. Sit down." Allyn pushed his wife into her chair.

"What I'm saying is, why couldn't I teach her? Right here. And maybe Evelyn, too... Then next year they can both go to school together. I think I can teach her just as much as she could learn at school. Besides—" She took a breath, then said again, "Because... she's ahead of most beginners. And... and she wouldn't need new clothes."

Allyn sat with his elbows leaning on the table, his head in his hands, in a prayer-like position. Jessie stirred her cold tea, with no intention of drinking it. Her mind was on the dirty dishes scattered over the table; she wanted to clear up, but was afraid to move, afraid of interrupting her husband's thoughts.

Suddenly he lifted his head. He grabbed her hand. "Yes, Mama. You're right. You *should* teach her. You could use the Bible for a reader, and—" He jumped up and went out. Discussion was over. Jessie had won, without a battle.

Chapter 23 — School

September - December 1935

    The same evening that she and Allyn had discussed school, Jessie had written to Gertie, asking for her girls' cast-off school materials, if they had any. It had paid off. Gertie had sent seven partly filled scribblers, two half-used pencils, a ruler — broken off at nine inches — a few chewed erasers, and a grade four reader. These, as well as the Bible, an old calendar, the Simpson's catalogue, and the books from Grandma, which Clara had so well memorized, that they would be of little use for school, were piled neatly at one end of the table, ready for school to begin.

    It was two days after Evelyn's fifth birthday. Jessie settled her and Clara at the opposite end of the kitchen table from the school materials, giving them each a piece of paper and a pencil. To Evelyn she said, "You draw me a picture." She placed a pencil in her hand, and after guiding her for a minute to give her the idea, she turned to Clara. "I want you to show me how much of the alphabet you can write, and then how many numbers you know."

    Clara tipped her head to one side, and with her tongue wagging across her lips, she tackled her work. This was nothing new to her; she had done it many times at Grandma's.

Evelyn, on the other hand, took the pencil her mother had placed so correctly in her hand, grabbed it in her fist and scribbled over the page. Then after biting the end off the pencil, she threw it across the room and jumped down from the chair. "Don't want to go to school," she said, stamping her foot.

Jessie shrugged her shoulders. "So much for that!"

"Can I go help Daddy cut wood, Mama?"

"Good idea. Yes. That's a very good idea."

Evelyn bounded for the woods, grabbing one end of her daddy's crosscut saw. Her *boopy-boopy, boopy-boopy* — an expression she had used since she was two, for each time the saw cut through the log — could be heard all the way back to the house.

"Well that's that problem taken care of, for today," said Jessie, letting out her breath in a long sigh.

One morning about two weeks after Jessie had started Clara on her schooling, she awoke earlier than usual. Lifting her head from the pillow, she dropped it again. "Oh, how am I going to get through this day?" she thought, putting her hands to her head and lifting it from the pillow. She eased her feet onto the floor and into her slippers, listening to the gentle breathing of the children. She felt the thrashing of the bed as Allyn turned with a snort.

She was glad she hadn't wakened him. She tiptoed to the kitchen, lifted the lids off the stove, shook down the ashes, laid paper and kindling, and threw in a lighted match. By the time she had dressed and combed her hair, the kettle had begun to sing. She previewed her day: get baby out of crib, change and dress him; supervise girls' dressing and washing; get breakfast—oatmeal and bread; after morning devotions, see Allyn off for day of work; supervise children's chores—getting water, washing dishes, bringing in wood; tidy house; prepare bottle for Alfred, and put him down for morning nap; feed chickens; get lunch; put Helen and Alfred down for afternoon naps—Evelyn, too, if she needs one—or send her out to play; then settle Clara at the table for her lessons.

Her head spun at the thought of yesterday's struggle. *How would it be to teach a slow child, if it's this difficult to teach a bright one?"* she thought. *"That's the problem: she's too bright for her own good!"*

Yesterday she had stood by her daughter, pointing out the sound, "th." Clara had said it. Then Jessie had shown her the word, "the."

Clara had insisted on saying, *"tu-hu-e."* Over and over, Jessie had shown her sentences, like: "The cat ran," or, "The girl threw the ball." Each time Clara would read the sentence correctly. But whenever she saw the word, *"the"* by itself, she would insist that it should be pronounced *her* way.

Finally, at her wit's end, she had flipped to the Gospel of John. "Here," she had said, "read this, as far as you can." She had turned back to her breadmaking.

By the time Jessie had shaped the bread into loaves and set it to rise, her daughter had read to the end of the third chapter, sounding out any unfamiliar word — without help, and without a mistake.

Now as she stirred the porridge, she let out a deep, shuddering sigh. Where should she go from here? How should she approach Clara's lessons? "Well, one thing I know for sure," she said, straightening her shoulders, "I'm not going to give up, no matter how hard my student makes it for me."

She pushed the porridge pot to the back of the stove, opened the door to let the cat in, went to the broken mirror over the washbasin, and began to brush her hair. To her reflection she said, "Well, I'm feeling a little better than I was earlier, though this mirror belies it."

Just as she was spinning her hair into a bun and pinning it to the back of her head, she heard her family begin to stir: her day had begun.

After her walk through the swirling December snow the jingle of the bell above the door at the general store in Meanook was a welcome sound to Jessie. A blast of warmth from the pot bellied stove in the middle of the floor felt like a hug to her. She wiped her steamed glasses with her gloves and went to the post office window for her mail.

"A telephone message for you, last night," said Hunter, handing Jessie a note. "I was just about to send someone out to deliver it to you. It's important."

Dad died last night, read the message. *Phone me collect.* It was from Bell, in Stettler, where Jessie's dad had lived since spring.

She hurried with her grocery shopping, then called her sister. There was a lot of arranging to be done before tomorrow, Friday, the day the tri-weekly mixed train (passenger-freight) came into Meanook.

Back home, she dropped the groceries onto the counter. She hung up her coat and put on her apron. "I'm going to Stettler on the train tomorrow," she said, her back to Allyn. "Dad died yesterday. Bell's arranged for tickets for me and the older girls." She swung to face her husband. "Think you can manage the little ones?"

Allyn had already begun to put the groceries away. At her announcement, he swung suddenly around, a bag of salt held in mid-air. He stood staring at her, his mouth opening and closing, like a fish out of water. The salt went, *splat* on the floor, the contents spilling. "Sure," he said, swallowing. He jumped to where Helen was, grabbing her and swinging her over his head. "I can manage the babies. We'll get along fine, won't we, Helen? We don't need Mama, do we?"

Jessie felt a stab of pain for her husband. Optimism was in his voice, but pain was on his face. She knew he was remembering last winter. "Don't worry," she added quickly. "We'll be back right after the funeral." She walked over to him and placed her hand on his arm. "I promise."

He grabbed her by the waist and spun her around before kissing her. "Sorry about your dad," he whispered.

"Brr! It's cold!" Jessie dropped the suitcase inside the door and blew on her hands. The girls stumbled in behind her, holding their faces.

At the sound of his wife's voice, Allyn jumped, nearly dropping the baby. He had just gotten Alfred up from his nap and was changing his diaper. "Back so soon?" He jumped to Jessie's side. "You were only gone a week. I thought... I didn't... expect you until at least Monday. He kissed her, then the girls. "How was your trip?"

"Fine," said Jessie in a nonchalant way, stooping to help Evelyn take off the two pairs of heavy socks she was wearing over her shoes, as overshoes. "And how were things here?" Her eyes slid over the topsy-turvy kitchen.

"Got the ceiling up," he said, his eyes following his wife's glance at the kitchen. Together they gazed above their heads at the new building-paper-ceiling. "But we had a near-accident," he continued. "Saturday I decided to work on the rafters so I could nail the building paper to it to help keep the wind out. The babies were playing in the kitchen. I was up top with the boards an' hammer for, oh, maybe ten minutes, when the board I was working with slipped from my hand. I heard a scream. I jumped down; and right by Alfred's knee was the board I'd dropped, with a two-inch nail sticking out. Guess he'd crawled over to see what I was doing." He picked his son up and rocked him, just as he had the morning of the accident. "Thank God for His protection. All he got was a scratch. If that nail had —" He shut his eyes.

Jessie took the baby from her husband, nearly buckling from his weight. "Oh, you're getting heavy, my man." She inspected the scratch on his face. "I can hardly lift you. Time you started walking," she said, cuddling him in her arms.

Alfred chuckled, first grabbing Jessie's chin and biting it, then throwing his chubby arms around her neck and hugging her.

"It's good to be home," she said. "Really good."

Chapter 24 — Make Her Cry

December 1935 – January 1936

Her eyes flew open. She lay for a few moments watching fingers of light gyrate through the window and dance across the floor. It was only midnight, but she felt wide-awake. Slowly she eased her way out of bed and tiptoed to the kitchen window. The aurora borealis had always fascinated Jessie. As she stood watching the vacillating colors, she could hear a tinkling, like miniature teaspoons being struck against tiny glasses; and she imagined the angels having a party, playing marimbas and dancing, as they might have done on the night of Christ's birth, when they announced: "Behold, I bring you glad tiding of great joy." (Luke 1:10)

Christmas. A time for joy. She smiled, remembering the girls' excitement at seeing the carolers on the station platform in Edmonton a few days ago; and how excited they had been about the Christmas decorations in each of the little towns the train had stopped at; and how, when they had gone through Edmonton, Evelyn had pressed her nose flat against the train window, not wanting to miss a single glimpse.

What could she do to make this Christmas one the children would never forget? Since returning from her father's funeral, she had been busy sewing dresses for the girls and rompers for Alfred. But that wasn't enough. Clara and Evelyn would remember the sleigh rides, the caroling, and the decorations at their aunties' last year. She wanted to do something special. But what?

She turned from the window. Her insides felt like they were being ripped apart by some giant snowplough and her head felt twice its normal size. She shuffled to the stove, pushing the teakettle to the hottest spot; then she lit the lamp.

"That's it!" she said, snapping her fingers. "That's what I'll do." On her way back to the table with the teapot in her hand, she grabbed the old Simpson's catalogue from the shelf. Intermittently, as she drank tea, she snipped, placing her cuttings into a used envelope.

Later that day she and three excited girls made paper chains, strung colored popcorn, and cut snowflakes from pages of Clara's notebook to paste on the windows. And in the evening Allyn helped the girls make snow-candy. This was his specialty — sugar taffy, cooled and hardened by dropping it into a bowl of snow.

Jessie tucked four exhausted children into bed. Now she could complete her surprise. By nestling a bed sheet into the corner of the room and adding snow (beaten Ivory Snow soap and water), she created a winter scene, using the figurines she had cut from the catalogue.

The scene featured groups of people on their way to church. In the top corner of the sheet she arranged the manger scene, cut from a grocery bag. Above that she hung the sketch of singing angels, which she had drawn with Clara's crayons.

After arranging the gifts among the scenes, gifts she had made, as well as ones she had brought back with her from the aunties, she stood back to survey her work. "Like it?" she asked, glancing over to the table to where Allyn sat reading his Bible.

"Hm," he answered, without looking up. "Say, Mama, listen to this."

She sighed, poured herself a cup of tea and sat down. How she wished her husband would take more interest in special activities. While she half-listened to what he was reading, she mentally prepared the meal for the next day: mashed potatoes, turnips, and the rooster Allyn had been given as pay a week ago. She'd wait until he was in bed to prepare the stuffing and gather together the ingredients for the carrot pudding. She yawned.

The next morning she crawled out of bed and staggered to the kitchen. Her head was swimming, and she was trembling. "Too many late nights," she said to herself. While she stirred the ingredients for the pancakes her stomach began to heave. She felt her knees buckle.

The buzz of voices and rattle of dishes oscillated inside Jessie's head. Slowly her eyes unglued. What ever was she doing on the Winnipeg couch, a blanket thrown over her, and a cup of tea on a chair beside her? She flung the cover aside and began to swing her legs over the side of the couch.

"No!" Allyn's voice cut through her head like a knife. "You stay there, Mama," he said. "Today *we* are going to do everything. You can supervise from there." He waved his hands in an arch. "You've made everything look so... wonderful, so... so Christmassy. Right, girls?"

"Yea. It's just like... like real Christmas," said Clara. Her eyes sparkled as she gazed at the winter scene, "'member last year? That... ah... thing at that church at Aunt Carrie's?"

Jessie smiled. "Yes. The pageant we went to."

"Yea. The Chris'mas paj'nt."

"Can we open our presents now?" Evelyn jumped up from the table and bounced to her mama's side.

Smiling and sighing at the same time, Jessie lay back on the couch. It *would* be a Christmas they all would remember. She just knew it would.

The New Year howled its way in. For days the wind blew. Jessie tried hard to forget the struggle going on inside her body, but as she stood now at the window, holding back the curtain, she shuddered. An eerie sort of light filtered through the swirling snow as it flung itself against the house and circled the woodpile. Everything was total whiteness. It made her feel as if she were in an igloo at the North Pole. She was inexplicably frightened.

"Just the strain of the funeral, and of Christmas," she told herself. "If this blizzard would only let up I'd feel better." She dropped the curtain and went to the stove. "I know we needed oil and groceries, but how I wish Allyn hadn't gone to town. And on foot, too."

The horses had been boarded at Erwin's for the winter, and up until this morning—when Allyn had insisted on going to town—Jessie had been glad that the only livestock to worry about were the half-dozen chickens in the shelter attached to the house. But now she wished he had had the team to take him through the blizzard. It was four o'clock and beginning to get dark. He'd been gone since ten.

As she was preparing supper, she heard the jingle of horse harnesses. Then she heard Allyn's voice, yelling his thanks to a neighbor, for the ride home. She let out her pent-up breath and dropped her shoulders, hurrying to the door to let him in.

The following day the wind died down and the sun came out. But on January twelfth another blizzard hit. As Jessie was preparing for bed, a pain gripped her; and with the pain, a fear — far stronger that of a few days ago — overwhelmed her. It was as if the *Angel of Death* were hovering outside the door, waiting amidst the blizzard... Waiting? Waiting for what? Suddenly she clutched her stomach, holding her breath to keep from screaming; she flopped onto the edge of the bed.

"Honey," she gasped. "Do we have plenty of coal oil?"

"Yes. Of course. You know that. I just got some." Allyn jumped into bed, pulling the covers to his chin. "Why?"

"Well, because —" The question seemed incongruent now that she had asked it, but she had to think of something to quell her fear. "Because I... have a... feeling that —" She got up from the bed. Lifting the lamp from the bedside shelf, she headed for the kitchen. "I think I... might need... the light left on tonight... and the fire stoked up."

"Why? What are you saying? Why do you feel — ?" Jumping out of bed, Allyn followed her into the kitchen. He turned her around to face him, looking into her eyes. By the dim lamplight she looked like a gray ghost. "Mama, you do look... awful. What's... what's wrong?"

"I... I'm a little scared. I —" She walked to the window, flipping back the curtain and peeking out a frost-free corner at the howling blizzard. "What'll we do if I... if I need... ah, need someone? —"

"What... what do you mean, Mama? 'Need someone'?"

"Well, what if I —? What if the —?"

"Jessie!" He jumped up from the table and ran to where his wife was staring out at the storm. "You don't mean... you don't think... you're not going to have your ba— No! You can't be— This isn't even the middle of January. You said... you told me the middle... of March. Oh, Mama! Oh, Jessie!" He gripped her hand and led her back to the table.

"Allyn! Oh-h—" She doubled over. "Don't... don't panic. Please." Between gasps she added, trying to force a smile, "I said *I* was scared. Don't *you* be." She grasped his hand.

Trying to relax her rigid body, she walked to the washstand and poured a dipperful of icy water into the basin. She wet a cloth and put it to her face. "Listen! Yes, I *do* think I'm going to have this baby tonight, or at least tomorrow. Listen," she repeated, looking into her husband's panic-stricken face. "I'm going to need you, so please don't panic. I'll give you step-by-step directions. We'll do fine." She wished she felt as confident as she was trying to sound. She knew the implications — and complications — of having a premature baby. She knew, and was terrified; but she must not let Allyn know just how frightened she was. She needed his help, his strength, his optimism. She took a deep breath.

"First," she said, forcing herself to straighten up, after a pain ripped through her body. "Bring that couch over here and open it out. I'll need to be close to the heat. And... and when the baby comes... it must be kept warm." Her head told her that there would be no need to keep it warm. It would be dead.

"Take that top drawer and empty it." She pointed to the factory-made cupboard, grabbing the edge of the table and squeezing her eyes shut. After getting her breath again, she tore an old flannelette sheet in half to line the drawer. "Put this on the oven door," she said. "And keep the fire moderate. Add one stick at a time. And Allyn, *don't* drop it in like you usually do. We can't have ashes flying all over the place." She threw him a weak smile, while she folded the other half of the sheet and placed it, along with a towel, in the bottom of the drawer. "Make sure there's always plenty of hot water."

"What... what's the hot water for?"

"Well to start with—" She smiled teasingly at her husband, whose face was the picture of devastation. "I think we could use a cup of tea."

For the next half hour, while the couple sipped tea and timed the intervals between pains, Jessie explained the procedures of childbirth. Then checking the room to see that everything was ready, she reminded Allyn what to do if she became unconscious during the delivery. By this time, it was well past midnight.

"I think... it's... time." Jessie stifled a scream. Doubling over, she grabbed her stomach. "Take the dishes off the table," she said, when she found her breath. "And don't touch these things." She picked up the towel containing the items she would need for the baby (tape, sterilized scissors and tweezers, etc.) and placed them where she would be able to reach them.

"Now spread this flannelette sheet on the table. Oh, you better put another stick in the fire. You might not have time for it later. Then scrub your hands with soap and warm—not cold—water. And I mean, *scrub*. Then wash them again just before the delivery." She dropped onto the couch, gasping, waiting for the giant of all preceding pains to pass.

Just then Alfred cried. "Give him another bottle... and check... the girls, too... Make sure they're... covered." She took a deep breath, praying that she wouldn't faint.

The cat jumped onto the couch beside her, rubbing against her arm. "Put... Buddy in... with... Clara... I certainly don't want... him out here."

Allyn scurried around obeying Jessie's orders. Just as he returned to the kitchen after removing the cat, the door blew open, letting in an icy blast and a gust of snow; the lamp flickered, belching out a puff of smoke.

"Allyn!" Jessie gripped the side of the bed, stifling a scream.

As if with one motion, Allyn shoved the wood box in front of the door, rinsed his hands, and was by her side.

She could hear the moan of the wind, the swish of dry snow hitting the cabin, the snapping of wood in the stove. She bit down on her bottom lip to keep from screaming. Her senses were aflame. She longed for the relief of unconsciousness; but she prayed, *Oh, God, please don't let me faint.* She shut her eyes, holding her breath as she bore down. Suddenly the pain subsided; she sank into semi-consciousness.

Sometime later—she had no idea how long—Jessie forced her eyes to open: something was wrong. She listened; she heard no sound. She lifted her head. Her husband was standing by the bed, holding a blood-streaked form in his hands, staring at it. "Allyn! The baby!" she heard herself shriek. He didn't move: he just kept staring. She flailed her arms, trying to reach him. "Allyn!" she shrieked again.

"It's... it's a girl. Mama," he whispered, as if just recovering from a stupor. "It's a girl."

"Make her cry! Allyn!" She reached out toward where her husband stood, but fell back onto the pillow. "Oh, Daddy, make her cry. Make her cry." She tried to roll over to prop herself on her elbow, straining to get to her baby; but she couldn't move. Her muscles felt like butter. "Make her cry! Turn her upside down. Hit her on her backside. Make her cry!" Tears were streaming down her face by this time, but she had no strength to move.

Still mesmerized, Allyn stared at the tiny, lifeless body he held in the palm of his hand. Slowly he lifted his hand, then dropped it. He couldn't do it. He couldn't. What if he hit her too hard?

"Do it. Hit her." By now Jessie was sobbing. "Oh, Allyn. Make her cry. Please! Make her cry."

At last—it seemed like forever—she heard the soft smack of Allyn's hand. After what seemed like another eternity, came a faint cry, like the mewing of a kitten. She let out a volume of breath, straining again to get to her baby.

Trembling, Allyn placed the small body onto the bed by his wife, then collapsed to his knees. He dropped his head onto the bed, his arms going limp by his side.

Jessie stared down at the bluish—almost transparent—form beside her. "She won't live to see the morning," she said to herself. She had the strong urge to weep again, but she daren't. She had too much to do. She willed her arms to reach for the sterilized material.

Nudging her husband a few minutes later, she handed him the infant. "Sponge her gently, like I told you; then wrap her loosely in a diaper and lay her on her side."

When Allyn returned from nestling the baby into the makeshift incubator, Jessie clasped his hand. "You were wonderful," she said. "You'd make a good midwife."

"I sure did a lot of praying," he said. "You know, I could have lost you, Honey. I heard just last month of a women who had a premature baby at home, just like you did, but—" He swiped at a tear. "The baby died. So did she."

"I know." Jessie tightened her grip on her partner's hand. "I know. I saw more than one case like that while I was nursing... And even in the hospital, many times both the mother and baby died. But we are far from being out of the woods yet." She struggled to a sitting position so that she could see the baby. "She's awfully blue... If she'd been born in a hospital, she would have been put right into an incubator, with controlled temperature and humidity; and she would have been given regular doses of oxygen, and been fed intravenously... I doubt she's even three pounds. *Blue babies* are what they're called," she said, flopping back onto her pillow. "Usually their blood has to be replaced. Usually... it indicates a congenital heart or lung defect... from fetal underdevelopment." She shut her eyes, letting the tears trickle down the side of her face, onto her pillow.

The persistent howling of the wind outside brought back to Jessie the dreaded presence of *Death*, waiting to snatch her baby. She felt certain now that *she* would survive; but she felt just as certain that the infant would not.

She should have been aware that things were not right with this pregnancy, actually, she was, and had been for quite some time. But she had been so busy making the new place livable; and then with Clara's schooling, and her dad's death, and Christmas, she had just not taken time to think about it. Her eyes drooped shut. She dozed.

"Daddy!" She awoke with a start. "We can't both sleep. One of us has to keep the fire going, and the kettle boiling. We have to keep the air moist, and keep her warm. We have to keep turning that drawer. We have to—"

"Whoa! Slow down, Mama. I know what to do. After all—" He let out a dry laugh. "I should. You've told me a dozen times. Besides, I couldn't sleep if I wanted to. I just want to sit here and thank God for this little miracle." He bent down and adjusted the diaper on top of the baby, feeling the side of the drawer nearest the oven. "And I just want to watch you sleep. See?" He held up the four-ounce bottle she had prepared before the birth. "Got the bottle of sweetened water all ready for her."

When he turned back to the couch, Jessie was asleep again. He stood for a moment looking into her face. It looked so peaceful. Then it struck him: everything seemed peaceful. The only thing he could hear was the crackling of the fire. He jumped to the window. From the pitch-black sky, millions of stars twinkled down on the white world below. The wind had stopped blowing. "The storm is over," he said. "Praise the Lord!"

His eyes slid to the Big Ben clock on the warming oven: *five o'clock, time to check on the children.* The room was cold, but not icy, like often when he would fall into a dead sleep and let the stove go out. "I'll have to keep the place warm for our little miracle baby now," he said, creeping back to the kitchen.

After checking the stove, he knelt beside the baby. Reaching in with his work-rough hand, he raised her head slightly, gently pushing the nipple into her tiny mouth. She gagged, making a gurgling sound. He began to panic, but checked himself, turning her onto her side, and listening, until he heard her breathing evenly. "Guess I'll let Mama feed you," he whispered, easing his hand out from under her head and setting the bottle back into the warm water.

"Mama... Mama... Mama."

Allyn jumped. The rattle of the crib, and Alfred's husky voice, roused him from a kind of a trance. He had been sitting with his head resting on his hands at the table for the past two hours, and had forgotten, momentarily, where he was, or what a bizarre night he'd just come through. Relieved that Jessie had not awakened, he headed for the bedroom, lifting Alfred from his crib. "Hi! Big boy. Wait 'til I show you the visitor that came in the night," he whispered.

Alfred chuckled, slapping his daddy on his bald head.

"Daddy? Me get up?" Helen sat up and rubbed her eyes.

"We're awake, too," rasped Clara, crawling out of bed, Evelyn right behind her. "Where's Mama?"

"Sh! Sh!" whispered Allyn. "Mama's sleeping. Come. I've a surprise for you."

Setting Alfred, still bundled in a sheet, on the table, Allyn lifted back the diaper from the drawer on the oven door.

"What is it?" Evelyn dropped to her knees, screwing up her face. "Is it a doll?"

"It's ugly." Clara turned when she heard her mother stir. "Why's Mama sleeping there?"

Jessie forced her eyes open. She saw three white forms bending over the oven. She thought at first that she was still dreaming, and that these were the angels in her dream. Gradually her mind cleared, and she remembered the baby she'd had in the night. A feeling of warmth and peace flowed through her; the sense of dread had left. She lay for a few moments, then wormed her way out of bed to where her family was gathered around the stove.

Chapter 25 — Lily

January 1936

"Mama? Did we have another baby? It sure doesn't look like a baby."

Jessie smiled down at her daughter. She guessed she should have explained to Clara about the coming baby, but she had thought she'd have plenty of time for that. "Yes. We had a baby. A baby sister." She shuffled past the girls and lifted the baby out of the drawer.

"Mama!" Suddenly realizing that Jessie was up, Allyn turned from where he was attending Alfred. "You'd better go back to bed." He took the baby from her and assisted her back to the couch.

The baby lay motionless on her mother's chest, making no attempt at sucking. "Well it wouldn't do much good anyway," breathed Jessie. "Again, no milk." She squeezed her eyes shut, refusing to let the tears escape. What should she do? How was she to get nourishment into this tiny body? "Daddy," she said, "did you give her any of that water?"

"Tried. But she just spluttered. Here. You try. She's too tiny to handle the nipple." He handed Jessie the bottle.

She squeezed the nipple, letting the water trickle into the baby's mouth; she swallowed. Trickle by trickle, she dribbled about a quarter of an ounce into the infant.

"Canned milk. That's it," said Jessie suddenly. "Allyn, look in that cupboard. Is there a can of milk?"

"Yea. Here's one." He waved a small can of Cherub milk. "Didn't know we had it. Don't remember getting it."

"Well I didn't know we did, either, but I had a dream about it." She furrowed her brow, trying to remember some of her confused dream, something about an angel carrying the baby and singing, *"Evangel, Evangel."* The angel in her dream looked like the one on the can of milk Allyn was holding.

"Later I'll add a few drops of milk to this." She looked down at the small bottle in her hand. "This is the only baby bottle I have. Glad I saved it." She smiled into the impish face of her fourteen-month-old son, scampering around on the couch beside her. Then squeezing the nipple into the infant's mouth again, she said, "Your brother's hard on bottles."

The bottles she was using for Alfred were vanilla, ketchup, or liniment bottles she had saved over the years. Right now, he was getting only sweetened water in them, as a sort of pacifier. Their milk supply from Rolland's, as of a few days ago, had been cut off. His cow was about to freshen.

"I'm telling you, young man," she said, rumpling Alfred's bright-red hair, "you're going to grow up mighty fast now." He had paid no attention to the little bundle in his mother's arms; but very soon he would realize that this little intruder would occupy most of his mama's time, and a good deal of his daddy's, too. "Oh, yes," she said, "you'll soon notice that you've been replaced." She looked down at the bluish, almost transparent face and her heart constricted. *If she lives,* she said to herself. *If she lives.* It pained her to watch the baby struggle with each drop she swallowed. *Perhaps it would be best if*— She left the thought unfinished.

"Mama? Do I have school today?" Clara squeezed in beside her sisters on the couch as they watched their mama coax liquid into the mouth of the doll-baby that was their sister.

"No. No school today. It's Saturday. But you could read a story to your sisters."

With the children tucked into bed that night, Allyn brought a tray for Jessie and sat down on the couch beside her. "Mama," he said, taking her hand. "God has been so good to us, hasn't He?"

"Yes, Daddy, He has." She smiled. "And do you know what I'm thinking? You haven't slept in over thirty hours. You go to bed. I've slept most of the day. I'll keep watch tonight."

"No! No—"

"Yes, Allyn. You must. Remember, I need you again tomorrow."

He kissed her, a worried frown furrowing his brow, but he flopped back onto the foot of the couch and was instantly asleep. Jessie thought to waken him and send him to his own bed, but she didn't have the heart. Instead she flipped one of the blankets over him and crept to the kitchen with her dishes.

On her way past the oven she peeked at the baby. *So fragile looking, almost like porcelain,* she thought. She recalled her dream and the words the angel was singing: "Evangel. Evangel."

Evangel means 'Good news.' Well, this baby certainly is that, Good news. She shouldn't be living. She's truly a miracle.

After puttering around in the kitchen, tidying it, she fixed a bottle of sugar-water mixed with a few drops of milk. Then she went to her bedroom and brought out her nursing book to refresh her memory on how to care for a premature baby. After reading for a few moments she slammed the book shut. *Hm! A lot that tells me. It gives advice for what to do under hospital conditions, not in an impossible situation like this.*

She went to where the dishpan hung. "Whether or not she lives, I must bathe her," she said aloud, taking down the pan. While she scrubbed and sterilized it, she berated herself, *Tsk! I've never been so unprepared; I don't even have any oil on hand.*

As she lowered the baby into the warm water, she felt the tiny frame squirm—almost imperceptibly. She was reminded of a baby bird she had found once, when she was a child: the bird had fallen from the nest. She had picked it up, cradling it in her hand. She remembered crying because its skin was so blue. It had wriggled, ever so slightly, in her warm hand. She had taken the cold, naked bird into the house and placed it in a matchbox on the oven door, to warm it. But now as Jessie trickled warm water over the bluish body of her baby, she put the memory from her: the bird had died.

Her shoulders aching from having slept on the couch for the past five nights, Jessie picked up the tin of milk, draining the last drop into the bottle. She knelt by the oven door, easing the baby into her arms for her two a.m. feeding. As she sat coaxing liquid into the infant, she worried. With Rolland's cow dry, and no one else nearby with a cow, and with the snow having been falling steadily for the past two days, how were they going to get milk for the baby?

The sound of the wind whipping snow against the window sent shivers down her spine. The stove made sputtering noises as snow was swirled against the chimney; the wind howled through the cracks in the windows and doors; and Jessie's head throbbed from weariness. She set down the bottle and took a sip of tea, noticing the little devotional book, *Daily Light*, open at the reading for March seventh. The thought struck her: *March seventh, the day I had estimated as the day my baby should be born. Here it is January eighteenth, and she is already five days old.* She reached over and pulled the book to her.

Allyn had a habit of opening the book anywhere and reading the passage for that day. Jessie supposed that he had been reading the March seventh reading before going to bed last night and had just left the book open. The evening passage grabbed her attention, reminding her again of God's care: "My times are in thy hand. Take no thought for your life, what ye shall eat, or what ye shall drink... Your heavenly Father knoweth that ye have need of these things. Trust in the Lord with all thine heart... Casting all your care upon him; for he careth for you." (From: Psa. 32:15; Matt. 6:25; Prov. 3:5 and I Peter 5:7)

The following morning the sun was out. From where Jessie stood, staring out the window, the walls of the cabin looked like the sides of an igloo, and the world, one big white sheet. She dropped the curtain and turned to the stove.

"Mama. I'm going into Meanook to get milk." Allyn ran outside, returning a minute later with an armload of wood. "Maybe I can find some work for the day, shoveling snow or something." He dropped the wood onto the floor, then began chucking it into the wood box. "You be okay for the day?" He kissed her and was gone.

Swishing the crumbs from the table into her hand and grabbing a handful of wheat to go with it, Jessie headed toward the chicken pen. With her hand on the door latch, she watched her husband wade through three-foot-deep snowdrifts on his way to the road. She puckered her brow and shook her head, then walked the few steps to the chickens. For the past several days they had been huddled together in one corner of the pen, looking miserable; but today they greeted her with singing. They too, must have been happy to see the sun. Their cheerful greeting lifted her spirits. She returned to the house with a lighter heart than she had had for days. She knew Allyn would get through. She knew help was on the way.

About three o'clock that afternoon Clara and Evelyn were at the window blowing peepholes through the frost. "Mama. Mama." Clara jumped to her mother's side, tugging on her dress. "Come look. Daddy's coming home. He's got a cow. He's got a black and white cow."

Jessie strolled to the window, carrying Alfred on her left hip. She bent to peek out. "Sure enough!" She threw back her head and laughed. "Sure enough. He's got a cow. Want to put your coat on and go meet him?" Her heart was singing as she ushered Clara out the door.

A half hour later, after they'd settled the cow in the barn, Allyn came into the house, carrying Clara on his shoulder.

"Mama, she likes me. She licked my face. Her name's 'Lily,' and she ours... to keep."

"Well, not exactly —"

"Where'd you get her?"

"Well, as I was about to explain," said Allyn, smiling down at his over-eager daughter. "This woman, Emma — lives just on the other side of Meanook — her barn burned down last night. She was in at Bird's Grocery store. Heard me telling about the baby. Asked if I'd keep her cow for her 'til spring.

"By the way, Bird said to congratulate you on the baby. Sent this." He dropped a paper bag onto the counter, spilling its contents — flour, sugar, eggs, and lard — then popped back outside to bring in more wood.

Death and *Life* seemed to be having a tug-of-war over the tiny piece of humanity in the drawer on the oven door. At times her skin was so blue, and she would lie motionless and death-like. Jessie had often dropped to her knees, listening, sure that the baby had breathed her last. At other times her skin seemed to take on a pinkish tinge, and she would screw up her wizened little face, moving her body ever so slightly. Both parents took turns watching her, turning her, and dribbling nourishment into her mouth.

"Does our baby sister have a name?" Evelyn poked her fork into the side of her cheek, looking over to where her miniature sister was sleeping. She took another forkful of food and turned to her mother. "Doesn't everybody 'spose to have a name?"

"Yes, you're right," said Jessie, exchanging an amused glance with her husband. "How about all of us naming her? She's ten days old. It's high time she had a name."

"I've told you about my dream, how the angel carried her while singing, 'Evangel.' So, how about 'Evangeline'? But for a middle name. I don't like it for first name."

"'Mary.' Let's name her 'Mary,' after Jesus' mother," suggested Allyn.

"I don't like 'Mary' for a name." Clara slammed her fork onto the table.

"What about 'Annie'?" Evelyn's eyes sparkled, "'member that story about 'Annie' you read, Clara?"

"'Annie Evangeline,' doesn't exactly sound right together." Jessie puckered her brow. "I know," she said, with a snap of her fingers. "Marianne Evangeline. She's such a tiny baby. Maybe a big name will make her grow strong."

So, "Marianne Evangeline," it was.

When Marianne was eight weeks old—about the time she should have been born—and had reached five pounds, according to the kitchen scales Allyn had recently borrowed from Hunter's store, she was finally moved off the oven door.

One morning, after the dishes were cleared away, Evelyn and Helen stood watching their mother get their baby sister ready for her bath, the highlight of their day. Jessie lowered Marianne into the basin. "Oh, you skinny little runt," she cooed, bending to kiss her. "I think I'll just throw you in the garbage."

The girls each let out a sharp gasp.

"Mama!" said Evelyn. "You aren't gonna throw our baby sister away, are you?"

Jessie smiled, her heart welling with love. She thanked God for all her children: for the little miracle daughter she held in her hands; for her son, still a baby, too, asleep in his crib in the bedroom; for the two eager-eyed girls at her elbow; for Clara, out with her dad, milking Lily; and for her husband, who tried so hard to keep food on the table. And she gave a special thanks to God for Emma, whom she'd never met, for giving the family a wild, stubborn Holstein cow, named Lily.

Chapter 26 — Three Quarters

May 1936

"Look what I just picked up at the post office." Allyn struggled through the door with a large box. "From Medicine Hat."

"Medicine Hat? From whom?" Jessie proceeded to open the parcel, wondering who knew them in that small southern Alberta city, a place to which neither she nor Allyn had ever been.

Inside the box was a note: *We have heard from an anonymous source that you are in mission work. Our ladies' group has collected these items, hoping you can use them. If not, we're sure you will know of someone who can. God bless you.*

Jessie turned the note over. "It doesn't even say what church. We don't know where to send a thank you." She looked at the outside wrapper. "Not even a return address, just the postmark."

After lifting off three pairs of small hands, which wanted to pull everything out all at once, Jessie began to take the items from the box: four squashed hats of assorted colors; a leather bag; dresses, one about her size and a few of smaller sizes; a layer of flannelette nighties of assorted sizes; a bundle of cotton underwear; a pair of men's pants and a shirt about Allyn's size; and a couple of rompers about right for Alfred. When she lifted out the next things, a bundle of baby clothes for a newborn, her eyes misted. Marianne, almost four months old, was six pounds. None of the clothes Jessie had on hand, apart from a couple of nighties she had made, fit the tiny baby.

"Oh! Look at this!" she said, coming to the next layer. She waved a wad of like-new diapers above her head. The ones she had been using for the baby and Alfred were ones she had had since Clara. They were so thin, Jessie had often said, "You can spit right through them."

Up to this point Allyn had been sitting at the opposite end of the table looking on with mild interest. But when Jessie came to the bottom of the box and waved a bundle of little red *Gospel of John* booklets and three used Bibles in his direction, he bolted from his chair, throwing his arms around her. "Praise the Lord! Praise the Lord!" he shouted. "I've been praying for these. I've promised folks I'd get them a *Gospel of John*... And those Bibles? I know just who I'll give *them* to. Praise the Lord!"

When the children were in bed that night Jessie dropped the pile of felt hats onto the table. She picked up her scissors and began ripping them apart. "I've been asking the Lord for shoes for the children," she said to Allyn. "There were no shoes in the parcel, but there were these hats and that leather bag, so by the end of today they'll all be shoes for the girls."

At the present time Allyn was cutting brush for the Canadian National Railway. Although the pay was scant, a few cents a day, at least he didn't have to scout for work, and he knew that the pay was certain. But it meant being away during the week.

It was an unseasonably hot day in mid-May, Wednesday, three days before Allyn would be home with any money. The last scrap of bread and the last oatmeal, Jessie had used for breakfast. Lifting the trap door to the cellar, a hole about six feet deep and four feet wide, she stepped down the four rungs, grabbing a jar of blueberry jam. Fretting, she analyzed the family's situation: Allyn gone; a delicate baby; big hungry Alfred and three girls to feed; three hens, each setting on six eggs; (they had eaten the rooster last week, and the other hen hadn't survived the winter); the one laying hen was producing an egg about every other day; and *this* was the last jar of jam. She set the jam on the counter. What would she make for lunch?

When will I learn not to fret? she scolded herself. *I know God will take care of us. He always has.* No sooner had she finished that thought, than the song, "Count Your Blessings," popped into her head. 1

"Well, at least there's milk," she said aloud, skimming the cream off the pail of milk and adding it to the half-quart already soured and waiting to be churned. Her mind turned to Lily, how God had supplied her so miraculously four months ago, on loan at first, but now theirs to keep.

She picked up the cream jar and began shaking it, not allowing herself to think past lunch. When she heard the splash, splash of the butter congealing and separating, she stopped to rest.

"Oh! That note. I've got to get that note to Rolland's." She tore off a strip from the discarded April calendar and wrote the note.

"Bring Alfred in," she called to the girls. "I have an errand for you to run."

"Me, too? Me, too?" Helen scrambled up from the ground, running after her sisters.

"I want you to take this note to Mr. Rolland's. And take Helen along," she said, wiping her little daughter's face and arms and brushing the dust from her dress. "Watch her, though. Remember, she's pretty little. Take her hand."

By the time the girls had reached the railway crossing, about a mile from their house, Helen was tired and had begun to whimper. Rolland's gate was just across the tracks, but his house was still nearly a quarter of a mile beyond.

"I got a good idea," said Clara. "Helen, you wait for us here." She pointed to a spot in the ditch at the edge of the tracks. "We'll be right back. Now don't you follow us." She shook her finger at her sister as Mama often did, to emphasize a point.

"It's too far for you. See those pretty flowers? Pick some for Mama."

Clara and Evelyn scampered across the tracks, swung a couple of times on Rolland's iron gate, then headed through the field to his house.

As Helen sat in the ditch making mud pies with her toes in a tiny puddle some late-melting snow had left, she heard a strange *putt-putt* noise. She scrambled to the top of the gravel incline, watching, as the noisy thing approached her. The flat, funny-looking yellow putter came to a screeching stop beside her.

Three men on a Canadian National Railway speeder-car stared down at the little *urchin* standing by the tracks, her thumb in her mouth, smudges of mud on her face, her arms, her legs, and her dress. Looking from one to another, they began discussing who this little rag-a-muffin could be. An abandoned child of some impoverished family? They'd heard of such things. A runaway? Not likely. She was too young. But what was such a little one doing away out here by herself?

"What's your name, little girl?" asked one of the men. "You all alone?"

Helen pulled her thumb out of her mouth and squinted up at the men, "Waiting for —" Then just as quickly as she had taken it out, she shoved her thumb back into her mouth and said no more.

A second man stood up, reached into the pocket of his striped coveralls and pulled out a coin. "Here," he said, tossing it at Helen, go buy yourself some candy."

"Come on," said the third man, not wanting to get involved with an abandoned child — if that's what she was. He looked at his watch. "We'd better get going." He put the speeder in gear.

Just then Clara and Evelyn popped over the tracks, stopping short when they saw the men on the strange looking car talking to their little sister.

"A car on a railway track?" Evelyn squinted, screwing up her face. She'd seen cars, and she'd seen trains. But a car on a railroad track? And what a funny car it was! She ran toward it.

"Howdy, girls. This your sister?" The man who'd thrown Helen the coin reached again into his pocket. "Go buy some candy," he said, tossing out two more coins. Before the girls had even had time to retrieve the money from where it had landed, the men had sped away.

Clara inspected the coins, comparing them. "What is it?" she said, turning hers over again. "Daddy's never thrown one like this on the floor. This one's got a moose or somethin' on it. It isn't a nickel."

"Maybe it's a dime," suggested Evelyn, opening out her hand to look at her own coin.

"No, silly, dimes are little." Clara frowned. "Here Helen, I'll hold yours. We gotta hurry home and ask Mama what this big nickel is. Evie, you hold onto your money, tight. Don't drop it. Take Helen's other hand. We gotta run."

When the girls got within sight of the house, Clara, followed by Evelyn, dropped Helen's hand and ran.

"Mama! Mama!" screeched Clara, racing into the house. "Look what we got. And it isn't a nickel, either. It's got a moose on it."

The girls presented the three coins to their mother.

"Where did you get these? They're quarters. And that's a reindeer, not a moose." Jessie looked at Clara. "Where did you get them. That's an awful lot of money for three little girls."

Over the howling of Helen, who was just now stumbling through the door, Clara told her mother the story of the men in the funny yellow railway car.

Flopping down at the kitchen table, Jessie rested her head in her hands. *"Seventy-five cents! Thank You, Lord. Oh, thank You."* Tearing another strip from the April calendar, she began making a grocery list: flour, potatoes, cream of wheat, sugar, eggs, lard. She added the cost of the groceries. "Hm! That leaves ten cents. Girls? No. Helen? Since you were the one that got us this money, what special treat would you like me to bring back from the store?"

"Puff wheat," she said, pulling her thumb from her mouth. "Me want puff wheat."

"Yea! Puffed wheat," shouted the older girls together.

Jessie smiled. If only those railway men had known! They were God's ravens, sent to supply bread to the family. Only that morning she had read to the children from I Kings 17, the story of Elijah: how God had looked after him by sending ravens to bring him bread each day.

Footnote: 1 "Count Your Blessings" — Author: Johnson Datman Jr./ Edwin D. Excell.

Chapter 27 — The Fleece

June 1936

Rake in hand, Jessie headed for the garden. Stopping at the radishes, she pulled a few. "These should be ready by now," she said, tossing aside the spindly greens. She poked her rake around the lettuce, beets, and carrots. Despite the dozens of trips to the well she and the girls had made each day to keep the seedlings watered, the long, rainless days of June had taken their toll. She leaned on the rake handle, looking down at the rows of shriveled vegetables. "Nothing. Not even pickins for the chickens," she said, her shoulders slumping. "Oh, when will it rain?"

As her eyes turned automatically to the cloudless sky, a shadow crossed her face. "Shoo! Shoo! Get! You ugly vulture." She ran from the garden toward the house, waving the rake above her head. "You've already gotten two, and you're not getting anymore," she screamed at the chicken hawk, already beginning his dive to grab one of the ten new chicks.

She had watched the incubation of these chicks so carefully. Two weeks ago when she had noticed one of the three setting hens becoming restless, she had removed her eggs and had given them to the others. She had been a little disappointed when only twelve out of eighteen eggs had hatched; so now, when she saw the marauder overhead, she wasn't about to let him rob her of any more of her flock.

At family devotions the following morning, Allyn read from the sixth chapter of Judges, the story of Gideon. The children fidgeted, eager to begin their day.

Their chores finished, Clara and Evelyn joined hands, and skipped down the well-worn path to their playhouse. To the girls, their playhouse had real walls, not just a few sticks of wood in the shape of a square on the grass; and a real ceiling, not just green leaves and blue sky.

Jessie had nearly finished her wash, which on days like this, she did outdoors. "Helen," she said, picking up the water bucket, "you keep an eye on your brother and the baby, will you? Mama has to get water." She would go past the playhouse on the way and send the girls back to mind the little ones.

As she neared the playhouse she heard the girls conversing: "Ev," said Clara, "what's a fleece?"

"I dunno," she heard Evelyn answer. "Guess it must be a cloth, though, 'cause Gideon wringed it out."

Jessie stopped. She could see the girls through the trees. Nothing but the cat's purring as he lazed in the sun broke the silence of the following few moments. She stood, barely breathing, surprised that the girls had even heard the morning Bible reading.

Clara gave a big sigh. "Sure wish I knew what a fleece is."

"Why?" Satisfied with the ribbon she had been struggling with on her doll's bonnet, Evelyn wrapped her in a blanket.

"Because."

"'cause why?"

"Because I want to know for sure if I'm s'posed to go to Africa to be a missionary. It would be terrible if I got way out there, then found out I belonged in China or somewhere else. If Gideon found out that he was s'posed to lead the army by seeing if there was water in his fleece, I can find out if I'm s'posed to go to Africa the same way... If I on'y knew what a fleece is."

Evelyn jumped up from the ground. "I should find out if I'm s'posed ta go ta India, too." She put her finger to the side of her face. "A fleece *must* be a cloth, though."

"I guess it is." Clara rose slowly from the ground, letting out a long sigh... "Let's put out a cloth tonight... Here." She pointed to a spot. "And see if it's wet in the morning. If it's wet, we're s'posed to go to

Africa and India. If it's not, we're s'posed to go to some other countries."

Jessie glanced toward the house, where she could just make out that the little ones were still in the same spot, playing with the clothespins. She hadn't intended to spy or eavesdrop on the girls, but their discussion intrigued and amused her: she wanted to hear it out.

"But we need two cloths," said Evelyn, looking at the spot on the ground. "One for each of us."

"That's right." Clara swooped down and snatched at her doll's blanket. "We could use Peggy Anne's and Eva's blankets."

"But... but they'd be cold tonight."

"Oh Ev. They're only dolls. Besides, they can sleep with us."

"No. I don't like a doll in bed with me, and I won't let Eva sleep all night without a blanket." She hugged her doll to her.

"I'll tell you what," said Clara. "We can't wring out cloth very well anyway. We'll get two tins and put them here... to get water in." Again, Clara pointed to the spot. "It was God that put water in Gideon's fleece, and He can put water in our tins if He wants us to be missionaries in India and Africa."

The girls turned and ran from the playhouse, letting their dolls tumble to the ground.

"I'll get water later," said Jessie, heading back to the house. She didn't want to interrupt whatever it was the girls were about to do.

As she began to hang the clothes on the line, Jessie saw Clara and Evelyn routing around in the garbage at the back of the shack, and a few minutes later, scampering back toward the playhouse.

The girls set their tins in place, picked up their dolls, and headed back to the house.

"Clara?" Evelyn grabbed her sister's arm, pulling her to a stop. "When Gideon put his fleece out to get water in it, didn't he pray that God would make it wet, so he'd know if he was s'posed to lead the army? We should pray, shouldn't we?"

The girls joined hands. "Dear God," they prayed together. "Put water in our tins, if you want us in India and Africa. Amen." Still holding hands, they skipped up the path toward the house.

After the children were in bed that night, Jessie crept down the path to the playhouse. She stood beside the tins, looking up at the sky, bright with stars. Daily, the family prayed for missionaries from all over the world. They often got letters from two of Allyn's maiden aunts, Jessie and Laura Allyn, a doctor and nurse team in India, as well as from other missionaries. And now her girls, in their childlike way, were dedicating their life to the Lord.

"Oh, God," she said aloud, thinking of the *special work* God had called her to while she was in nursing, "all the hardship, the sacrifice of my career—all of it—has been worth it after all."

She turned to go back to the cabin, glancing again at the tins. The light from the full moon shimmered through the leaves. Tipping her head, she winked at the grinning moon. "I see you laughing at the strawberry jam tin and the Nabob coffee can waiting to be filled with water. I hear you saying, 'There'll be no water tonight, my little ones.'"

The next morning just as the sun was peeking over the horizon, Clara and Evelyn raced each other to the window.

"Oh, Ev! It rained! It rained!" Still in their nighties, the sisters ran down the path to where two tins, spilling water over their brims, waited for them.

Jessie rolled over... "Rained," she groaned, pulling her legs up towards her chin.

Suddenly, her eyes flew open. She sprang to a sitting position. *Rained? Did they say, 'It rained'?* She jumped out of bed, grabbing her housecoat. *It hasn't rained for six weeks. The garden!* She ran up the path and through the garden gate. The lettuce, beets, carrots, and even the radishes seemed to be smiling at her. "Oh, I'm so glad I didn't dig you up, or let the chickens have you. Maybe we'll have vegetables from our own garden after all."

Footnote: Part of this chapter, the story about the little girls in the playhouse, is adapted from a composition written by Clara in her Junior year at Prairie Bible Institute, in 1949, its original title: *Water in the Tins.*

Chapter 28 — Fire!

July 1936

Tick-tock-tick-tock. The Big Ben alarm clock throbbed in her ear. She sat up and struck a match. The sky was beginning to lighten, but it wasn't quite light enough to see the clock. *"Four thirty! Where is he? He should have been home by dusk."* Jessie threw back the sheet and crawled out or bed, carrying the lamp to the kitchen.

"I'd give anything for a cup of tea," she said, "but I'm not lighting a fire to add to this heat." She lifted the lid of the teapot. "Oh, well, I guess tepid tea is better than none." She poured out the last of the tea in the pot. Her head throbbed and her stomach heaved. She was still feeling nauseous, as she had all day yesterday.

"Where is that husband of mine?" she said aloud. She hit the side of the cup with her spoon. As she took the first sip of the lukewarm liquid, a niggling from her subconscious surfaced. *Smoke! I smell smoke.* She ran outside to the north side of the house, where she could just barely see the outline of the newly constructed barn.

Just as she was approaching the barn to check on the livestock: Lily, Bunt (Gilly's colt), and the chickens, which just two days ago she had moved there, a blaze towered to the sky and she heard a crackling.

"Bush fire…! The barn! The house! Oh, Allyn, where *are* you?" Tears sprung to her eyes.

Suddenly the whole sky was ablaze. She ran back into the house. "Clara. Evelyn. Wake up." Although panic was building inside her, and her heart was pounding, Jessie shook the girls gently. She needed their help; she must not frighten them. "Listen, girls," she said, sitting on the bed and helping them into their clothes. "Mama needs you." Evelyn yawned and started to climb back into bed.

"Listen!" Jessie shook her daughter again. "Mama needs your help. Daddy didn't get home last night because he's helping put out some fires." To herself, she thought, *I hope he's putting them out, and not caught in one.*

Evelyn's eyes were suddenly wide with fright. Jessie held her cheeks between her hands and leaned close to her face. "Don't be frightened," she said. "Remember the verses we were learning today? Let's say them together."

While the girls finished dressing, they repeated the verses from Psalm 46:1-2: "God is our refuge and strength, a very present help in trouble. Therefore will we not fear."

"We're going outside now to watch the fire, and to pray," Jessie said. "I want you girls to stay with the little ones while I take Lily and Bunt down to the well. Understand?" She bundled Marianne in a blanket and handed her to Clara. After hauling Helen out of bed and leading her to Evelyn to hold by the hand, she lifted Alfred from his crib and led the family outside.

The jingling of horses' harnesses and the frantic voices of men, one of whom she knew to be Allyn's, grabbed Jessie's attention. She let out an involuntary sigh of relief.

"Where did the other men go?" Jessie dumped the pail of water into the barrel and tossed the empty bucket back to her husband.

"Fire's out of control." Allyn handed her another pail of water, reaching again, almost at the same time, into the well, as the two of them filled the forty-five gallon barrel on the back of the wagon.

"It's swept several farmers' fields. They've gone to the next farm to help. I said we'd be okay."

Allyn steered the team between the barn and the house. He began throwing water on the roofs of the two buildings. The fire by this time was just a few feet from the barn. "Oh, God," he cried, "save our house."

Jessie, in the meantime, was grabbing the chickens two at a time and carrying them to the woodpile at the south side of the house. After the last dazed chicken had been settled on its new perch, she ran to the west side of the house, to where she had left the children. Clara and Evelyn were staring, wide-eyed and frightened, in the direction of the barn, with the babies fast asleep between them. Helen sat sucking her thumb and whimpering, resting her head on Evelyn's shoulder.

Swooping her little daughter into her arm, Jessie whispered, "Don't cry. Daddy's here now. And so is God. Everything is going to be all right." She set Helen down, grabbing the older girls by their hands and pulling them to their feet. "Come," she said, "let's join hands and pray. The house is *not* going to burn."

"The barn! The barn!" Allyn jumped from the wagon, from where he had been sloshing water onto the buildings. "The roof's caught fire," he said, running to where his family stood. He removed his cap and wiped his head with his hand. "Only a miracle will save the house now. With that tarpaper roof, it would take only a spark to start it on fire. Only a spark." He turned and headed to the well to refill the barrels.

Jessie wasn't sure whether to run into the house to rescue some of their things, or to stay with the children. They were calm now that she was with them, so she stayed, watching the fire consume the barn.

"Look!" she said suddenly, dropping the girls' hands and running toward her husband, who for the past fifteen minutes had been dousing the house roof with water. "Look! The wind must have changed direction. The fire's burning back on itself."

Allyn's head jerked toward the barn. "Praise the Lord! It'll burn itself out now," he said, jumping from the wagon. "Our house will be safe."

"Mama." Evelyn tugged at her mama's dress. "It's raining. I wanna go in."

Chapter 29 — The Shadow of Death

August – October 1936

  Allyn followed Jessie to the kitchen. "Good rain we had," he said, sitting down at the table and pouring himself a cup of tea. "Shouldn't be any more fires this year." He dipped his wet spoon for the third time into the sugar bowl, glancing over to the washstand where Jessie was doing her hair. *Poor Mama*, he thought. *She looks sixty. What is she? Oh! She's thirty-four! Today's August tenth--her birthday. I wonder what--?* He shut his eyes tight to squeeze out the worrisome thought. *She's just tired,* he told himself, swallowing his mouthful of tea.

  Had Jessie known her husband's thoughts of that moment, she would have agreed about her looking sixty: a few strands of gray had snuck their way into her darkened auburn hair, giving it a muddied look; her complexion, once like a tree-ripened peach, was ashen, her cheeks hollow; her eyes, once a lively blue, were dull, sunk in the middle of dark circles; and her shoulders were beginning to be permanently slumped.

  Taking the hairpin from her mouth, she plunged it into the bun at the back of her head. She straightened her shoulders, forced a smile and turned to her husband. She knew what he was leading up to. She had seen his restlessness growing for the past week. "Allyn," she said, "why don't you go? I know you want to. You want to check on those Sunday schools you started, way up there in—"

"Mama. You mean it?" Allyn jumped to his wife's side. "Think you'll be okay? I heard yesterday about some brush cutting up near Lac La Biche, but I... I was worried... about leaving you—" Should he remind her it's her birthday? But being Allyn, he didn't. He never mentioned birthdays, not even his own.

"Go. I'll be fine." She gave him a little push.

"Monday. Wash day," Jessie groaned and rolled out of bed. The thought of hauling the boiler onto the stove; of trip after trip to the well to fill the boiler and rinse tub; of rubbing and scrubbing the clothes on the zinc wash board, then wringing them out by hand and hanging them on the line—especially on a warm day, such as today— just the thought of it, made her want to crawl into a hole and pull the dirt around her.

Her stomach heaved. She put her hand to her mouth and ran out the door to the outhouse. For over a month now she had known she was carrying another child, but she hadn't mentioned it to Allyn. He would have grinned, jumped up and hugged her, and then would have quoted: Psalm 127:5: "Children are a gift from the Lord, happy is the man who has his quiver full."

"A quiver," he had explained once to Clara, when she had asked, "is a bag a shepherd carries his arrows in. Seven arrows is a quiver full."

But Jessie didn't share her husband's enthusiasm of having a quiver full. She loved every one of her five children. But another one? Alfred, twenty months, twenty-four pounds, was still not walking; and at almost seven months, Marianne was still very delicate and sickly, and not yet nine pounds. Another baby by the time she was just over a year? She pushed the thought away. She just didn't have the strength to think about it right now.

By noon she had completed the wash. She sent Clara and Evelyn to town for a few groceries. Marianne was asleep. "Helen," she said, seeing that she and Alfred were playing quietly on the floor. "Mama has to hang up the clothes. You watch your brother. I'll be in, in a few minutes."

She was just pinning the third sheet to the line when she heard a scream. Letting the sheet drop to the ground, she ran toward the house.

"Mama! Mama!" Helen met her at the door. "Alfred's mouth's on fire."

Jessie rushed to where Alfred sat screaming, holding a handful of burning matches. She grabbed the flame, extinguishing it, just seconds before it would have reached her son's hand. She pulled his other hand away from his mouth. His lips were beginning to blister, his tongue, fiery red.

Snatching him from the floor, she sponged his mouth with cool water, then swabbed it with olive oil. "Where'd he get the matches?" she said, turning to her daughter.

"I dunno, Mama. He lighted them on his teeth." Helen backed into a corner and plunged her thumb into her mouth.

After having rocked him on her shoulder for nearly an hour, Jessie laid Alfred in his crib. "How's my poor little man going to survive without his bottle?" she said.

When Alfred awoke he reached for his bottle, filled with water, waiting in his crib beside him. Sputtering and grumbling because his mouth was too sore to suck, he stood up, and with the pitch equaling that of a professional baseball player, he flung the bottle to the other side of the room. A look of requited anger spread over his face when he saw the contents spilling over the floor.

For days Jessie spooned gruel down her son's throat. Whenever he cried for his bottle, she would give it to him, knowing full well it would end up on the floor, smashed. It had now become a game with him.

One afternoon, after about a week of his bottle crashing — she was running out of ketchup, vanilla, and liniment bottles — Jessie laid him down for his nap. "Now look here, young man," she said, "your mouth is better now. You break one more bottle, and it will be your last." She turned to leave the bedroom... *Crash!* Another bottle. She stooped to clean it up, glaring at her son. He stood in his crib grinning down at her, a twinkle in his sky-blue eyes.

"You didn't believe me, did you?" she said, plunking him down onto his pillow. "Well, you'll see. Now you go to sleep." She left the room.

Alfred cried himself to sleep, but never asked for another bottle.

One morning about a week later Jessie struggled out of bed, lit the stove, fixed and warmed a bottle for Marianne, changed and fed her, and laid her in her homemade cradle. She tossed a flannelette sheet onto the couch, pulling the cradle close to it.

"Six o'clock. I'll just snatch a few more winks before the children get up," she said, dropping onto the couch. For days she had dragged herself around, hardly able to hold her head up. How she wished Allyn would come home. But in his last letter he had said that the brush cutting would last until about the middle of September. That was still three weeks away.

School, she had thought, when she had read his letter. *Clara and Evelyn will have to start school before he gets back.* How would she ever manage? But right now, she didn't care. She shut her eyes and was asleep.

"Mama! Mama! Mama!" Jessie could hear the children crying, but she couldn't get to them. She was falling... falling... into a deep hole. The children were tumbling in after her. Where was she? Where was Allyn? Why wouldn't he come to help her? She was in a pool... a pool of muddy water. No... a pool of blood.

"Mama! Mama!" The children were crying again. She couldn't reach them. She was sinking, sinking deeper into the pool. Alfred... He was drowning. She could hear his husky cry. His mouth was on fire, but he was drowning. And the baby...? Was that her cry? It sounded muffled. Was the baby drowning, too?

"Mama! Wake up!"

Jessie struggled to pull her eyes open, but they closed again.

"Mama! Mama, you're bleeding, Mama." Clara shook her mother. "Mama! I got Alfred out of bed. Mama, but he's wet. He's crying, Mama. Mama! We need you, Mama."

She forced her eyes open again.

"Alfred?" Jessie's head was in a fog. She strained to sit up, but flopped back onto the couch, wiping at her wet eyes. What? Who? Everything was fuzzy... Bleeding...? Did someone say she was bleeding? She struggled again to sit up. She opened her mouth to speak, but no words came. She wormed her way to a semi-sitting position. She saw a pool of blood on the sheet under her. She gasped.

Her mind snapped to attention: *I can't let the children see that.* She struggled to get up. What should she do? Her head was spinning, but she was slowly coming to reality.

"Clara." Her voice came out in a croak. "Will you make breakfast? I'll tell you what to do. Evelyn can set the table."

It pained Jessie to ignore Alfred, who sat in his saturated diaper, howling; but first she must attend to herself. She gathered the sheet and blanket to her, shuffling to the bedroom. She was still bleeding. Groping her way around, she clutched another sheet and spread it on a chair. While cleaning herself up, she called directions to Clara. Over the howling of both the babies, she managed to supervise the breakfast making, as well as to direct in Alfred's diaper changing.

"Can you lift Alfred into his highchair?" she called.

"Yes, Mama. He's in. We're all sitting down. Do you want me to give the baby her bottle?" Clara hollered over Marianne's piercing cry.

"No. I'll feed her in a minute. She had a bottle a couple of hours ago." Jessie glanced at the alarm clock by her bed. *Ten o'clock? No wonder she's crying. It was four hours ago that I fed her.* Four hours! She couldn't believe it. She had just shut her eyes for a minute.

"I made you a cup of tea. Mama," said Clara, sounding like an adult, when Jessie returned to the kitchen.

After filling a bottle for Marianne, Jessie took the tea her daughter had made her and went to the couch. She would feed the baby, drink her tea, then begin her daily routine.

"Mama. We're hungry... Mama. What's for dinner, Mama?" Jessie forced her eyes to open. Clara was shaking her. Had she fallen asleep again...? Her eyelids closed.

It sounded like the screech of an eagle far across the valley. She heard it again. It was coming closer. She put her hands over her head and crouched. It was right upon her, ready to snatch at her hair. She opened her eyes a crack. She heard it again... But it wasn't an eagle: it... it was—? She reached out her hand, touching something. The screeching subsided. Where was she? She groped for her bearings. Was she still on the couch...? But it was dark... Where were the children? The screeching started again— It was her baby. She put her hand on the cradle, rocking it; then worming her way off the couch she staggered to the kitchen. Fumbling around for the matches (which, since Alfred had burned his mouth, were on the top shelf of the cupboard), she lit the lamp.

What time is it? She peered at the clock. *Eleven? At night? It can't be...! The children. Where are the children?* She stood, dazed, staring at the clock, trying to get her mind to focus. Her head was spinning. She started for the bedroom, but after nearly falling, she grabbed the table. Reaching for the broom to use as a crutch, she shuffled into the bedroom. The children were there, in bed, and in their nightclothes too... Was she dreaming? Could this whole day have passed and she not have known? Wobbling back to the kitchen, she grabbed the clock, clutching it as if to choke it. Its hands, unmistakably, pointed to the eleven and the one.

I can't believe it! Where did this day go? She glanced around the kitchen. *Who...? Did the girls – ?* A weak smile snuck across her face... "Yes," she whispered, "I guess the girls *were* my angels of mercy." The loaf of bread lay butchered on the cupboard; the jam, what wasn't on the cupboard, was on the outside of the bottle, the lid on the floor; the dishes were washed—sort-of—and thrown helter-skelter into the cupboard; clothes were strewn from one end of the living area to the other. No doubt, Alfred and Marianne's diapers were there, too.

"But, who cares? At least the children ate and are in bed," she said, spooning soft boiled egg into the baby's mouth. "What else matters?"

The next morning when Jessie opened her eyes, she was again on the couch. She hadn't remembered going to sleep there. She just remembered putting Marianne into her cradle and rocking it... Once...? Twice...? Now it was morning. Her head fell back onto the pillow. It felt like it was a balloon blown to its fullest, about to burst. She struggled off the couch, to the outhouse. Returning, she flopped again onto the couch... "I must light the stove," she muttered... "I must change, feed, and bathe the baby. I didn't bathe her yesterday. I must give Alfred a bath... What day is this? Wash day? Bath day? Sunday?"... She closed her eyes. She heard the prattle of children in the background.

Jessie opened her eyes, forcing them into focus. The baby, in the cradle beside her, was asleep. But then her eyes fell on Alfred, sitting on the floor on the other side of the room, rocking back and forth, whimpering. Holding out her hand toward him, she said, "Come to Mama."

Using his right foot as a propeller, he thumped along on his bottom to the couch, leaving wet spots on the board floor. Tears streaking his face, he climbed into his mama's arms. Jessie took the sheet and wiped his eyes, her own spilling over when she saw his chafed legs and bottom. How she longed for strength to bathe her babies, to comb the tangled mass of brown, red, and blonde hair of her girls, to wash their faces, and to feed them properly... She must get up, or she must get help... Yes. That's what she'd do. She'd write a note today, and send the girls over to Mrs. Strang's... But right now, she would just shut her eyes again. Just for a minute.

Allyn urged the team homeward. "You'll just love my wife," he said to his companions. "And will she ever be surprised to see me! It's three weeks earlier than I told her I'd be home."

"Mama? Jessie, I've brought—" Allyn stopped short at the door, throwing a fast glance back to the two young Canadian Sunday School Mission workers he had brought home with him.

"Jessie! Mama!" With one leap he reached the couch. He hadn't noticed the putrid smell of dirty diapers, the sheet with dried blood in the corner, the clothes littered from one end of the house to the other, the spilled milk, the topsy-turvy kitchen. He hadn't seen the smudges of soot on Clara's and Evelyn's faces and hands, the tangled hair of his daughters, or the tear-streaked faces of Helen and his son. He didn't hear the shriek of the baby. One quick glance told him that his Jessie was... was—

Dropping to his knees, he gazed into the deathly white face of his wife. He grabbed her hand: it felt like ice. He laid his head on her chest. He could neither hear nor feel a heartbeat.

"Jessie! Mama!" he sobbed, his head remaining on his wife's chest.

"Mama's been sick for a long, long time," sniffled Evelyn, her teary eyes peering up at the young men. She took them by the hand and led them to her mother's side.

"We tried real hard to wake her, Daddy. And she was bleeding." Clara, her eyes flooded with tears, leaned over to touch Allyn's shoulder.

Slowly Allyn lifted his head, his face wet with tears. Rising, he pushed the children aside, running to the cupboard to where he remembered having seen a bottle of olive oil: it was lying empty on the shelf.

"Brethren," he said, turning suddenly back to the young missionaries, "James 5:14 and 15 says: 'Is any sick among you? Let him call for the elders of the church; and let him pray over him, anointing him with oil in the name of the Lord; And the prayer of faith shall save the sick, and the Lord shall raise him up...'"

"Well, brethren, the only oil we have in the house is coal oil." He ran to the porch, grabbing the five-gallon can of lamp oil. With his Bible and the oil, he returned to the side of his wife.

Jessie still had not stirred. Allyn felt again for her pulse. He listened for her breathing... Nothing. Pushing the children to their knees by the couch, he fell on his knees at her head. "Brethren, pray for her. Pray for my Jessie." He groaned, grabbing his wife's cold hand.

The young men, both having moistened their fingers with coal oil, touched Jessie's forehead. They poured out a prayer—over the screams of the two babies—a prayer, deep from within their hearts, for this saint to whom they had not yet been introduced.

Jessie heard singing. She saw a light, with Christ standing in the midst of hundreds of shining angels, at the top of a golden ladder. And then she saw a river, a muddy river—was it the same river she had fallen into...? The children? What about the children? They had fallen in too... She must rescue them. She could hear them crying. She reached for them, but they were gone. She tried to cry out, to scream; but no sound would come... She was cold, so cold.

She heard the far-away sniffling of her children, the shrieking of her baby, and the hoarse cry of her son. She thought she heard the groan of her husband. Maybe he had come to rescue her after all... She felt as if a trickle of warm water were running through her. She felt a feather on her forehead... No, not a feather... It was someone touching her. She heard confusion of unfamiliar voices... It sounded like praying... She heard Allyn groan again. He *had* come.

She felt her body begin to relax... to warm... to tremble. She opened her eyes.

It was October. Clara and Evelyn had been in school for a month, Clara, well ahead of her other two grade two classmates, and Evelyn, one of three beginners. Clara handed her mother the letter she had picked up from the post office after school.

Dear Mrs. Splane: — The letter was from Miss Thomas, the secretary for the Canadian Sunday School Mission, in Three Hills. *We heard from our two young missionaries, of your miraculous recovery two months ago. And of how, immediately after, you put together a meal so quickly — and so effortlessly, it seemed to them — while picking up litter, washing children's faces, combing hair, changing diapers, and fixing bottles.*

We are thankful to the Lord for raising you up. Now, to get to the purpose of this letter. As you know, each summer we hold a Bible camp at Gull Lake. We require a camp nurse...

Jessie sat, her chin cradled in her left hand, while she drummed a rhythm on the table with the fingers of her right hand. "Well, why not!" she said suddenly, a smile spreading across her face. "Now that there won't be another baby in the spring, why not?"

Dear Miss Thomas, Jessie wrote. *In answer to your letter, I am happy to accept your invitation to be camp nurse next summer. My daughter, Clara, is already beginning to memorize the three hundred Bible verses required for free admission as a camper. My younger daughter, Evelyn, who will not be of the required age of seven until September, would also like to go, if, because I will be there with her, you would be able to stretch the age rules...*

Holding Marianne on her left hip, Jessie stirred the porridge. Alfred, having just learned to walk, toddled across the floor on his chubby legs and was trying to climb up Jessie's dress, while Helen, in one of her temper tantrums, sat in the corner of the kitchen, her mouth open, her face blue from holding her breath.

"Now say it again, Evelyn," said Jessie. "Clara. Don't rush ahead. You know that Evelyn can't read the verse like you can. Help her. Evelyn, it's not 'Nicomus'. It's 'Nic-o-de-mus'. Say it."

Jessie pushed the porridge pot to the back of the stove, put Marianne into the high chair, hoisted Alfred onto his stool at the table, carried Helen, screaming, into the bedroom, and came back to listen to Evelyn repeat John, chapter three, verses one to three.

"Except-a-man-be-born-again, he-cannot-see-the-kingdom-of-God," chanted Clara and Evelyn together.

"Good. Now, go get Helen. Let's have breakfast." Jessie sighed and spooned porridge into the six bowls set around the table.

Chapter 30 — Mad Dog

November 1936

"Remember now, Clara," said Jessie, pushing the girls out the door for school. "Don't forget to look after your little sister. She's not used to long walks in the snow like you are." It was the first snowfall of the winter, and about eighteen inches had fallen overnight. Clara loved the snow, often accompanying her daddy on his treks through the woods.

"Follow me," said Clara, stepping into the footprints made earlier by her daddy. After leaving Allyn's tracks, she broke a trail through the bush, Evelyn puffing along behind.

"Wanna go home the long way home?" asked Clara after school that day. She grabbed her sister's hand and led her down the railway tracks and along Rolland's fence. Scuffing through the fresh snow, the girls headed up *Camel Hill*, so named because of its resemblance to the hump on a camel.

About ten feet from the top, Clara stopped, her hand flying to her mouth. "Evie." She turned to where Evelyn was crawling up the hill on her stomach. "Come here," she whispered. "Re-al sl-ow. Don't make a sound."

"What?" Evelyn crept up beside her sister. "Why are we whispering?"

"Shh! That dog." Clara lifted her mittened hand and pointed. "It's a mad dog."

A silver-gray dog, almost as tall as they were, stood on the crest of the hill, his tail erect, his ears perked, his steely-gray, slanted eyes focused on the girls. The sisters squeezed hands, as they stood staring at the massive dog.

Evelyn's mouth was dry. She was too scared to cry. One leap and he could be on them. That day in school, the teacher had read to the first-graders the story of "Little Red Riding Hood," and had shown them a picture of a wolf. To her, it had looked just like the dog staring her in the face. "It's a wolf," she whispered, swallowing the lump in her throat.

"No. It's a mad dog," rasped Clara.

"What's he mad at? Us?" Evelyn turned her frightened face toward her big sister.

"No, silly. A mad dog means he's gone crazy. Look. There's foam coming from his mouth." The sisters gazed at the white froth surrounding the dog's muzzle. "That's called 'foaming at the mouth'." Clara continued her explanation in a stage whisper. "That means he's got hyder... hyder-something — the mad disease."

The sun was resting on the horizon. Up until then, the dog hadn't moved. Suddenly, he lifted his head and howled, a howl that would send shivers down the spine of a seasoned woodsman. The girls threw their arms around each other, dropping to the ground.

Slowly, eerily, the sun began to spread shadows across the snow. Too frightened to move, the girls watched as the shadow of the dog grew bigger and bigger. He bent his head, creeping closer and closer. It soon would be dark. Then the mad dog — or wolf — would pounce.

Clara's heart pounded so loudly in her ears that she was sure the dog would hear. She had to do something. But what?

"We gotta run," she said suddenly. "Run home fast. And not look back." She bounded to her feet, pulling Evelyn with her.

"Mama! Mama!" Clara fell through the door. "We saw... a mad... dog."

"You saw a what?" Jessie set her mending down and listened as the girls panted out their story. A frown puckered her brow; inwardly she was smiling. "Get changed," she said abruptly, "and get to your chores. It's nearly dark."

She sat strumming her fingers on the table. "A mad dog!" What an imagination her eldest daughter had.

The following day when Jessie went to town, she ferreted out the facts: one of the men who sat warming his hands at the pot-bellied stove in Hunter's store said, "Yea. Old Terry, the trapper, got himself a shepherd-wolf cross. Real friendly. Sits atop that hill. Kind o' like *king o' the castle*. Can see the whole countryside from there. Looks for rabbits. Name's 'Wolf'."

"I saw your 'mad dog' today." Jessie met Clara at the door. "His name's 'Wolf,' and he's not a mad dog. And he's not a wolf," she added, turning to Evelyn.

"But... but he *is* a mad dog. He was frothing at the mouth. That's how you tell if it's a mad dog, if he froths at the mouth." Clara looked indignant. "Teacher said so. She said it means he's got hyder... hyder—"

"Hydrophobia," finished Jessie. "But he doesn't. It was frosty yesterday; remember? I'd guess, Wolf was eating snow. That could have been steam coming from his mouth. Anyway, next time you see him, call him by his name. I did today. He wagged his tail and licked my hand."

Clara screwed up her face, unconvinced that what her mother told her was true. But she never saw Wolf again, so she forgot about him.

Chapter 31 — Hayrack

November 1936

Jessie stood by the window staring out into the blackness. "Where ever could they be?" She turned to the stove, added a stick of wood and made herself a cup of tea. While it was steeping, she went again to the window. "Oh, where are they?" she said, wringing her hands and pacing. "They've been gone since early morning. I knew I shouldn't have let the girls go."

That morning when Allyn had suggested taking Clara and Evelyn with him to trade Bunt, Gilly's colt, to a neighboring farmer for some loose hay that he'd had in his barn for two or three years, Jessie had hesitated. "What if a blizzard hits, or you have some trouble? What if—? You'd better go by yourself," she said. But with pressure from Allyn and begging from the girls, she had given in.

After swallowing the last of her tea, which hadn't alleviated her worrying, she went outside, and to the woodpile. *Where could they be?* she said again, craning her neck and peering into the darkness, as if by looking she could will her family into sight.

As she turned to go back to the house, panic building inside her, she stopped, cupping her hand to her ear. Was that crunching of snow she heard? Holding her breath, she listened. There it was again, closer. Then faintly, she heard the voices of her girls and the snorting and scuffling of the horses. Stumbling and slipping, with only house shoes on her feet, she ran towards the familiar voices. As she drew closer she heard a groan.

"What's wrong?" she gasped as she approached the entourage. "What happened?" She grabbed Prince's halter, pulling the team to a halt.

"Oh—h," Allyn groaned, struggling up from where he had been stretched on the bunker of the sleigh.

"The hayrack tipped," said Clara.

"Where is it...? Never mind. Let's get Daddy home. You can explain later." Jessie let go of Prince's halter, allowing him to continue the remaining few yards to the house.

Unfastening the horses' harnesses, leaving them where they fell by the door, Jessie slapped the rumps of Prince and Gilly, sending them off on a trot to the barn (a rough log shed, chinked with mud, which Allyn had just finished building, replacing the one they had lost in the fire).

"Your knee's not broken," said Jessie, after cutting away Allyn's pant leg. "Just a bad sprain. But you'll be off it for a long, long time."

More comfortable after a cup of strong tea, Allyn told his story: "We were nearly home with the farmer's hayrack full of hay when the sleigh runners hit a hidden rut. The girls had been sitting on top of the hay just minutes earlier, but I had told them to get down. They were on the back dangling their feet, when I felt the hayrack swerve. I hollered for them to jump. They did, just as the team lurched. I guess the horses felt the swaying and it startled them. They bolted; the hayrack tipped, breaking loose and spilling me and the hay down the bank. I jumped clear of the hayrack, but my knee hit a rock." He groaned.

He ended his story with, "You know, Mama, I don't know how we got home. It was a miracle. A miracle." He slumped back on the couch and was immediately asleep.

One morning a few days after the accident, when Jessie came into the house from milking Lily, she found Allyn hobbling around the kitchen. "I wish you'd stay off your feet and give that knee a chance to heal," she scolded. "You're just making it worse." She plunked the milk onto the counter... "That cow! I'd swear she hates me. Every day it's a fight. Today I thought I'd fool her. I put on your pants, shirt, and hat. And I thought for a while I *did* have her fooled. She stood quietly while I milked the first half pail full. Then calmly, turning to look disdainfully at me with those bovine eyes, she lifted her foot and set it into the pail. I was so mad I poured the milk over her; then I began again." She laughed an embarrassed laugh. "This is all I got." She tipped the pail toward her husband.

"I'll milk her." Clara jumped up from the floor, where she was playing with her sisters. "I'll milk Lily."

"Don't be silly. You can't milk her." Jessie frowned at her daughter.

"Yes, I can. Yes, I can. Can't I, Daddy? Daddy lets me milk her sometimes. Don't you, Daddy?" Clara flashed her dad a teeth-missing grin.

"Yes, I have let you milk her, but I don't think — Remember, I told you that if you don't milk her dry each time, she'll dry up; then we wouldn't get any more milk from her 'til she freshens with a calf?"

"Of course I remember, Daddy." Clara set her feet apart and put her hands on her hips, as she had often seen her mama do. "B'sides, who do you think milked her when Mama was sick?" She cocked her head toward her mama.

Jessie shrugged her shoulders, turning to hide the smile that played at her lips, at her daughter's impudence. "I guess I lost that one," she said. Actually, she'd been too sick at that time to think even about her children, let alone a cow.

That evening Jessie accompanied her seven-year-old daughter to the barn, watching her through the window. With Buddy, the cat, rubbing against her leg, Clara sat on a three-legged milking stool, carrying on a conversation with Lily, who stood, without so much as a flick of her tail, letting the child milk her. Jessie watched, amazed, as the little girl took her thumb and index finger and deftly squeezed the last drops of milk from the cow, just as her daddy had taught her.

When she had finished, Clara threw her arms around the cow's neck, hugging her. "Thank you. Lily," she said, looking into her eyes. Lily responded by giving Clara a slurpy lick.

"Well! I never!" exclaimed Jessie, chuckling. She went into the barn, picked up the pail of milk, and together they walked to the house.

From then on, until Allyn was well, and whenever he was away, Clara milked Lily.

Chapter 32 — "And The Meal Wasted Not." I Kings 17:16

March – August 1937

    The brisk March wind blowing full in her face, nearly taking her breath away, Jessie stood studying the dozens of icicles, which hung tenaciously to the eaves of the shack. The biggest one, at least a foot around and extending from the roof to the ground, was right outside the kitchen window. As she chopped at the giant icicle she could hear the whooping of four of the children inside. She was especially worried about the baby. At fourteen months, Marianne was not quite fourteen pounds, and with the whooping cough sapping her strength and dehydrating her, how much more could her frail body take?
    Pushing the door open, she dropped her armload of ice into the boiler, which she kept going day and night to humidify the air; then she ducked back out for another load.
    Evelyn was the one to come down with the infectious disease. When the health inspector had come in his horse-drawn sleigh to plaster the *Under Quarantine* sign on the door three weeks before, Jessie had been furious. "How do you think my daughter *got* whooping cough?" she had said. "The whole school is full of it. Your daughter, she goes to the school. Did you quarantine yourself?" She had been sorry since, for her outburst; but with Allyn away,

everything seemed to be piling on Jessie all at the same time. And that sign had been the last straw.

"I'm... sorry, Mrs. Splane," the inspector had replied. "I'm just doing my duty." He had smiled wryly at her. "Someone will come out once a week to see if you need anything," he had added quickly.

"Don't bother." Jessie had stepped back into the house, slamming the door and leaning against it.

"You'll have to stay in quarantine until I come back and remove the sign," he had shouted at the closed door.

As Jessie entered the house now with the last armload of icicles, Marianne was gasping for breath. She plopped the ice into the boiler, dropping her coat in a heap by the door. Grabbing the baby and holding her upside down, she reached into her mouth with her finger to clear her throat. After what seemed like an eternity, Marianne gagged, coughing up phlegm. After another choking gasp, the baby started to cry.

"Oh, my baby. My baby." Jessie hugged Marianne to her, letting her own tears spill onto her baby's golden hair. "That's the most wonderful sound I've heard in days. Cry, my little one, cry."

She pulled the rocking chair to the window; and as she sat rocking her baby, she reviewed the last three weeks, particularly the last three days. She had been afraid to go to sleep for fear that one of the children might choke. For the past two nights, she had heard strange noises: *hissing, laughing, creaking and banging,* then *more hissing.* At first she had thought it may have been ice melting, but that was unlikely, since it was the middle of the night. She recalled now that she had told herself then that she must have been dreaming. But of course she wasn't, because she had been rocking first one child then another.

Last night it had been Alfred she was rocking when she had heard a kind of scratching noise. Thinking at first that it might be Buddy, she had glanced toward the couch where she had last seen the cat; he was there, sleeping peacefully. *What was it then?* she had wondered. After carrying Alfred to his bed, she had gone to the window. The stars, thousands of them, were winking down at her, as if mocking her; and the moon, with his sinister grin, she was sure was sneering just at her. Although she knew no one was out there — she could see all the way to the woodpile — she thought she could hear what sounded like a cackling laugh.

She had turned then from the window, deciding that her sleepless nights were getting to her. Ousting Buddy from the couch, she had blown out the lamp and had lain down, thinking to catch a few winks while she could. No sooner had she closed her eyes, than the hissing-cackling-scratching noises started again. She had jumped up, lit the lamp and made a pot of tea.

On the table lay her open Bible. Her eyes fell on Psalm 34:7. "The angel of the Lord encampeth round about those who fear him, and delivereth them." Reflecting on the promise given to the psalmist, words from one of Charles Wesley's hymns popped into her mind:

"Angels, where 'ere we go,
Attend our steps whate're betide.
With watchful care their charge attend,
And evil turn aside."

A feeling of inner peace began to seep through her tired body. She could feel herself beginning to relax. She blew out the lamp and went to her own bed. Three hours later she was up again, rocking one of the children.

That was at six o'clock this morning. And now in late-afternoon, as she sat rocking Marianne after her choking spell, she reviewed her present situation: today she had used the last of the flour; there hadn't been enough even to make a batch of bread — she had made biscuits instead; the hens were laying only occasionally lately, and she had scrambled the last six eggs for dinner. What about supper? What was left to scratch together for supper? And even if she *did* have money — which she didn't — how would she get any groceries? She couldn't leave the children alone. She was virtually a prisoner.

As she sat pondering, her head began to nod in rhythm with the rocker; she dozed. Suddenly, feeling someone at her elbow, her head jerked up. "Hello," she said, looking into the pair of dark blue eyes staring into her face. "Feeling better?"

"A' better now." Helen flashed a dimpled smile. "I hungry."

"Good! What would you like for supper?"

"Maconi."

"All right. Come rock the baby while I make supper."

After returning from the barn with one late-laid egg, Jessie scraped the edges of the flour bin with a knife. She measured two cups of flour into a dish, added a pinch of salt, a dab of melted lard, and moistened the mixture with milk and the egg. Scratching the bin once more, she scraped another handful of flour, spread it on the counter, placed the ball of dough in the middle; then stretching and rolling, she flattened the dough to an eight-inch square. Cutting long thin strips of dough, she draped them over the back of a towel-covered kitchen chair. She put a kettle of water on to boil before coming back to take Marianne out of Helen's arms.

"Go wake your big sisters," she said to her four-year-old daughter. "They've slept the afternoon away."

Dropping the macaroni into boiling water and opening the last jar of tomatoes, Jessie said, "Thank the Lord for simple tastes of children."

"Mama," said Evelyn the following morning, swallowing the last mouthful of the boiled wheat that her mama had fixed just the way she liked it—soaked for a day, then simmered until it was soft and mushy. "Will you read us the story of Elijah and the widow-widow woman this morning for devotions?"

Jessie turned to I Kings 17: 8-16. In her own words she told the children the story of how God sent Elijah to the widow woman of Zarephath, who would feed him until the drought was over.

"'But,' said the widow, 'I'm just going to gather a few sticks to make a fire to cook the last meal for my son and me before we die. I have no more flour and no more oil'." *Oil,* Jessie explained to the children, "was what the people used in those days, instead of lard.

"'Bring me a drink of water and make a cake for me first,' said Elijah.

"The widow made a pancake for Elijah and one for herself and her son. And until the famine was over and the rains came, Elijah stayed with the widow and her son. The oil and flour lasted, and lasted, until the drought was over."

By the time Jessie had finished telling the story, her eyes were filled with tears, but her heart was renewed with faith.

For the next week whenever Jessie went for flour, she was able to scrape enough from the sides of the bin for macaroni, or biscuits, or pancakes—or hardtack if the hens forgot to lay. Each time she approached the bin, her mind told her there could be no flour left, but her heart reminded her of the story of Elijah, and the oil and meal that never ran out.

Allyn was still away. The quarantine sign was still up. No one had come to check on Jessie and her family. And it was now four weeks. Jessie wasn't sure if it was because of the mud, because of her saying, "*Don't bother,*" or because they had simply forgotten.

Finally, one day near the end of March, the health inspector plodded to the door. "Would have been here a week or more ago, Mrs. Splane," he said, "but the mud was too bad. Are the children better?"

"Yes. For nearly two weeks now—" She glanced down at his gumbo-laden boots and her reserve was broken. The poor man had walked through a mile-and-a-half of mud, just to release her from her quarantine prison. She threw the door open wide. "Come in," she said. "I'll make you a cup of tea before you go back."

It was later that same day that Jessie heard a scuffling outside. Recognizing her husband's step, she dropped her sewing and ran to the porch. She threw back her head and laughed when she saw him, partly at the pleasure at seeing him, and partly because of how he looked. He was covered with mud from head to toe. "You look like a mud puppy just out from his hole," she said, throwing open the door and pulling him into the porch. "I'll bring you some clothes. Take those off out here."

"Sold the horses in Athabasca," Allyn told her when she returned with his clothes. "I walked home cross-country." He reached into his muddy pants' pocket, pulling out a handful of crumpled dollar bills. "Not much work around. No need for the team." While stripping off his muddy clothes, he continued. "Met a wonderful Christian family just north of here—four boys, and a baby on the way. The missus is not very well."

July

Eight year-old Clara and six-year-old Evelyn, each carrying a bundle of bedding, skipped down the path toward Meanook. Jessie plodded behind them, a suitcase in each hand. The excitement of the day before in packing hers and the girls' clothes for the Canadian Sunday School Mission Bible camp, her sleepless night, and the noisy chatter of her family at breakfast had left her head spinning; but her lips were smiling at her daughters' excitement. And she had to admit that she, also, was excited.

During the time of the quarantine of a few months ago, Jessie had concentrated on teaching the girls their Bible verses for camp. Clara, who found learning easy, could recite any one of the three hundred verses she had been required to learn for her entrance fee. Evelyn had managed only a few.

The ten days of camp passed quickly for Jessie and the girls.

"I'll never complain about the chatter of my family again," said Jessie at the supper table the day she and the girls arrived home. "When you get ten or twelve girls in a room about the size of this—" She waved her arm in an arch. "Or a hundred and fifty boys and girls together at a meal, it makes our noise seem like whispering."

"I said all my Bible verses, Daddy. Perfectly," said Clara, cocking her head.

"Me, too—"

"Oh, Evie." Clara cut in. "You did not. You couldn't hardly say any. You forgot most of them."

"I did not. I'll say them now to prove it. 'For God so loved—'"

"Oh, Evie. Everyone knows John 3:16." Clara threw a disdainful look at her younger sister, while the rest of the family laughed.

"It's good to be home," said Jessie. "Really good."

Chapter 33 — And Four Makes Nine

September 1937 – April 1938

"Mama, I have lots of news." Allyn had been away for the past three weeks, and as he bounced into the house, he emptied his pockets of change, tossing the coins onto the floor. He unloaded his bag onto the counter—a slab of bacon, a jar of blueberries, a partly eaten sandwich, and a handful of grubby peppermints, which he threw onto the floor where the children were scrambling for the coins.

"Daddy! Don't—" Jessie stooped to pick up the candy, but Alfred had already popped the last one into his mouth, looking up from his crouched position with a mischievous grin. Jessie sighed, shrugging her shoulders as she smiled at her son.

"What's the news you had?" She turned back to her husband, who was helping the girls count the change they'd retrieved.

"Remember that family I told you about? The one with the four boys and sick wife? Remember, I told you how Alex, the father, wanted so badly to go to Bible school?" Allyn cleared his throat while diving for the stove to push the teakettle on to boil.

"Yes," said Jessie. "Go on." She detected that her husband was in position for playing one of his stalling games again. "What about it?" she persisted, dropping a pinch of tealeaves into the teapot and handing it to Allyn at the stove.

"Well." Allyn cleared his throat again. "His wife died. Left the poor man with five boys." Removing both the lids, as well as the middle section, he stirred around at the fire, then dropped in a large block of wood.

Jessie watched the sparks and ashes ascend to the ceiling. *One of these days,* she thought to herself, shaking her head, *he'll start the house on fire.*

"Jessie." Suddenly Allyn turned to face his wife.

"Put the lids back on," she said. "You'll burn the place down." Now, she knew he had a bomb to drop. He never called her *Jessie* anymore. It was always *Mama.*

"Jessie," he repeated, going over to where his wife was sitting at the table. He grabbed her hand. "Jessie... the man was just heartbroken. He's so lost without his wife, and he did so want to go to Bible school. So—" He took a big gulp of air before continuing. "So... so I told him to come by here next week. I told him... I said we'd... keep his boys for the winter... so he could go to Bible school... I knew you'd agree." He disappeared out to the woodpile for an armload of wood.

"Next week...? Five boys...? Did he say, *'five boys'*?" Jessie stood up, her mouth agape, staring at the door.

Although the addition was only partly finished by the time the week was up, Jessie and Allyn moved the three girls into it, freeing the bedroom for the boys.

At about four o'clock, on a crisp early-October afternoon, a beat-up '29 Chevrolet chugged into the yard. Like spiders being chased from their nest, four boys tumbled from the back seat. Carrying a baby and a suitcase, their father shepherded the group to the door.

"Gootday, Meesus," he said, before Jessie had had a chance to fully open the door. "Kindly I t'ank you for carink for my boys for da vinter." He dropped the suitcase in the middle of the floor, his big hand grasping Jessie's, nearly crushing her knuckles. He began his introductions: "My name ees Alex. And dis here beeg boy ess Steve. He ees eight." He placed his hand on the dark head of his oldest son. "Then cums Pete here." Alex pointed to a lanky red-haired, freckle-faced lad. "He ees seex. But Pete vill not be stayink. He vill cum mit me. T'morrow. He ees goink to be adopted." He smiled fondly at the lad. "And dis here rascal," he said, pointing to a dark-haired little fellow, "ees Cho (Joe). He ees four. Then leetle Neek (Nick) ees soon t'ree. Baby Paul, ees chust about seex munts."

Jessie took the baby from Alex's arms, nestling him on her shoulder; she reached for Nick's hand. The blonde-haired little mite pulled away, running to his daddy.

"No, Neek, go to your new mama. Vhat shoud da keeds call you, Meesus?"

"Well, they could call me *Mrs. Splane, Aunt Jessie,* or *Mama.* Let them choose. Let's have supper." Jessie propped the fair-haired baby in Marianne's highchair, and turned to the stove.

"No! Mine! Mine!" twenty-month-old Marianne screeched, shaking her chair, trying her best to shake the baby out of it.

"No, no. Look. Here's a big grown-up chair for you." Jessie lifted her tiny daughter onto the high stool Allyn had built for Alfred. After a loud protest from her son, Jessie finally got the families settled around the table for the evening meal.

It was after Alex's car had chugged down the road the following morning, and after she had ushered the girls and Steve out the door for school, and after Allyn had left for the day, that Jessie discovered that neither Joe nor Nick spoke English. And she didn't speak Ukrainian. What was she to do? How was she to communicate with the little fellows?

For two weeks Nick would have nothing to do with Jessie. He clung to Joe by day, and to Steve by night. Whenever he would look Jessie's way, it was with daggers in his blue eyes. However, he always seemed to know when it was mealtime. Communication? What did he need it for? A mother? Who needed one? As long as there was food.

Joe had his own way of letting Jessie know what he wanted. He just took it. Then with his big, defiant brown eyes, he would look at her as if to say, "Try and stop me!"

Each morning, rain, snow, sleet, or shine, the two little boys would gulp down their breakfast; then without waiting for family devotions, or dismissal, would bolt outside to climb on the woodpile, the barn roof, the trees, or in and out of the unfinished lean-to addition. When they weren't climbing, they were terrorizing the chickens or Lily. Instinctively, however, at mealtime they would rush into the house, gobble their food, then rush out again.

"How will they ever learn English at that rate?" said Jessie one day as they raced past her.

One afternoon on a beautiful, late-October day, Joe and Nick, in their usual manner, raced around outside for an hour. Then just as Jessie was about to put the bread into the oven, she heard a husky voice. "Affer. Come oushi!" it said. Jessie gasped. It was Joe's first attempt at English. Of course, only she — and he — understood.

"Alfred," she said, looking into the corner of the room where her son sat playing with Helen. "Joe wants you to go outside to play. Come on. You, too, Helen. The fresh air will do you both good."

Despite her daily encouragement for Alfred and Helen to join Joe and Nick outdoors, her two youngsters shied away from the rough-necked boys.

As Jessie closed the door behind her two, she smiled. At last Joe belonged to the family. Nick, she knew, would soon follow. Paul, satisfying his baby needs for a mama, had taken to Jessie right away. And Steve? Well, Steve lived in his own little world.

Jessie went about her daily routine, whistling, thinking no further about the children. When the older three arrived home from school, they occupied themselves with their chores. At supper time the family gathered around the table, Joe and Nick storming in as usual. They began their food gobbling.

"Boys!" Allyn banged his fist on the table. "We are not heathen in this house. We don't eat without thanking God for our food. I've had enough of your rowdiness and ill-manners."

It was then, when silence fell and eight pairs of startled eyes gawked up at Allyn, that Jessie noticed. "Where's Alfred?" She jumped up from her chair.

All eyes turned to the vacant place at the table.

"Helen. Where's Alfred?" Jessie repeated.

"I dunno. I came in with Clara and Evelyn." Helen looked with innocent eyes at her mama.

"Joe? Nick? Where's Alfred?" Jessie gripped an arm of each boy.

Silence. One pair of rebellious brown eyes stared at Jessie. One pair of blue eyes stared down at his plate of partly eaten food.

"No one eats a bite 'til we find Alfred." Jessie lifted the two babies from their chairs. To the other children, she snapped, "Get! All of you."

Allyn bolted for the door, the children scrambling behind, while Jessie, a child on each hip, followed. It was nearly dark, but six pairs of young feet scampered all over the yard, in every direction.

Instinctively, both Allyn and Jessie headed for the well. With dread, Allyn lifted the lid, peering into the shallow water. Together, they heaved a sigh of relief. Even in the semi-dark, they could see that he wasn't there.

Fifteen minutes later the dejected group, all but Joe and Nick, shuffled back to the house. No Alfred. And now it was too dark to see. One by one they sat back at the table, their heads hanging low.

"Where? Oh, where could he be?" Jessie set the babies back into their chairs, and clutched at her hair. Just as she headed back to the door to continue her search, she was startled by a voice.

"Mama! Mama!" cried the husky voice from somewhere in the yard. "Come qvick!"

Joe? Calling, "Mama"? Jessie headed for the door.

"Mama! Mama! Come here!" came a softer, but just as insistent, voice.

"Joe? Nick?" Jessie, with Allyn right behind her, carrying a lantern, ran toward the voices.

Gingerly they stepped into the barn to where the little boys had led them: they feared the worst. They approached the spot where Joe was pointing. What was it he was pointing at? They dropped to their knees.

Through a crack in the barn, shone a thin beam of moonlight. A wisp of red hair sticking out from a mound of dusty hay was all they saw at first. Allyn pushed back the hay, fearing the worst." With his heart pumping the blood with a swishing sound through his head, he lifted his son. Alfred's head flopped onto Allyn's shoulder; he jerked, sighed, and opened his eyes.

"Our *'little-boy-blue,* fast asleep in the hay,'" said Jessie, reaching over and kissing her son. "Come boys," she said to Joe and Nick, taking a hand of each of them, "let's go back and finish our supper.

It was to a meal of cold hash-browned potatoes and greasy fried eggs that the group returned, but at last they were a family. From that day on the boys accepted the family routine, rules, and discipline, sharing in the laughter and joy.

The extra hours Jessie spent sewing and knitting and creating special gifts for Christmas that year, she did with a heart filled with love for each of the nine children — equally — in her extended family.

But for Allyn she had a special surprise: "Sorry I didn't have time to make you a gift," she said on Christmas night, snuggling close to him. "But I do have something for you. However, I'm afraid you'll have to wait awhile." She kissed him on the ear then turned over.

"What do mean, *'Have to wait?'* How long? What is it?" He rolled his wife over, making her look at him. "When do I get this special gift? Come on. Tell me. You know I don't like waiting for things."

Jessie gave a deep sigh, pretending that she had already fallen asleep, but her slight giggle gave her away. "Oh, next summer some time," she whispered.

"What?" he said, finally catching on to what she meant by *'special surprise.'* "How long have you known?" He jerked to a sitting position.

"Oh, about a couple of weeks. I'd say your little surprise should arrive in plenty of time for your birthday. Maybe before. But let's not say too much yet. Remember the last time? And almost the time before? Let's keep it our own little secret — 'til we're sure."

It was two days after Paul's first birthday. For the past week Jessie had been mending and sewing for the boys, making sure their clothes would be ready. And although she knew when he would come, she had been dreading the sound of Alex's car chugging up to the door: and now it was here.

She thought she would choke on the lump in her throat when she handed Paul to his father: his baby arms clung to her neck. And when Marianne began crying, "Pauly. My baby, Pauly," and ran after Alex to the car, Jessie could scarcely keep her tears from spilling. But when Alex placed the baby on the car seat and shut the door, and both Paul and Marianne were howling, it was sheer willpower that kept Jessie from joining them.

With effort, she forced her eyes to Steve. He stood, one hand on the car handle, waving goodbye to Clara and Evelyn. Were those tears Jessie saw in his eyes...? Or were the tears in her own?

With one last race around the yard. Nick ran to Marianne, giving her a shove and knocking her to the ground; then grabbing Jessie's legs and peering up at her with eyes that looked like two pools of water, he said, "Bye, Mama." Then, like a bullet being shot from a gun, he flew to the car, slamming the door behind him.

The lump in Jessie's throat had now grown to the size of a baseball.

"Come on, Choe." Alex turned to Joe, who was still climbing the woodpile. "We must go."

The little boy tumbled to the ground and ran to Jessie, looking up at her with mischievous brown eyes. Suddenly he turned to Alfred, punching him in the arm. Then he fled to the car, diving in through the open window.

Alex gave the crank handle a pull. The car spluttered. He jumped behind the wheel. The car pulled away.

Jessie stood, choking back tears, her children beside her, until she could no longer see even the dust behind the wheels. Part of her heart went down the road with that beat up old Chevrolet carrying Steve, and Joe, and Nick, and baby Paul.

Chapter 34 — A Quiver Full

August 1938

"Lo, children are an heritage of the Lord: and the fruit of the womb is his reward. As arrows.. so are children... Happy is the man that hath his quiver full of them." Psalm 127:3-5

"What are you sewing, Mama? Can I turn the handle?" Evelyn stood with her elbows resting on the table, her chin in her hands. She loved watching her mother make things on the sewing machine.

"*May I?* corrected Jessie. "*May I* turn the handle?"

"Well, can I?" insisted her daughter. "What are you making? Doll clothes?"

"No. They're baby clothes."

"Who for? We don't have a baby."

"Well, we soon will have." Her mother picked up a worn flannelette sheet and tore it into pieces. "You may turn the wheel for these diapers," Jessie said, lowering the pressure foot onto one corner of the material.

"What baby? Is Paul coming back?"

"No. Besides, Paul isn't really a baby anymore. He'd be a year-and-a-half by now. Turn the handle."

"Are we gonna get another baby?" Evelyn wrinkled her freckled nose, pushing her head to within two inches of her mother's.

"Keep your eyes on what you're doing if you want to turn the handle. Yes. We're going to have another baby."

"Don't we have enough already?"

"Well, whether we do or whether we don't— Stop the wheel. I have to turn the corner."

"Can't we send it back? The baby, I mean."

"No. You can't send babies back. It's already on the way." Jessie repressed a smile.

Turning the wheel in silence for a while, Evelyn concentrated on the straight lines her mama was sewing. While Jessie prepared the next diaper, Evelyn put her hands in her chin again, her mind mulling over the matter of the coming baby. Suddenly she stood with her arms akimbo, letting out an exasperated sigh. "Do you *want* the baby?" she asked.

"Yes, I s'pose. Start the wheel." Jessie began sewing the last diaper. "But there'd be nothing I could do about it now, anyway."

"Why? Don't you have any *say* in the matter?" She lifted her hands from the wheel, putting them back on her hips. She stamped her foot, letting out another exasperated puff. "Where's this baby coming from anyway? When is it getting here? Is it gonna be a boy?"

"Enough questions now," Jessie said, turning the wheel herself. "You run and play."

While she put the diapers away, she thought of last Christmas, when she had first told Allyn that she was expecting this baby. "Almost a quiver full," he had said, pulling her to him.

"Not almost," she had answered. "This is the seventh, and final one."

"What do you mean, *the seventh*?" He had pushed her from him, shuffling to a sitting position.

Just like my husband, she mused now as she cut and pieced together the remaining material for a tiny nightie. *Just like him. Whenever he's frightened about something he blocks it out.* She recalled his reaction when he had learned that it was a miscarriage that had nearly taken her life almost two years ago—total rejection of the fact. To him she was just sick. So when she had told him that they would have their quiver full with this baby, he had for the moment, been almost hostile.

"Just because the Master Archer had another use for that last arrow and removed it from the quiver, doesn't mean it was never there," she had said to him just before they had fallen asleep, last Christmas night.

And now, her mind swinging back to her conversation with Evelyn, she smiled. *Guess it's time I told my daughter where babies come from.*

One day in mid-August, in a hurry to go to town to get some iodine for Evelyn's infected foot — she had stepped on a rusty nail — Jessie grabbed the milk bucket and headed to the barn. Black flies and yellow jackets swarmed through the air, waiting for prey. As she crunched through dry grass, disturbing lurking grasshoppers, she glanced toward the rising sun. How different it looked from yesterday. She remembered having noticed it as she had watched Allyn pedal away on his bicycle. It had appeared like a ball of fire dropping into the midst of the forest of poplars. Today it was hazed over, giving the whole atmosphere an eerie look. She spun her head around. A funnel-like cloud billowed in the southwest.

"*Fire!*" She dropped the pail by the barn door and ran back to the house, stopping short at the door. "*I mustn't panic,*" she told herself. She took a deep breath before entering.

"Clara, I know I said that I'd milk Lily today, but I was being selfish. You've been at Grandma's most of the summer, and Lily really missed you, so you go milk her. But don't dawdle. I have an errand I want you to run." She didn't at the time, but she had to think of some reason to urge her to hurry.

Pouring salt into a pan of warm water, Jessie, as quickly and as calmly as she could, bathed and bandaged Evelyn's swollen foot. "*It's infected — badly,*" she said to herself. "*It needs to be attended to immediately. A rusty nail infection can lead to--*" She pushed the thought away. She had to get the children out of here, to some safe place. The fire was fast approaching, heading directly for the woodpile and the house. But where could she take them...? And how?

"Oh, God," she prayed. "What am I to do? With Allyn not here, my baby due in a few weeks, my little girl on the verge of blood poisoning, two toddlers, and no neighbor for two miles; God, what am I to do?"

"He maketh me to lie down in green pastures: he leadeth me beside the still waters." Psalm 23:2. The answer came like a bolt from heaven. As the verse flashed through her mind she became calm: she knew what she would do.

"Listen, kiddies," she said, as soon as Clara was back from milking (she was glad, with Clara's daydreaming mind, that she hadn't noticed the smoke on the horizon; panic was the last thing she needed), "I want you all to listen to Mama... and to stay calm. There's a fire headed this way.

But! —" She held up her hand to still them when the older girls let out a gasp. "Remember how God helped us before? Well, He will again. Clara, I want you to take this to Brooks. And Helen, you go along, too. Just follow Clara, and don't cry if she runs ahead. Do you hear?" She handed Clara the hurriedly scribbled note: *Ned, Jim: Fire headed our way. Allyn not home. Can you help?* She pushed the girls out the door, watching for a moment as they ran down the path toward the well.

To Evelyn, who had hobbled to the door and was standing beside her, she said, "I'm going to take the little ones down to the well. I'll need you down there to watch them. Can you hobble there on your own? Take the broom for a crutch."

Evelyn had always been afraid of going to the well. One of her daily chores was to carry water, but she always managed to go with Clara or Helen, or trade chores with them to avoid going. "Will you be there, Mama?" She looked into her mama's face, her eyes wide.

"Not all the time. I'll get you settled, but I can't stay."

"Mama! The caterpillars!" Evelyn pulled her collar up around her chin, her eyes filling with tears.

"Evelyn." Jessie took her daughter by the shoulders. "The caterpillars are gone, long ago. That's all those butterflies you see flying around. You know that. I'll be bringing Lily down, so she'll be with you... And so will Jesus."

Evelyn swallowed, gave her eyes a quick wipe on her arm and turned toward her little brother. "Come on, Alfred," she said, grabbing his hand. "Let's go down to the well."

The flames were licking across the field, just southwest of the house by now. After having moved the woodpile away from the fence, Jessie began raking away the leaves that had gathered along the fence line. As she raked, every minute seeming like an hour, her fears grew. *Oh, why did I send the girls away?* The more she worried, the faster she raked, despite the screaming pain in her back. *What if the fire has — ? What if... they got caught — ?*

She dropped the rake and ran to the top of the hill. "Evelyn," she called, "are Clara and Helen there? Did they get back?"

"No, Mama," Evelyn wailed. "They're not here?"

Oh, God, what did I do, sending my children into the middle of a fire? How could I have? She snatched the rake from the ground, fear gripping her heart. *What can I do? What can I do — ?*

She dropped the rake and ran toward the gate: a wagon was rumbling into the yard.

"Mama! Mama! We went through fire." Helen jumped off the back of the wagon, Clara right behind her. "And the water from the barrels splashed all over us. It was fun!"

With the girls having joined the other children at the well, and with the men already busy ploughing a firebreak, Jessie again picked up her rake. That her back felt as if it were about to break made no difference to her: her children were safe. Now she must save her house.

When she had finally raked all the way to the house she laid her rake down. "I'm sure the men could use a drink of good cold water," she said, wiping her brow with her apron. Clutching at her back she picked up the bucket from the porch. As she headed for the well she looked over to the fence, sure that by this time the fire would have crossed it. But what she saw made her drop the pail: the fire, instead of advancing, was burning back on itself.

"Gentlemen," she yelled to the men. "The wind's changed direction. Look!"

For the first time in over an hour the men looked up. "So it has," said Ned, taking off his cap and wiping his brow. "So it has."

It was August twenty-fifth, a week after the fire. When Jessie heard Allyn banging around in the kitchen building a fire, she lifted her head from the pillow. It flopped back onto it. For the past week she had been having excruciating back pains and headaches. But this morning it felt as if her head was about to explode, and her back felt like Lily was stepping right in the middle of it. She rolled onto her side, gingerly lowering her feet to the floor.

"Tea ready?" she said, shuffling to a chair in the kitchen. She threw Allyn a weak smile, leaning her elbows on the table and propping her head in her hands.

"You okay?" Allyn slid a cup of tea across the table. "Not time for the, baby yet, is it?"

"No." Jessie laughed. "Not for a couple of weeks. Do I look that bad?" The look on her husband's face told a whole story.

Jessie took a sip of tea. *Florence*, she mused, savoring the name and at the same time thinking of her sister. She reached across to the shelf beside the table, touching the soft, blue towel Florence had sent her for her birthday two weeks ago. "I'll save it for the baby's first bath," she had said at the time.

Rubbing her hand across it now, she returned to her musings: *If this baby's a girl I'll name her Florence... Florence Ruth.* Her mind drifted to names she and Allyn had discussed for a boy. She liked the name, 'Richard,' after Allyn's youngest brother, Dick, whom she was so fond of. Allyn wanted 'Ernest,' after the brother next to him, who had died of typhoid when he was nineteen. Allyn had refused to discuss girls' names. "This one will be a boy," he would always insist. End of discussion!

"Florence," Jessie said again, this time out loud. Allyn wasn't listening anyway. She got up from the table and began breakfast preparations. "Florence Ruth... That's what we'll call her."

As the day progressed, Jessie knew that it would not be two weeks until the baby came. As she and Allyn sat having their before-bedtime cup of tea, she said, "I think you'd better run and alert Mrs. Brooks." Their friend and neighbor, Ned and Jim's mother, had offered to help at the birth.

"What? What do you mean?" Allyn slammed his cup onto the table. "I thought you said—"

"I know. But I don't think—" She looked into her husband's frightened eyes and suddenly felt sorry for him. He could stand up to any pain or hardship for himself, but whenever anything threatened her health, or one of the children's, he panicked. She reached for his hand. "Honey. It's all right. A baby coming two weeks early is not unusual. Remember what I went through a week ago? It's not surprising that it's early. Will... you go see Mrs. Brooks?"

Allyn jumped up, stepped into his rubbers and grabbed his cap and bicycle clip. "I wish. I wish—" He bolted out the door and mounted his bike.

"Yes," said Jessie to the closed door. *I know what you wish. You wish we could afford for me to go to the hospital. I know, Daddy. I know.* She had hidden the last bill they had received from the Athabasca Hospital, the one for Helen's birth, nearly six years ago. It hadn't been a demand for the balance, just a friendly reminder. *We'll pay*, she had said to herself when she had read the note. *At a dollar a month – like we've been paying – it may take years, but we'll pay. Yes, we'll pay.* And they did.

"Six sharp!" said Mrs. Brooks to Allyn who stood at the door fidgeting, one hand on the doorknob, the other clutching his cap.

"No need to panic, Mr. Splane," his neighbor called after him as he ran back to his bike. "No need to panic. That baby won't be here for at least another week. I know babies; believe me! But I'll be there at six sharp tomorrow morning." She shut the door.

Chapter 35 — "Pauly, My Baby"

August 1938

"Allyn! Wake up. Wake up."

"What? What time... is it?"

"It's five, but I don't think this little one is going to wait for Mrs. Brooks."

Allyn scrambled into his clothes and went to the kitchen to build a fire.

"Mama? Can we get up?"

Allyn rushed into the children's bedroom. "Yes," he whispered. "You can get up, but it's real early, so be quiet." He lifted Marianne from her crib, grabbing her clothes.

"Why?" asked Evelyn in a whisper loud enough to wake the dead. "Who's sleeping?"

"Nobody. But we might have a surprise for you — after breakfast. But you've got to go to the kitchen and stay there 'til I call you. There's porridge on the stove."

"Where's Mother?"

Mother? Allyn threw Clara a look, then grinned. Just yesterday he and Jessie had been discussing the *culture* their daughter had been practicing, learned during the summer from his mother. He let it pass. She soon would be back to *Mama* again.

Through the clinking of spoons on bowls, and childish prattle at the breakfast table, came muffled sounds and a stifled cry.

"What was that?" Evelyn dropped her spoon, jumped up and headed for her parent's bedroom. At the same time, came a knock at the door.

"Evelyn!" Clara's sharp voice brought her sister to a halt. "Father said to stay here."

"I'm just going to answer the door," said Evelyn in a wounded voice, changing direction.

It was exactly six o'clock. Mrs. Brooks pushed past Evelyn, dropping her coat onto the couch.

There was no longer any prattle at the breakfast table. Five pairs of eyes were glued to the doorway between the bedroom and the kitchen as the puzzling sounds continued.

Then came a cry, so distinctive that even Marianne knew what it was. "Pauly! Pauly! My baby, Pauly," she cried, pushing at the table, trying to break free from her stool. "Want my baby, Pauly."

Running from the bedroom to the table, Allyn lifted Marianne from her stool. "Come, kids," he said. "Come see the surprise I promised." He led them into the bedroom, lining them up along the wall opposite their mother's bed. "Mama had a baby. A new baby sister for you," he said, beaming from ear to ear.

"About six pounds of it." Mrs. Brooks held up the screaming baby.

"Mama?" Evelyn's face puckered into a puzzled frown. She remembered the conversation she'd had with her mama a few weeks back. "Our baby?" She looked first at her mother, then turned to Mrs. Brooks. "I didn't... see it when—You didn't bring—? Mama?" She turned back to her mother.

"Yes." Jessie gave her daughter a weak smile. "Yes. It's our baby." She closed her eyes. "I *must* tell her... about the facts of life," she said to herself.

Clara looked down at her younger sister. "Honesty! Don't you know *anything*? Tsk!" She shook her head in disgust at her sister's ignorance.

"Is it... really ours? To keep?" Helen smiled a dimpled smile and looked up at her daddy.

"Pauly. I want my baby Pauly." Marianne tried again to struggle free from her daddy's arms, her face turning as red as her hair.

"No. Not *Pauly*," said Allyn, tightening his grip on his little daughter. "It's a girl. Your baby sister."

"One… three… six… ten girls…! And I'm the on'y boy." Alfred, not quite four, glared at his daddy and fled from the room. He climbed onto his chair at the table and grabbed a piece of bread, smearing it with butter. He took the sugar bowl, dumping the contents onto the bread. Stuffing the whole piece of bread into his mouth, he ran outside.

Four pairs of blue eyes followed Mrs. Brooks as she scurried around making preparations for the baby's first bath. (Alfred excluded. He was having nothing to do with another sister.) Checking Jessie's ready materials, she discarded first one thing then another, replacing it with things she had brought. "I'll not use that dirty old rag on a baby," she said, flinging aside Jessie's brand new birthday towel. She reached into her own bag, producing a dazzling white towel.

For weeks after Paul had left, Marianne had gone around the house whining. And now since the baby had arrived, she had not stopped singing about *'her Pauly'* being back. No amount of persuasion, explaining that the baby was a girl, or allowing her to see the baby, would convince her that this baby was not *'Pauly.'*

One day shortly after the birth of the baby, as the family sat around the supper table discussing names, Jessie said, "I thought Florence Ruth would be nice."

"Pauly. My baby, Pauly. Back. Back." Marianne began her chant again.

After the laughter of everyone at the table had died down, Allyn said, "Well, I guess we'll just have to call her, 'Paul.' But since she's a girl, it'll have to be, 'Pauline'."

"'Pauline'." Jessie closed her eyes as if registering the name. "Pauline Ruth."

"Pauline Ruth," repeated Allyn, his tone indicating that the matter was settled: her name was, "Pauline Ruth."

"You, my little Pauline Ruth, are the only one of my babies I've been able to nurse." The rocking chair squawked in rhythm to Jessie's cooing conversation with her baby. She told her how badly she had needed to nurse sickly Evelyn, how she had no milk for Helen. "And your brother," she said, "I couldn't nurse him, either, and he was *always* hungry." She smiled down at the infant, then told her of the miracle of Marianne's birth, and of how Lily had come to them.

Pauline opened her eyes, squinting—almost smiling—at her mama, tugging and pushing, as if trying to sit up.

"My little 'Pauline Pusher'. You may be my last, but you're not going to be left behind, are you?" Lifting the baby to her shoulder, Jessie continued her one-way discourse with her as she rocked her back and forth.

It was two weeks later. Allyn was awakened from a deep sleep by the squeaking of the rocker. "Mama?" He reached across the bed. "Mama? Funny, she usually brings the baby into bed for her two-o'clock feeding." He jumped out of bed and went into the kitchen.

"Mama! What's wrong?" He touched her on the shoulder. "You usually—" As he struck a match to light the lamp, he realized that she had been up for quite some time. She had lit the stove but not the lamp. "You're not... nursing her?" he said, seeing his wife holding a bottle to the baby's mouth.

She didn't answer.

Allyn bent down, putting his index finger under her chin, raising her head. "Mama, you're crying!" He dropped to his knees beside the rocker.

She sniffled, shifting the baby to her shoulder. "Oh, Daddy," she said, "I was so happy to be able to nurse at least one of my babies... Remember? I nursed Clara for two days, and then—well, you know about the others. Oh, Allyn... Why...? Why?"

Allyn took the baby and placed her in the wicker clothesbasket Mrs. Brooks had brought. He took his wife's hands, pulling her to her feet and gently rocking her back and forth, letting her cry on his shoulder.

At last Jessie pulled away. She went to where she kept her first-aid supplies, gathered up what she needed and went to the table.

Allyn sucked in his breath when his wife pulled off the bandage that was covering the running sore on her right breast. "How... how long... have you had... that?"

"Quite awhile... more than a week. But I so wanted to nurse, and I had the milk this time. So despite the pain, I—"

"Shouldn't you see a doctor—?"

"You know we can't afford—" When she saw the look of hurt on Allyn's face, she stopped, sorry she'd snapped at him. She reached over and touched his face.

Chapter 36 — A No-Win Situation

1939

Jessie shifted the baby to her shoulder and rested her own head lightly on the soft, blonde curls of her ten-month-old daughter. Tears stung her eyes as she glanced down at the pock-covered face; she stroked her hands, gloved with socks to keep her from scratching. "My poor baby," she sighed, kissing her. "Well at least your fever has broken."

About a month ago the girls had been sent home from school because Helen had broken out with chicken pox. Again, for the third time in as many years, a sign hung on the door of the mud-plastered log shack: "Under quarantine." How Jessie detested the stigma. *Leprosy.* That's what it made her think of: a neighbor would come to the gate and whistle; Jessie would run out to give, or receive any messages; but no one would come near the house. And again, Allyn was away.

What angered Jessie most, however, was that her three girls had had to miss a chance of their lifetime, a school trip to Edmonton for the Royal visit. King George VI and Queen Elizabeth. Although all three girls had been over the chicken pox for nearly a week, the younger children—who didn't even go to school—were still sick with the disease. And until the quarantine sign was removed, the whole family was prisoner.

"Prisoners!" Jessie said aloud now as she sat rocking her baby, at five o'clock in the morning. "That's what we are, prisoners. Trapped. Trapped in a no-win situation: no work, so no money to move to where we can find work."

For months she had been fostering a dream (or desire, or wish): "If only we could move to the city, maybe I could get work, go back to nursing—" But every time she entertained the thought it would vanish and be replaced with: *How? How can I? I'm a mother of six. A mother's place is in the home... And anyway, how can I? We're trapped.*

As the days wore on Jessie became more and more obsessed with the idea of moving to the city. Every time she would sit down to read her Bible, or would kneel to pray, she would visualize herself living in the city, going to church, visiting friends, and perhaps nursing part time? Then, *Crash!* would go the picture, like the shattering of a looking glass. They were trapped.

In her devotions Jessie was reading the book of Habakkuk. Because she was reading through the entire Bible, she was dutifully plowing through the Minor Prophets, not her favorite part of the Bible. One morning, half concentrating, she read through to verse seventeen of the third chapter, receiving no heart-message. But on verse seventeen she stopped. She read it again.

"This is it. This is our situation exactly." She read the words aloud: "Although the fig tree shall not blossom, neither shall fruit be in the vines, the labour of the olive tree fail, and the fields shall yield no meat; the flocks shall be cut off from the fold, and there shall be no herd in the stalls..."

"Exactly," she said again. "It's been that way with us for—"

She read on: "Yet I will rejoice in the Lord, I will joy in the God of my salvation.' (v. 18)

"That's the hard part," she said aloud, "to rejoice." She read verse 19: "The Lord God is my strength, and he will make my feet like hinds feet, and he will make me to walk upon mine high places..." She put the Bible down.

"Well, whether or not we move to the city," she said, going to the stove to stir the porridge, "God has promised to 'make me to walk upon high places.' That's enough for me." She thought again of His special promises of years ago: "I will walk with you..."

Her heart felt lighter. Humming a tune, she set the table for breakfast. It had been weeks since she'd felt like singing.

One day about a month later, while Jessie was in the garden weeding, Allyn came bounding up the path, waving a letter. "From your sister," he called, before even reaching the garden gate.

Jessie rose to her feet. On her apron she brushed the dry garden dirt from her hands, then took the letter and began to read. First a smile, then a frown, crossed her face. She handed the first page to Allyn.

He gasped. "Florence and Louis? Coming here?"

Florence had married a local Hawaiian in 1933, a bookkeeper for a sugar plantation. This was their first trip to Canada since. Allyn had never met Florence, but from what he had heard, and from her letters to Jessie, he knew that she did not think too highly of him for, "snatching her baby sister away from a promising career," and for, "taking her into the wilderness."

He passed the page back to his wife. "Well, what are we waiting for?" he said. "Let's get busy and brighten this dump up." He turned and ran from the garden.

On the morning of her sister's arrival (they were to be driving a rented car from Edmonton), Jessie hurried the children through their morning activities of dressing, breakfast, and chores. She cleaned the kitchen, trimmed the wick and shined the chimney of the lamp. She tore pages from the catalogue and polished the stovetop.

"Wonder what my sister will think of *this* place," she said, tossing the old fly sticker, black from its catch, into the stove. Her mind explored the *Paradise* her sister lived in: the house with the palm tree in the middle of the living room (they had built a garbanzo around the tree to incorporate it into the room); the perfect view of the ocean and mountain; the papaya, lemon, and guava trees; the fragrant flowers; the warm ocean breezes. Of course, she had never been to Hawaii, but with Florence's vivid description, she could almost feel the breezes and smell the flowers.

Her eyes surveyed her own surroundings: a shabby log shack — with a thrown-together addition — building paper covering both the mud-plastered walls and rough-board floors; low four-paned windows with a view of... of — She shuddered. *My sister? Coming here?*

She went to the trunk, pulling out a linen tea cloth, wrapped still in its original tissue paper, the only remaining wedding gift of eleven years ago. It was with a caress that she smoothed it on top of the table, noticing once again, the dainty flowers embroidered in each corner:

"A mixture of plumaria, hibiscus, and bougainvillea, flowers of Hawaii," Florence had explained on the card accompanying the gift.

Holding the tatted lace edging between her fingers, Jessie was seven again, sitting beside fifteen-year-old Florence, who was patiently teaching her how to tat. *Wonder if I'll get the time – or money – to indulge in pleasurable handwork ever again,* she thought just now.

"Mama! Mama!" In the middle of her reverie, the children burst into the house, their arms laden with wild flowers: brown-eyed Susans, daisies, buffalo beans, Indian paintbrush, and baby's breath. "Look 't what we got for Auntie Florence and Uncle Louis," they chorused together.

"Oh no! Not now," groaned Jessie. But when she saw the sparkle of excitement beginning to fade from their faces at her rebuff, she said, "Oh well, all right. They *will* brighten the room. Put them on the cupboard; I'll arrange them."

"We have *years* of catching up to do," said Florence later that evening, when at last the two sisters were alone.

They had had little time to chat earlier in the day. While Jessie had been preparing a meal of roast chicken, potatoes and gravy, garden salad, and blueberry pie, (and Allyn had been entertaining Louis), the children had given Florence a grand tour. Not only had they shown her the garden, the barn, and the well, but they had brought her Buddy to pet (she disliked cats); had shown her the half-grown chicks (which made her shudder); and had introduced her to Lily, taking her hand and urging her to stroke the cow's face (she had grimaced, yanking her hand away).

And now as Jessie and Florence sat sipping tea and talking, the crackling of the fire in the stove; the flicker of the coal oil lamp, throwing eerie shadows across the table, the walls, and the ceiling; the sleeping noises of the family; the clinking of cups on saucers; and the stifled giggling of the two sisters, gave an atmosphere of tranquility to the Spartan surroundings. Florence had kept well hidden, the shock she'd had when she first laid eyes on the place her sister called home.

Chapter 37 — The Hitchhiker

October – 1939

"Canada's joined the war." Allyn dropped the groceries onto the counter. "Heard it on the radio in the store. Everybody's talking about it, all excited. Imagine! They say it's the best thing that could happen to this country, what with the economy the way it is, and everyone out of work."

Jessie's mouth dropped open, her mind flipping back to when she was thirteen and her brother, George, joined the last war. Would it now be her husband? (And them with six children!) But just as quickly as the thought — and fear — came, she shoved it from her, thinking instead of her secret desire. Maybe now, if, as Allyn had said, 'men would be joining up,' there would be a few more jobs available in the cities.

In bed that night, taking the opportunity of Allyn's talk of war, Jessie shared with him her dream, leaving out the part of her getting part-time work.

"The city!" he exploded, bouncing to a sitting position. "Where would I find a job in Edmonton? And where do you think we'd live — with six kids?" He flopped back onto the pillow, turning his face to the wall. "The city!" It took him back to his early days of childhood in Edmonton. He'd started school there and had dreaded every day he'd had to trudge down the sidewalk to enter the gigantic doors of that school. He squeezed his eyes shut now to block out the memory.

Jessie was sitting up, hugging her knees. She knew her husband: she knew it was best to let things sink in before pursuing an argument—or discussion. Finally she ventured, "Actually, I was thinking more... of Calgary." She cleared her throat then continued. "Grandma, Bill, Claribel... they're all there... And what future is there *here* for us? For the children?"

Allyn bounced up. Copying Jessie in her knee-hugging position, he rested his chin on his knees. "Hm!" was all he said. He sat there for several minutes, not moving—scarcely even breathing. Suddenly he jumped out of bed, went to the kitchen and lit the lamp.

A half-hour later, since Allyn still hadn't returned to bed, Jessie too went to the kitchen. She found him with his head resting on his arms, his Bible open to Psalm 32. Verse 8 was underlined with heavy blue marking: "I will instruct thee and teach thee in the way which thou shalt go, I will guide thee with mine eye."

Sitting down beside him, placing her hand on his shoulder, Jessie shared with him her verses from Habakkuk, which had kept her buoyed up all summer. "I've been praying for months for some kind of change in our situation," she said, going to the stove to make a pot of tea.

When Jessie brought the teapot to the table, Allyn grabbed her hand. "I *could* try getting back on with the CPR," he said. "But you know their policy: once you quit, they won't take you back on. But maybe now with the war—" He squeezed his eyes shut for a moment. "Let's ask God for a sign," he said, popping them back open again.

"God says that He will guide us with His eye," Jessie said, pulling her hand free of his to pour the tea. "So let's keep our eyes on Him. That's sign enough. He'll show us what to do." She believed more in conviction and deep inner peace than she did in signs; but she knew that Allyn needed the comfort of a sign, something like Gideon.

Together they bowed their heads. After a short prayer Jessie continued, "I believe God will take us out of here before winter. I hope so—but that's not important."

"Well, I know one thing for sure." Allyn shoveled sugar into his tea. "My Sunday school work will be over, the way everyone around is talking about joining up, going to war. Don't know if there's any truth in it, but—" He took a gulp of tea. "But I've done all *I* can here anyway."

A month later Allyn came home from town waving a letter. "From my brother, Bill," he called, still yards from the house. "It's our sign." Puffing, he entered the shack. "It's our sign. He sent us some money. Says, 'Just wanted you to have this. Tho't you could use it. Not much, but all I could spare.'"

Jessie smiled as she lifted the eight dollars from between Allyn's extended fingers. *Eight dollars! All the sign my husband needed.*

It was six o'clock. Jessie tiptoed into the bedroom and planted a kiss on each of her six sleeping children. Passing the crib on her way out, she dropped a second kiss onto the baby's forehead, swiping at the moisture in the corners of her own eyes. Back in the kitchen she stood looking long and hard at her husband, wanting to say something to him but not knowing what. He was dropping sticks of wood into the stove, sending a shower of sparks to the ceiling. As the ashes settled back onto the stove, the cupboard, the table, and him, he turned and glanced at her, then jerked his head away.

She picked up her bags and stepped out into inky-blackness. The crisp October morning threw its clammy cloak around her: she shivered.

Crunching through frost-stiffened grass and leaves, she stopped at the gate, turning to look for a final time at the place she was leaving behind. "It still looks like a friendly, vacant-minded man," she mused, feeling the suggestion of a smile pull at her lips. "But now it has a soul."

The smoke belched from the rusty stovepipe; light from the flickering lamp tossed shadows through the frosty windows, shadows that Jessie knew to be her children, up now for their day. In her imagination she could hear them calling, *Come back, Mama. Come back.* Her heart quivered: she wanted to go back, back into the warm shack, back to the comfort of her family, back to—

She wanted to forget the whole thing: how could she leave her children? She swiped at the tear that had trickled down her cheek. Then, turning abruptly, she threw back her shoulders, took a deep breath, and walked away. Her head was flooded with memories: memories of sorrows, joys, trials and triumphs, memories that formed the soul of the house she was leaving behind.

As she passed through the tiny town of Meanook, she saw a light flicker on in a house, a lantern swing. A whiff of frying bacon and perking coffee coming from one of the houses gave her a warm, but sad, feeling. These people, behind these doors, had been her neighbors, kind, but distant. Many of them had been in her home, she, in only a few. And she would never see these folks again. Her heart lurched. How could she do this—walk away? But what choice did she have?

She walked on.

A couple of cats dashed across her path, tangling seconds later with spine-chilling screams. She shivered. The distant yipping of coyotes, the nearby howl of local dogs, the lonely hoot of owls in the trees, all added to the turmoil of her mind. A fall fog floated in and out of the trees, touching her face like clammy fingers. With the fog, came snatches of conversation she'd had with Florence a couple of months back: *Why?* she had asked, looking around at the frugal surroundings. *Why did you choose this…? You had a career… How could you have thrown it away for… this…?*

At the memory of the sting her sister's words had left, Jessie's eyes misted. She stumbled on a rut in the road… She felt so alone, so lonely… And it was so dark. "Oh my dear sister," she said aloud now." If you only knew! If you only knew the half of it!"

She plunked her bag on the side of the road and checked her nurse's watch: seven-thirty. *"The traffic from Athabasca to Edmonton — if there is any — should be along any time now."*

She strained her eyes, watching for headlights. The bush beside her rustled. She started, her eyes darting in the direction of the disturbance. Putting her hand to her heart, she drew her eyes back to the north, continuing her vigilance. Another rustle diverted her attention, but this time she could see enough to recognize it to be a rabbit, dashing off into the bush. She checked her watch again: eight. She shivered in the cold.

The sky was just beginning to grow pink when she saw the headlights of a car. Her heart began to pound. Until this moment she hadn't considered the risk she was taking—a 37-year-old woman, hitchhiking on a lonely road. Was she crazy? But what else could she do? With only eighteen dollars in her purse—and no prospects of more to come; with a family of eight to relocate, what choice did she have? She couldn't afford the train. And *Allyn* certainly wouldn't have been able to find the family a suitable home.

She began to tremble as the car came closer. She stuck out her thumb. *Was this the way one did it when one hitchhiked?* She looked at the thumb sticking straight up in the air, like it was a thumb belonging to someone else—someone she didn't know. The car came alongside her, slowing, as if to stop. It chugged on by. Her heart sank. She began to shiver, this time from both cold and fear. She dropped her hand, her head falling heavily onto her chest. She closed her eyes to squeeze back the tears that were forming behind her eyelids.

The car stopped, shifted gears, and began to back up. Her eyes popped open. Her heart started its pounding again. She felt as if she had turned to a pillar of salt as the car came to halt beside her.

The passenger door swung open. A man's voice bellowed, "Lady! Don't ya' know the chance you'se takin'? Hitchhikin' on this road? Don't ya' know the kind of people what's out there? Hop in."

Jessie felt as if her knees were incapable of holding her up as she stepped onto the running board, and into the 1930 Ford sedan. She glanced warily into the unshaven face of the middle-aged man behind the wheel. Not only did he have a stubbled chin and a mass of frizzy, dirty-looking hair, but also his overalls were greasy, and he smelled of body odor and chewing tobacco. She sat tense, on the edge of the seat, wishing she were still standing in the cold.

"Where ya' goin' lady"? he rasped. Then, without giving Jessie a chance to reply, he added with a motion of his head, "Reach back there and fetch that there box."

Shaking, Jessie pulled the box over to the front seat and set it between them.

"Open it." He grinned, displaying a nearly toothless mouth. "It's grub. Bet you're hungry."

Recalling the words of reprimand to her before she climbed into the car, Jessie glanced again at the man. He was smiling, strumming a rhythm on his steering wheel. *I guess he's harmless,* she said to herself, letting out a volume of breath, *despite his physical appearance.* Opening the lid to the lunch box she clutched the thermos, pouring out two cups of sweetened, black coffee. Normally, she hated sweet coffee, but as the hot liquid trickled down her throat, she thought she had never tasted anything better. She sat back in the seat, relaxing her cold, aching body.

PART II

Prologue

September 1951

She sat cross-legged on a chair by the kitchen door, swinging her leg back and forth. A tear slithered under her horn-rimmed glasses, trickled down her cheek and into her mouth as her mind reviewed her years in this house, the house that her husband had built: a slant-roofed, two-room mud-plastered shack, with a pre-fabbed-barn addition, and gable windows jutting from each side of the peaked roof. Her eyes roved the room, the room that had her touch to it: her oil paintings hanging on the walls, her embroidered runners edged with tatting covering the chiffoniers, a doily she had crocheted and edged with tatting, gracing the top of the dome-shaped radio.

The children rumbled down the stairs. Quickly swiping her hand over her eyes she turned in their direction. *How can I say goodbye?* she thought. *It sounds so final.* Would she ever see them again? Or would she ever again talk face-to-face with her eldest daughter, now so far away?

She watched, as her husband grabbed his cap, stepped into his rubbers, and slammed out the door. She watched, as three of her children picked up their bags and followed him. She watched, as her two youngest stood by the window, waving goodbye to the group. She could feel the lump in her throat swelling. *What was to become of her children?*

She felt as though she were being enveloped by a fog; her head begin to reel. Her mind slipped to the visit she'd had a month ago with her sisters and brother: "Why?" they had asked her, "when you had so much talent, did you choose to throw it all away...? Throw it all away... Throw it—" The sting of their words still rang in her ears.

"'Why?' indeed!" she said aloud now, kicking at a cat toy as she rose slowly from her chair. *Oh, my dear, dear brother and sisters, if you only knew the half of it. If you only knew!* Her shoulders slumped. Her eyes blurred. She stumbled on a shoe in the middle of the floor on her way to her bedroom to dress. *How could she do this? How could she leave her children?* –

Chapter I — Surprises in Store

November 1939

She forced her eyes back to the two-story house in front of her, pushing at the gate. It fell from its hinges onto a pile of decayed boards, once a sidewalk. Through a tangled mass of weeds and snow-sogged wisps of uncut lawn grass — hiding broken boards, garbage, and discarded toys — she picked her way to the door. While struggling with the rusty lock her eyes scanned the tattered screen on the full-length veranda, the diagonal crack across the front window, and the peeling paint on the broken shingles.

When she had fought her way past the labyrinth of cobwebs just inside the front door, dank and musty air invaded her nostrils. She stood gaping. How long had this place been vacant?

For two weeks Jessie had searched for a feasible place to rent and had jumped to the phone when she had read the ad: *Large, furnished, three-bedroom, two-story house for rent; spacious kitchen, roomy living area. Apply...* But now, standing in the hall, her eyes adjusting to the dim light and her nose to the smell, her body gave an involuntary shudder.

"Well what did I expect for eighteen dollars a month?" she said aloud. Placing her handkerchief over her nose, she proceeded down the hall to look at the rest of the house. She was here; she'd paid the rent; she'd make the best of it. As she mounted the steps she could hear the scurry of hundreds of tiny feet. *Mice!*

With the little finger of his left hand Earl Smith lifted the lace curtain of his living room window. "Why did I ever let myself get talked into this?" he growled, dropping the curtain to check his watch. He glared at his brother.

Henry shifted from one foot to the other, twisting his cap in one hand and jingling the car keys in his pocket with the other. His eyes dropped to the floor.

"Five minutes to seven." Earl shook his watch, wound it, and then placed it to his ear. "What time did you say they were coming?" He lifted the curtain again, squinting into the blackness of the mid-November morning. Just barely, he could make out the outline of the utility trailer (piled high with ungainly furniture, and covered haphazardly with a tattered tarp tied down with binder twine and haywire), which was attached to his immaculate Essex sedan. His lip curled.

He and Hank had bought the car four years ago — new — and had both treated it like it was their baby.

"Why did you get us into this?" he growled, turning again to his brother. "Where *is* that guy we're supposed to be taking to Calgary, anyhow? And six kids, you say? You must have been mad!"

Hank pulled his hand from his pocket and began twisting his cap with both hands. "Well... we... we wanted to visit our sister," he stammered. "And he *said* he'd pay for the gas. Besides, I... I... ah, I saw the children. They're... they're—"

"Here they come." Earl dropped the curtain and headed for the car.

Picking up his valise. Hank switched off the light, pulled the door shut behind him, and padded after his younger brother.

"They'll be so tired when they get here," said Jessie, amidst a yawn, as she climbed the stairs to turn down the beds. Her heart skipped a beat. It seemed so long since she'd seen her family. Back downstairs she whistled as she swished her dust cloth for the dozenth time over the oak dining room table, checking again to make sure that the seven high-backed, padded oak chairs and one matching captain's chair were precisely in place. She scanned the room, satisfied with the result of the scouring that she, Grandma Splane, and her friend, Mana, had done.

How majestic her Mason Risch would have looked in this room! She sighed a nostalgic sigh. But her piano was gone, long gone. Gone to pay for Allyn's Bible school training.

The 1935 Essex purred down the Edmonton-Calgary highway at thirty-five miles an hour. Hank was behind the wheel, Earl beside him, stoically enduring the chatter of the man on his right. The baby sat on her father's lap, mouthing a jam sandwich. The five children, squeezed into the back seat of the car, intrigued by their first car ride, or eager to see their mama, or lost in a book, added no extra stress to the brothers. However, when the baby flashed Earl an impish grin and offered him a bite of her mucky sandwich, he cringed, and his lips curled. "Can't you make this thing go any faster?" he snarled at his brother. He shoved the baby's hand off his knee, throwing a scathing look toward the father.

Hank gripped the steering wheel tighter, putting a little more pressure on the gas petal.

Jessie tapped her watch, putting it to her ear. *Whatever is keeping them?* She could feel the tendons in her neck tightening. *Nine-thirty! They've been on the road since seven this morning.* Dropping into the recliner chair and pushing it into the recline position, she closed her eyes.

Midnight. An explosion in Jessie's head brought her to a sudden upright position. Her heart was pounding; she stared wildly around her.

Three girls raced past her, running up, then down the steps. "Stairs! We're rich!" Evelyn squealed, first to reach the bottom. Only a few times had she seen houses with stairs. Anyone affording such luxury *had* to be rich.

"And flat walls!" Helen rubbed her hands up and down the smooth surface. "We *must* be rich." Lumpy, mud-plastered, whitewashed walls were all she had ever known.

Clara, a dreamy smile spreading over her face, ran her hand over the shiny oak table as she scanned the rest of the room.

Her heart still pounding, Jessie rubbed her eyes, rose slowly, grabbed her sweater and a flashlight, and went out to the car.

When Allyn heard her voice he crawled from beneath the car, scrambling to his feet and giving her a bear hug. "Had a near-accident at Lacombe," he explained, swinging her around. "Hitch broke. I cried out, 'Oh, Lord, save us,' and that instant the car righted itself. It was a miracle!" He removed his cap, gave his forehead a swipe, and then continued. "I fixed it, but—" He turned and grinned at the men. "These good brothers insisted I ride out back on the utility trailer to watch it—" With that, he clamored back under the trailer to finish undoing the haywire he had wound around the hitch to hold it together.

Haywire Splane — her husband's well-deserved nickname. A smile crept across Jessie's lips. What couldn't be fixed with haywire couldn't be fixed, according to Allyn.

Jessie stooped to lift the sleeping baby from the car, touching the awkward bandage on her foot. "What happened here?" she asked, crouching to talk to Allyn.

"Rusty nail." Allyn shoved himself from under the car, grabbing his tools and flashlight.

"Oh, by the way," he said, "I sold the lumber from the floor and ceiling of the shack to a guy for eight bucks. Paid for the trip." He turned abruptly to the Smith brothers, who were already climbing into their car to make their escape, thanking them again for bringing his family down.

"You take Marianne," Jessie said to Allyn. Cradling Pauline against her neck, she reached into the back seat and took her sleepy son by the hand. "Come on, my boy, let's go see our new house.

"What about Lily?" asked Jessie, as the group headed for the house. "What did you do with the cow — and Buddy?"

"Gave her back to Emma. Gave her the cat, too. Lily dried up, you know. Her milk got less and less the last couple of weeks. Just like she knew we didn't need her anymore. Almost four years she gave us milk, and never once freshened."

Meanwhile, inside the house, the girls explored.

"Come on. Le'me show you something." Clara tossed her head in a knowing way, proud of her city knowledge. She led her sisters into the bathroom. Flushing the toilet, she lifted the seat. Evelyn and Helen dropped simultaneously to their knees, bumping heads as they hung over the toilet bowl.

"Where's it go?" Helen put her hand into the toilet drain, feeling the swirling water. "Do 't ag'en. Do 't ag'en," she squealed.

"That's nuthin'." Clara waved her hand. Having been at Grandma's many times in her young life, she knew where to find the bathroom wonders that would make her little sisters' heads swirl. "Wait'll you see this!" She flipped aside the curtain.

"What's that?" Helen's hands flew to her mouth.

"A bathtub, silly." Evelyn pushed her younger sister aside to get a better look. "I 'member. Aunt Bell had one o' these."

"How... how can they dump it?" Helen's face rumpled into a puzzled frown.

"They don't, you goose. Watch." Clara turned on the taps, watching her sisters staring wide-eyed at the water pouring from them. She turned the taps off and reached for the drain plug. For the second time the younger girls bumped heads as they dropped to their knees to watch the water swirl down the tiny drain.

They were still discovering amazing things — like real toilet paper in a dispenser (instead of an old catalogue hung by a string on a nail in the outhouse); and real cupboards built into the wall; and a mirror where they could see themselves from head to toe — when their mother called the family into the kitchen for a snack.

Helen watched her mother take a quart of milk from the icebox. Her eyes grew big. First the stairs; then the front porch, that Clara had called a *veranda*; then the toilet; then the big bathtub, where the water swirled down a tiny hole; then milk in a funny bottle from a box in the kitchen! But when her mother turned off the gas burner of the stove, her eyes nearly popped out of their sockets. A fire that disappeared when you turned a knob? This was too much! Too much! She flopped onto a chair at the table.

Alfred stood with his head tilted toward the ceiling, his mouth open. His dad had just come from the bathroom and had flicked off the light. The little fellow ran toward the darkened room, gazing up to where the light had been. "Daddy?" he asked, gawking at the light bulb. "How did the light get up there? And where'd it go?" His head dropped back again.

"By a switch. See?" Allyn showed him how the switch worked.

"Is there a pipe to take the light up there?" The five-year-old ran to the switch on the kitchen wall, flicking it off. The light disappeared. He pushed at the switch again. The light re-appeared. No match! No lamp! He stood staring back and forth from the ceiling to the light switch.

The parents exchanged amused smiles. Oh, what a lot of surprises were in store for their children!

After their midnight repast, instead of going to bed as Jessie had expected they would, the children investigated every nook and cranny of the rambling house, from the dust-choked attic, where the mice skittered out of sight, to the spider-infested crawl-space in the cellar. The full-length veranda, they used for a racetrack. Never in all their combined imaginations could they have thought there could be so many wonderful things or so much space in one house. It was nearly 2 a.m. before their parents could coerce them to their beds.

Chapter 2 — Adjustments

November 1939 - 40

"No jobs to be had. Nothing." Allyn shoved the paper aside, dropping his head onto his hands and letting out a half-groan, half-sob.

"Here's something," said Jessie, after scanning the ad section of the paper her husband had just cast aside. "Not much, mind you, but it's something."

He grabbed one side of the paper. She pointed: *Be your own boss; sell Lee Products; no previous experience necessary; work your own hours. Contact...*

"You've had selling experience." Jessie tried to sound consoling when she saw the look of disappointment on her husband's face. "You sold life insurance once. Remember?"

"Lee products! *What* are Lee products?" He jumped up and went to the stove, turning on the gas burner, then striking a match.

"Allyn!" Jessie sprang to the stove. "Light the match first. Do you want to blow the place up? Here." She brushed her husband aside. "I'll make the tea."

"I don't have a car. How can I — ? What *are* Lee products, anyway?" Allyn stirred his tea, absently dipping his wet spoon into the sugar. The couple drank their tea in silence.

Early the following morning Allyn was again scouring the newspapers for work when his eyes fell on an ad: *Do you want a fulfilling career...? See the recruiting officer... between the hours of...* He dropped the paper and disappeared into the bedroom, returning ten minutes later, dressed in his Sunday best. He grabbed his cap from the hook and his bicycle clip from the table and dashed out the door.

With his cap stuffed into his back pocket and his application clutched in his hand, Allyn stood in a long queue of men, waiting his turn to be interviewed. His knees knocking against one another, he watched the facial expressions of the recruits as each one left the interview booth: *Dejection? Elation? Disappointment? Anger? Relief?* What would his reaction be when it was his turn?

"NE-XT!"

Stepping into the booth, not sure that his knees would hold him up, Allyn swallowed, feeling as if his Adam's apple would choke him. He handed the officer his application.

"Splane. John, *Allyn*, 5' 6", 145 pounds; Health, excellent."

"Hm!" The recruiting officer scanned the application, then eyed the recruit in front of him. His penetrating green eyes bored holes into Allyn's sky-blue ones. "What experience have you had, Splane?"

"In what?" Allyn muttered, shuffling from one foot to the other, his eyes searching for a safe place to rest.

"*SIR!* It's *SIR*, to you," bellowed the officer. "In anything. What have you done with your life for the past twenty years?" His voice made the pictures on the wall vibrate.

"Well... sir... I... worked ten years on... the Canadian Pacific Railway, as a tender truck repairman... in—"

"That was ten years ago," snapped the officer. "You *have* that on your application. What about the last ten years? What do you have to offer the army, Splane?"

"I'm... I'm willing to do anything... sir."

"Have you a family, Splane?" The officer glanced back to the application. "That part, you left blank."

"Yes, sir. I.... have... a wife and children."

Again, the man glanced at the application. "Age 39; Education, Grade 11..."

"How many? How many children? How old?" He rose part-way out of his chair, his face almost touching Allyn's.

Squeezing his cap, which he had been twisting around in his

hands, Allyn shut his eyes and blurted, "Ten, nine, seven, three — No. Ten, nine, seven, five, three, and one."

He jumped; his eyes popped open; he dropped his cap. The officer, with a bang that sounded like a gun being fired, stamped Allyn's application. He shoved it across the table, with a glare that sent Allyn withering from the room.

Rejected! Rejected! Rejected! The words hammered in Allyn's head and gushed out his ears with each push of his bicycle pedals on his way home.

Monday morning, with his bicycle carrier loaded with spices, liniment, flavoring, ointment, brushes, cough syrup, etc., Allyn, his face grim and his jaw set, pushed his bike away from the house. He was off for his first day of selling *"Lee products."*

"We just can't do it. We can't make a living at this." Allyn slammed the account book shut, brushed his head with his hand and moaned. He had been tallying the proceeds of his first week of selling. "Five dollars and ten cents net profit for six, twelve-hour days. That for a month, won't even pay the rent, let alone put grub on the table and shoes on the kids."

Jessie pulled the book toward her, scanning the figures. She went to the stove; and while she waited for the kettle to boil, she watched her husband rolling his head back and forth on his hands. *Whatever happened to my carefree, optimistic husband?* She pursed her lips, puckering her brow.

"Next month is Christmas." She poured out two cups of steaming tea and sat back down beside her husband. "Maybe sales will pick up — with the Christmas cards you've got to sell. And besides, I've several sewing projects on the go now." She rubbed her hand across her husband's shoulders, forcing herself to smile. A twinge — just a twinge — of guilt flashed through her: it had been her idea to move.

"I... I guess we're all having a bit of trouble adjusting to this new life," she said, removing her hand from her husband's shoulder. "The girls, at least Evelyn and Helen, are not having too easy a time at school, either. Helen cried all her first day. The teacher had to send for Clara."

"Why? Why was she crying?" Allyn's head popped up. He'd been out ringing doorbells until nine every evening. He hadn't seen the children, except for a short time at breakfast. And then he didn't feel like talking, knowing what he had to look forward to for the day. "What was she crying for?" he asked again, suddenly forgetting his own anguish.

"I never really did find out." Jessie took a swallow of tea, which she'd let get cold. "She said her eye was sore; but I really think she was scared and lonely, being in a classroom with so many children—and without her sisters, for the first time since she started school. And the work, too. The school is months ahead of that little one-room, nine-grade Meanook School. It's a struggle every day to get her—and Evelyn—out the door. Their looks of terror and panic nearly rip my heart out. Clara has adjusted, of course."

Allyn jumped from the table, running up the stairs two at a time. He dropped to his knees by the girls' bed. "Oh, God," he moaned. "Help us. Help us all."

It was one o'clock in the afternoon. Jessie had just bundled Alfred and Marianne up, shuffling them outside for some fresh air. Pauline, she had put down for her afternoon nap. "Now," she sighed, brushing the palms of her hands together, "maybe I'll get somewhere."

She had been having difficulties fitting the sleeve into the suit jacket she was working on. "Only two weeks 'til Christmas. I just *have* to get Mrs. Phillip's suit finished."

She had just begun to sew when she heard the thump of Allyn's bike hitting the side of the house.

"What!" What's he doing home so soon?"

"Mama!" Allyn burst through the door, the children following him. He tossed his cap onto the dining room table. "Mama! Praise the Lord! Praise the Lord! Good news! Good news!"

"You kiddies go on back out," Jessie called. "You haven't been out ten minutes. Play on the veranda if you want."

"I visited Gramma today." He paused, rubbing his hands together then blowing on them. "Remember my old CPR foreman? Well, just yesterday, Mother was talking to his mother. They're old-time friends, you know."

Jessie didn't reply. She continued working on the suit.

Allyn went on. "She told Gramma that there's job openings on the railway because of all the men joining up, goin' to war. So, guess what

Mama...? Mama, are you listening?"

"'course, I'm listening." Jessie nearly choked on the pins protruding from her mouth. "Go on," she mumbled.

"I went to see the foreman right away. He took me over to the CPR office." Allyn jumped up, grabbing Jessie around the waist and pulling her to her feet. Pins scattered everywhere. He kissed the top of her head. "They hired me. I'm in."

"What! What do you mean...? I mean, when do you start?" Jessie unruffled herself from her husband's hug, bending to gather up her pins. She sat back down at the machine.

"In two weeks, right after the New Year. But—" He swung around and headed for the kitchen.

"'But,' what?" Jessie pushed back her sewing and followed him. "What? What is it you're not telling me?"

He filled the teakettle, dropped tealeaves into the pot and rattled two cups out of the cupboard, plunking them onto the table.

"Allyn." Jessie's voice was sharp. "'But,' what?"

"Well..." He squeezed his eyes shut, facing away from her. "The job's in...in Medicine Hat. A pipe fitter. Fixin' boilers, or sumpthin', on engines." He plunked onto a chair at the table, squeezing his eyes shut again.

"Medicine Hat? What do you mean, 'Medicine Hat'...? You mean—?"

"I'll... I'll have to go first," he put in quickly. "And... and send for the family later."

Everyone else was in bed. Jessie sat at the dining room table, a map of Alberta stretched before her. "Let's see." She wormed her finger down the map. "Medicine Hat, Medicine Hat... About forty miles from the Saskatchewan boundary, and very near the U.S. border, too."

Shuffling through a few books beside her on the table, she located Clara's school atlas. After looking in the index, she flipped to the page of information on the little city that would soon be home. Neither she nor Allyn knew anyone from there, and only once since she'd been married had she even heard the name of the place, until today.

"'Population: close to ten thousand,'" she read. "Hm!" she said aloud. "I wonder how up-to-date this information is?" She checked the date of copyright. "Oh well, close enough I guess. 'Industry: farming, gas plants, flour mills, pottery.' And...oh yes. I recall something about this. *'Redcliff.'* It has that big glass factory. It's only seven miles from Medicine Hat."

She read a few more tidbits on the "Hat" (as she had just now read was Medicine Hat's nickname): about the red cliffs where the clay came from; about the caves and coulees surrounding it; about the bad lands — with their "hoodoo" hills — just miles from the city; about the cactus; the sagebrush with its ticks; and about the rattlesnakes —

Her eyes began to droop. She shut off the light and crawled into bed by her sleeping husband. As she was dropping off to sleep, her mind reviewed what she had just been reading: how Medicine Hat got its name. The Blackfoot medicine man (or was it the Cree?) was crossing the South Saskatchewan River that winds through the area; he dropped his hat into the churning water; it was swept away. So the other side won. Thus, Medicine Man's hat became *Medicine Hat.*

"Quite the folklore!" A smile played at her lips. She floated from the fuzziness of pre-sleep into the unconsciousness of sleep.

Chapter 3 — Medicine Hat

1940

The yellow light filtering through the falling snow cast eerie shadows down the long wooden walkway to the train coach Jessie had been directed to. The baby straddled her left hip, and in her other hand she lugged a cumbersome suitcase. Her head throbbed in rhythm with her purse, which bumped her with each step she took. Halfway up the walkway she dropped the suitcase, turning to see where her children were. Clara, just behind her, was struggling to hang onto Marianne, who wiggled and squirmed, trying to free her hand. Helen was still back at the gate, her head back, her mouth open, trying to catch a snowflake. A stick in his hand, Alfred banged his way along the fence rail; while Evelyn, with the small bag she was carrying, was making imprints in the snow as she inched her way along.

"Children! Come along. We'll miss the train." Jessie's voice sounded shrill to her ears. "Hush!" she snapped at Pauline, who was fussing in her arm. She hastened her pace, forcing one foot ahead of the other.

"Evening, ma'm. Need help?"

Jessie felt the suitcase leave her hand. She jumped, tightening the grip on the handle. Beside her, appearing it seemed out of nowhere was a handsome young man in a trainman's uniform, who in the haze of the platform light looked seven feet tall. She shot him a quick sideways glance, noting the deep cleft in his chin.

"Name's Gallinger." He winked. "Dave Gallinger, friend of Bill Splane. He told me you'd be leaving on the train to the *'Hat'* tonight. Asked me to keep an eye on you, since I'm on this run. Looks like you've got your hands full."

Jessie shuffled the baby in her arms, "Thanks," was all she said to the young man, but she took an immediate liking to him; and in years to come, whenever he was on a stop-over in Medicine Hat, he was a welcome visit in the home.

"Think you can handle it from here?" he asked, after turning the coach seats on both sides of the aisle to face each other.

"Oh yes." Jessie smiled at her new friend. "You'd best be getting to your own duties now... After all, it *is* nearly midnight. They'll likely fall asleep immediately." She reached into her bag, pulling out a diaper.

She had just unfastened the first pin in Pauline's saturated diaper, when a screech from the other end of the car pierced her ear. She jumped, stabbing her finger on the pin. "Evelyn," she said, blotting away the blood, "watch the baby." She dashed to where Clara was fighting to bring Marianne back to her seat. As she was turning to go back down the aisle with the screaming youngster, she bumped into Alfred and Helen, who were dashing in and out between the seats.

"Get back where you belong," she scolded, shuffling them ahead of her. "And stay put."

Evelyn had no sooner finished pinning Pauline's diaper, than the toddler wiggled from her sister's grip, slithering to the floor and thumping her way down the aisle on her bottom, her style of crawling. Because of her infected foot of two months ago, setting her back to crawling, she had only recently relearned to walk. But crawling was quicker, and safer.

"One, two, three... six? Are these all *your* children?" A middle-aged woman in the seat ahead of Jessie puckered her brow, and then smiled.

"Yes..." Jessie let out a long sigh. "I'm afraid so. And I'm sorry if—" She plunked Pauline into the seat and sat down beside her. "I'm sorry if the children have—"

"My! How brave you are!" The woman's husband dropped one side of the newspaper he was reading. He shook his head, a half-grin on his face. "Marj here couldn't even manage one." He chuckled, hiding again behind his paper.

And from then on, until the children fell asleep, Jessie had two willing helpers.

"Re... ed... cliff." The conductor's voice boomed in Jessie's ears at five the next morning. She rubbed her eyes and straightened her hair, glad that the night of fitful sleep was over.

"Medicine Hat, next stop... All passengers for Medicine Hat..." The conductor smirked—it wasn't a smile—at Jessie. "Medicine Hat... next stop," he repeated and passed on.

The night before when he had taken Jessie's ticket, he had snarled, "Just 'cause you got a free pass doesn't mean you can let your kids run wild, disturbing folks, you know." He had glanced at the brood: Alfred, munching on a sandwich, flashed him an impish grin. Clara, her nose in a book, didn't even look up; Evelyn, with Helen fidgeting beside her, sat twiddling her thumbs; and the two little ones, by then, had fallen asleep.

Jessie had thrown the conductor a scathing look. With a toss of her head, she had replied, "I am *always* in *full* control of my children." But inwardly she had quivered. Had he heard of their misdemeanors of a half-hour earlier?

The conductor had then passed a surveying eye over the group of children, a fleeting smile crossing his face. "Yes," he had said. "Yes. I believe you are. I believe you do have control." Giving Alfred a tweak on his cheek, he had passed on down the aisle.

And now as the train crept across the bridge, then began its slowing process, nearing the station, Jessie glanced out the window. Ghost-like shadows, floating around hazy yellow light from the street gaslights, and the haloed headlights of a half a dozen cars waiting for the train to pass, filtered through the haze.

She lifted Pauline from the seat and nudged the other children ahead of her. As she neared the exit of the train, the acrid smell of natural gas invaded her nostrils. *All Hell for its basement,* came to her mind. She had just recently read of Medicine Hat's being described that way; and she could well agree with it, if her nose was any judge.

Almost before she realized what was happening, Jessie was sitting beside her husband in a taxi, the baby on her lap, and five sleepy children packed in the back seat. The drone of Allyn's voice mingled with the buzz of the motor, spun around in her head. And then the taxi stopped.

"It... it's all I could find," said Allyn, leading the family through a door and up a flight of stairs. "Nobody wanted six kids."

Jessie wandered as if in a stupor, from the kitchen to the living room and into the two bedrooms of the upstairs suite. After ushering the children into beds, clothes and all, for a few more hours sleep, she flopped onto the bed that was to be hers and Allyn's. "We'll talk later," was all she could manage to say before she fell asleep.

The front steps of the two-story house led directly onto the sidewalk. The houses on either side were so close, it gave the impression that one could reach out of the window and shake hands with the neighbors. The back yard was about ten feet square. And the folks in the suite below were elderly, with a mentally handicapped, adult daughter, who constantly wandered upstairs, all the while tapping her watch and asking, "What time is it? What time is it? Somebody tell me, what time is it?"

It was Saturday. For five days Jessie had searched the newspaper ads for a more suitable place to rent. Living in an upstairs suite, she knew would not work. How could she keep the children quiet? And how could she keep Amy downstairs where she belonged?

Since Allyn would be finished work at noon, Jessie left Clara in charge of the children and walked to town. She went into the first real estate office she saw.

"Yes. We do have one place for rent," said the agent. "But it won't be available until March." He reached under the glass and pulled out the description. "It's a two-story, older house, with two bedrooms downstairs, and three upstairs. But it's 'way out on Seventh Street, five blocks west of Division Avenue. And its—"

"What's the rent?" Jessie took hold of the piece of paper the man was reading.

"Just a minute, missus." The agent put his hand on her arm. "Just a minute. There are some things you should know about the place. It has plumbing, but no electricity. Everything's gas, both heat and lights. Your nearest neighbor is about seven long blocks away. I don't think—"

"How much?" Jessie looked into the man's eyes, while reaching into her purse.

"Fifteen dollars a month. The landlady's Mrs. Donnald. She's away, but will be back in June. She wants two months rent up front. But—"

Plunking fifteen dollars onto the counter, Jessie said, "This is for March; you'll get April's in two weeks."

She left the office with a light heart, the address and receipt for the house folded carefully in her purse. Instead of going home, she walked to the place she had just rented. The two-story house, with dirty white paint and peeling green trim, several cracked or broken windows, and an upstairs balcony, stood vacant and alone. She picked her way past a broken toy wagon, the frame of a tricycle, dog litter and other rubble, to the back door. It wasn't locked.

Her stomach heaved as she stepped into the kitchen. Putrid water lay in a pool in front of a broken icebox. Moldy bread (rejected, she guessed, by the mice), empty milk, pork-and-bean, and salmon cans littered the floor. The living room was no better. Stained wallpaper hung in shreds on the wall; stuffing from a non-existent sofa lay in mounds on the floor, accompanied by a shoe here, and a sock there.

Pressing her temples between her thumb and fingers, she scouted the rest of the house, mentally measuring the windows for curtains.

The bell above the door of the real estate office jingled. The agent glanced up, a look of surprise on his face when he saw Jessie.

"Have you *seen* that place you rented me?" she asked, before she had even reached the counter. "Have you seen it? I just came from there." She gave the man a brief description of what she had just witnessed. "You should be paying *me* to live in that place."

"I... I'm sorry. I tried to warn you, but I had no idea it was *that* bad." He opened the till. "You want your money back, I presume."

"No." Jessie placed her hand lightly on the man's arm. "But I want a month's free rent for cleaning the place up. And I want a key now — although, as I told you, the place was unlocked — so we can start cleaning. We'll take occupancy in March, like you said, but I want the rent I gave you today, to be for April; furthermore, fifteen dollars a month is too much." She smiled, softening her voice. "But that's not your fault."

"Tell you what, Mrs. Splane." The man began writing. He'd do anything to get rid of that Seventh Street house. It had been nothing but trouble ever since he'd agreed to look after it.

Paid in full, until June 2, read the receipt he handed to Jessie. "After that, you'll be responsible to the landlady. By then she'll be back." The man shook Jessie's hand, retreated into an inner office and closed the door.

Chapter 4 — "A Lot Of 'Splane'n"

February 1940

The weather was mild, only a few degrees below freezing, on that first Sunday in Medicine Hat. After the family had trudged what seemed like miles (it was actually a mile and a half) through falling snow, Allyn stopped in front of a building. The sign read: *The Church of the Open Door.*

"This?" Jessie wiped the snow from her glasses. She stared at the gray, narrow two-story building. "It's... a... house!"

Ever since their arrival in Medicine Hat six days ago, Allyn had talked about the little church group he had been attending, with Reverend and Mrs. Gunn, the ministers. "Yes," he had said, "they both preach. And Mrs. Gunn is as dynamic as her husband. Wait 'til you meet 'em."

Inside, while Jessie peeled off coats, hats, mitts, and boots, her eyes wandered around the room: a handful of people sat on straight-backed, higgledy-piggledy arranged, runged wooden chairs (which she was sure had earlier been in neat rows); the piano stood in the front left-hand corner of the room; a raised platform to the right of it, with a slender pulpit in the center. In the front row, on the right, sat a man and woman, their heads bowed in prayer. (No doubt, the "Gunns.")

Allyn nudged his family to the third row on the right, where eight chairs, as if waiting just for them, made up the row. While the red-haired young woman sitting at the piano played the prelude, a few more people trickled in, each one glancing to the row of newcomers.

Suddenly, the slender man Jessie had earlier observed in an attitude of prayer jumped onto the platform and began swinging his arms around. As if the resurrection had taken place, the congregation sprang to their feet: the service had begun. After a few animated choruses, such as: "Climb, Climb up Sunshine Mountain," and "Running Over," Reverend Gunn motioned the people to be seated.

"Now, folks," he began, in a voice that seemed to rattle the chairs, "today, we have a lot of *'Splane'n'* to do. Thanks to our brother here," he nodded in Allyn's direction, "our numbers this morning have almost doubled."

The congregation laughed.

"Brother Splane, bring your family up. Let's meet them."

With Pauline clinging to her neck, Jessie rose slowly to her feet and followed her husband. Clara bounded in front of Allyn onto the platform, while the others hung back, each trying to hide behind the other.

"We all know Al here—Mr. Splane," the minister began. "And now, here's his good wife." He shook Jessie's hand. "I understand you play the piano. Well, Margaret there," he nodded at the pianist, "will be glad, I'm sure, to share the piano playing with you."

The girl at the piano—and Jessie noticed now, that she was just a girl—nodded her head, smiling at Jessie.

"And this must be Clara, and Evelyn, and Helen…" He went down the line, touching each head.

Each member of the congregation stood, in turn introducing him or herself and welcoming the family into the group. Jessie's heart was warmed. No longer was she trembling in front of a group of strangers. She was standing in the midst of friends. It was as though they already knew the family—and perhaps they did. During the introductions, the memory of the "love-box" of many years before flashed into her mind. These were the anonymous donors of those gifts of love; she was sure of it.

Mr. Gunn (Jessie learned during the introductions that he did not wish to be referred to as *Reverent*) was a wiry, balding man, of about sixty. Exuberance, wit, and love bounced off him, and on to the whole congregation. His wife, standing now beside him, was rotund, her face like the moon on a shimmering summer night. When she smiled, her twinkling eyes disappeared, leaving only slits behind her wire-rimmed glasses. Earlier, when she had moved to her husband's side for the introductions, it had seemed more like rolling, than walking. And now as she gripped Jessie's hand and said, "God bless you, sister," her rich mellow voice enveloped Jessie, giving her the feeling of being wrapped in love. Jessie *knew* she was going to like Medicine Hat. And she already loved this congregation of friends.

Chapter 5 — The Singer Sewing Machine

February 1940

"Good afternoon, ma'm. The lady downstairs said you'd be interested in what I have here."

Jessie was sitting at the sewing machine making curtains for the house they would be moving to in less than two weeks. She jumped, turning to see who had entered the room. A middle-aged man, who had knocked on the wall at the top of the stairs, then had entered, began to undo a large carrying case.

"Who are you?" she said, slowly rising from her chair. "And I'm not interested in anything you may have. Please leave." She pointed to the stairway... "A sewing machine!" Her mouth dropped open when she saw what the man had in his case. "I have one." She held up the curtain. "And it has worked..."

"Oh yes," said the intruder, glancing at the hand-operated *Singer* Jessie was using. "And a good one, no doubt. But *this*..." he pointed to his wares. "This is a treadle machine. The rest is in the car. It has a cabinet and... and it's yours. Today. For only fourteen dollars down and seven dollars a month for two years." He glanced again at Jessie's machine. If you use that as a down payment, you..."

"I'm not interested in buying anything on time, and I certainly don't have the cash. Now, if you'll excuse me." She turned toward the bedroom. "The children are awake from their naps now. I have to see to them." She expected, with that dismissal, that the salesman would take his leave. But he left only long enough to snatch the rest of his equipment from the car. By the time Jessie had returned from the bedroom, her three preschoolers in tow, he had set up the whole package (how could he have done it so fast?) and was sewing on a piece of cloth.

He looked up and grinned at her. "See? Look at what this wonderful machine does." He held a ruffled strip of cloth in his hand. "This, and many more things. See this box of attachments?" He pulled out a drawer and lifted up the box.

Whether or not the salesman had Jessie's attention, he certainly had the children's. Alfred dove to the floor to examine the mechanics of the treadle; Marianne did her best to worm her way onto the salesman's lap, while the Pauline lunged for the cabinet drawers, yanking out the box of accessories, and spilling the contents over the floor.

Two hours later the salesman was still demonstrating the wonders of the treadle machine; and Jessie was still insisting that she could not, and would not buy. She had, however, made tea, and when the three older girls burst in from school she was sipping tea with the salesman. Time slipped by. The man remained. Before Jessie knew it, Allyn was pounding up the stairs.

"My husband's home. I've got to get supper on." Jessie hurried the tea dishes off the table, expecting the salesman to begin packing away his paraphernalia.

Undaunted, the man continued his demonstrations to Clara, Evelyn, and Helen, who watched, enthralled, at the tucks, hems, zigzag patterns, gathers, etc., which the marvelous machine turned out.

"Buy it," said Allyn, after Jessie had explained to him the persistence of the man. Then, in a voice intended for the salesman to hear, he said, "Buy it, so the man can leave, and I can have my supper." He winked at Jessie, kissed her and disappeared into the bathroom to wash.

So the contract was signed, and the salesman left. It was probably the hardest sale—albeit, perhaps the most interesting—he had ever made. But the *Singer Sewing Machine*, through the years, proved to be all he had said it was, and more.

Footnote: And the old 1940 model, Singer sewing machine, still stands proudly in Alfred's house; although it has since been converted to electric.

Chapter 6 — A Reason To Cry

1942

Swirling the cloth around the soap, making the squishy sound that she knew would make her little girl giggle, Jessie lathered Pauline's back and tummy. Tears trickled from under her glasses, mingling with the rinse water she poured over her child.

"Are you cryin', Mama?" The pupil of her right eye almost disappearing behind her nose, the 4-year-old squinted into her mama's face.

Jessie swung a fluffy towel around her little one and lifted her from the tub. Snuggling her face next to her daughter's as she sat on the toilet seat cuddling her, she thought how pretty her youngest child was, except for her eye.

Her mind flipped back to two-and-a-half years ago: a month after moving into the Seventh Street house, Helen had come down with red measles, followed in turn by the others, except for the baby. After the other children had recovered, Pauline had broken out with it. Since she wasn't really sick, she would not stay in bed, and certainly not in a darkened room. The darkened-room bit was just an oldwives' tale, anyway — in Jessie's opinion. According to the doctor, however, the measles had weakened the child's right eye.

Another tear splashed onto her daughter's head.

"Mama!" Pauline threw back the towel. "Mama, you *are* crying. Why are you crying, Mama?"

"Well, my little one." Jessie carried her to the kitchen and set her on the edge of the table, rubbing her head briskly with the towel. "There are a lot of reasons for crying. Some are sad, and some are happy." She picked up the green gingham dress with the little eyelet lace ruffle at the bottom, which she had made for her just yesterday.

Pauline lifted her arms, letting the dress slip over her head. She didn't need help dressing; she'd been doing it herself since she was two; but bath time was her special time with her mama, a time when she would have her all to herself. "Is yours a happy reason, Mama?"

"Yes. I s'pose." Jessie began brushing her little girl's blond hair around her finger, into ringlets.

"Why? Why are you crying happy, Mama?"

"Well," she gave her a hug, lifting her to the floor. "I guess it's because, because I have you all to myself." She tickled her under the chin. "Now you run and play. Tiggy's waiting for you."

She couldn't tell her little daughter the *real* reasons for her tears: last week Allyn had brought home a radio. "Now we can hear what's going on in the world," he had said, plunking the dome-shaped, two-foot-high tube radio onto the table and plugging it into the outlet. He had slapped the five-dollar radio permit to draw to Jessie's attention that he had, indeed, gotten one, as required by law.

Two hours ago on the news, Jessie had heard that the Japanese on the west coast (Vancouver, where her sisters, Carrie, Bell, and Gertie now lived) had been expelled from their homes, their market gardens, and their fishing villages, into detention camps in obscure parts of British Columbia and Alberta... For what? Just because Canada was at war with Japan? And because they were Japanese? But they *weren't* Japanese. They were Canadians, just like herself. It just wasn't fair. But then, war was never fair.

Yes. That's why she cried.

And a further cause for her tears—and she couldn't tell her little girl this reason either—(she swiped at another tear): the howl of her second youngest daughter just an hour ago, as her brother dragged her out the door for her first day at school, was still ringing in her ear. And the panic written all over her wee face as she left the security of mama and home, still haunted her. She had wanted to run after her, to bring her back, to enfold her in her arms, to keep her there forever.

She smiled mentally now, at the proud look on Alfred's face when she had said to him, "You look after your little sister, now, won't you?" He had flashed her a smile, revealing two crooked, half-grown front teeth, his freckled face reddening to match his brick-colored hair. "Don't worry, Mama," he had said, gripping his sister's hand.

"I won't let *anything* happen to her." And then they had left, Marianne howling at the top of her lungs, the syrup pail containing her lunch bumping against her leg with each step she took. As she had struggled to free her hand and run back to the house, Alfred had pulled her down the sidewalk toward the primary school, seven blocks away.

Yes. That's why Jessie cried.

"Mama." Pauline, having forgotten all about the discussion on the reasons to cry, was tugging at Jessie's skirt. "Mama, will you help me find some new places to hide? Tiggy knows *all* the places I hide."

"Yes, perhaps later, but you run along and play with him for now. I want to write a letter. You try on you own to find new hiding places. But you know, Tiggy watches where you hide? He doesn't shut his eyes like you do. That's why he finds you faster than you find him."

"That's cheating, Tiggy. Tiggy, you shouldn't cheat." Pauline shook her finger in her kitten's face.

Chapter 7 — The Victory Garden

1942

It had been such a long time since Jessie had written to her nursing friend, Mana. A wave of sadness swept over her: she'd lost contact with the others of the five-some friendship from her nursing days — Evelyn Kadey, Ida Huxley and Sadie Nash. They were all married, she knew; she'd received wedding invitations from them years ago, but of course, couldn't attend. But over the years, all but Mana had dropped out of her circle.

Sitting now, tapping her unopened pen on the table, her chin resting in her hand, Jessie scanned her memory for news she may have missed in the few letters she had written to her friend in the past two years. Her mind flashed back to the Seventh Street house, its trials and triumphs. She tried to close out the memory of the bitter battles she and Allyn had had with the landlady: how, when Allyn had changed the water tank from upstairs to downstairs for better efficiency, she had demanded that he change it back — he had refused; and how, when he'd dug a cellar without her permission, Mrs. Donnald had threatened to throw the family out — in the middle of winter.

She smiled a wry smile now, thinking of the time Marianne had stuffed her nose full of buttons. Jessie had had to rush her by taxi to the emergency ward of the hospital, after her own efforts to remove all of the buttons had failed. She thought, too, of another hurried taxi trip to the hospital, three miles from that house, when the wind had slammed the door on Helen's finger, almost severing the end. The finger was saved.

Another smile crept on to her face now, as she thought about the puppy that had *followed* Alfred home from school his grade one year. Oh how the children had wanted to keep that puppy. But she had insisted that it must belong to someone; it was wearing a collar.

"But, Mama," Alfred had wailed. "It *wants* to belong to me."

"Tell you what," she had said. "We'll advertise. If no one claims him, we'll keep him."

For four glorious weeks the children romped with the black-and-white terrier pup, whom Alfred had named *Spot.* Then one day, alas! The owner knocked on the door to claim the pup. Spot confirmed the ownership by his exuberant welcome. It was a tearful group at the supper table that night, Jessie remembered.

The recollection that the four oldest children had given their hearts to the Lord, while living in that Seventh Street house, came to her now like a refreshing breeze from heaven.

So, despite the cold and bitter winds that swept through the uninsulated, poorly constructed run-down house; despite the children's constant illnesses; and despite the termagant, Mrs. Donnald, the house on Seventh Street had left its happy memories. And now they had their own place.

Last spring, for twenty-five dollars, they had bought a lot on Ninth Street, just west of Division Avenue, diagonally across the street from *Connaught Elementary School.* Allyn had thrown together a two-room shack, and the family had moved in. Much to their delight, the four oldest children had slept in a tent in the yard for the summer. Then in September, Allyn had purchased a well-constructed, discarded barn, which he had had hauled to the lot. It became the shell for their present, four-bedroom house.

Although the house was not up to the standard of the other houses on the block, it was better than any other they had lived in since they had been married. And it was *theirs.*

Jessie smiled to herself when she reread her account to Mana of the *barn raising* they had had back then — one year ago now. (She had a habit of keeping carbon copies of her letters, to refer to now and then, as she didn't often get to write to her friends.) This is what she had written: *Early one Saturday morning, a couple of men from the CPR yard, where Allyn works, and a couple from the church, converged on us. With ropes tied to the flattened walls, within a matter of four hours the walls were up and fastened. It was time for refreshments. That was my job. I passed out sandwiches and lemonade.*

One fellow from Allyn's work, Mr. Novisky, said, 'What! No whisky?' He was joking, of course. Allyn takes a lot of that kind of ribbing from his fellow-workers. His nickname, as you may well imagine, is 'Preacher Splane.' But now, after that, the kiddies lovingly refer to the man as 'Mr. Nowhisky.'

The blended fragrance of roses, carnations, four-o'clocks, and a myriad of other flowers wafted through the house on the warm September breeze. Through the open door Jessie watched a sassy robin tilt his head, then pounce on some unwary worm. From where she sat, she could see just the tip of the *Blue Ribbon* attached to the sign: *Best Garden of the Block.*

It had been a struggle to plant the garden. With money she had earned earlier in the spring from sewing slipcovers for a four-piece living room suite, Jessie had bought the lot next to the one the house was on. She had paid fifty dollars for it, double the price of the first lot, a year ago.

"Tiggy!" Pauline scrambled after the cat. Tired of being dressed in doll clothes, he had escaped her custody, jumping onto the table. He stopped within inches of the open inkbottle, jolting Jessie's mind back to the letter she was writing.

She dipped her pen into the ink and continued her letter: *Since everyone seems to be talking 'Victory Gardens' these days,* she wrote, *I decided I'd use the extra lot for my 'Victory Garden.' Besides peas, carrots, tomatoes – the usual – I wanted flowers, lots of flowers. You should have heard Allyn's hue and cry when I told him what I was doing.*

'Flowers?' he said. 'Why not potatoes and corn? You can't eat flowers!'

'You've got potatoes and corn. All over the place,' I argued. 'I'm planting flowers.'

And that's just what I did. That's why I call it my 'Victory Garden': I was the Victor.

You can imagine my elation when I won the award for the best garden of the block! Allyn was pleased too. I know he was, although he'd never admit it.

Better than any award, though, was to hear passers-by remark, 'Oh, isn't it wonderful to see beauty in the midst of the doom and gloom of these war days;' or to hear, 'My! Look at those gorgeous flowers! Every kind you can imagine!' And once I heard, 'Now there's the garden of an artist.' It did my heart good.

Incidentally, my vegetables are abundant, too. What wonders a hose can perform! How well do I remember, in days gone by, carrying buckets of water from a well to pour on a garden, which in the end the grasshoppers ate.

We got a phone last week, the first on the block. It certainly has helped to advertise for work. Sewing is rather slow right now because of wartime rationing. But I can get all the housework I can handle, for thirty-five cents an hour.

Speaking of rationing. Of all the restrictions, gasoline, coffee, butter, sugar, etc., the hardest to cope with in our family is sugar. The children all inherited their dad's sweet tooth. The sugar coupons always run out before the week does. So I came up with an idea. I filled and labeled seven, quart sealers, one for each member of the family (except for me; I don't use sugar). After setting the jars in a row on the counter, I announced, 'The one with the most sugar left in his or her jar at the end of the week gets to choose what treat they'd like me to make.'

The idea worked well – for the three older girls. They run their own contest to see how little they can use. But Allyn and the three little ones – Allyn is the worst – go through theirs in three days. After the first week, though, I said, 'No borrowing.' Now they've learned to conserve. All but Allyn. I've caught him on several occasions trying to snitch from the children's jars.

As for getting back to nursing? Alas! I have been away from the profession too long. I checked just last week. It would mean upgrading and going through the final exams again. The cost is far more than I am able to scrape together. So for now, it's scrub board and scrub brush for me.

Well, I guess it's lunch time. Pauline is tugging at my dress. It seems the kitty is plain tuckered out. He's off some safe place having a sleep.

Come see us some time. We'd all love to meet your little girl. Your friend, Huddy.

Chapter 8 — "Train Up A Child"

Spring - 1945

"Where *is* that child?" Jessie went to the window, craning her neck in order to see the full length of the block. At first she thought she saw some activity at the corner, but after studying it awhile, she determined it to be only April fog floating around the streetlight. "Midnight! And she's not in. This has got to stop. It's the third time this week she's been out late. But *never* this late. It has just got to stop." She dropped the curtain, turning back to Allyn.

He sat at the table, rolling his head on his arms. "Oh, God," he moaned, "don't let the devil have our daughter. Oh, where did I go wrong? Where? Where?" A sob escaped with the last words.

"Daddy." Jessie touched his shoulder. "Don't blame yourself. She thinks because she's sixteen, and working, she can do what she wants. She thinks — I should have insisted she stay in school."

"Oh no, Mama. It's not your fault. She could have gone wild even at school. We saw it beginning —" He grabbed Jessie's hand, pulling her onto a chair beside him. "It's... it's that delivery boy... What's his name? He's the one that's led her astray."

"No, Allyn. Not him. Not anyone. Clara knows right from wrong. But let's not — Anyway, I know what I'm going to do. You go back to bed. You have to be up early for work."

"What? What… are you going to—?"

"Never mind. I'll let you know." She pulled the bedroom door shut behind her husband. Going to the chiffonier, she took out her writing materials.

In elementary school Clara had been an honor roll student. Popular among her peers, she had several like-minded friends who enjoyed biking, hiking, singing, and were interested in art. She sang at church, taught Sunday school, and enjoyed family and church activities. But plunged in with five hundred other ninth-graders from all over the city when she entered high school, she was like a gold fish in a lake full of carp.

At first she had mingled without mixing, her interests still keenly distinct from the majority of her peers. But soon her priorities began to shift. Her spiritual enthusiasm sagged. She began to balk when asked to sing; she made excuses for not wanting to attend church or family activities; she became moody and irritable. Her sparkle had gone.

"It's just a phase," Jessie had defended to Allyn. "She'll grow out of it."

At the beginning of October that year (a year-and-a-half ago), in order to help make ends meet, Jessie had hired herself out to do washing or cleaning by day, taking Pauline, age four, with her. Then during the evenings she did tailoring for clients.

In early November Clara had found an after-school and Saturday job as a clerk in a small grocery store. Both Allyn and Jessie had agreed that perhaps this outside stimulation was what she needed. She loved the work. Her jovial spirit revived, for a while.

One Wednesday in mid-January the following year, since the store closed Wednesday afternoons, Clara had arrived home from school about four-thirty. She threw her books onto the table, running outside to where her mother was hanging clothes on the line. "Mom," she said, picking up a wet towel and handing it to her mother. "I had a good idea at school today… Why don't I quit school? I could look after Pauline while—"

"What?! Why don't you, what?"

"Quit school, so I could help you—"

"I heard you the first time. Don't be ridiculous. You're not even fifteen. You couldn't, even if we gave you permission—which we wouldn't. Don't talk nonsense." Jessie turned back to the clothesline, pinning on the last sheet.

"I'll be fifteen in two months. I could take correspondence. I could help you. With what I earn, and by you not having to lug Pauline with you wherever you go—"

"Stop right there. I don't want to hear another word. You can't quit. That's all there is to it."

"But Mom!" Tears were near the surface. It wasn't usually like Clara to use crying as a weapon for getting her way. "I'd learn more by correspondence than I ever will in *that* school. All the kids ever do is fool around… and talk about boys." Now her tears were flowing in earnest.

Jessie went into the kitchen, dropping the stiff laundry she'd just removed from the second clothesline, onto the table. Clara followed her, wiping at her eyes. She began to help shake out the frozen towels, her composure slowly returning. The next minute she was chatting animatedly about how she and her friends, Joan and Ella, had foiled the nasty plans of a cluster of boys who had plotted a trick to play on one of the teachers.

"And what will happen when the boys find out that their joke backfired?" Jessie smiled, amused by her daughter's story.

"I dunno. Don't care, neither. Oh, Mom, *please?*" Clara's spirits plummeted again. "You *gotta* get me away from that school. I really could be a big help by taking Pauline off your hands and doing the housework and all."

Jessie looked at her daughter. True. She could be of help. But quit school? "Look," she said. "Just five more months 'til school's out, and—"

"Five months! M - o - m! That's a lifetime. *Please?*"

"Let's not argue about it any more. We'll talk it over with Daddy."

"Talk to Daddy? M-o-m! *Nobody* can talk to Daddy."

"That's enough now. Daddy will decide."

During the war many children dropped out of school to help their parents, for many reasons. So, by special permission from the school board, Clara dropped out of school six weeks before her fifteenth birthday, in order to help at home.

A month later, however, tired of being at home all day doing menial household duties, and entertaining a 4-year-old, and being denied correspondence because of her minor age, Clara took full-time employment at the grocery store.

Now it was fifteen months later. Pauline was in school; Clara was still employed at the grocery store; and Jessie still scrubbed floors, and did other people's laundry, and tailored for clients in the evenings.

She sat now at the table at twelve minutes past midnight, her writing tablet before her, waiting for her wayward eldest daughter to come home. "Well," she said, opening the plunger to her fountain pen and plunging it into the blue-black ink, "even if I have to scrub floors the rest of my life, I'm going to do it. I'm going to send Clara—and Evelyn—to Prairie Bible Institute in the fall."

Evelyn was in grade nine at Alexander High School this year, but unlike her older sister, she was shy, introverted, and submissive. She didn't enter into school activities. Setting her head toward home the minute school was dismissed; she never once looked back until she was safely in the folds of house and family.

Jessie began her letter. *Dear Miss Thomas:* She wrote to the secretary of the Canadian Sunday School Mission in Three Hills, requesting an application for her daughter to be a junior counselor at summer camp, reminding her of Clara's years of camp attendance. She mentioned the few difficulties she was presently having with her daughter. *But they are actually quite minor,* she amended in conclusion. She licked the envelope, stamped it, and began another letter. This one was to the Prairie Bible Institute, asking for information, applications, etcetera, for both the Bible school and the high school.

After sealing the second letter she went again to the window to peer down the road. It was now one-thirty. Through the still-floating fog, under the corner streetlight, she saw the silhouettes of two people in animated conversation. She watched until she saw them separate, one, whom she had determined to be Clara, heading the half-block toward home. She dropped the curtain, popped the letters into her purse, and headed for the bedroom. She'd talk to her daughter in the morning.

Jessie had learned through her years of child rearing with Allyn, that diplomacy, not dogma, was the best way of handling difficult situations, especially with her head-strong eldest. She had asked Allyn, knowing his explosive, impulsive nature, to let her deal with their daughter. *How* she handled the matter, only God, Jessie, and Clara ever knew.

IF YOU ONLY KNEW

Tears stood in Jessie's eyes as she waved goodbye to her daughter. She had said many goodbyes to her during her sixteen years, but this one was different: she knew that from now on whenever Clara came home she would be just a visitor. As she watched the train disappear from sight on that warm morning in late June, taking her daughter to Gull Lake Bible camp to be a junior counselor for the summer, Jessie knew that her oldest daughter was no longer a child. She had taken her as far as she could. The rest was up to her — and God. All she could do now was rest on God's promise: "Train up a child in the way he (or she) should go, and when he is old he will not depart from it." Proverbs 22:6.

Chapter 9 — One Bleak November Morning

Fall – 1945

November was *not* one of Jessie's favorite months. On this particular morning as she sat having her cup of *quiet tea*, (as she had once called it to her friend, Kathleen — it was a time just after the children had left for school, when she felt a need for quietness in her life), her eyes drifted to the window. Sleet slithered silently down the windowpane, settling in a sloppy slush on the sill. The branches of the tree in the neighbor's yard, each swaddled in a soggy silver sweater, slunk sullenly close to the tree trunk.

"Poor birch tree," said Jessie, "it's really weeping this morning. And I don't blame it!" Other drab November mornings of years gone by came to her mind, mornings she would rather forget; but they were part of her history. Her mood matched the weather.

As she sat now, tea in hand, she had one ear on the radio, listening to the first session of the *Prisoner of War* murder trials. The murders had taken place in July 1943, and July 1944, at the Prisoner of War (P.O.W.) camp on the south hill of the city. It had been a well-kept secret until recently. But now, since V.E. day, in May, the trials were big news all across Canada. The news matched her mood.

The mailman rattled the mail into the box; the front doorbell gonged; and the telephone rang, all at the same time. Jessie's day had begun. Snatching the mail, she ran to the phone, yelling, "Come in," to the front door caller. Shuffling through the bills, fliers, and personal mail as she answered the phone, she opened an envelope from Clara and Evelyn. The phone call was from Mrs. Johnson, setting an appointment for Jessie to clean her house at two o'clock.

The caller, standing just inside the door nervously twisting his dripping cap in his hand, while slipping off his toe-rubbers, was a young man Jessie had seen at church. Hiding her annoyance at the interruption, she dropped the letters into her apron pocket and invited the visitor into the living room.

Two hours later, an Electrolux vacuum cleaner richer, Jessie ushered the happy young man out the door. She had not wanted a vacuum cleaner. She had always insisted, "My duster and my dust mop have worked fine for me all these years, and they will continue to do so." But because of the young man's persistence, and because he was from the church and she felt sorry for anyone trying to make a living in such a manner, she had signed the contract and paid the ten dollar down-payment. The rest was to be paid in six installments.

"Now," Jessie sighed, closing the front door and giving her purchase a kick as she passed, "I can read my girls' letters." She'd had a few previous scratches from them during the month they'd been at Prairie Bible Institute, but they had been so busy settling in that their notes had been brief. This letter looked like a book.

Dear Mom and Dad: Jessie read Clara's letter first, smiling when she read, *The rules are strict. Evelyn is terrified that she may unintentionally break one. Me? I don't let them bother me. Since you were always so strict with us, I guess they just come naturally.*

"Strict!" Jessie snorted. "She should have had my dad for a father!"

Because I'm only sixteen, and actually too young for Bible school, I was put in the high school girls' dorm, Clara continued. *I'm really enjoying the subjects and the studying. It's so different from what I've known as school, 'til now.*

Remember the time Evie and I put out the tins to ask God if He wanted us in India and Africa? Way back when I was seven? Well, I wrote about that for my first English composition. I called it 'Water in the Tins.' Guess what? The teacher has asked to use my composition as a sample, in other years. Imagine!

And guess what else? Out of the two hundred and fifty who tried out for the radio choir, I was one of the twenty chosen. I was thrilled!

Gotta go now. I love it here. And I love you... Clara.

Jessie swiped at the moisture at the corner of her eyes as she began reading Evelyn's letter. Hers wasn't quite as long. She could sense the homesickness that oozed from between the lines; yet never once did Evelyn actually mention it. She told of her studies, naming the teacher for each; she mentioned how much more she enjoyed school at PBI, than she ever had at high school at home. *"I don't mind getting up in the mornings,"* she wrote. She ended her letter by relating how the Lord was meeting her in new ways and how determined she was to become a missionary in India.

Jessie sat rubbing the letters between her fingers, savoring them. Oh, how she missed her daughters! But she wouldn't want them home for all the world. She was glad — so glad — that God had directed her and Allyn to send them to PBI, the school that had meant so much to *them* years ago. *Yes,* she mused. *I'll scrub floors for the rest of my life, if it means —*

She was jolted from her reverie by the slamming of the door: the children were home for lunch. She jumped up to put the soup onto the stove.

The sun had come out; the sleet had vanished; the birds were chirping; and Jessie no longer had the November blues.

Chapter 10 — The Invasion

1946-1947

"You always seem so happy, Mrs. Splane," said Jessie's employer, passing the bathroom door and hearing Jessie humming.

"I am happy, Mrs. Nickel. I have a lot of reasons to be."

"Reasons? You do have children, don't you?" She laughed a humorless laugh.

"Yes. Six."

"Six kids, and you can sing? ... I have two." She stood with her hand on the bathroom door, watching Jessie. "Last night Tom— Well... never mind. At least my daughter's married now, but she gave us enough trouble. Don't you worry, Mrs. Splane? About... well, about what they're doing when they're not under your nose?"

"Oh yes, I worry. But not about what the children are doing. I know what they're doing."

"You know...? All the time?"

"Well... most of the time." She turned slightly, so she could see her employer's reflection in the mirror, yet keep on working. "My oldest two daughters are two hundred miles away, at school. And my third daughter is in grade nine at the high school—"

"At the High...? And you don't worry? Tom goes there, also in grade nine. Always in trouble; never gets home 'til— I never know what Tom will get into next... What about their spare time?"

"Spare time?" Jessie laughed. "The older girls live in a dorm at a Bible school — Evelyn's in high school there — and they *have* no spare time. Helen and Alfred are so involved with the church young people that *they* don't have time to get into mischief. And Alfred gets up at five to deliver papers; he has a second route after school. The younger girls are only eleven and eight… They all keep pretty busy." She looked up at Mrs. Nickel, feeling sorry for her. "Maybe having a lot of children, it's easier?"

"Hmm!…" Mrs. Nickel walked to the kitchen, pushing the teakettle onto the burner; then she went to the bedroom to get ready for work. She was a nurse at the hospital. By the time she got back to the kitchen Jessie was cleaning the cupboards there. "Week after week I've watched you work, Mrs. Splane," she said, pouring water over the tealeaves. "You're so thorough, so organized. You'd have made a good nurse." She laughed.

"I *am* a nurse." Jessie began replacing the dishes onto the shelves, wiping each one. "At least, I was," she said, as if to herself.

"You're what!" Mrs. Nickel stopped in the middle of pouring the tea. She plunked the teapot onto the table and placed her hands on her hips. "Do you mean to tell me you're a nurse, and you're cleaning *my* house…? Get down from that stool right now. And get back to your profession." She stood for several seconds just looking at Jessie. "Incredible!" she said at last, shaking her head.

Over tea Jessie explained the difficulties to Rene (upon learning that they were fellow nurses, her employer had insisted that Jessie call her Rene) she had encountered in getting back into nursing. "I can't afford the time off," she said.

"You just leave it to me. I'll fix it," said Rene. You can upgrade while working on the general ward at the hospital. Did you know that?"

"No. No one ever informed me of that."

"Well, you leave it to me."

"Meanwhile," said Jessie, getting up from the table and removing the empty cups, "I'll continue to clean your house — and anyone else's who asks." She laughed. "And thanks. I'd like nothing better than to get back to nursing."

The perfume of apple blossoms, the fragrance of lilacs, and the pleasantly pungent aroma of new leaves permeated the early June air.

This, and the newly learned possibility of getting back to nursing, gave Jessie a feeling of euphoria as she sat later that day reading a letter from the girls. "Only three more weeks and they'll be home." Her heart skipped a beat.

She jumped when she heard the thump of Allyn's bike hitting the side of the house. "He's home early. Wonder why?"

The screen door slammed behind Allyn. "Mama," he panted. "You know where we go for Sunday school? Skunk Island...? Well, I heard today that those poor people are about to be flooded out. I'm going down there to see how I can help."

As usual, whenever he was excited about something, he talked non-stop, giving no opportunity for questions. Jessie just listened.

Skunk Island, as it was referred to, was actually a small peninsula on the flats of the South Saskatchewan River, in the southeast corner of Medicine Hat. Here, a group of people, whom Jessie called, *The Hat's forgotten few,* lived in houses — or shanties — made of discarded scraps of lumber, metal, cardboard or wooden boxes, broken culverts, or anything else they could find. Their beds consisted of cast-off clothing, rotted mattresses, or whatever they could salvage from the garbage dump.

It was here Allyn, along with Jessie and some of the children, went each week to hold Sunday school. They would pack saxophone, autoharp, hymnbooks, and a few little "Gospel of John" booklets, into their 1929 Essex — used only on Sundays or special occasions — and chug down to Skunk Island. This was the highlight of the week for many of these folks, especially the children. Along with the Sunday school equipment, often there would be boxes of clothing (gathered by Jessie from clothes too small for her children, or from the neighbors), as well as groceries, homemade preserves, or toys.

Sleep had all but claimed Jessie when she heard the car choke to a stop in the yard late that night. Pulling on her housecoat, she went into the kitchen, setting the teakettle on to boil.

"Two families are flooded out," said Allyn, tossing his cap onto the lid of the wooden garbage box by the door. " And the river hasn't peaked yet. If it gets any higher, the whole place'll flood." Scraping a chair by its legs across the floor, he plunked it at the table and sat down. "Henry—you remember Henry—begged for my help. I told him he could bring his wife and kids, and stay in our basement. I knew you wouldn't mind. It'll only be for a—"

"When?" While pouring boiling water onto the tealeaves, Jessie gawked at her husband. "What about beds...? And cooking...? And bathroom?" Her face puckered into a frown.

"Mama, don't worry. You know they don't live fancy. They'll do like they do at their own place... throw mattresses or rags on the floor, and they have a camp stove. But... they *will* have to share our bathroom."

"When are they coming?"

"Tomorrow."

"Tomorrow? I have to work tomorrow."

"I know. I know. I told them that. I said they could go into the basement through the outside trap door. There's only six of 'em." Allyn trailed sugar into his tea.

"Oh me! Oh my!" Jessie dropped her head into her hands, a surge of burning indigestion hitting her, as it had been doing a lot of late, whenever she was upset. Her tea sat untouched. "I'm going to bed," she said.

It wasn't until she was within sight of her house on her way home from her cleaning job the following day, thinking only of pulling off her shoes and relaxing with a cup of tea, that Jessie remembered about the house guests. The activity in her yard had arrested her attention. Her hand flew to her head. She could see youngsters, at least a half a dozen of them, bouncing all over the place. Her eyes flipped to the trap door. Heads were appearing and disappearing through the opening, like popcorn. Slowly she approached the house.

"What! I thought he said six were coming. Six! Who are all *these* people?"

"Hallo, Mrs. Splane. I'm Henry." A tall robust man of about forty strode toward her, his hand outstretched. "I met you a few weeks ago. Remember? And this here's my brother, Ben, and little sister, Aggie. She ain't married. And this's Wilma, my wife." He turned, wrapping his arm around a giggling roly-poly woman, then continued; "and here's Fanny, Ben's wife... Thanks for openin' your home t' us... Oh," he added, as another couple popped up from the cellar. "This here's Mary and Charlie, Fanny's sis and her ol' man." Seeing Jessie looking past him, to the children flitting like flies around them, he added, "Oh, the kids... They'll make th'mselves known. Don't you worry 'bout that." He laughed.

Jessie's head was spinning. Wordlessly—she hoped at least she was smiling—she shook the extended hand of each one, as Henry's introductions proceeded. Then involuntarily squeezing her temples between her thumb and fingers, she fled to the shelter of her kitchen, where she flopped onto a chair.

Jessie could barely wait to leave the house every morning during the stay of the nineteen guests. After her day of scrubbing floors or washing windows for her clients, she dreaded returning home. She knew that her own floors would look like the barn after the cows had left; the bathroom sink would resemble the sink at the CPR round house; the tub would have a scummy ring around it; and every window in the house would be steamed and gummy. There wasn't an inch of the house that had escaped the guests' explorations.

The children—twelve in all, ranging in age from six months to twelve years—had climbed on every stick of furniture in the house. Outside, they had terrorized the chickens, strangling three of the four-week-old chicks. They had broken the fence, pulled the basement trap door from its hinges, and scattered Allyn's cement sand all over the yard. The garden, which until the invasion, had been doing nicely, had been trampled or pulled out. The '29 Essex, a favorite place for the children to rampage, had had every moveable wire yanked out, the air let out of the tires, and the steering wheel pulled off.

"Sorry you had to walk into such a mess," said Jessie to the girls, who had arrived home from PBI just the day after the visitors had left... "But am I ever glad your home!"

Armed with scrub brushes, hot soapy water, bleach, rags, and fumigant, Jessie and her daughters began what the girls called, "operation, invasion-mop-up." Not only had cast-off clothes, rags (no doubt used for bedding), rotting food, and human feces (some of them, it was apparent, hadn't bothered to use the bathroom) been left behind; but what was worse, cockroaches and bedbugs had taken over the basement.

"If I thought for a moment, that God's love had penetrated even one of those nineteen souls who spent the last three weeks under our roof, I would feel it had been worth it," said Jessie to her daughters, over a much-appreciated cup of tea they were enjoying after two hours of scouring.

"Every evening your dad played his sax for the children, sang, and read Bible stories to them, even sitting with them sometimes until they fell asleep, while the grown-ups went to town to whoop-it-up. We had forbidden either alcohol or smoking in the house, but we couldn't very well control what they did away from the place. Sometimes they would be away all night, then sleep away the next day." She stood up and carried her cup to the sink.

"Where'd they get money for their shenanigans?" asked Clara.

"Search me!" said Jessie. "As far as I'm concerned, we were just used for baby sitters — or taken for suckers!"

"Only God knows," Evelyn said. "Mom, Clara and I'll finish up. The kids'll be home for lunch soon."

Chapter 11 — To entertain Strangers

1947

"Be not forgetful to entertain strangers: for thereby some have entertained angels unawares." Hebrews 13:2

So it's no Mason Risch! Jessie hastened her steps as she neared her house. How excited her family would be when she told them the news! *A legacy,* she thought. *I guess I'll just have to consider the out-of-tune, beat-up old Schmidt — with one broken key — an extension of Dad's legacy. At least it's a piano!*

She had dusted the piano many times during the year she'd worked for the Nickels. In a dreamy mood one day recently, she had said to her employer, "I had a piano once—"

"You did? Do you play?" Rene had been an accomplished pianist at one time, but her life now was too busy, and too filled with problems; it had been years since she'd set her fingers on the keys. "What happened to it? Why did you give it up?" she had asked.

Briefly, Jessie had told her employer about the Mason Risch her father had given her, and how they had sold it so that her husband could go to Bible school.

The thought struck her now: *One hundred forty dollars, I paid Rene for it (and ten dollars for the delivery man tomorrow), the same price PBI gave me for my Mason Risch fifteen years ago.*

"And for my other news?" she said, hastening her steps even more for the last half block. "Allyn, at least, will be happy. Something I've waited for, for twenty years!"

She stopped at the door, her hand on the door latch. "A baby? That sounded like a baby." Cautiously she opened the door.

"Hi, Mom!" Helen jumped up from the floor, where she and her younger sisters had been huddled. "That's Richard." She pointed.

"Why... how come... here?" Jessie knew that her daughter had gone babysitting that morning, in response to an ad she had put in the paper, but here? "Does the baby's—Richard's—mom know you're here?"

"Yea, Mom, she said to."

Slowly Jessie approached the pallid baby, lying passively on a blanket on the floor. "How... how old is he?" To her, he looked far too young to be in the care of a child.

"Seven months," said Helen.

Lifting the baby into her arms, Jessie noted his sour-milk smell, his grubby rompers and the scaly feeling of his skin. His head flopped onto her shoulder. She lifted an arm then let it go; it flopped to his side. When she put her finger into his hand to check for his grip, to which there was no response, she saw his dirty uncut fingernails. She puckered her brow. "Are you sure he's seven months?"

"Yea, Mom. She said his birthday's December first. I always ask about ages."

"Yes. I know you do." She turned her attention back to the baby; he just wasn't right for seven months.

"Let's get him cleaned up and fed. Where's his food?"

Helen held up one empty baby bottle.

"That's all?"

"Yea. But we filled it once from our milk."

Jessie shook her head. "And his clothes?" She glanced down at the grubby canvas bag on the floor. "That's it...? Are you sure his mother said you could bring him home?"

"Yea, Mom." Helen let out an exasperated sigh. "When I knocked on the hotel room door the lady answered an' pulled me in, real quick. She just handed me the baby an' said, 'This is Richard. Here's his clothes an' his bottle. I'll be back at ten.' She picked up her purse an' was gonna' leave. That's when I asked how old he was. Then I asked, could I bring him home, 'cause you and my sisters would be here. An' she seemed kinda' glad. An' Mom... the hotel was dark and dirty... an' it stunk. I was... kinda scared to stay there... by myself."

"Yes, well, I'm glad you didn't. Let's get Richard cleaned up."

A few hours later Richard looked like a different baby. After bathing him, Jessie had rubbed him with baby oil, massaging his head to remove the scales and scabs. And while he slept, she had washed his clothes, which consisted of two pairs of rompers, one undershirt, and four grubby looking diapers.

"*Eleven!*" Jessie glanced at the clock, then went to the bedroom to check on the sleeping baby. Since ten she had paced the floor, checked the baby, then paced the floor some more, becoming more worried by the minute. Visions of the police knocking any minute at her door and arresting her for kidnapping — of course she knew they wouldn't — bounced around in her head. "Didn't you say she'd be back at ten?" she said to Helen, who sat at the table resting her head on her folded arms. "What did you say the mother's name was?"

Helen lifted her head, a dazed, half-asleep look on her face. "Huh? Her name? I... I don't... I didn't... ask... and she doesn't... I didn't... tell her my name, either. Only... only the telephone number on that ad."

Jessie sighed. "You'd better go to bed. You're *sure* she said — What was the room number? I'll give her 'til midnight, then I'll call the hotel."

It was five minutes past midnight. Jessie flipped the pages of the telephone book, looking for the hotel number. She had her hand on the phone when it rang. "Hello?" she said, grasping the receiver as if she were choking it.

"Is this...? Are you...? Do you...? This is—"

"If you're the mother of Richard... yes. You have the right number... *Where* have you been? Where *are* you? How could you—? I'm the mother of the girl you hired to baby-sit... She's only fourteen. How could you—?"

"I... I'm sorry. I... couldn't... ah... call. I... Please, missus. I'm real sorry. I... could you—?"

Jessie heard the choke in the woman's voice. "Is there a problem?" she asked, her voice immediately softening.

"Well... ye... es. Me and my husband... well... and I—"

"Look," said Jessie. She could hear the woman sobbing now. "Would it help if my husband were to come down and talk with you and your husband...? Would you like that?"

"Well... yea... maybe... okay... I... Room 211. And thanks. "

When the phone went dead in Jessie's ear, she thought, "The woman didn't even ask how her baby was!"

"I think they'll be okay now," said Allyn, returning from the hotel at six the following morning. "We talked and prayed all night. Then just before I left this morning they asked if we could keep the baby 'til noon. They want to have breakfast and talk things over, try to patch things up."

It wasn't until ten past three that afternoon—she was sure of the time, because she'd checked the clock every ten minutes since noon—that the phone rang again. Jessie lunged to answer it.

"Missus Splane? This is Irene," came a whiney voice on the other end of the line. The previous night Allyn had learned that Richard's mother's name was Irene Johnson and that she wasn't really married to the man whom she called "Mel,"—Mel Jones.

"Me 'n Mel... well, we wanna go to Grand Prairie," she continued. "Mel's got a job up there, 'n all." She cleared her throat. "But we got... no place t' go to; so we was wonderin', 'n all... would you'se be so kind, 'n all... to keep Richard?"

"Keep him?" Jessie frowned into the phone while looking over at the baby, who lay on a blanket in the middle of the kitchen floor, surrounded by pillows. He was staring at the ceiling, moving his head from side-to-side, as if studying his surroundings. He was much brighter, Jessie thought, than when he'd come to them thirty hours ago. "Keep him for how long, Irene?"

"Well... say 'bout ten days, 'n all?"

"Ten days? Hm!" Jessie hesitated. "All right, Irene. Ten days. But no longer. I work. And it's not right leaving an infant in the care of a fourteen-year-old." A mental picture of her tree-climbing tomboy, with her hair straggling loose from her braids, her dress torn, and smudges on her face, flashed before her, and to herself she added, *At least not my fourteen-year-old!* To Irene, she said, "Get back sooner if you can."

"Oh, I promise, missus. I promise. I really do. And thanks loads."

"Where — ?" The phone clicked in Jessie's ear. She groaned, a flash of anger tearing through her. Irene hadn't yet asked how her baby was. "Some kind of a mother! Poor Richard. No wonder he looked like he did when he came yesterday."

Still holding the receiver in her hand, Jessie thought about the news she had been so excited about yesterday, the news she had been so eager to tell the family. Well it would just have to wait now. She placed the receiver back onto its cradle and walked to the piano. She hadn't had a chance to look at it since it had been delivered four hours ago.

It had been well over two weeks and still no word from Mel and Irene. Jessie sat with the phone to her ear. She had just phoned the hotel where they had been registered in town.

"No," said the clerk. "We haven't heard from them. All I have here in my records is that they left owing two nights' lodging."

"No idea where they went?"

"No. But they left a suitcase. You can have it if you want... But you'll have to pay the fourteen dollars they owe."

Allyn retrieved the suitcase. Together they opened it: a couple of smelly, men's shirts, a cigarette package — *Players* — with one cigarette left in it, a pair of dirty socks, a tie, and a wallet.

Jessie opened the wallet: a torn theatre stub, a hidden penny, a stick of wrapped Wrigley's spearmint gum, and an outdated driver's license for a Mel Green.

"Mel Green!" Jessie handed the license to Allyn. He looked at it, turned it over, frowned, and handed it back to his wife.

"We've been had!" he said, slamming his fist into his hand.

Jessie went to the phone. She dialed the operator. "Give me the names and phone numbers of all the hotels in Grande Prairie, please."

Before beginning to dial the numbers the operator had supplied, she sat for a moment, her crossed leg swinging back and forth. She rested her elbow on her knee, her chin cradled in her hand... What would she do if she couldn't locate Richard's mother? She glanced at the baby. He was sitting on the floor — by himself now — playing with the eggbeater. He peeked up at her, his blue eyes twinkling. He flashed her a dimpled smile. Her heart welled with mother-love, which was immediately replaced by rage. *How can a mother abandon her child? How can she?* She turned back to the phone and began dialing.

"Yea," came the reply from the desk clerk of the third hotel Jessie called in Grande Prairie. "Yea—*snap-snap*—we 'ad a couple registered 'ere that sounds like it might o' bin your people—*snap-snap*. I 'member 'em well. 'adda go up twice't ta their room ta 'ush 'm up. The man, large, burly, bushy hair, dirty beard, 'ad a foul mouth, 'e did. 'is ol' lady, she was a straggly mousy kinda' woman—*snap*... Scream? She was screamin'—*snap*—like she was bein' murdered. Jist a minit. Gotta call on th' other line."

Jessie sat tense and rigid, relaying to Allyn the information she had received so far.

"'Allo agen—*snap*—" came the raspy voice with a sloppy British accent. She continued from where she had left off. "Then after th' screamin', dead silence—*snap*... Next mornin' thay was gone. Left owin' sixteen bucks, thay did—*snap-snap*—"

"What names did you say they registered under?" Jessie was standing now.

"Ay didn't say. But—*snap*—jist a sec. Ay'll check, 'ave to look back. Ah, oh, 'ere 'tis. Ah, Irene and Mel Janes? John? Oh, their writin'! Can't 'ardly read it—*snap-snap*—"

Jessie squeezed her eyes shut. If that girl snapped her gum one more time, she was sure she would scream. "What address?"

"Ah, address, address... hm? Don't see none. Wonder how—? Oh, no, 'ere. No... jist a phone number. 3697—"

"What? It can't be!" Jessie said when she heard the number. That's—" She was about to say, *"That's our number,"* but not wanting to be stuck with paying another hotel bill of theirs, she checked herself. "That's funny," she said instead... "Thanks. Thanks for your help." She hung up, giving her head a quick shake to get rid of the annoyance of the gum snapping, still ringing in her ear.

"This is a matter for the police," she said, turning to Allyn, who sat at the table making faces at the baby on the floor, and gulping down scalding tea. She gave him a full run-down of the conversation, minus the gum snapping, then turned back to the phone.

"And you'll be willing to keep him until we can locate the mother?" asked Constable Summers after hearing Allyn and Jessie's report.

"Well… not for too long," replied Jessie. "I'll be starting a job at the hospital soon." She glanced at Allyn; she hadn't told him yet… "Can you locate someone with that little bit of information?" she asked the officer.

"We'll locate her," assured the constable picking up his cap from the table and striding toward the door. "No matter how long it takes. We'll locate her."**1**

"I haven't got, *'No matter how long it takes'*," said Jessie to herself, leaning her head against the door as she closed it behind the officer. In just a little under a month she was to begin general duty at the hospital, taking up-grading courses on the side, to regain her nursing status. That was the exciting news she had had to tell Allyn the day the baby had come. She had kept waiting for just the right time, a time when she didn't have Richard to think about.

She walked now into the bedroom, peeking into the crib. "So cherubic-looking!" She let out a long sigh. He lay on his tummy, his legs tucked up under him, his dimpled hand curled close to his rosy cheeks. His dark eyelashes, a contrast to his sand-colored hair, lay splayed across his cheeks. "So different from when you came to us," she whispered, kissing him… Did God intend for her to be this wee tyke's mother? Was this one of His *"angels"* that she was entertaining, unawares? If so, what was His purpose? Tears formed behind her eyes.

"Oh, and I was so looking forward to—" As she brushed away a tear she felt her husband's comforting hand on her shoulder. They embraced.

Mrs. Ford, a middle-aged widow with one grown daughter, was nicknamed *Dolly* because of her large doll collection. Actually, Dolly herself looked like a doll—at least Jessie thought so. Petite, dainty, a mask of bright makeup, her hair dyed jet-black, she walked with small mechanical-like steps.

Jessie always looked forward to her once-a-month afternoon at Dolly's. She could hardly call what she did there, *work*. It took no more than two hours to vacuum and dust the small house, and to wash out the kitchen and bathroom, which were never really dirty. For the remainder of the four hours, for which Dolly insisted on paying her,

Jessie and Dolly would sip tea and talk. Today as they chatted, Jessie told her friend about Richard: how he had come to them, and of the disappearance of his parents.

"And what concerns me right now, Dolly," said Jessie, "is that I am to start work at the hospital in a couple of weeks. What am I to do with the baby? I refuse to give him over to the authorities, not knowing into what kind of a home he'd be going. He's such a sweet baby, and so very little trouble.

"The younger girls will be back in school in a day or so; and Helen, who got us into this, will be going *away* to school with her older sisters in about a week." She let out a deep sigh and took another sip of tea.

As a rule, during their chat-time, Dolly would pour a constant tale of misery into Jessie's ears, telling of her many illnesses and past misfortunes. But today it was Jessie who had done all the talking. Dolly sat tapping her slender fingers on the tabletop as she listened. Subconsciously, Jessie's mind registered the fuchsia nail polish on her employer's long fingernails, a perfect color-match to the loose-crocheted cardigan thrown over her slight shoulders.

Dolly leaned one elbow on the table, her chin resting in the palm of her hand, her brown eyes—usually dull and sorrowful—sparkling. A suggestion of a smile played at the corners of her rosebud, lipsticked lips, making the "worry-lines" on her face more predominant. Suddenly she broke into a broad smile, grasping Jessie's hand. "What would you think of me?"

"Think of you?" A quizzical expression flashed across Jessie's face.

"Oh, how silly of me," said Dolly. "I'm always doing that. My daughter tells me I always keep people guessing. I mean, what would you think of *me* being Richard's mother?"

"You?" Jessie gasped. "But your health."

"Oh, my health, pshaw!" Dolly flapped her hand. "Just the other day my daughter said to me, 'Mother, all you need is to find something to do to keep your mind off yourself. All you have to keep you busy are these inane dolls.' I was cross with her at the time, insulting my babies." She looked over to her rows and rows of dolls, all sizes, shapes, and colors, arranged around the living room. "But you know? I think she's right. Yes! I really do." She walked over to the dolls, picking up one she'd dressed as a little boy and carrying it back to the table. "I *do* need something more than these inanimate dolls—

much as I do love them—to keep my mind off my problems. Would you... do you think I—? Would you consider *me* a suitable 'mother' for Richard?"

Jessie clasped her friend's hand and smiled. "Dolly, the best. I would consider you to be the best mother in the world for Richard, judging from the looks of your present family." She waved her arm toward the dolls. "Yes, Dolly. I would consider you the very, very best."

Dolly set the doll back into its place and poured two cups of fresh tea. She lifted her cup in Jessie's direction and said, "To Richard! And to Motherhood!"

Standing by the crib that night, Jessie reflected on the many *strangers* she and Allyn had entertained, from the four boys of years ago, to the most recent, baby Richard. With a shudder she recalled the experience of three months ago, and those basement *strangers*.

Then with a warm feeling flowing into her heart she recalled the *strangers* they had entertained last year, how she had stumbled across the *tent* people. She had seen the Morrises at church. The next day, walking home from the store with a shopping bag full of groceries in each hand, her head down, she had stumbled into a tent peg. The tent was right in the middle of a shortcut she often took on her way home from the store. Just as she was about to veer around the tent, a lady popped through the opening.

"Excuse me," Jessie had apologized. "I wasn't intentionally intruding on your privacy... Say! Haven't we met?"

The young lady had scrutinized Jessie for a few seconds. "Yes!" she had said. "Yes, we have. At church on Sunday."

"Oh, that's right. I felt I wanted to invite you and your family over to the house, but we had an afternoon Sunday school; so I couldn't." Jessie had then taken another look at the tent. "Is... I didn't realize... Is this where you live?" she had asked.

"Won't you stop for a cool drink?" the lady had invited. It was over a glass of lukewarm lemonade that a long friendship between Jessie and Mrs. Morris had been born.

For two months, until the basement of their new place was finished, Mr. and Mrs. Morris, their five year-old son and three-year-old daughter had lived with Allyn and Jessie and family. A month after moving into their own basement Mrs. Morris had their third child, a daughter.

As Jessie stood now, looking at Richard, a surge of warmth flowed through her. "Yes," she said. "Dolly will make a wonderful mother to you, our latest 'stranger'. And, yes, Richard, I do believe that you are an angel in disguise. You will be just the medicine that my friend needs."

Footnote: 1 As far as we know, Richard's mother was never located. The last we heard, Richard was still in the home of Dolly. This was long before the days when "Child Welfare" would step in and take abandoned children into their care.

Chapter 12 — Blind?

1947 – 1948

After reading the note on the table Jessie's eyes darted to her daughter's report card. Pauline? Quick as a whip at everything she put her hand to? A whiz at the piano? A voice like a bird?" My baby? Failing at school? Impossible!

She squeezed her eyes shut; her insides were ablaze. She stirred a teaspoonful of Krueshen salts into her tea, grimacing while she took the first swallow. Had she been so wrapped up in her new job career that she had failed to notice? It wasn't as if she never saw the children. She was with them for an hour or so in the morning before school, and an hour at lunch, and every weekend. How could she have missed noticing her daughter's sight loss?

She read the note again: "Pauline is having difficulty seeing... In fact... she is virtually blind... Please contact the principal's office"

Blind? Incredible! She crumpled the note into a ball and tossed it toward the garbage. *Blind!* For nearly an hour she sat at the table, her head in her hands, half praying, half thinking, subconsciously aware of the sleeping noises of her family. It was 11:30, and she had just come home from work.

As her mind began to mull over the problem, an episode came to fore, one she had witnessed the previous Saturday: Marianne had been practicing the scales and songs her piano teacher had given her. She enjoyed the piano and was doing fairly well, but she had not yet grasped the meaning of the squiggles on the page in front of her, or what relationship they had with the keys on the piano. Stumbling over a difficult passage, she had slammed her fingers onto the keys, sending up a cacophony of sounds; then she had begun again.

"No! No! No!" Pauline had shouted at her from the kitchen. "That should be 'C', not 'D'. Hit 'C'."

Marianne had gritted her teeth, slamming down the lid of the piano. "I'll *never* be able to play. Who can practice with *her* around?" She had jerked her head in her sister's direction and had run outside.

"You're doing fine. Just practice when she's not around," Jessie had followed her daughter, consoling her.

Her mind now coming back to the present, Jessie thought of how Pauline had taken immediately to the piano. After having had only a few lessons she was already completing her second book... "And they tell me this girl is failing in school?" Suddenly something clicked in Jessie's mind: "Hm! I wonder how she is able to *see* to read the piano book?"

She jerked her head up, got up from the table and went to bed. She knew what she was going to do. Tomorrow was Saturday. She would keep mum about the contents of the note; she would ignore, for now, the failing grades. It would be her special weekend mission to observe her daughter—to spy on her, if necessary.

It was shortly after nine on Monday. Jessie walked up the steps of Connaught Elementary School, headed for the principal's office. Just as she was about to enter she bumped, literally, into Miss Meeks, the school nurse.

"Oh! Mrs. Splane," she said, a sickly smile sneaking onto her insipid face. "You're just the person I want to see."

"And *you* are just the person *I* want to see," Jessie retorted. This wasn't the first encounter she had had with the school nurse. From the day she had entered her children into the schools, she had had run-ins with Miss Meeks: *Marianne*, she had classified as undernourished in her first year at school and had put her on a special nutrition program: *infuriating!* And *Helen*, she had sent home on numerous occasions for rashes of one description or another (scabies, seven-year-itch, or some other outlandish ailment), diagnosed solely by Miss Meeks. "Seven-year-itch:" *ridiculous! Evelyn,* she had dubbed as anemic because she had fainting spells: *preposterous! Alfred,* she said had blood that was too thin because he had frequent nosebleeds: *comical!* And *Clara,* she had checked for T. B. because of her chronic cough: *ignorant!* So now, when Jessie came face-to-face with her archenemy, she was ready for a good war — looking for one, as a matter-of-fact. Her daughter, blind! *This* was the last straw. She followed the nurse into the principal's office.

"What!" Jessie jumped to her feet when she heard what the principal and the nurse had to say. "I should say not! And furthermore," she said, "Pauline is not blind. It's all a game, exaggerated by the attention she's getting from all of you."

"But, Mrs. Splane," said Miss Meeks, standing as well. "Are you not concerned about your daughter's welfare?"

"Of course I'm concerned," snapped Jessie. "That is exactly why I will not hear of sending her to the Brantford, Ontario, School for the Blind. She is not blind. And," she turned now to the principal, "she *will* do better in school. Imagine! The teacher giving her coloring to do while the other children are doing their regular work —

"And why Brantford?" She snapped her head back to Miss Meeks. "That's clear across the country. Are there not schools closer?" Not waiting for an answer, she continued. "Regardless. She is not going to *any* school for the blind. And that's final." Turning her head again to the principal, she said, "And she is not to be treated *special.* Understand?"

She snatched up her hat and stormed out of the school. *Never* had she been so steamed! Her heart was pounding, a swishing sound throbbing out her ears.

For the remainder of the school term Jessie was barraged with information about schools for the blind. She received numerous notes from the school, threatening her of the consequences of refusing to allow her child the opportunities available for the handicapped. She ignored them all, expecting at any moment a visit from the authorities insisting that she was an unfit mother. But then she thought of Richard: the authorities hadn't seemed all that concerned about the fitness of *his* mother. But for her own peace of mind — and because of the insistence of the school — she took her daughter for eye test after eye test, all with the same result: "Your daughter has a weak right eye with considerable sight loss, but she will (partially) grow out of it. When she is older you may want to have her eye operated on."

In the meantime Jessie kept an observing eye on her daughter, noticing the little games she would play. All of a sudden, remembering that she was supposed to be blind, Pauline would squint, moving close to an object, pretending she couldn't see it. Ignoring these antics, Jessie coached her in her lessons. Her school marks picked up; she passed her grade; she forgot her *games*.

But because of the pressure put on her, Jessie made herself a promise: *If I receive word from the School For The Blind by the time school starts in the fall, I'll send her – for one term. If I haven't heard by then she'll attend the regular school.*

Two weeks after school had started, an application for attendance at the Brantford school arrived. Jessie read the material, walked to the garbage and dropped the package in. Pauline, newly fitted with glasses, had already settled into her fifth-grade year. Having dropped her façade of blindness, she began to do well in school.

Chapter 13 — Full Circle

1949

"Cheerup-it's-gonna-rain. Cheerup-it's-gonna-rain." The robins were singing their rain song again. And on this muggy morning in early June as Jessie sat down at the kitchen table, her heart was singing along with them. A smile on her face, she shuffled through the mail: electric bill, phone bill, a grocery flyer, a letter from Alfred and Helen, soon to be home from high school at PBI. Seeing that, she hugged it to herself, intending to read it first—she always read her children's letters first. But when her eyes fell on an envelope from the *Department of Nursing* in Edmonton, she dropped her children's letters; the smile faded from her face; and a severe attack of nausea hit her. Pouring out a cup of leftover breakfast tea, she stirred into it a teaspoon full of Krueshen salts. That antidote wasn't helping her indigestion much any more, but she hoped it would alleviate a little of the pain that attacked her at the sight of the ominous looking letter she now clutched in her hand.

What would she tell Allyn if she hadn't made it? What would she tell the girls? Everyone was awaiting the news. Everyone knew she'd pass. Everyone, but her.

It had been a difficult two years: studying, keeping house, getting the older girls and Alfred off to Prairie Bible Institute, sending them letters and parcels, coaching the younger girls with their school work, going to church; and all the while, tramping the halls of the hospital — for five dollars a day. And always, always, there was the burning indigestion and nausea. Had it all been worth it? Had all her hard work paid off? Well... the contents of the envelope would tell her. But she couldn't look — yet.

Her mind flashed back to some of the patients she'd nursed over the two years. "All things work together for good, to those who love God... and are called according to his purpose." The verse, Romans 8:28, came to her mind, the one she had quoted recently to a patient.

Mrs. O'Reily and her husband were pastors of the newly formed Pentecostal Church, and good friends of the family, although Jessie herself did not attend that church. Jessie had just come on duty and was making her rounds. Upon entering one room, she had checked three of the patients. When she approached the bed of the fourth, she had heard a sniffling. "Anything I can do for you?" she had asked, stooping to read the name: "Mrs. Isabel O'Reily."

"Isabel?" she had said, surprised. "It's Jessie. Jessie Splane. May I do... something for you?"

Isabel had pulled the sheet off her face, wiping her eyes with it. "Oh, Jessie," she had said, grasping her friend's hand. "Why? Why did the Lord permit this to happen to me? I came in during the night with pains. Chronic appendicitis they think. They'll know more after my tests." She had doubled over then with a spasm of pain. "But why do I have to be here? My family needs me. My husband needs me. I don't want to be here." She had begun weeping again.

It was then that Jessie had quoted Romans 8:28. Isabel had dried her eyes and smiled.

Later Isabel had related to Jessie that God's Word had proved true. There *had* been a purpose in her stay in the hospital: the young woman in the bed next to her had, with her husband, attended O'Reily's church, against the wishes of the girl's parents. Her dad had classified the O'Reilys and their church as *nothing but a bunch of fanatics!* But during a visit to their daughter in the hospital, they had met Mrs. O'Reily as well as her husband.

"Come see for yourselves whether we're fanatics," Pastor O'Reily had invited.

The following Sunday both couples had attended church and had come into new relationship with the Lord. They became regular attendants.

Now, thinking of that incident, she knew that Romans 8:28 was for her, too.

"And Marge!" Jessie's head popped up. "How glad I am that I met Marge!" She had been so very ill. Not only had Jessie been able minister to Marge's physical needs, she had also been able to encourage her spiritually. A warm friendship had developed, a friendship Jessie hadn't had since her early nursing days, well over twenty years ago.

"Yes!" She glanced again at the envelope. "Regardless of what this letter contains it *has* been worth it."

She clasped the envelope with both hands, ripped the end and slowly pulled out the contents. Lifting the certificate to her lips she kissed it. Again, after so many years, she was "Huddy, R.N." She had come full circle.

Chapter 14 — "That's Not Flu"

1950-51

The train whistle blew, long and rasping, pouring volumes of vapor and smoke into the warm June air. Jessie stared absently out the window at the tufts of shrubs peeking up through the tiny valleys scattered over the patchwork farm fields. She'd been this way so often in the past five years that she felt there was nothing new to see. It had been only two months since Clara's Bible school graduation, and here she was again, minutes from the station. She hadn't wanted to come again so soon, but how could she have disappointed her daughter? Being that she was able to travel on a pass with the C.P.R., she had no excuse not to go. She recalled her first trip to Three Hills, when Helen was a baby. And now she was graduating from high school.

Waiting for the train to go the last familiar miles, she closed her eyes, swallowing her nausea. For years she had tried to ignore the burning pain that gnawed at her insides, telling herself that it would go away. And for the past year she had tried to ignore the growing lump in her right breast, keeping her fears to herself. She'd waited too long—twenty-four years—and had worked too hard to regain her R.N. status to allow her health to deprive her of her career.

Forcing her mind to think of something pleasant, her thoughts flipped to Clara, in Montreal, where she was studying French in preparation for her going to French West Africa. Oh, how Jessie missed her! But she was happy for her. She thought about what Clara had written in her most recent letter: ...*The son of my French professor, an arrogant, know-it-all photographer, has appointed himself as my private French mentor,* she had said. Jessie recalled her remark to Allyn: "Sounds like love at first sight to me."

The train jerked to a stop at the familiar Three Hills train station. The pleasure on Helen's face, at the sight of her mother stepping down from the train, made Jessie forget her own pain. She was glad she had come to see her third daughter graduate.

Since receiving her certificate, almost two years ago now, Jessie had chosen the field of specialized nursing, private cases who needed round-the-clock care. This way she could choose her own patients, allowing her breaks between jobs. Not only was the pay better, but the pace was a little less strenuous than on general duty.

This was Jessie's first day on a new case, after a week's break. Unlike her last one, six weeks without a day off working the four-to-twelve shift, this one was to be short, perhaps ten days.

It was two o'clock on a mild March day. Jessie had lain down for a nap after lunch. Struggling to a sitting position, she eased her feet onto the floor. As she donned her uniform, her insides ablaze, she was reminded of her checkup. She had told Dr. Charles that she would step into his office before she began her shift, to have him examine her. No longer could she ignore the signs that struck fear to her heart; she knew she must have a confirmation of what she already knew. And now as she placed her starched cap into a paper bag, she wished she hadn't told him that she would see him. But he'd said, "three-o'clock," and he would be waiting.

"No!" Jessie yanked her gown around her, staring savagely at the doctor. "No! I won't have an operation."

"You must. Or you'll not see your next birthday."

"I want a second opinion." Jessie snatched her glasses and ducked behind the screen to dress.

"You can *have* a second opinion, or a third, or a tenth, but they'll all tell you the same thing. You *must* have an operation— immediately. Whom shall I call for a second opinion? My son? Or another doctor?"

"Never mind. Doctor," she sighed, swallowing the lump in her throat. "Never mind. I could have diagnosed my own case; I've known for a long time. Schedule me for the operation. But give me a week—maybe ten days. I've just taken on anoth—"

"No! No, Jessie, not ten days. You've already waited—" His voice, almost tender, dropped to barely above a whisper. He peered at her over his glasses then grabbed the operating schedule, studying it.

"I want you here Sunday, *this* Sunday. I'll operate first thing Monday."

Slowly she made her way to the ward where her new patient's room was. As she passed the admission desk she spotted her friend standing at the charts. *An angel,* she thought, staring at her for a few seconds: the sun rays from the window, shining on Bernice's red hair, made it look like she had a halo. "Just what I need right now, an angel."

Bernice looked up and smiled, her blue eyes sparkling. "Jessie!" she said, setting down the paper she was examining. "Are you all right? You look a little peaked."

"Bernice," Jessie replied in a kind of gasp, "may I talk with you for a minute?" She eyed the student nurse at the desk. "In private?"

Taking Jessie's arm, Bernice steered her into the vacant admitting office.

"My friend." Jessie swallowed, then continued. "Would you be able to find a replacement nurse for Mrs. Kindle? I'm afraid... I'm afraid... I won't be able to... I... I have to have surgery."

"Cancer?" Bernice gasped when Jessie told her the prognosis. She placed her hand on her fellow nurse's arm. "Never you mind about Mrs. Kindle. And you sit right here 'til I get back." She pushed Jessie gently into a chair.

Resting her head on her arms at the desk, Jessie felt suddenly overcome with exhaustion. How would she ever make the two-mile walk back home?

A cup of tea in her hand, Bernice returned a few minutes later. "A taxi will be here in fifteen minutes to take you home," she said, setting the tea in front of Jessie. She patted her arm and left the room. She knew her friend needed to be alone right now.

It was three-forty-five when the taxi dropped Jessie at her door.

"Time for a short nap before the girls get home from school," she said to herself, her hand on the door latch.

"Oh, Mom... you're home!"

Jessie jumped, startled by Marianne's voice. "What are you doing home at this time of day?" she said.

"I... I'm... Teacher sent me home. She slumped in her chair, her head flopping onto the table. She started to cry.

Jessie placed her hand on her daughter's forehead. "You're burning up, girl." You'd best get to bed." She helped her into hers and Allyn's bedroom, just off the kitchen. Suddenly her own illness and exhaustion were forgotten.

Jessie stirred Burgundy dye into the laundry boiler, steaming on the stove. She thought back on a couple of months ago. She had been with Allyn, driving back from the tiny town of Seven Persons, where Allyn held a once-a-month Sunday school. It had been her first Sunday off in many weeks. Just as they were nearing the airport on this particular Sunday, she saw something.

"Allyn" she said. "Stop. Back up."

Slamming on his brakes, Allyn skidded to a stop. "Why?" 'He jerked the gear into reverse.

"There." Jessie pointed to a blob, blending almost with the snow, at the side of the road.

"What is it?" Allyn craned his neck, trying to see what his wife was lifting into the car.

"It's material," she said, plunking the goods into the back seat. "A whole bolt of white satin material."

Since no one had responded to her week's advertisement about the found material, she was putting it to good use. She lowered five yards of it into the dye, thanking the Lord, and the unknown person, for the gift.

The following morning, Saturday, as Jessie began to sew the housecoat she had cut out for herself the night before, from the now-Burgundy satin material, she glanced over to where Marianne lay burning with fever. For four days she had nursed her, forcing liquids through a straw down her throat and sponging her to bring her fever down. Four days! The symptoms indicated flu, but why hadn't the fever broken by now? Jessie puckered her brow. How would she ever be able to leave her to go to the hospital?

Sunday was bright and sunny. Allyn and the girls were to go to Grassy Lake, a town fifty miles from the *Hat*, for a meeting where Mr. Maxwell, the principal of PBI, was to be the special speaker.

"Mom," said Helen, "with Marianne being so sick, and you having to go to the hospital this afternoon, we'd better cancel our trip." Helen had chosen not to return to PBI for her first year of Bible school, in order to help out at home.

"No, no. You go," said Jessie. "You've had this trip planned for weeks. I'll arrange to have Myrtle from across the street come over to sit with Marianne 'til you get back. And I can take a taxi to the hospital."

"That's not flu that child has," Myrtle screamed at Allyn, scarcely waiting until he was through the door after their trip to Grassy Lake. "That's not flu. You get her to the hospital. Immediately! How dare you to have gone off like that! You should be reported for child neglect." She snatched her sweater and slammed out the door.

Allyn's mouth opened and closed and his body twisted like a fish on land, as he gawked at the door through which his hysterical neighbor had just exited. He blinked his eyes, swallowed, then turned on his heel and went to the stove to make a cup of tea.

Helen, in the meantime, had changed her clothes in preparation to go to work. Back in the kitchen, she stared at her dad. He sat at the table gulping scalding tea, his eyes glued shut, his chin trembling. Tears squeezing from his closed eyelids trickled down his cheeks and into his tea.

"Dad?" Helen bent close to his ear and touched his shoulder. "I have to go to work," she whispered. "You be all right?" She had to go, or lose her job. Without having received an answer she left the house and pedaled the five blocks to the confectionary store, where she worked. But her mind was on her mom, her sister, and her poor, devastated dad, not on her work.

Allyn paced the floor between the kitchen and the bedroom. "Oh, God," he moaned, wringing his hands as he walked. "Oh, God. Oh, God." Suddenly he grabbed Pauline, pulling her into the bedroom and shoving her onto her knees. He fell beside her, dropping his head onto the bed where his second youngest daughter lay.

"Lord, heal her," he prayed, his mind as much on his beloved Jessie as it was on his near-to-death daughter.

IF YOU ONLY KNEW

It was midnight. **1** "Standing somewhere in the shadows. You'll find Jesus." The mournful tones of the alto saxophone poured out into the dark kitchen. Slumped in a chair, his eyes closed and his chin trembling, Allyn propped his sax on one knee as he played.

For the two hours she had been back from work, Helen had paced between the kitchen and bedroom, checking on her sister. The dim light in the bedroom made it difficult for her to see clearly. This time when she checked the thrashing body on the bed, she dropped to her knees to get a better look. "Dad! Dad! Come here!" It was almost a scream. "Look...! Her mouth."

Allyn dropped the sax on the table and ran to his daughter's side. He fell to his knees to examine Marianne. "Blisters!" he gasped. "Her mouth is full of blisters!"

"So is her head," said Pauline. "Dad," the girls said, "We've got to *do* something. We've got to get her to the hospital."

Pauline collapsed to her knees by her sister's bed. "Oh, Marianne," she wailed. "Don't leave me... Oh, please don't die.

Lunging for the phone, Allyn dialed a number. "Send an ambulance," he screamed into the mouthpiece. "Quick!"

Footnotes: 1 "Standing Somewhere in the Shadows." Author: E.J. Rollins c. 1943. 1947 Assigned to Haldor Lillenas.

Chapter 15 — Only A Miracle

1951

She could see lights, hear music. She was a feather on the wind, floating... without pain... peaceful....

Voices... voices... like a buzz saw they cut through her bliss... Allyn's voice... Bernice's voice... Words... words.

"Marianne. A miracle... it's Marianne... as you've never prayed before." Her ears registered the words. "... pray now... Only a miracle..."

"Miracle... miracle..." She strained to hear what the voices were saying; she couldn't concentrate. She tried to force her eyes to open; they were glued. She tried to lift her arm; it was a piece of cement. She was being strangled, choked...

She was forcing a tube down the patient's throat and into her nose. She was fastening needles to the patient's arm, needles with tubes leading to intravenous and blood transfusion bottles. She was pulling up the sides of the bed and tying the restraint securely to them.

Jessie's eyes unglued... *She* was the patient. It was down *her* nose and *her* throat and in *her* arm that the tubes and needles were. She fought to sit up, fought the restraint, fought to try to get past the obstructions. She had to get to her daughter.

A needle penetrated Jessie's skin. Her eyes glued shut again. She was a leaf being tossed by the wind. She must stay awake. She must get to Marianne. "A miracle... a miracle. If you only knew... If you only —"

"Jessie? Can you hear me? Can you wake up? Jessie?"

With effort Jessie opened her eyes. She squinted at the face that was close to hers. In slow motion she turned her head from side to side. Only one tube remained, the one running from a needle taped to her arm, to a bottle hanging on a stand above her head. She could move. The restraint was gone. Beside her bed was a blanket-covered wheelchair... What was it for? Surely she wasn't expected to get into it? She closed her eyes.

"Do you think, if I helped you, you could sit in this chair?" Bernice was easing her hand under Jessie's head.

"What for? I just want to sleep."

Bernice cleared her throat. "If you want to see your daughter alive... you'll have to see her now." The words sounded cruel, but how else was she to tell her friend that her daughter was dying?

"Your husband's with her now." Bernice steadied the swinging IV bottle as she wheeled Jessie toward Marianne's room.

Allyn was sitting by the bed rolling his head in his hands. As she passed him, Jessie placed her hand on top of his for a second, then withdrew it. She gasped: that person—connected to tubes and covered with blankets—in that bed couldn't be that of her little girl? She stifled a sob.

1 "*Stephen Johnson's* disease," her friend had explained on the way to the room.

Jessie looked again at the body in the bed, slowly recalling a lecture in which Dr. Charles had shown a picture of a *Stephen Johnson's* case he had once doctored—his only previous case of this rare disease. But the difference between the mental picture and what she saw before her was that *this* was supposed to be her daughter. (And the person in the picture had no hair—and had died!) Her head was spinning. She gazed at her daughter then shut her eyes.

When next she peered down at the creature in the bed she moaned. With a slight movement of the head, gobs of dull golden hair lay unattached on the pillow. The mental picture of the hairless creature of the lecture flashed again before her: she clasped the arms of the wheelchair.

"Shall I take you back?" Without waiting for an answer Bernice wheeled Jessie from the room. "Come sit in your wife's room for awhile," she said to Allyn. "I think she could use some company. *I'll come back here.*"

Clasping his cap in both hands Allyn stumbled, robot-like, behind the nurse.

2 Marianne had been aware of her parents' presence in the room. She had been floating on the ceiling watching the whole affair: She saw the still form on the bed; watched the head rolling on the pillow leaving hair where the head had been; she heard the groans of her father and the gasp of her mother; she felt the emptiness of the room when they left. She watched bodies floating around the form—that was supposed to be her—on the bed: one white-clad creature peered at the body, one shook the I.V. bottle, while still another checked the tubes in the patient's nose and down her throat... Then they left—all but one. She watched that one pull curtains around three sides of the bed.

Death curtains, she thought. *Yes, death curtains. So this is what death was like!*

She felt herself float from the ceiling; she was back in the bed. The quietness in the room was screaming at her. She *had* to open her eyes. She *had* to—just a crack. A night-light above the door was all the light there was in the room. On the stark-white wall straight ahead of her— the side where there was no curtain—she could make out an oval-shaped mirror. She made her eyes peer at it, bring it into focus. A light diffused in the mirror; the face of Jesus appeared, ever so faintly at first, then clearer. She knew it was Jesus by the way He smiled at her. She smiled back. She was with Jesus. Yes, she guessed she was dead. Then, just as the image had come, it faded. Her eyelids closed.

"Mrs. Splane? Mrs. Splane?" A nurse stood over Jessie's bed, shaking her. "Time for your medication."

"Why don't they ever let me sleep?" Slowly she opened her eyes, glancing at the empty chair by the bed where, last she recalled, Allyn had been sitting. Her fuzzy brain began to unravel the events of the past few hours—or was it days—?

The nurse was saying something. "Wh... what did... you say?" she croaked.

"I said, 'Your medication.'" The tiny nurse smiled and handed Jessie a miniscule paper cup.

Jessie squinted. She didn't recall ever having seen this nurse before. "Where's my husband?" she asked.

"He left at six, a couple of hours ago. Said something about already having missed one day of work."

"What is today?"

"Tuesday... Want to see your daughter?"

"My daugh—? Marianne...? You mean—?"

"Yes." The nurse smiled, locking the wheelchair in position by the bed.

Back in her room Jessie stared at the ceiling, the sight of her daughter—deathly pale and without hair—still haunting her. Her mind flashed back fifteen years, when the death angel first hovered, waiting to snatch her premature blue-baby—Marianne. But she had struggled then, and was struggling now, to rob Death of his prey.

"Thank you, Lord," Jessie said aloud, "for sparing our *Miracle Daughter* once again. And thank You, too, for lending *me* a little more time.

Footnotes:

1 Nothing further could be found about *Stephen's Johnson* disease, but that is the actual name of the disease that struck Marianne.

2 Author's version of the story, as told by Marianne.

Chapter 16 — All Is Well—Or Is It?

1951

It had been nearly three months since her operation. For six weeks Jessie had to travel back and forth to Calgary for radium treatments, but that was finished now. And a further six weeks she had spent trying to get her strength back. Marianne had recovered, and was back at school. Jessie felt it was time for her to start getting her life back on track. She had put her name in at the hospital again for special nursing. As far as her family knew—and judging from their happy chatter and oft-times irritating bickering, she was assured of it—all was well with her. And that's just the way she wanted it.

It was nine-thirty on a warm June Monday morning. She had just sat down at the piano when she heard the rattle of the mailbox. As she walked down the hall to pick up the mail, the phone rang. "Why does it always happen at the same time?" she said, changing direction to catch the phone.

"Mrs. Splane?" It was the hospital. "We have a case for you. Would you be able to start today? A young man with polio was just brought in."

"Polio!" Jessie furrowed her brow. She thought about young Don from church, a polio victim of a few years back. A teenager now, he had been left with a permanent limp. "Polio," she said again, grabbing the mail from the box. "What a dread disease!"

Her face brightened. "A letter from Clara." Setting aside the numerous bills, she settled in with a cup of tea to read her daughter's letter: *Dear Mom, Dad, and Kids.* She smiled. Clara's typical short-cut greeting. ... *And now for the best news,* Jessie read. *Stanley and I are engaged. No set date yet for the wedding. But, Mom, Dad, put us on your calendar for early next summer...*

Yes, Jessie's prediction of a year ago had been right, *that egotistical, pig-headed know-it-all,* who had appointed himself her private French tutor, was soon to be Clara's husband.

She set the letter aside. "I wonder, my dear eldest child," she sighed, "if I'll be—" She stood up, glancing at the clock. She had to be at work by three.

"He's twenty-one. His name is Allen." Jessie told the family the next morning at breakfast about her polio patient. "His fiancée, Amy, told me that their wedding date is set for June 21st." Swallowing a lump in her throat she continued. "Only three weeks away. I doubt he'll— He's in an iron lung."

It was a few days later. The family had just sat down to supper when Jessie stepped through the door. It had been only two hours since she had left for her shift at the hospital. "Allen— My patient died to day," she said, "the day he was to have been married." She disappeared into the bedroom to hide the tears streaming down her face. "All the world goes on like nothing's happened. People keep on eating; keep on laughing; cars keep on driving; and a young man who was to have begun his life today lies dead—in an iron lung. And nobody cares! Nobody cares!"

As she was pulling her uniform over her head, wiping her tears with it, she felt the soft touch of a hand on her shoulder. And then she was crying into Allyn's shoulder.

For the next week Jessie's eyes filled with tears every time she thought of taking on another case. "I just can't take it. I just can't stand to see people suffer—and die."

"What's the matter with me?" she reprimanded herself a few days later as she sipped her morning tea. "All my life I wanted to be a nurse, to help people get well, to minister to their needs. It was the happiest day of my life when I finally held my nursing certificate in my hand. And another happy day when I got it a second time two years ago. And now I can't—"

When she heard the mail rattle in the mailbox she pushed her depression aside. As she walked back to the kitchen, she quickly sorted through the mail, spotting two letters with familiar handwriting. "A letter from Gertie," she said, dropping the bills and junk mail onto the table. "And one from Florence!"

"Hello? This is Jessie Splane," she said into the phone after reading her sisters' letters. The blood swished through her ears, and her left breast felt like it was on fire. "Put me on your schedule. I will be available beginning today. And book me solid 'til mid-August." She hung up the phone and began her housework, whistling as she dusted. She hadn't whistled since young Allen had died.

Florence will be arriving in Vancouver from Hawaii in early September. We'll all be here. Think you could make it? We'd love to see you. The words of Gertie's letter rang like music in her ear. Carrie, Bell, Gertie, Florence, and even Eugene—her whole family—all in one place; it was more than her wildest dream! She hadn't seen her only living brother since she was sixteen.

Think you can make it? Gertie had asked. And *I do hope you will be able to make it to Vancouver. I'd love to see you,* Florence had said.

Make it? You bet I'll make it! If it's the last thing I do, I'll make it!

Chapter 17 — The Coat

1951

"Last day I'll have to make this trek." It was a sultry mid-August day. Jessie forced one foot ahead of the other on the two-mile walk home from the hospital. *"The last day?"* She sighed. *"Well, for now anyway."*

Monday she and Pauline would be leaving for Lacombe for a visit with her niece, Muriel, Bell's daughter; and the following Monday, was her trip to Vancouver. Her heart did a flip-flop. *"How good it will be to see my sisters and brother again!"*

Suddenly, like a swollen river, a flood of gloom engulfed her: after the trip she would be back at the hospital — as a patient. "I will not have another operation," she had told Dr. Charles a week ago when she had gone to him for her checkup.

"Then you'll die," he had shot back. "You waited too long the first time. You *must* have the surgery."

"If I must, I must," she had replied with an exasperated sigh. "But not until after my trip. I've worked too hard, and waited too long, to miss it."

Jessie sat cross-legged on a chair in the kitchen, swinging one leg back and forth. Her bottom lip pinched between her thumb and forefinger, she let her eyes rove the room, as if assessing it — or seeing it for the first time. Hearing the rumble of the children on the stairs, she brushed her hand across her face to remove a stray tear that had trickled under her glasses.

When Evelyn, Helen, and Alfred, their last-minute belongings gathered in their hands, approached her to say their "goodbyes," she stared absently at them. "Goodbye" sounded so final. She wanted to jump up and hug them. She wanted to enfold them in her arms, to keep them there forever. She wanted to, but she just sat there, staring at them.

She watched, as her husband picked up his cap and keys from the kitchen table, stepped into his rubbers and slammed out the door to the car, the children following him. They were on their way to the train station — off to school, off to the rest of their lives. She brushed at another tear.

Her eyes wandered to the small kitchen window, where Marianne and Pauline stood waving a cheerful *goodbye* to the group as they left. She recalled the laughter and giggling at the breakfast table earlier. She thought about Allyn's glib remark, "When I get back from the train, let's all go on a picnic."

A picnic!

As she watched her daughters, still in their nightgowns, standing at the window snickering, while nudging and digging each other in the ribs, suddenly she was angry. She could feel that familiar lump in her throat. How could she leave these carefree, happy-go-lucky youngsters in their father's care? How could she? How could he care for them? He, whose whole life was one big *picnic!*

Picnic! Didn't he know? Didn't he care? Didn't *anyone* care? If only they knew! But she couldn't, she wouldn't tell them. Let them *have* their picnics.

Ever since returning from her visit with her family, depression, like early morning fog, had hung over her.

"I feel I failed my mission with my sisters, my brother," she had confided to her friend. Marge, on her return home. "It was so hard to talk to them about God, and what He means to me. I tried to tell them that I had chosen the difficult path I've walked, because God promised long ago that I would not walk alone; He would be with me to 'make the crooked places straight.' But always, the conversation with them got turned around to, 'But Jessie, you had so much talent. You could have been an artist, a singer, a pianist — anything you wanted to be.'

"I told them, 'I was, I am, what I want to be.'" "Oh, Marge, I've failed. Failed God. Failed myself." She had started to weep.

"No, sweetie," her friend had answered, taking Jessie's hand in hers. "You haven't failed. You planted the seed; God alone will do the rest. It is He who will make it grow." The two friends had embraced, and Jessie had felt comforted at the time.

Now, on this late-September morning—Helen's nineteenth birthday—as she sat watching her children leave, the sun was creeping over the hazy horizon. It was the promise of another glorious, southern Alberta autumn day. But Jessie didn't notice: she could not shake the gloom that had settled on her.

She should have been over any post-operative depression by now. She had had the surgery in mid September—*a success,* by the doctors' first diagnosis. "Just a matter of healing," so they had said. "No radium treatments necessary this time," had been their announcement.

So why the gloom? She should be *happy* to see the children getting on with their lives. *She was!* Both Evelyn and Helen had hesitated about leaving her, but Jessie had insisted, in fact, had been emphatic.

"No! You go," she had told them. "That's where God wants you. We'll manage."

After all, is that not what she had worked for all her life: to see each of her children pursuing a God-chosen career? And Helen had already sacrificed one year. So it wasn't their leaving that caused this empty feeling, this sense of abandonment. But what was it? Was it because... because she knew—?

Day after day Jessie forced her body from the bed, promising herself, "Today I'll feel better. Today my strength will return."

The October winds had blown the leaves from the trees. What weren't lying in mounds on the lawn, were mingled with the dregs of the garden. Jessie struggled into her clothes, urging herself toward the door. Rake in hand, she scuffed through the crisp leaves. As she began to rake, she began to shake; she couldn't control her arms.

"Guess the girls will just have to do it," she said, letting the rake slip from her hands. She hated to ask any more of her daughters. They—and Allyn—were already doing most of the housework. But— She shuffled to her room and flopped onto the bed.

It was late October. Jessie glanced out the window at the early winter storm. "You need a winter coat," she said, watching her youngest daughter grab her summer coat and sling it over her shoulders. "You'll freeze in that one. After school we'll hop the bus and go look for one."

Jessie had always made her girls' clothes. The usual procedure was to open the catalogue—Eaton's or Simpson's—and have the girls pick the model of garment they wanted. She then would buy the appropriate material and create a replica of the garment each had chosen, always, to their delight. But her cancer had left her weak. It didn't take a person with even her nursing knowledge to know it was advancing, despite two radical mastectomies, both within nine months. So, she felt that it would be easier to buy her daughter a coat this time.

"Oh Mom! This one." Pauline took her mother's hand, leading her to a mint green coat with a plaid-lined hood. She put it on, mincing toward the store mirror. Her first store-bought coat! She was ecstatic. "It's just per—fect!" She tossed her head and strutted back toward her mother. With one knee slightly bent, her left hand poised with the little finger stretched out, she raised her right arm gracefully above her head in a curved position, imitating the mannequin in the display window.

Jessie smiled. How she would love to indulge her, to buy this coat for her. She sized her daughter up and down, pursing her lips and puckering her brow. She opened her purse, rustling around in it for her wallet, checking her cash again. "Take it off," she said suddenly. "It's not for you." She began to walk away.

"But Mom!"

"Take it off." She waved her hand. "The color's not right. You'd have it filthy in two days. Take it off."

"But—" Pauline stroked one sleeve, preening once again in front of the mirror. Then in slow motion, she slid her arms from the coat, hanging it on its hanger, but not placing it amongst the other coats on the rack. With her eyes still glued to the coat she followed her mother from the store.

"Here," called Jessie to Pauline the following day as she sorted through the front hall closet. "Here's a coat. It was Evelyn's. I can make it down for you."

Pauline inched toward the closet. Wrinkling her nose, she crooked her little finger through the neck loop of the coat her mother was handing her. She remembered the coat. It had looked okay on her big sister when she'd worn it a couple of years ago.

"But Evelyn is a red-head, and big. Gray suits her. I'm blonde, and petite," she said to herself, sniffing and giving her head a toss. "I need bright colors." Reluctantly, she slipped her arms into the sleeves. They hung four inches beyond her hands, and the coat reached almost to her ankles. "Mo-om! This'll *never* fit me."

"You wait and see." Jessie approached her daughter, tucking and folding, measuring the coat with her practiced eye. "You just wait and see."

Together, mother and daughter ripped, turned, sized, and stitched the main seams of the gray coat, Pauline, all the while chattering about how *green was her colour – a light green, like the coat in the store.*

It was Monday. By sheer willpower, Jessie forced her body from her bed and struggled into her housecoat. She staggered to the bathroom. "Another day. How am I ever going to get through it?" She splashed cold water onto her face.

After making some tea she wobbled back to the bedroom, setting her cup on the wing of the *Singer,* treadle sewing machine. She crawled onto the bed. "I must get that hem in," she gasped, hauling the coat to her. With her fingers trembling, she threaded the needle.

Just as she was plunging it into the material for the first stitch, she heard the familiar *chug-chug-splutter* of Marge's Thames station wagon as it came to a stop in front of the house. Her heart flipped. *Just what I need, the cheery presence of my friend.*

"Honey?" Marge entered the kitchen without knocking. "Brought you some soup." Not seeing her friend, she dropped the jar of soup onto the counter and hurried into the bedroom, where she found Jessie propped up by pillows, a cumbersome coat on her lap.

"What in the world are you doing?" scolded Marge.

"Hemming this for Pauline." Jessie flashed her friend a weak smile. "She doesn't have a winter coat."

"Well by the looks of you, you should be in the hospital. You can hardly hold your head up... Here." She reached for the coat. "Let me finish it."

"No!" Jessie jerked the coat out of her friend's reach. "I've got to do it. I *want* to do it. It's the last thing I'll ever be able to do for her. After all, she's my baby." She swallowed the tears she could feel forming behind her eyelids.

Marge wanted to protest the statement, "It's the last thing I'll ever be able to do for her," but the look on her friend's face made her decide to let it pass.

While the needle continued to plunge in and out, in and out, in and out, the two friends chatted and giggled.

"Oh, Marge, I don't know what I would have done without you these past few years." Her face flushed, her words coming in puffs, Jessie dropped the coat onto her lap and swiped at a tear, brought on partly by the laughter, and partly by—

"And, sweetie, I don't know what I would have done without you," replied Marge, swallowing the lump that threatened to choke her.

They embraced, fear clutching each of their hearts: Marge's, because she was afraid she wouldn't *have* her friend much longer, and Jessie's, because she *knew* she wouldn't.

Jessie pushed away, grasping at her sewing again. Her head feeling like a ton of lead, and her insides like they were on fire, she continued her needle plunging.

While Marge went to the kitchen to warm the soup and arrange a tray, Jessie wormed her way out of bed. Slithering to the floor, she crawled to the bathroom.

"Honey!" Marge looked up when she saw her friend creeping across the floor. She ran to help her. "Please let me take you to the hospital... Now."

"Marge..." Jessie's voice was coming in gasps, but she managed to force a smile. "As soon as I've... finished the coat I'll go... I promise."

For two more hours Marge chatted, forcing herself to be jovial. It wasn't usually hard for her, but watching her friend suffer, she found any conversation difficult.

Jessie's eyes misted over; her breath was coming in short puffs; concentration was an effort; she wasn't hearing her friend anymore; her hands constantly made mistakes; she couldn't see the needle. But by force of will, she urged her fingers to continue.

"Fin... finished!" she gasped, snipping the thread and pushing the heavy coat from her lap. She flopped onto the pillows. "Call... the am... ambulance. What... are... you... waiting for?" Her lips stretched into a forced smile; her eyelids drooped shut.

Chapter 18 — The Coronation

October 29, 1951

Exhausted after his workday Allyn lay asleep under his wife's hospital bed. "Don't let the nurses see me," he had said, pulling one side of her blanket over the edge to hide him from view. Jessie had snickered at this.

Pillows surrounding her head, the hospital bed slightly inclined, Jessie lay reading, giggling to herself.

"Hi, honey. How 'ya doin'?"

At the voice of her friend, Jessie's head popped up. Marge and her daughter, Joan, along with Marianne and Pauline, approached her bed.

"Whatchya readin'?" Marge flipped to the cover of the book in Jessie's hand: it was a book of nursing experiences.

"Reminds me of my training days." Chuckling, Jessie told the group about her escapade of traveling down the long, dark laundry chute with the laundry. "Oh, so long, long ago now," she added with a sigh.

The jocular mood, enhanced by Allyn's place of reclination, continued throughout the visit.

"Can't you get me out o' this prison?" Jessie said suddenly, looking at the windows in a conspiratorial manner.

"Tell you what." Marge hunched close to Jessie's ear, feigning a whisper. "I'll bring the wagon 'round — under your window —"

"And we'll tie the bed sheets together," cut in thirteen-year-old Joan, her twinkling brown eyes roving the room. She crouched, snatching at the sheet.

"Yea! And all of us will lower you into the van," said Marianne in a hoarse whisper.

"And we'll whisk you away... And we won't tell *him*," added Pauline, pointing her finger in the direction of her dad, still lying under Jessie's bed.

"And we'll all live happily ever after." Allyn shot up from the floor and joined the group.

Jessie's head slumped against the pillow. Her charade of gayety had been a strain, but her loved ones' laughter was like medicine to her ears. Were they also just pretending to sound so happy? Or had she fooled them into believing that she was going to be all right — as she had Allyn?

"Visiting hours... now over." All too soon the loudspeaker crackled out the unwelcome announcement. "Visiting hours are now over. All visitors please leave the hospital. All visitors please leave."

Unwilling to leave, but knowing she must, Marge stooped and planted a kiss full on her friend's mouth, turning quickly away, to hide her tears. She grabbed her daughter's hand and together they left, leaving Jessie with her family.

Cap in hand Allyn shuffled toward his wife, bending to kiss her. Taking his face in her hands, Jessie turned his ear to her mouth, whispering something to him. He jerked away, a look of shock crossing his face. Then, characteristically, he chirped, "Bye, Mama. See you tomorrow." He stepped into his rubbers and trotted down the hall.

Jessie's head turned slowly toward her daughters, standing hand-in-hand by her bed waiting their turn to bid her goodnight. It was a look of pleading she read on her youngest daughter's face, as the light from the overhead globe reflected on one lens of her thick glasses. She tilted her head then rushed to her mother, kissing her quickly on the cheek. Tears glistening in her eyes, she pulled away and rushed from the room.

Panic was in Marianne's eyes as she hung back a moment before bending to kiss her mother goodnight. Jessie was reminded of the day she had pushed her wee girl out the door for her first day of school. Her eyes had said then, as they were pleading now, *Mama, please don't make me go away from you.*

During the drive from the hospital to home, while Pauline and Marianne sat silently huddled beside him, Allyn pelted out strains from a favorite hymn of his: **1** "Praise the Lord! Praise the Lord! Let the earth hear His voice... "

Pushing his way past his daughters when they reached home, Allyn ran into the house, lunging for the phone. He dialed the long distance operator: "I want to make a person-to-person call —

"Hello, Evelyn?" he shouted into the mouthpiece when he heard his daughter's voice. "Good news! Good news! Mama's coming home tomorrow..."

Jessie slumped down into her bed, switching off her bedside light. Her head lolled to one side of the pillow, the memory of her daughters' faces haunting her. She thought of Pauline, just barely into her teens. Who would guide her through the difficult decisions she would face during adolescence? Who would protect her from wrong choices? And Marianne? What of her? She, too, was still a child — so vulnerable, so naive. She thought about the *problem* Marianne had asked her about. Since her illness her body wasn't functioning as it should be for a girl her age. Jessie had promised, just a few minutes ago as she said her goodbyes that she would take her to a doctor as soon as she was out of the hospital. But she knew that *that* was an easy way out. She just couldn't bring herself to tell her little girl that she didn't think she'd be coming out of the hospital. She recalled a conversation she'd had with her a couple of months ago when Marianne had brought home a kitten from her babysitting job. "Can I keep him?" she had asked. "He's the cutest one of the six." Jessie thought of her reply: "Perhaps in the fall you can have a kitten. I won't be here?"

And now she closed her eyes to blot out the memory of the look of fear and puzzlement on her daughter's face at the time. She had the same look on her face tonight.

Oh, how could she leave these youngsters in the care of their father? How could she? She loved Allyn, loved him dearly. But how could he care for these tender children? She lay thinking of the shock on his face at her whispered message a few minutes ago: "Allyn, you were not meant to live alone. Go out and find yourself a good wife to look after you." And she meant it. He was incapable of caring for himself, and she knew he couldn't look after the children. For one fleeting moment — until a searing pain ripped through her whole body — she wished for a little more time, a few more years.

In the gray-darkness, her eyes roamed the chalky-white ceiling of the hospital room, before resting on the window. The blackness outside screamed at her: she wanted to scream back. *Never,* had she felt so alone. She squeezed her eyes shut. The gushing in her ears made her feel as if her head were about to explode. She felt so far from her family, so separated. She thought of Clara's upcoming wedding.

She wanted desperately to see her eldest married, to meet her first son-in-law... And her three children away at school, how she wanted to throw her arms around them, to tell them how much she loved them... She wanted her family around her, at her bedside, hanging on to her. But they were gone. All of them. Gone to carry on with their lives — without her.

As she lay there she thought of Jesus, hanging on the cross. She felt just a wee bit of the pain *He* must have felt when His Father turned His back on Him: the loneliness! The despair! The blackness!

"Yea, though I walk through the valley..." and "I will walk with you..." Snatches of promises from the past began to trickle into her mind. "I will never leave you..."

Turning, she switched on the bed light, reaching at the same time for her Bible. She didn't feel like reading, but she wanted the comfort of God's Word near her. Idly she flipped the pages, her eyes closing again. She dozed.

Just before midnight the nurse came in with her medication. "Just leave it there," she said, a weak smile struggling on her face. "I'll take it in a bit."

Slowly and painfully she raised her knees, bringing her Bible into reading distance. Her eyes fell on a passage, marked in red: II Timothy 4:7 & 8. "I have fought a good fight, I have finished my course, I have kept the faith: Henceforth there is laid up for me a crown of righteousness, which the Lord, the righteous judge, shall give me at that day — "

Had she fought a good fight? Had she done all she could to raise her family? Her life flashed before her. Given a chance, what would she do differently? How would she advise her children? What further sacrifices would she make? What more would she have taught them?

A feeling of inner peace began to ooze its way past her despair, her loneliness, her fear. She could feel her body begin to relax.

Her knees flopped to one side, her head lolling to the other. With a splat her Bible landed on the floor...but she wasn't aware of it. She had taken her flight from this life, for a better one. She had gone HOME for her Coronation.

This is not the end of Jessie's story, only the beginning. Her influence lives on in the loved-ones she left behind, and in everyone with whom she came in contact.

Footnote: 1 Author: *"To God be The Glory"* — Fanny J. Crosby — Text: William H. Doane. Descant and choral ending c. 1986 — Norman Clayton Pubco (a div. of WORD, INC.)

Epilogue

October 1989

    I stood on a knoll overlooking the Tawatinaw Valley, my eyes drinking in the splendor of the panorama. The aspen, poplar, and birch trees had exchanged their summer attire for a wardrobe of gold, orange, and brown; and the underbrush looked like a multicolored plush carpet. Canada geese, on their southbound migration, patterned the sky, their dissonant chorus echoing through the hills. A soft breeze caressed my face; then with a cold slap, it reminded me that it was October.

    My eyes wandered over the valley, stopping at the spot where I knew the shack had been, *and I was seven again.* In my mind's eye I could see that shaggy log shack my father had built. I always imagined that its two front windows, on either side of the slab-wood door, were its eyes, and that it was a friendly giant, always ready to protect us. I recalled that October morning — when Mama left.

    I was standing tiptoed beside my sisters at the six-paned window in the kitchen, blowing peepholes in the lacy designs Jack Frost had painted, so that we could peer out into the inky blackness. I could still picture the flickering lamplight behind me, and hear the crackle of the wood in the stove. I remembered watching the smoke from the stovepipe spiraling downward, twisting and twirling past the window, like dancing ghosts. I remembered grabbing my sisters' hands when I saw Mama standing, looking back at the house. I had wanted to shout, "Mama, come back. Come back." I was afraid I'd never see her again. A tear trickled down my cheek.

A gust of wind lifted a few dry leaves and swirled them around my face, whisking me back to the present. I stared down at the casket in front of me, *and I was nineteen again.* It was six o'clock on a warm, late-September day — my nineteenth birthday. Bags in hand, ready to leave for the train, I stood in the kitchen with my brother and sister, staring at my mother. I wanted to rush at her, to throw my arms around her. I wanted her to shout, "Don't leave; don't leave." I was afraid I'd never see her again. A tear trickled down my cheek.

My eyes returned to the pile of dirt at the side of the grave; then I glanced at the *green* around the hole. I didn't want to look again at the coffin. To me, he wasn't in it. He was with *his* Jessie — my mother — for whom he had waited thirty-eight years to rejoin.

"Go out and find yourself a good woman," Jessie had whispered to her husband the night she died.

And that's just what he did. Eight months after Jessie's death Allyn married a woman twenty-two-years his junior, who gave him four sons and two daughters. The girls both died at birth, and their oldest son drowned at the age of twenty. Standing now, with moistened eyes, next to Allyn's wife were three fine looking young men — her sons, Allyn's sons.

Allyn spent his latter years back in the country where he had been the happiest. And it was here, in the beautiful Meanook valley, where family members — as well as a few friends — gathered to pay their last respects to him. It was just a simple graveside service — no fuss, no bother — just like he wanted it.

But the family was not complete.

My mind wandered to Clara. I reflected on excerpts from her memoirs:

So this was Africa, the land we had struggled toward... elegant palms, tropical foliage, white, match-box-like houses, squalor and sordidness... and heat, oppressive heat...

I stood gazing into the starry African sky, where the big dipper sat at a frightening angle and the whole galaxy looked so... different... so hostile. I was alone, alone in a strange land, with strange culture, strange customs, and strange people. I was frightened.

"*I closed my eyes for a minute, and I was seven again, back in Meanook, in the stick-and-leaf playhouse with my sister: The moon — which now seemed so unfriendly and distant in this strange sky--was the same moon that smiled down on the Nabob coffee can, and strawberry jam tin, brimful with water, so long, long ago.*

"This — Africa — was where God had called me. I was not alone."
(excerpt taken from Clara's manuscript about her life in Africa.)

Clara and her husband (married in July, 1952), spent ten years in Senegal, as missionaries. Three of their four children were born in that land.

In November 1975, in Sterling, Ontario, their life's work was over. They were both killed in a car crash.

They would be standing now with Jessie, I thought, greeting Allyn, telling their story.

I shuffled closer to my husband as I glanced at the black hole into which they would soon lower my dad. Evelyn, having just arrived back from India in time to spend the last remaining days of Allyn's life, nursing him, was beginning to relate a few of her memories. I recalled her brimful tin of water. Her story would fill another whole book. But an excerpt from a recent letter will paint a small picture of her life:

1 *As I entered the *India for Christ headquarters in Chilakaluripet, immediately fifty pairs of brown hands and arms were raised, palms together in traditional manner of greeting. The children were standing in two lines facing each other to form a lane through which I walked. A shrill chorus of little voices greeted me with, 'Vandanalu' — 'Praise the Lord'.*

These are Evelyn's children — God's children — the fulfillment of her calling, the water in her tin.

Alfred couldn't be present at his father's grave; but he was here, because this was his heritage, too. He sent his memorial:

In loving memory of a mother and father who had no university degree in psychology; spent nothing on child-care programs; never attended sessions on 'communicating with teens; had no bank accounts; received no government assistance; yet molded the lives of their children through dedication and example.

This is the key to parental success and to the survival of our nation.

Alfred and his wife have a son and a daughter, the daughter having spent several years as a missionary in Senegal, Africa.

I glanced again at the spot across the valley from the cemetery, recalling the time Evelyn and I stood watching our mother bath our little *Miracle Sister*. We had gasped when we heard her coo, "Oh, you skinny little runt; I think I'll throw you in the garbage."

Smiling to myself at the memory, I made eye contact with Marianne, standing next to her husband. She has no recollection of this place; she was only three when we left. But this was the place of her birth, the place where *Death* and *Life* competed for her. Had not *Life* won out, many children would have missed the blessing of having been brought up in her home.

2 Marianne and her husband raised six children, a daughter and two sons born to them, and three boys born to someone else, but given to them by God to be raised in their home. (Several foster children have also passed through their home.)

The minister was saying the committal now, "dust to dust," etc. The burial service was nearly over. But I wasn't finished my reflections yet. I wanted to cap my memories of this sacred place. I may not be back this way again.

I recalled the excitement on our dad's face when he stood us all against the wall, in order of age, to show us the surprise he'd promised us at breakfast that morning. "You have a new baby sister," he had announced.

Pauline couldn't be with us here, standing by our father's grave. She couldn't be, but had wanted to be. She would have liked to see where she had been born; she wouldn't remember. She had been only fourteen months old when we left.

Pauline and her husband have a daughter and a son.

I left the cemetery feeling — not sad — as I suppose I should have felt; I felt as if I owned half of Alberta. Only months before I had stood at my mother's grave in the southern part of the province, reminiscing on our life in Medicine Hat. Now, at the geographical center of Alberta, I have just finished saying goodbye to my father. What a rich heritage I have been given!

This story of Jessie — and Allyn — is my legacy to my siblings and their offspring.

Not **THE END**, only **THE BEGINNING**

Footnotes:
1 "India for Christ," an independent mission, headquartered in Chilakaluripet, Andhra Pradesh, S. India, was founded and is chaired by Evelyn Splane.

2 One of the adopted sons was adopted back to his birth-parent when he was 15.

Update on Family - 2004

Clara: At age 46, Clara and her husband, Stanley, were killed in a car crash. Her four children are married and live in Eastern Canada and the United States. Clara's memory lingers on in each of her children and in her siblings.

Evelyn: Most people are retired at age 74, but Evelyn still makes trips back and forth from Canada to India in her duties with India For Christ. She is well, and says that she has no intention of retiring until God 'retires' her to a better place—Glory.

Helen: (the author) is still writing. She and her husband, Hartson, live in beautiful British Columbia, where they enjoy their life with their dog and cats. They had no children of their own, but shared in the raising of many.

Alfred: resides with his wife, Dorothy, in Ontario. His son, Lyle and his wife, Bertha, with their five children, live in the Maritimes. Their daughter, Sheryl, who spent some time in Senegal as a missionary, now lives near her parents. Sheryl is a prolific writer of poetry.

Marianne: lives with her husband, Louis, in British Columbia, not far from Hart and Helen. Her children are all grown and away from home now, and live in British Columbia, Alberta, and the United States. Marianne has been blessed with several grandchildren.

Pauline: resides with her husband, Ken, in British Columbia. Her daughter lives in Ontario and her son lives in the United States.

Our Stepmother, Helen: is in a nursing home in Alberta, close to her sons, Dan, Ernest, and Stephen. She is 82, and in poor health. We all thank God that she shared in our life.

BIBLIOGRAPHY

Archives, Medicine Hat News.
Archives, Three Hills News, Archives.
Authorized King James Version, *Holy Bible.*
Barnes & Noble, *Roget's University Thesaurus.*
Dian Dincin Buchman & Seli Groves, *The Writer's Digest Guide to Manuscript Formats.* Cincinnati: Writer's Digest Books, 1989.
MacGregor, J.G., *A History of Alberta.* Edmonton, Alberta, Hurtig Publication, 1977.
Prairie Bible College, *Prairie Harvester.* Three Hills, Alberta, Prairie Bible College *Pub.*
Webster, *Webster's Encyclopedic Dictionary* Canadian Edition & *Webster's Dictionary and Thesaurus.* Lexicon Publications, Inc., N.Y., 1988.
William E. Messenger/Jan De Bruyn. *The Canadian Writer's Handbook — Second Edition.*

Printed in the United States
52562LVS00004B/24